# Dorflin's Daughter

**Book One**

**in** *The Vana Avkomling Saga* **by**

**S. Leigh Jenner**

## Mead Hall Press
**Evanston, IL**

**www.meadhallpress.com**

*Dorflin's Daughter*

©2005 S. Leigh Jenner

All rights reserved. No part of this book may be reproduced in any form or by electronic or mechanical means, including information storage and retrieval systems, without permission in writing from the publisher, except by a reviewer who many quote brief passages in a review

Mead Hall Press

848 Dodge Avenue

Evanston, Illinois 60202 U.S.A.

www.meadhallpress.com

Jenner, S. Leigh
    Dorflin's Daughter / S. Leigh Jenner—1st ed.
    ISBN 0-9764771-0-6
    1. Fantasy—General—Fiction 2. Historical—Fiction
I. Title
                Cover art and content by S. Leigh Jenner

Printed in the United States of America by
Wave Graphics, Mattoon, Illinois

This book is dedicated to all our loved ones who were so understanding and supportive—our parents, our siblings, our children, our friends, our pets—and most especially Kurt Chapman and David Mansen, whose tenacity almost overmatched our own.

# Prologue

In the center of the gods-world of Æsgard, almost as if the rest of the heaven has been built outward from it, stands stately Idavoll, the Peacestead. Thereon is built the hall called Gladsheim—the High Thingstead of the Gods, the Æsir Court of Judgment. In all the Nine Worlds, no structure equals it in beauty or impressiveness, for within and without, the hall is resplendent with graven and burnished gold; it is roofed in silver and lighted by the phosphorescence of the sunset. In this vast hall, surrounded by the twelve seats of the gods who sit with him in council, stands the massive golden throne of Odin, and in it sits the All-Father himself, Chieftain of the deities.

"Silence!!" roars Odin, fixing his single eye on the gathered gods. Instantly, all murmuring ceases, and Odin All-Father inclines his head toward his wife to hear her counsel.

"Ever you have played harsher with Lokji than with the others," Frigga Cloud-Spinner reminds her husband sharply, tossing her snowy locks. There is an unsurpassed love between Frigga and her handsome step-son—a tragic fondness, the roots of which are lost in the tangled mystery of Lokji's parentage. Her *heart is filled with a yearning to see the comely youth, and she has long been wroth that Odin remains so unrelenting.*

*"Our Lokji you have barred from your home for his careless-ness in losing your toys—yet you sit ready to bestow still another favor on Lord Freyr, who has been far the more reckless. Of the four great magick gifts crafted by Dvalin, most powerful of the Darkelves, not a one returned you to Lokji, though 'twas he who brought them to you. The ring, you kept for yourself and the magick hammer you gifted to our son, Thor—but to Lord Freyr you gave the sorcerer's sword, which he rashly traded away. Also, in his hand did you put Skidbladnir, that most wondrous magick ship, and seems he did lose it, most heedlessly—"*

*Before them, in an unusual mood of defiance, stands the Vanir god, Lord Freyr, a majestic personage clad this day in court robes of sky-blue moreen, his golden hair held faultlessly in place by a gleaming boar-headed band of remarkable workmanship. Freyr speaks fiercely. "You know the sword I gave freely, of my own will, in exchange for the hand of fair Gerda, and 'twas a bargain that gives me yet much contentment. My ship, though—'twas stolen from me, certain!"*

*Odin's voice waxes fiercer yet. "Is't you were slumbering, Freyr, to allow so measureless a treasure to be stolen?"*

*"'Twas lost to me by enchantments!"*

*"Nay, 'twas lost to you as your sword was lost—because you had not the care to value its true worth!"*

*Ever since the end of the grave Winter Wars, when the Æsir and Vanir gods at last quelled seasons of bitter warfare by an exchange of hostages, Freyr has lived as a trust-pledge in Odin's world, along with his twin, Lady Freyja and their father, Njord. Bold, young, vital, and startlingly comely, Freyr has in the count-less ages since his arrival there proven himself so powerful that oft he is considered second in rank only to the All-Father himself.*

*Odin, in truth, loves him as a son, and, of all the immortals, only one bears Freyr any trace of ill-will: Lokji, the handsome god of cunning, once favored of Odin, now displaced in his step-father's affections as much by Freyr's uprightness and virtue as by Lokji's own lack of it.*

*Lord Lokji's high seat stands empty this day, as it has these many councils past, a quarter of a century as reckoned by the mortals below in Midgard. Lokji, in his human-form, wanders amongst men there now as Lord Lodur, banished from Æsgard for his carelessness in misplacing some treasures of Lord Odin's, and for the cruel words of spite that escaped him while denying his own blame. His entry to Æsgard is barred till he can find and return the missing chess pieces.*

*There has been some satisfaction for Freyr in this turn of events; unbeknownst to all, it was he and his sister who contrived the banishment in retaliation for Lokji's many malicious insults against them. Despite their happy adoption into the clan of Æsgard, the two are secretly devoted to preserving and passing on the powerful magick that is the heritage of the Vana-gods, preferring to share it with elves, humans, and halflings rather than with the warlike and oftimes abusive Æsir. Apart from Odin All-Father, who respects it as part of their nature, Lokji alone of his race suspects and covets their might, and has put himself to the task of equaling it, swelling even more the bitter contention between them.*

*It is a deep-seated resentment, akin to human hatred, that has grown between the two, further fueled by Lokji's consuming passion for the beautiful Freyja, Freyr's twin and consort, who has oft ungently spurned Lokji's bold advances.*

*In peaceful Idavoll, no voice is allowed to rise in anger, no shadow of a quarrel may fall. Oft had Lokji and Freyr sat anext each other there, though, and glared silent threats and curses one to the other, undetected, for both were masters at hiding their thoughts. If ever Freyr expected to be chastised in council, he feared it would be for that and never a thing more.*

*This day, he approaches Odin's throne with confidence, having come to ask a boon of the All-Father, as is indeed his earned right. He voices his plea low, having no wish to share so private a matter with others. Odin bends forward and listens intently, then rises from his seat roaring an exclamation of distress. "How can you dare request immortality for another when you so recently endangered us all by your carelessness, and have yet made no move to right your foolishness?"*

*Freyr stiffens, looking bold and sullen, but he is sage enough to make no defense.*

*Odin stands, looking past him to the other gods assembled, and speaks again. "'Tis one matter when an object of such power is held by one of us, but when it is allowed to pass from our hands to another race—by fecklessness or by treachery—then might be brewed disaster of the worst sort. Think you on Skidbladnir—a ship that will grow in size to carry even the largest army, that will fly on command through the air to any named destination, that can travel in flashing instants, then folds so small it can be carried in a pouch unseen. Now, picture such magick in the hands of an unworthy—one bent on gaining wealth and power, or even...."*

*Odin's thunderous voice trails off. Of a sudden, Freyr and Freyja—alone of all the gods assembled, for their powers are more acute—realize for the first time that Odin All-Father knows fear, and that the thought which dreadens him is that his own son, brother, and stepson—Lokji, master of falseness and trickery and transgression—will find the thing, and use it to further increase his own ill-gained might. It is a thought which pales them both.*

*Moments pass in ringing silence. Then Odin speaks again. "Good and faithful have you ever been, Lord Freyr, and I am minded to bestow the boon which you beg. 'Twould be a failing on my own part, though, to let it go unheeded that you have been careless of hallowed things, and so have unwittingly helped to undermine the strength of the gods gathered here. Wherefore let this be my decree: If the one for whom you seek immortality can find the ship, hold tight to it against all the powers that seek to wrest it, then return it to your hand, I will consider your plea. Let your halfling son prove himself worthy of the trust and able of the attainment, with no interference from you or yours, other than that within reach of any Holy by the power of the Runes, then this boon will be granted."*

*And so began the first quest of the Vana Avkomling.*

# Chapter One

There was only a single ship but it was immense, richly carved, and gilded in the Viking style. Any who saw it would know it was certain to carry no fewer than fifty marauders. Surely, as soon as it was spotted, looming ominously off the craggy coastline, crashing through the crests of waves in the growing darkness, the villagers—all but the strong men of arms-bearing age—would have fled inland.

"Odin's breath! Is it the shadows that hide them, or are there but a score sitting mounted and armed to meet us?" cried a young man with the unmistakable air of a great warrior, who stood at the prow of the fast-moving ship. He was tall and slender, but strongly built. His honey colored hair was sun-streaked, and he had a handsome, open face, browned and freckled by the sun. Now, he squinted into the waning light, scanning the rocky promontory before him.

A decaying wooden fort stood proudly on the headland. Beyond it, an ancient Roman signal tower crumbled down the craggy cliff, still seeming to warn seafarers against seeking welcome in the vast, sandy cove.

"Could there be a smaller vill in all the Anglish Danelaw which you might have chosen for this raid, brother?"

The man next to him, taller yet and every bit as bold-looking, lifted his helmet and loosed his long, white-blond hair to the cooling sea wind.

"'Tis the wealth of the treasure that matters, Roric Grim-Kill," he said with a thin-lipped smile, "and not the size of the city."

Roric eyed him dubiously. "Aye, Vanaash. So you tell me every time that strange second sight of yours leads us to such a gods-forsaken hamlet!" He started to say more, then bit his tongue. Truth was, for all his merry nature, Roric was reluctant to jest about his foster-brother's special sense. It had brought them, and all of their many loyal men, great riches in the two years since Vanaash had agreed to let it guide the warship. In fact, they had more than doubled the already appreciable wealth of their family estates, making theirs the vastest and richest holdings in northern Skog.

What was more, that sense had saved Roric's life. He would have been off to Valhalla more than three years since, had Vanaash not accompanied him when he kept a dangerous love-tryst at that Icelander woman's house. Keeping watch with his other-sight while Roric and the lady toyed with each other elsewhere, Vanaash had called out a warning late one evening after seeing, in his mind's eye, the woman's husband, with eight armed men behind him, making his furious way back across the frozen bay. Roric had not stopped to wonder how his foster-brother had seen beyond the walls, over the miles and through the mountain; the two of them were high on a ridge four or more furlongs away when the riders finally thundered into the courtyard far below them. Aye, Roric would have paid dearly for those long nights of lingering had the husband caught him, but the woman had been well worth the dangerous adventure of that hard ride away. Roric scarce could suppress a fond smile at the thought of her, but soon as his gaze grew distracted, Vanaash nudged him ungently and spoke in a sharp whisper.

"Think about her some other time, brother! Worry now about how to stay close beside me when the burning and commotion starts. The dwelling I seek is somewhere up the steep rise by the forest there." He gestured north toward the Roman ruins with a sweep of the arm; Roric glared at him.

"Can't be you still hope to find that holy woman here! Think you all your dreams and visions will come true just for the having of them?" Obviously exasperated, Roric shook his head with wonder, but Vanaash's stoic features had already taken on a grim determination. It was a look Roric knew well and found useless to resist.

Once the ship was secure in the shallows, Roric unleashed the men with three stinging blasts of a bull-horn trumpet. Vaulting over the lapstraked sides of the ship, they lunged waist-deep through the sea, shields and weapons held high, then tromped up the stony shore, senses numbed by the chill of the water and their own thundering roar: a raucous, yet somehow poetic, drone composed of threats, snatches of old Norse songs, and Wulf Shin-Griever's continual chanting of that damnable hymn he had composed to the goddess Frigga.

They made short work of the defenders. Most were young and untried, and it did not take long to scatter the rest. Then, like ravens swooping to a calf two full days dead, the men of the Chieftains of Skog came upon the hapless Anglish village of Scarbyrig. Lost in the excitement of their fast-sweeping surge, Roric felt a rush of disappointment when Vanaash stopped suddenly and reached roughly to stop him.

"Our way is back there!" Vanaash gestured with a toss of his head. He shouted to be heard above the din that ensued as men set flame to the ancient ramparts that surrounded a score or so of timber dwellings, and brought them down with a mighty crash that lit the darkness. Raising his shield to ward off the shower of embers and sparks this caused, Roric signaled two more men, their most trusted. Ivar Half-Hand argued a bit, using exaggerated expressions of frustration more than words. Bull-shouldered Wulf Shin-Griever was young, hot-headed, and addicted to adventure, though. He turned and followed, still hoarsely repeating his rambling chant, and taking mock swings with the battle-axe that had earned him his known-name.

Good that Vanaash, at least, finds this duty gladsome, Roric thought glumly, aggravated at the thought of missing the glorious climax of what was certain to be the last sea raid until after the harvest. All too soon, his days would be filled with plowing and planting, weeding and watering. Oh, how he loathed farming! He kicked angrily at a heavy endpost of the newly fallen fortification. So easily did it give way, shattering and splintering, that he gave it a moment's perusal and found it had been purposely hollowed. Stooping, he reached deftly inside, fished around a scant minute, then drew out a heavy leather pouch. A quick glance inside was enough to pacify him, and his expression eased to one of satisfaction at the sight of gold and silver bracelets and rings, and an odd stone near a quarter the size of his clenched fist, scribed with intricate blood-red markings of rare and wondrous beauty.

Roric bit back a smile as he quickly thrust the heavy pouch down the neck of his leather hauberk. Then, somewhat lighter of mood, he hurried after his foster-brother, leaving the others to scour the huts for more prizes. 'Twas well indeed that he had found such worthy treasure. He would not have liked returning to the homestead with naught in hand but an old hag of a holy woman.

Alone in the cottage, Iseobel fingered her amulet of carved amber cats as she read. Stretched on her pallet, she had tucked herself in with a light bed fur and now leaned against a bank of pillows, crushed flat from the length of their service. Her little calico cat, Machthild, curled comfortably beside her, she craned, holding the precious thong-bound vellum closer to the burning taper, the awkwardness of her pose as habitual as her early morning stiff neck.

Her need to learn was surpassed only by the imperative that no one must guess how urgently she studied. With Dorflin, her father, suddenly and mysteriously gone, Iseobel could not guess what might lie ahead. Now she had abandoned attention to her surroundings for the knowledge on these pages, wisdom which she hoped would bring her the skills and power to fend for herself. Dorflin had always intimated in his couched way that hers was a special purpose. Special because she was to become a priestess ... or something beyond? He was never quite forthcoming on that point. Now her desire to know was desperate.

Though Dorflin's priestly duties sometimes took him away from their vill for days, this time he had disappeared unannounced and had been too long gone for her comfort. The uncertainty tormented her, not only because she loved him dearly and it pained her to consider life without him, but because he had kept her so sheltered from the ways of the world that she could scarce imagine facing life without his guidance.

She had never met any others of their kind. No other shamans or magickers that she knew of had ever come to their hamlet. If Dorflin did not return, she would be called upon to serve as sole shamaness to her village. Where would she turn now? Who would instruct her? She worried that she as yet lacked much of the necessary wisdom, though many healing skills were under her mastery, and it was clear that the villagers already respected her. In fact, they had set her apart, as they had her father, from their own ways and lives. Except for her friend Geir and a few other childhood friends, she was quite alone in the world without Dorflin.

Therefore, it was necessary that she study and strengthen her skills. According to Dorflin, all the keys to wisdom and magick were bound within the two books he had gifted her on her last birthday. Yet study as she might, little in the first book made any sense to her, and the second book was indecipherable. Not that she had any trouble with the actual words; she had long ago mastered the meanings of the runes of the FUTHARK, had come a fair way in the working of rune magick, and was familiar with many of the prayers, meditations, incantations, and spells contained in the volumes. There was more to these books, though, than the instructions lettered on the vellum pages: ancient, esoteric knowledge written in riddles to ensure that only those chosen to understand them could ever hope to interpret the sacred mysteries. If all the books' many riddles could ever be fathomed, she would be considered wise beyond measure. For now though, despite fleeting moments of hopeful inspiration and insight, the hidden meanings taunted and teased her mercury eyes, causing head-pain if she pondered them too long.

She had to keep trying, though! Her father had often cautioned her with tales of powerful enchanters who could bring less able Holies under their power and sap raw magick from them to enhance their own, all the while draining those more helpless of their vitality and growth. Determined that his daughter should never become such an unwilling thrall, Dorflin had taken great pains to impress on her the need for strength, and dutifully she pored over her studies with fervor. She would be stolid enough, she vowed, to stand victorious against any dark magicker who confronted her!

Moreover, Dorflin had stressed the worth of these volumes. At his insistence, she had often practiced movements to speedily conceal the books and cause any physical display of her rune-working to disappear. No precaution seemed too outlandish.

This night she was glad for her own wariness for she felt a vague uneasiness. In truth, only the boldest villager would dare burst in on her unannounced, and no visitor would ever approach in the night, for the dense woods surrounding their property had the reputation of being spirit-guarded, even haunted. Why, then, did things not seem right?

Iseobel shivered, then brightened. Surely it was nothing but her worry for Dorflin, the loud howling of the wind, and her own weariness! Reaching, she tickled Machthild's silky neck, smiling as the cat rolled over, purring.

"Silly of me to be nervous, dear one, when you are so obviously comfortable and content—" she started, but even as she spoke, she stiffened with a surge of fear, and the cat sprang to all fours with a surprised yowl. There was noise in the distance, strange and foreboding: the sounds of a great many approaching. Faraway cries, carried on the wind, rose to shouting and seemed to move closer.

*Marauders!* Iseobel's fingers gripped the amber cats on her necklace, and she froze. Why, by all the gods, would any invade this tiny hamlet? It was not a spot that boasted vast wealth or rich treasure. Even so, the clamor was unmistakable, and a faint smell of smoke convinced her the vill was under attack.

Trembling, Iseobel considered quickly. Should she arm herself to help with the fighting? Her sword skill was not terrible. She might be of some help. With Dorflin gone, though, there was no healer here but herself. She would serve the people better to stay whole and aid the wounded.

But she must hide! The hut near the sacred grove, she knew, was the perfect refuge. It boasted a marvelous hidden closet, undetectable from inside or out. Though doubtful the invaders would think to go farther than the cluster of cottages along the stream that ran from shore to vill, a sharp-witted one might notice the well worn path to the shaman's home and follow it. Granted, the little hut, which Dorflin fondly called the "goddess" hut, was only a furlong beyond, but it was well hidden, almost invisible among the trees.

Scattering the protesting little calico, Iseobel was up and into her kirtle in a flash, readying herself for flight in the way Dorflin had made her rehearse so often she could do it in her sleep. After dousing the smudge fire, she grabbed her leather satchel, always kept ready with a pair of shoes and a change of dress. She wrapped the two books in an oiled cloth and hid them and her pouch of runestones inside the bag, along with a few seedcakes and dried fruit. A skin of water and her small dagger completed her packing. Hauling on leather boots, she paused again to listen. "By the Norns," she murmured, "they're close!"

She grabbed her woolen cloak, heavy with embroidery and jeweled talismans, snuffed the candle, and made for the door. To her distress, a last look around revealed the rune of the Vana gods still glowing where she had projected it for protection while she studied. Actually, she was not sure whether any but the initiated could see it, but she could not hazard leaving it to announce the presence of a Holy. Even one young and untried like herself would be a rich prize for any seeking to use her powers for their own gain. She had to banish it! Reaching instinctively for the cats on her necklace, Iseobel strove to channel her thoughts. A dagger of lightning cracked the sky. Her already-thinning nerves jumped, but the hovering runeform glimmered and then, with an almost audible hiss, vanished.

As the door slammed behind her, the eerie glow of the fast-commencing squall revealed the gap in the woods that marked the overgrown path to the goddess hut. Pulling her cloak close, she headed for the safety of secret shelter. Trees cast skeletal shadows. The wind stung her face. Iseobel ducked under a branch, and her wind-whipped hair tangled in it, holding her fast.

"Tyr's hand!" she oathed aloud, unceremoniously yanking her dark tresses free. Sure of voices now, she began to run.

It seemed the marauders were following her! She panted more from fear now than from exertion. Maybe these invaders had determined to advantage themselves of women as boldly as they helped themselves to the vill's stores and treasures.

*Stores and treasures?* Hah! What Viking would waste his time on a place so small and poor? More to the point, she wondered frantically as the clamor grew closer, who would bother to climb to such a remote part of the hamlet? Could they know a maiden lived far back in the forest or could it be that somehow she was known outside the area and they sought her for her powers? No! That was ridiculous. She was still only a student of magick. It must be Dorflin they sought. Even so, they might well decide to take her in his stead.

More fearful now, she traded stealth for speed until she reached the fringe of the giant pine that draped the hut, hiding it well. She rounded to the door, lifted the heavy latchboard, and entered, all at once aware of the comforting scent of the place: lingering hints of rosemary, lavender and other familiar perfumes. Noiselessly closing the door, she scurried to the back of the hut, careful to obliterate any trace of her footsteps on the rush strewn floor. Behind a wall of hide, stretched tight and painted to resemble the stars in the midnight sky, was the harrow Dorflin had constructed for their rituals: a long low altar—no more than a thin slab of limestone, deeply carved, resting atop two wide trunks of lightning-killed oak. In the darkness, she made her way back to the wooden wall behind it and counted a space of five hand-widths in from the right, at knee height, then felt for the knothole. Finding it, she relaxed a little. Manipulating it just right opened the secret closet Dorflin had built behind the timber walls, and she climbed in and pulled the panel back into place behind her.

Safe at last, she drew a deep breath to still her pounding heart. Outside, the sky split again, this time fulfilling its promise. The rain came in torrents, cheering Iseobel somewhat with the thought that tonight's downpour would douse more than one marauder's fire. Smiling a bit, she savored the image until, realizing that she was exhausted, she dropped her sack on the floor and lay down, using the bundle to pillow her head. Though vowing to remain alert, once huddled in the total darkness, Iseobel dropped into sleep almost instantly.

An unearthly wail startled Iseobel awake. She must have napped for a moment, she realized with dismay. Blinking to clear her mind, she now recognized the eerie howl that had roused her. Poor Machthild was outside in the rain!

Carefully removing the false panel again, she started towards the front of the hut but had only gone a few steps when instinct stopped her. Closing her eyes, she willed herself to hear past the wind and the welling storm. She swept her attention in every direction, particularly on the narrow pathway that led hither. In just moments, she was rewarded by an awareness of tell-tale signals: the twang of a soggy twig's snapping, the squish of footsteps on rain-soaked grass and, at length, a hint of men's voices.

Heart pounding, Iseobel dropped to the floor and swiftly crept back into her hiding spot, just as the outer door swung open. Gathering her skirts and cloak after her, she silently pulled the panel shut. Safe!

She could hear two men searching the other room, though with less violence than she had expected. It surprised her somewhat to realize only a pair had come this far. On that she had misguessed, her fear making her imagine a larger and rougher company. She'd been right about who they were, though; they spoke Norse. Holding her breath, Iseobel strained, hoping to catch even a single decipherable word. When she did, her hand flew to her mouth to stifle an unbidden cry of dismay.

"... *vitki!*" one of them had said in a low voice. It was near the same as the Anglish word, "witki," the word for people like herself: wise ones ... workers of rune magick ... Holies who worked under the protection of the gods! She had not been mistaken; they *were* looking for Dorflin—or for her!

She shuddered, but before she could muse on it, a high-pitched yowl followed by a gruff oath jarred her. Machthild meowed insistently, the panel shuddered ever so slightly, and Iseobel grimaced. "May the nine mothers of Heimdall take you, cat!" she swore mentally. Machthild had led them to her very feet! Surely the pair knew she was in there now, and it would take them scant minutes to discover their way in. The advantage of surprise was her only hope.

Quietly as possible she groped for the bodkin in her satchel. Her legs ached and her palms were moist with fear but, happily, her eyes were used to the darkness. When the men discovered the secret closet, she would have a good chance to strike and flee before they saw her.

The panel rattled again; this time it was not Machthild's pawing. Iseobel steadied herself, dagger in one hand and satchel in the other. Suddenly, the panel opened wide. A dark, sopping figure edged a shoulder cautiously into the narrow space. With a warrior's wariness, he slipped farther in, nearly filling the entryway. As he groped forward in the darkness, Iseobel hissed, then slashed at the searching hand, connecting.

"Odin's eye!" the man bellowed, but instead of pulling away, he yanked her from the chamber, and deftly wrested her weapon away. A distant flash of lightning revealed him to be white-blond of hair and ice-blue of eye. Proud-looking, she thought, and fiercesome. Nevertheless, in the brief instant of light, their gazes met, and Iseobel was overcome with a strange trembling.

The moment passed quickly, though, and Iseobel bristled again with fear and loathing. She wrenched her arm away and, twisting hard against the man's grasp, managed to break free. Springing quickly, she took two bounding strides, but came up short, held fast by a fistful of her own long hair. It was the other warrior who had entangled his hand in her tresses and now turned her face to his. He laughed as she squirmed in his grip. Even in the darkness, she could see the white gleam of his teeth. He said something to the other as she struggled; his voice sounded merry and good-natured which enraged her the more.

"We shall see," she muttered defiantly. Gritting her teeth against the pain of her hair tearing from her scalp, she whirled violently, slamming her satchel under the man's chin. Caught by surprise, he let go of her, staggering backwards into the wall and, as fortune would have it, onto the cat.

With a snarl, Machthild sprang on him, sinking claws and teeth deep into his thigh. Again Iseobel darted for the open door, but the white-blond warrior ensnared her in a powerful grasp. Determined not to serve as sport for these men, Iseobel let her knees buckle momentarily, burdening him with her entire weight, and then began to flail and kick and bite. She felt his grip loosen and made ready to bolt again.

By now, the other had disentangled himself from the cat and came to aid his companion. Iseobel fought, writhed, and spit; but finally, though it took the pair of them to subdue her, the men wrested Iseobel to the ground and wrapped her, knapsack and all, in her cloak. Conversing nonchalantly over her high pitched oaths and curses, they carried her, kicking and struggling, into the storming night.

Thus bound helplessly, she was carried to their waiting ship.

# Chapter Two

The Vana goddess Freyja was astonishingly beautiful. Her lissome, high-breasted figure was unequalled in the Nine Worlds; her delicate complexion was exquisite; her silken tresses, which near swept the floor, seemed to reflect every light and motion around her; her commanding eyes were like mirrors of heaven. All craved her, none could resist her, and her mere presence had proven an arduous lesson in poetic love and yearning for many a man, mortal and immortal alike.

In gentleness, she was splendid; in anger ominous; and now, in anguish, she charged the air around her with a trembling nervousness, like the last blue and windy wisps of rain-streaked sunlight before the breaking of a midsummer storm.

"She is frightened and helpless! How could you let it happen this way?"

She closed her eyes as handsome Freyr—her soul mate, her twin, her lover—encircled her waist with his strong and reassuring hands. "You know our bounds of interference in mortal affairs are sore limited," he whispered soothingly, pulling her close in the way that always thrilled her. "If we help them too much, Odin will deny them immortality. I can but nurture hints in Vanaash's dreams and visions, else answer directly only what the lad thinks to ask the runes."

"But to let her suffer an abduction!"

Freyr tossed his head; a gentle smile lit his fair features which were so like her own. "Iseobel is in the hands of the very man whom we mean to have her! 'Twas my own daughter, not yours, who was the one cruelly snatched and used. Must be you know it is the worse for me—seeing my precious seed in the arms and service of our enemy, Lokji!"

Freyja shivered involuntarily. The Æsir god Lokji, even in his human form as the great Lord Lodur, always inspired her with dread, though he was comeliest of all gods and men. It had been hard to resist his advances, so intense was the heat he had inspired in his courting of her. Her wisdom and strength had proven his equal or more, though, and she had sore insulted him with her lofty rejection. She did not in the least regret it, for her power and Freyr's remained untainted because of it, but Lokji had sworn himself against them now and, worse, against the halfling children who were the only hope of their race. The dark lord knew their terrible secret. The Vana line was at a stalemate. Despite their abiding love and closeness, their health and fairness, Freyr and Freyja, unlike uncountable generations of Vana twin-god procreators before them, could not have children together.

Reading her as he always did, Freyr smiled wanly. "You know his secret, too, fairest!"

"Aye! That he is both Lord Odin's brother and son, born of incest."

"A bane to him!" Freyr added. "That which is the strength and essence of the Vanir, is an abomination to the Æsir, and ever they suffer hard from the consequences of it!"

He was right. To the Æsir, such a birth was a curse, though not one immediately discernable. All four of the sons Odin had fathered of necessity on his mother Jord were beautiful to look upon. The All-Father had pretended they were his step-sons to hide the shame, and had lavished them with every advantage of wealth and magick. Yet Hoder was blind, bold Thor was simple, Hoenir was cruel, and Lokji was—.

"Evil!" Freyr exclaimed in a tone that chilled her. "That is why we decided long ago 'twould be preferable to share our seed with humans than with the Æsir!"

He spun her gracefully to face him and kissed her brow before taking his leave. His words and manner, as usual, had calmed her somewhat, but she could not help worrying.

How much more promising the continuation of their line, they both knew, if they sired halflings by honorable Holies. Then they could mate their male and female offspring without the taints of the violent Æsir blood. Once Odin granted their children immortality, they could ensure the Vana lineage. Mighty Odin had decreed no Æsgarder could further the prospects of his halfling children. Were any to attain immortality, they must earn it. He had learned sadly by granting immortality to the first three halflings of Lokji, who had mated unwisely. Those offspring were tainted and dangerous. From thence, all aspiring to become immortal were bound to prove themselves to Odin. That was why she had sought Dorflin—surely any child he sired would prove worthy!

She thought about him now, as she often did. Whether he wore sueded leather breeches and a velvet jerkin of the finest making or rough-wove burlap and ill-fitting woolen leggings, Dorflin carried an air of elegance, presence, and power. The tall man with the wolf-silverbrown hair and sea-blue eyes could not pass through a village without turning heads and starting tongues. He bore an aura of mystery and charismatic charm. 'Twas no surprise she had noticed him and craved him for her most sacred of purposes!

Long had she searched Midgard after she and Freyr had made the decision. For this task she did not need the lusty, gamesome type she usually favored, but a stolid and mighty one: a worker of magick, dreamer of dreams, lover of cosmic order, and guardian of secrets. Try as she might to find a Midgarder with promise, none, she kenned, was right.

While she tarried in her choosing, her twin grew impatient. He'd been quick to father a girl child. Though the mother seemed holy and honorable, the girl, grown to womanhood and steeped in Vana power, served Lokji now and had given their comely, cunning enemy a halfling magicker son. Then, too soon for Freyja's liking, her twin had chosen another mortal and fathered a son.

Remembering this, Freyja felt again the bitterness. Sore had Freyr wounded her with his impertinence! She knew her own seed was imperative to properly perpetuate the balance of their race. Were Freyr's two halfling children to mate one another, her own powers would not be passed on and, though Freyr was content to believe he and she were alike enough to be as one, she knew there were aspects of herself he could not fathom: feminine mysteries he could never pass on.

With the birth of Freyr's boy child, she had hastened her search till she at length found Dorflin. Raised by Druids in the Cymry, he was strong in tree magick and exceptional in power and devotion. He had gained much of his prowess serving the White Goddess of the Celtic West, but his quest for knowledge had brought him to learn both the Æsa and Vana ways, becoming skillful at disguise and a powerful runester as well. She had never had a priest so loyal before. He alone, of all she had observed, was intent on serving the Vanir whole-heartedly. Though he made obeisance to Odin and the Æsir, a glance into his heart had shown he was sworn to her alone. He was the one!

Their trysting had been sweet, and Dorflin had understood that Freyja did not dare linger in Midgard. He had delivered her of the child himself, with the help of their lightelf friend Ridi, skilled in midwifery, in the small hut which he had ever after called the "goddess" hut.

Before she returned to Æsgard, Freyja had given him a sacred charm for the child's protection, and two books of knowledge, writ so that none but the girl could ever wholly decipher the sacred lessons therein. Freyja herself, though, could not tarry longer in Midgard, so Dorflin had been forced to raise their daughter alone.

Hurt by her brother's unfaithfulness to the pact they had made and suspicious that he might one day support his own daughter's claim as progenitor, she was intent upon making Iseobel the more powerful of the female Vana halflings. Though she felt no certain love for any other race of gods, not even the Æsir, with whom she lived and commerced, both she and Dorflin recognized the wisdom of favoring the White Lady, for the Celtic goddess might be of service in their daughter's safety and care.

This secret she hid even from her beloved twin-mate, that she had instructed Dorflin to rear the child first in the way of the White Goddess. The trees, stones, water, and air were the White One's domain in the land where Dorflin was sired. Who knew but that the time might come when they must hide the girl, not only from the Æsir but from the Vanir as well? So the agreement had been made and, beyond that, she could offer little hand in the parenting.

Bathed in the golden glow of the sunset, Freyja stood and stretched sinuously. Board would soon be set, and she must clear her mind and go merrily to feast. Still, there was a lingering sadness now she could not quite banish. She needed to see him!

It would be risky, she knew, to avail herself of Hlidskjalf, the Eye of Heaven, without formally requesting permission from Odin All-

Father, but she was too impatient now to wait. Besides, she knew he walked in Midgard this month, disguised as a one-eyed beggar, in his usual wont to test men's worth. In a trice, her decision was made. Opening a garderobe, she pulled forth her falcon cape and donned it. Save her necklace, Brisingamen, it was most powerful of her magick accouterments. So well did she love the freedom of flying in it, she had made herself forget that it came as a gift from Lokji in the days when he courted her.

Minutes later, she sat invisibly at Hlidskjalf. It was as if the Eye had been trained, or locked in place by some unknown power, for as soon as she looked toward Midgard, it focused on Lokji, noble and darkly handsome in his human-form, Lord Lodur. Mounted on his black steed, he argued with someone. There was a look of cold fury in Lodur's cherry-black eyes.

For more than twenty human years, Lokji had wandered Midgard, relentlessly searching for the tokens that would re-admit him to Æsgard. So well had she hidden those chess pieces that even now the dark one scarce had a clue! Odin would never let his stepson return till those magickal toys were returned. Looking on the makebate now, she could feel his wrath, rolling like waves of cold wind towards the heavens, and she shivered.

She was angry, having snuck here for the secret opportunity to look on Dorflin. She had done all that was required, but the Eye had focused not on him, but on this other, for whom she felt naught but loathing and meanness. Scarce seemed it possible, for ultimately the ruler of the Eye was the heart of the looker, and with all of her immense power, she had willed to see the other.

Lodur reared his horse now and started away, black hair flying on the belligerent breeze. Then the other man turned; she was clenched with an awesome dread. There was no mistaking the strength and power of his bearing, the determination of his look. The Eye had not argued its nature after all. This man now was indeed the one she had purposed to look upon—Dorflin.

So, at last they had found their way together, these two! Who knew how long they had commerced; both hid themselves well from the heavens. Could be the dark one already knew the maid's bind-ring was being forged and, by stealing it, meant to make her his own!

It had been a difficult decision not to warn the child of Lokji's human-form, but should the girl's mind or thoughts ever light on him, even in curiosity, he would swoop to her as surely as a hawk to its prey. No, she decided, she and Dorflin had chosen rightly. But the enforced vigilance ... the uncertainty was maddening. She, herself, was helpless, sworn not to interpose. But also she was frightened and fiercesomely angry. And she knew the time was at hand.

# Chapter Three

Having been unceremoniously dumped on a heap of straw in a closet on board, Iseobel alternated between anger and fright. She bashed at the door until it jolted on its hinges, but could not budge it open. Surely the Norsemen sailed swiftly home now across the Grey Sea. Soon there would be no hope of flinging herself overboard to swim back to shore. Mentally, she spat at herself. It had taken two of them, but they had bested her! Now she was captive, shut away until … until what?

What did these men know of her, and how had they fathomed it? How was it they knew where to find her? Had they only meant to have their way with a maid, would they have struggled so hard to get her aboard their ship?

The ship lurched, and Iseobel felt nausea welling within. "Mighty Njord," she invoked the god of the seas, "if I must be on water, please whisper the wind and waves to calm." Again the craft lurched. Faint, Iseobel sank to the straw.

She had known discomfort of water travel as a child, but now she felt agony. "My daughter," her father had cautioned long ago, "as your powers grow, you will find yourself less and less able to travel the seas. The whys and wherefores I cannot tell precisely, but it is ever so with our kind."

*Our kind,* Iseobel mused miserably, lapsing suddenly into worry for Dorflin again. Where *was* he? Her manic attempts at scrying had yielded nothing.

Oh, to catch a glimpse of those sea-blue eyes and that wolf-silverbrown hair! Already wretched, fret now grew heavy within her, too. Would Dorflin think that now, at eighteen, she had run off to escape the duties he foresaw for her or would he somehow know that she had been abducted and had not abandoned him of her own will?

Iseobel's fingers automatically reached for her cat amulet, a gift from the mother she'd never known. Aside from learning that her mother had left Midgard when Iseobel was only an infant, she knew nothing about the woman, and Dorflin had steadfastly managed to avoid her questions. Treating the amulet as a great treasure, Dorflin regularly exchanged its leather thong for a longer one as Iseobel grew, so that the talisman hung securely yet were easy for her to grasp when she needed their comfort. She could not remember a time when it wasn't there around her neck.

A high wave crashed over the sides of the ship and washed along the floor of the low closet where Iseobel huddled, shivering. She tried unsuccessfully to stifle a cry as her belly rose in her throat. Becalming herself, she determined to get to her feet. Surely someone would have pity and let her out so that she might take herself to shipside and be sick overboard. Feeling for a wall, she steadied herself and stood as high as she was able in the dark, cramped locker. A lurching roll flung her back onto the straw. Cloak and kirtle soaked by sea and rain, she crawled like a babe to the door and began to pound.

"For merciful Odin's sake," she cried, "let me out! Is there none of you with pity?"

She was sure no one heard her; the tumult outside was too great. The wastrels were too busy trying to save their ship to worry about the likes of her, she bemoaned. If the great boat capsized, *they* at least would have the chance to swim to safety, leaving her to sink; she was of no more value to them than any other piece of ill-gained treasure.

This notion angered her sorely; she was swept by a strong urge to curse them. She would bring them down, even if she had to share their fate! Shakily, she crept back to the straw and, mounding it high, crawled atop, reaching for her rune pouch.

Feeling delicately among the carven runestones, her fingertips lit upon the one she sought: LAGUZ, ⌐, the lake, the rune of the watery depths. Deliberately holding it inverted, she focused on it until a glowing blue runeform took shape in the darkness. Fists clenched, she began a murmuring chant, and in the language of the runes, described a curse. Suddenly the runeform wavered wildly, broke Iseobel's trance, and dissipated. Her heart was flooded with sure knowledge. *The rule of the gods decrees a gift for a gift. Seek to do evil, and evil you shall be henceforth.*

Chastened, Iseobel quickly returned the stone to her pouch and tremulously called to Dorflin and Freyja for forgiveness and guidance. Then, drained, she slumped over in the straw and abandoned herself to helplessness. All night long, unable to tell and hardly caring whether it was the ocean or her heart making her sick, Iseobel moaned on her sea-soaked bed. By the time light crept in at the chinks, the weather calmed, the ship ceased to pitch and roll, and Iseobel found the strength to push a small pile of straw, which she had of necessity soiled, off into a far corner. Drawing her knees up under her cloak and nibbling at one of her seedcakes, she rocked back against the closet wall, half-dozing until there came a sound at the door.

The hasp turned, and daylight flooded in. Iseobel shielded her face from the glare. A crouched silhouette approached her, a hand touched her shoulder, and a deep resonant voice, which she recognized too well from her capture, addressed her.

"Are you well?" He reached forward as if to comfort her.

Comfort, indeed! Surely he meant to.... Defiantly, Iseobel wrenched her shoulder away, retreated into the corner, and clenched her damp woolen cloak tighter around her. She cast the flaxen-haired man a withering look and, grasping the amber cats on her necklace, raised a hand menacingly. "Begone! You shall not use me in your ill sport!"

To her surprise, the man backed away. Nervously fingering the edge of her embroidered hem, she took satisfaction in realizing that she was not entirely strengthless, after all. Focusing her bleary eyes on him with renewed vigor, she watched while he set down a small pail and parcel, staring all the while at her, squatting to avoid bumping his head on the low ceiling.

"You will eat and drink shortly," he ordered in unsteady Anglish. "Mayhap it makes you wretched to think of it, but 'twould be best if we keep you somewhat strong."

She made no answer. He rose a bit and spaded the soiled straw into a bucket, then piled up some clean straw in an attempt to make a bed, searching out the driest to lay across the top.

Iseobel wanted to spit but her mouth was too dry to do it.

"Could be the drier straw will prove more comfortable," he said. She steeled her gaze, allowing no evidence of comprehension to stir her features.

"Elsewise, I have only a pile of cold and sopping hides to offer!" he said, but Iseobel only glared. Lifting the bucket, he retreated to the door and opened it. The smallest blast of sea wind made its way in as he did so, and Iseobel opened her mouth wide to savor its freshness.

The man hesitated at that very moment and turned sharply as if to say one more thing. Their eyes clashed like iron on iron. Iseobel, unnerved, clamped her jaw shut hard and suddenly.

The man stopped, eyes blazing, as if she smote him. "'Tis well you bit that oath back!" he said gruffly. "Know that I will suffer you not to spell or curse me, now or ever!" He stepped out, letting the door slam behind him with a thud.

Iseobel was not entirely displeased that her captor thought she had the power to work galdor spells to his disadvantage, but it was another indication that he expected her to be a magicker of far greater power than she knew herself to be. Feeling feeble and trying to formulate a way of using his misconception to her own advantage, she relaxed slightly, and felt more than ever the reeling dizziness that engulfed her. Despite it, she snapped back to her icy-eyed stare almost immediately as the man made his way back in to her prison. She thought he had finally taken his smug leave, but apparently he had only walked shipside to heave the contents of the bucket overboard.

Iseobel remained frozen. Seasickness or no, she would use what magick she could to hold her captor from her, although she had begun to doubt that he meant to have his way with her. She watched fiercely while he set down the bucket, reached to a hasp on the wall, and pulled a small shutter aside. Even from her low vantage point, she could see that the opening, while narrow, admitted a full view of the bow.

"You will feel less alone if you can see the others who stir and work round about you," the stranger said. She knew he was struggling to keep his voice steady. "Best you realize we keep you in here for your own safety and with no evil intent."

Iseobel moved not a muscle, except to follow him with her eyes as he stood up best he could in the low-ceilinged closet. Pointing to himself, he smiled, condescendingly she thought, and pronounced a phrase carefully: "Vanaav Komling."

She stared wordlessly. The name seemed strangely familiar, but she held her look purposefully blank.

"That is my formal name," he added, scanning her for acknowledgement. "You will hear the closest of my kith and kin address me as 'Vanaash.'"

He pointed to her questioningly. She knew this Vanaash expected her to share her name in return, but unrelenting still, Iseobel answered only with piercing silence. Outlined as he was in the doorway, his back to the sun, Iseobel could not read his face but knew it must register bewilderment and frustration. But it was only after he finally left, that she allowed herself a grim grin of triumph.

Satisfied that he was gone, Iseobel crept over to the small pail and took a sip. The cool beer felt soothing against her dry lips, She took a long pull to settle her stomach. Though the sea was calmer now, and the ship tossed less than before, she still felt a rushing dizziness. Not daring to partake of the food he'd brought, she crawled back to her straw mound and rested.

As the night fell, the air became chill, and Iseobel, much weakened, began to shiver in her damp clothing. She knew she would be warmer if she removed her sodden kirtle and shift but the thought of exposing her bare skin to the cold air made her tremble all the more. Railing at herself to be sensible, she finally steeled herself and hauled off her boots and stockings. Gritting her teeth to keep them from chattering, she removed her woolen cloak, lay it down and bunched straw around it, forming a nest to pull about her. Then, unfastening the kirtle, she spread it out in hopes that it might dry at least a measure.

By the time she heard the sails being lowered, Iseobel felt somewhat better; they would travel more slowly now, and the waves would less resist them. It might not be a bad idea to eat a little more. With effort, she crept to the bundle of food, but once unwrapped, the smell of dried fish and salted lamb turned her stomach. Hoping to calm her belly, she took a few small sips of beer and, once the heaving passed, she crept back to lie miserable on the straw. She had fasted many a time in her training without ill effect, but the retching combined with the abiding damp made her sicker, weaker, and more helpless than ever she had felt before.

*   *   *

Outside, Vanaash strode to the bow. No, he had not expected a warm reception from this woman, but for outright hatred and venom he had not been prepared. Her unearthly grey eyes had looked like liquid mercury when she opened her mouth to curse him, making her stare seem inhuman. 'Twas good luck she had changed her mind, he thought glumly; he would not have wanted to return to his homestead spelled with some crippling disease, or lunacy, or worse. That voice, too! It was as if she repelled him with the sheer force of it. Even so, he was certain she must be the very one he sought. Puzzling over her anger and hatred, he turned to look at the closet which housed her, half-hoping to see that she had opened the tiny window, but she had not.

Turning back to the prow, Vanaash reflected yet more on the comely creature. He was so lost in thought that he jumped when he realized that Roric was at his side, boldly insinuating that the woman had welcomed Vanaash's manly presence in the darkness.

Deeply shaken by his recent encounter and in no mood for Roric's jests, Vanaash faced his foster-brother squarely. "'Tis not the fact of it, Roric. Methinks rather she believes we would harm her, and most cruelly, too."

"Could be 'twas but the storm caused her to be affrighted, and the dark of the closet!" Roric, sobered by his brother's mien, stifled his first reaction, which was to scoff. "Surely in a pair of days, she will come aright."

Mildly heartened by Roric's attempt at reassurance, Vanaash mumbled in agreement and set about correcting their course by the early evening stars. His eyes turned now and again to the closet window but it remained ever closed.

Three times more, Vanaash brought Iseobel food, drink, and water for washing. Though he was careful to greet her every time, she sat still in the corner glaring at him, walling away her thoughts. Worse, the woman was obviously weakening. He saw clearly that she was more ill than could be accounted for by the sea motion, and that which might help her, food and drink, she refused. Too, he was sure that despite all his trying, he frightened her. Unlike Roric, who had wooed and bedded more maids than could be counted, he had never been one who waxed easy and comfortable with women. His foster-mother once told him that he lacked a certain gentleness of manner which women craved, and suggested he spend less time in work and study and more in gaming and poetry. He could not help but wonder whether their captive might be more yielding with a man more blithe and gamesome, like his foster-brother, than she was with himself.

Next morning, Vanaash, knowing Roric would be among the first to have risen, sought the Grim-Kill out and found the man draped casually at the prow, enjoying the damp and salty morning as he fed on sodden barley-cakes.

Roric grinned him a greeting, then sprang to his feet, apparently made uneasy by his foster-brother's dour look. "Everything is well, or not?"

Vanaash shrugged, facing himself into the wind and letting it blow the ice-blond hair out of his face. "I can't help but wonder, brother, how long a body can survive without sustenance. The Anglish woman has taken no food in three nights."

"Seems not a matter over which to worry yourself," Roric replied levelly, holding out one of the cakes which Vanaash accepted joylessly. "If she is of the Holies as you say you suspect, must be she can fast a good length of time."

"She looks pinched and weak now!" Vanaash grimaced. "It seems she is starving."

"That sly one? I doubt it!" Roric shook his tangled curls and gave a snort of genuine laughter. "Mayhap she carries her own food stashed in that precious satchel of hers. In any case, I scarce believe she will starve herself on a four-day voyage."

"You have not looked on her since we sailed, Roric!" Vanaash miserably tossed the unnibbled portion of his barley-cake into the foaming waves. "'Twould grieve me greatly if she somehow met death at our hands!"

Roric laughed again, turning his face to avoid a gust of salt spray. He clasped his hand briefly to the other's shoulder. "Worry more that she has sense enow to keep to the dry straw. Seepage from the rain and spray has certain pooled along the ribbing in the closet, no matter how much we bail out here. Even that, though, will make her chill and queasy, not dead!"

"More's the worse ...." Vanaash whispered numbly, picturing the woman's discomfort with a surge of guilt and horror.

Roric shrugged as if to downplay the seriousness of his own words. "She seemed strengthful enow when she struggled against us. She has, I hazard, more vigor than the men who have been rowing all night. 'Tis better we worry about raising the sails for the day than about her!" Realizing that his jests had not done much to lift Vanaash's mood, Roric shrugged, "Mayhap it would ease your mind if I were to look in on the holy woman today and see if any herbals can be of use to her."

"Aye," Vanaash said in a far-off tone, "I would that you looked in on her." Under other circumstances, Vanaash might not have trusted his lusty foster-brother to visit a pretty maiden alone without flirting. Oft had the man stolen a maid right from the arms of another man who loved her, merely by smiling a certain way and making himself irresistible, a great talent with him. But Roric was well skilled with herbs and remedies, and it was likely the man could help her.

Later in the day when Roric returned downcast from his visit to the little closet, though, Vanaash was sure that this time he had no worries on that account. It was obvious Roric had suffered the same freezing reception. He suspected, too, that Roric, as one who enjoyed unbidden the attentions of maiden and matron alike, was surprised that he could elicit no response from Iseobel for all his charm.

"You've a strange one there, brother," Roric had commented glumly after Iseobel's rebuffing of his proffered solace. Almost against his will, Vanaash was forced to agree. Those quicksilver eyes seemed to take in everything and emit nothing but ice! Holy or not, though, she was a rare-looking woman and he knew it, though it irked him to hear Roric say those words aloud.


By the time the door had opened at mid-day, Iseobel was so ill that she could barely sit upright to watch the new man enter.

He had bowed respectfully, and when he introduced himself, she recognized the voice—the second of her captors, the one who had laughed at her. Even fevered, seeing him, she wondered that she had been afraid of this man with disheveled hair, jangling jewelry, and a boyish, good-natured smile. He knelt next to her, searching seriously through the contents of a medicine pouch, as if it represented a real reason for his being there. She knew she should probably allow a bit of looking after, but could not bring herself to actually invite any ministrations.

Though the man had made every effort to be gentle with her, his gaze had been bold. She half expected, during his courteous solicitations, that he might let his touch linger a bit too long here or there. He did not, though, and instead dabbed her throat and shoulders with a cooling balm and rubbed her lips with a soothing nectar that at once made her calm and sleepy.

"Best you make yourself well, maiden," he had whispered as he left her, "else many a more heart will be broken than you can imagine." His husky voice had moved her somewhat as she drifted off; there was a kindly timbre to it that rang of hope. She was as yet unsure of the other, but certainly there was no malice in this one.

The day had drifted by in sleep made easier by the remedy. Later, Iseobel half-wished for another dose of it, but the healer had not come back. It was late in the night now, and she tossed and turned. Yet, despite her long slumber, Iseobel was exhausted. Raising herself weakly, she realized she was shaking violently, too, and her under-shift was soaked, not with sea-water but with the hot sweat of fever. She grasped the hem of it and pulled it off over her head. As she looked for a place to hang and dry it, the hasp unlocked, and before she could react, the door swung open. She dove for the warmth and modesty of her cloak, but not quickly enough. In the light from the oil lamp he held high, she saw his trembling gaze, a mix of confusion, apology, and desire. The man Vanaash was looking at her unclothed!

Iseobel stared daggers at him, willing him to turn his gaze, but she found no stores of strength to compel him. Even so, Vanaash glanced away quickly, as if her look had physically forced him.

"How dare you!" she hissed, biting on the words before she buried her face in the straw. *Dorflin!* Mentally she called on the one who always came first to her thoughts. *If he will have advantage of me,* she trembled, *then let it be, for I am ill and feckless upon the water. I can fight no longer.*

Though she had not spoken aloud, the man seemed to have heard her thoughts clearly. Embarrassed, he looked down at her and, hanging the lamp, removed his own wolf-fur cloak. He knelt and spoke gently, "Please, take my mantle."

Surprised by his solicitous tone, Iseobel glared first at him then at the proffered mantle, but its promise of warmth was too tempting to resist; she reached out and snatched it. Burrowing down into the fur, she lapsed into a confusion of thoughts, made more feverish by the fact that Vanaash was staring at her unabashedly now. When he reached over to cushion the straw, Iseobel found herself too feeble to protest, though his nearness bothered her.

Why could he not leave her be? If they were determined to minister to her, why had not the other one, that Roric, come with his assortment of herbs? She wanted nothing more than to sink back into the comfortable numbness of sleep, but this one seemed bent on tending to her now. In truth, though, when he lifted her head and held the rim of the beer pail to her lips, she slowly but thirstily sipped. Then tired from the effort, she watched listlessly as he opened the bundle. He broke off a piece of something, and held it to her mouth.

"Lutfisk," he said, as if it were something that should reassure her. "Let it bolster your strength, lady!"

At the first whiff of it, she groaned and, unable to stop herself, began to retch. Too powerless to lift her head, she choked. Quickly, the man turned her on her belly, lifted her by the middle, and held her forehead. How wonderfully cool his hand was! Even in her abject misery she savored it.

When her spasms subsided, he released her gently, then swiftly cleaned away the soiled straw. She looked up as he returned; even in the dim light she could see longing in his gaze. She cared no longer about her nakedness, in spite of her every certainty of what was about to happen.

Trembling, he pulled his eyes away. He turned, snuffed out the oil lamp, and tucked the fur mantle back around her before he lay down beside her in the dark. Iseobel gritted her teeth, crying silently to Dorflin as the man gathered her to him. She held her breath.

Vanaash did naught, though, but hold her, pillowing her head on his chest and gently stroking her hair. Though she was wroth to admit it, for the first time since she was forced aboard the *Windrider*, Iseobel knew comfort.

Hazily, she closed one hand over her amulet. Draping an arm around her captor's waist, she snuggled toward his warmth despite the fact that she was fairly burning with fever. Soon, his unwonted gentleness had lulled her toward blessed sleep. Tumbling fast into childlike slumber, she murmured softly for her father, leaving Vanaash wide awake to wonder about the identity of the man Dorflin for whom she so obviously longed.

# Chapter Four

Roric Grim-Kill was wide awake in the misty hours before dawn.
Savoring the kiss of the ocean wind, he stood in his favored spot at
the intricately carven neck of the proud dragon prow. They had put
down the sails for the night and re-hoisted them as tents over the
spars so the men could rest peacefully despite the sporadic
storming, but it had stopped raining a full two hours ago and, as
usual, he found it intolerably close under the waxed-woolen
awning. In fact, he greatly favored soft drizzle and an occasional
sharp bite of wind over the afflicting mixture of strong attars, stale
drink, and bodies long-unwashed which seemed to gather like a
malodorous cloud under that heavy canopy. It was chill enough that
he was glad for his mantle of marten's fur. They had already come
three of the four days' sail back to Sogn, and he meant to enjoy his
last night at sea.

She was a grand ship, *Windrider*, best of any long ship he had
seen, boasting thirty-four oars, a closet, a cargo hold, and glare-eyed
dragons bow and stern, each three times mansize. It had been his
father's ship, though he could not remember that Eirik Half-Dane
had ever stood beneath a hoisted sail. Nay, his father had been a

homesteading man and had financed the building of such vessels, but like many other rich landholders had paid others to do his raiding.

The man was dead four years now and no one, it seemed, ever had ill to say of him, but to Roric such a reticence seemed more a blot than a virtue. "Let me put *Windrider* on the waves, father," he had been wont to say when younger, "and I will earn you more riches in a single seafaring season than all you have amassed these many years of farming and husbandry."

But when Eirik Half-Dane lay dying, he had gifted *Windrider* to his foster-son instead. "Let Vanaash have her," he had murmured, speaking thickly through lips heavy with the rime of death. "Better gone to one who has heart and pride, if not a drop of my own blood, than to a bold-mouthed brat who can ne'er be aught than useless."

Thinking of it now, Roric shivered, less from cold than from anger. It was unfortunate that in his father's last days, the man had been so wroth with him. Eirik had never forgiven the deathwound the Grim-Kill had dealt his kinsman, Haftor. By the gods, though, it had been far more than the drunken, jesting swordplay he had pretended. His sister Beatta's honor might have been forfeit had he let on that he'd killed his cousin for attacking her, so he uncomplainingly suffered his father's contempt.

Too, there was the child Roric had fathered on the lowly byre-maid, Kirsten. His father would scarce let him forget *that*! Eirik had been implacable, though their retainer Wulf Shin-Griever had gladly taken the proffered silver and married the girl to give the child a name. Had made a good match of it, too, for Kirsten was a pretty woman, and so good with a needle that Wulf was counted the best dressed of warriors now, in his decorated sarks and embroidered tunics. Though he bore the Shin-Griever no ill and deemed him firmest of friends, Roric sometimes longingly imagined how differently his own life might have fared thus far had he been allowed to wed the servant woman himself instead. Useless picturings, for Eirik had made his decree and it was far too late now to change it. Long ago, Roric had taught himself not to care that his father had despised him, seemingly from his babyhood on. Still, it hurt so much to think on these things that he hurriedly forced his mind to other matters.

Apart from Ivar Half-Hand and a young Dane named Egil who were tending the tiller, Roric knew not that any other man was awake until he saw Vanaash emerge unsteadily from the small pine locker where they were keeping the holy woman. Roric tried, but not too successfully, to suppress a smug smile at the sight of him. His foster-brother was cloakless, loose and rumpled, and, as he walked, was picking bits of straw from out of his hair and the folds of his kidskin tunic. He had been with the woman six hours or more. Could be she had proven herself less than holy!

Scarce had he formulated the thought than Vanaash shot him a chilling glance. "She was ill from the pitch of the sea and fevered from the damp, brother," he said in a cold tone, "and I held and soothed her till she slept."

Roric shrugged and gave a casual laugh. "Must be her powers are not over-developed if she scarce can withstand the rock of the waves." He could not help being wary of this so-called holy woman; she seemed too young to have earned much knowledge, though her manner of control was uncanny.

"Could be she is one of the Holies—" Vanaash started, as if in answer. In truth, he knew she was, but his foster-brother was wont to scoff at such beliefs. As he'd expected, Roric threw his head back and laughed.

"If she was one of the Holies, she would have put an unbreachable shield up all around that miserable hut where you found her. Else she would have slipped invisible through our fingers 'ere we put her on this ship! The Holies all are hardy people, Vanaash. Secure in their power. This one seems too ... soft."

"Aye. Could be you are right in that!" Vanaash answered, still plucking twigs of straw off his clothing and throwing them, one by one, into the sea. "Why she was strengthless to stop us, I cannot say. But I sense her power."

Roric laughed again. "Know you what seems to me? That you have journeyed a long, hard way to claim a useless good luck charm. Think you she will be disposed to bless your endeavors after you snatch her from kith and kin and burn her village?"

"Mayhap she will be able to read why I took her," he whispered.

There was a long silence; they listened to the swell of the ocean a while before Roric spoke again. "Why *did* you take her?"

"Seems I cannot rightly tell till it all unfolds!" Vanaash exclaimed miserably.

Roric stared at him accusingly. "She will not bring us any good fortune. Best you be rid of her at Sogn!"

"Nay, Roric!" Vanaash turned his back and stared intently at the first lavender ribbons of dawn shimmering in the east. "She is meant to come with us."

"What mean you? That you will carry her to Skog and build a hall for her in the village there, so that freemen and lords will pilgrimage to hear her speak?" Roric sounded more interested now. He was thinking of a great jarl, Lord Lodur of Trondelag who, finding a holy woman on the Isle of Fyn, crafted a fine warship and housed her on it, perched outside his village. Then folk came from everywhere, far away as Tromso and Gotland even, for it was said she could speak directly with Frigga Cloud-Spinner, chief of all goddesses, and through her to Odin himself. Could be she had been one of the Holies, maybe even god-sired, for there were thousands who could attest to the strength of her magick, and it was ever rumored that evil Lodur was fond of stealing holy women for his own use. The jarl had grown magnificently rich on the many pilgrims' offerings.

"Might be she could bring us good fortune after all!" Roric mused excitedly. "We could house her in that ancient cairn near Bjorgvin!"

Vanaash stilled him with an impatient wave of the hand. "She is coming home to Skog with us, brother," he said wearily, "but only until we are willed to bring her elsewhere."

"To our very skaale you mean?" Roric's tone was incredulous. "Must be you have not wasted much thought on how Beatta will take to such an unexpected visitor!"

"'Tis not as if I am springing a surprise!" Vanaash answered hotly. "I told your sister most certainly that I expected to be bringing back a holy woman!"

"Aye, so you told me, too. And I was minded of that withered hag at Rogaland we were wont to buy wolves' teeth and hawks' claws of when we were youngsters!"

"Say you that this one's face is to her detriment?"

Roric let go a short laugh. "Well you know I would better look upon one finely wrought than any other. But Beatta—"

"What matters this to her?"

"First and foremost, 'tis her homestead!" Roric declared hotly. As the *Windrider* had gone to Vanaash, so Eirik Half-Dane had bequeathed his vast estates to his fiery daughter. She was far more capable, the dying man had proclaimed bitterly, than the willful and arrogant Roric. "'Tis her homestead, and she has a most jealous care of it. And of you!"

Vanaash flushed and looked away. Watching Vanaash curiously, Roric tried to fathom him. Surely he understood the customs! Beatta was newly widowed, and as her foster-brother, Vanaash was expected to take her on. It would be no great trial for him, either. Beatta was full-bodied and fair of face. What is more, Beatta craved the man, any fool could see as much! Her heart was set upon having him, and she was a hard one to sway from course. Vanaash knew the woman well, too. She was indomitable and had well proven the iron edge of her temper to all of them. Why in the Nine Worlds Vanaash would want to bait her by bringing home a chattel, especially one with a face and form like this one's, was beyond Roric's comprehension. To his reckoning, Beatta was one woman better left unriled.

Roric waxed angry as he thought on it. Could be he would have to deal with this would-be holy woman himself, and save them all the trouble....

A merry cry of thanks to the sea-god Njord went up from the crew. Land was in sight! The exhausted men hove to their oars and pulled with a new vigor. Soon they would be entrenched in the mead hall, telling of their adventures and showing prizes.

The May sun was gentle on their backs and baked the rain-sodden gear they had spread to dry. One by one, each left his post as instructed by Ivar Half-Hand to pack his trunk and prepare for landing. Roric himself stood at the tiller, looking for the markings that would guide them to Sogn's harbor.

Vanaash finished packing his gear, re-rolled the many oiled charts, and walked aft to relieve the Grim-Kill. "Surely," he said, amused by the faraway look in Roric's eye, one which he had come to know so well, "you must be anxious to ready yourself for the waiting ladies."

"Must be you know I never have need to ready myself for such," Roric replied flippantly, tossing overboard the remains of a small stick he had whittled near to nothingness. "But what of your Danelaw woman? Think you not she, too, would want to be made ready for the eyes of men? Would you bring her off the ship bounden like a prisoner, or do you have enow heart to present her as an honored one of your travel party?"

Whether he was more astounded by Roric's concern for the woman, or by his own lack of forethought, Vanaash could not tell. He had been so busy deciding how to handle the woman once they were off the ship that he had never given a thought to her grooming.

Roric tossed Vanaash an earnest smile. "Seems 'twould be fitting to give a care for the creature, brother. Methinks you should see to her this morning."

"May the great dragon take you, man," Vanaash laughed, pulling the tail of Roric's bounden hair, "if anyone has brushes and perfumes enow for a lady, Grim-Kill, 'tis you. I shall send for you and your oiled pack of primpings in time." So saying, he strode to the closet door, this time pausing carefully to knock.

Taking a soft moan as reason enough to enter, Vanaash ducked in and, closing the door behind him, opened the small window. "Look," he pointed, "we nearly are at journey's end. Soon you will look on Skog, our home in the Nor Way."

Iseobel made no response, only turned on him a dull and fevered gaze. Alarmed that she seemed to have taken a turn for the worse in a matter of hours, Vanaash left to fetch Roric. He was grateful that his foster-brother, as a youngster wishing to escape the unwelcome condescension of his father and siblings, had kept to his mother's side and learned much of household remedy. 'Twas an art that had oft proven of invaluable worth.

"By both ravens!" Roric breathed anxiously, bending to trace the shape of the rune WUNJO, ᛈ, on the maiden's brow with his fore-finger soon as he saw her.

"Aye! This one could well use that rune's bounty!" Vanaash whispered dully, watching him. "The joy of health would serve her well just now."

Roric nodded in stern agreement. His anxious look assured Vanaash that her illness was serious. He watched in admiration as Roric reached into his belt-pouch, withdrew a linen cloth, dipped it, and, after smoothing stray tendrils of her matted dark hair away, bathed the woman's hot face and hands. Then he fetched the pail of beer, lifted her head, and brought the rim to her dry lips. After taking but a couple of sips, the woman turned her head, refusing more.

Roric reached under his hauberk and withdrew a worn-velvet neededs pouch wherein he carried his healing herbs. Selecting from among the various physics a dose of dried nightshade, he placed it under her tongue, then daubed soothing oil on her cracked lips.

"Your second-sight may have led you aright to this beauty, brother," Roric growled while he tended to her, "but may the gods forgive you that she suffers so sorely at our hands."

Vanaash remained unmoved. He had not heard Roric's remark or the oath breathed after it. It appeared that the woman had, though, and she reacted to Roric's honest solicitude gratefully, lifting a hand and weakly stroking his newly shaven cheek as if to impart forgiveness.

Roric stiffened, then returned to his task with renewed fervor. Re-wetting the cloth, he placed it on her forehead, then turned to survey her clothing. The linen shift was dry, but the kirtle, stockings, and cloak were damp. Her boots, too, could use an hour in the sun. Gathering up her belongings, he handed them to Vanaash with orders to set them out to dry, then tried to extract the damp leather satchel that pillowed the woman's head. She clenched it so fiercely that he gave up.

When Vanaash returned moments later, he was certain that the woman now realized, too, that she was ill far beyond her seasickness. Her breathing was labored, and her heavy-lidded gaze wandered from his face to Roric's as the two of them spoke in low tones over her. She was listless yet she held tight to Roric's arm as if for strength. Seeing that, Vanaash tensed; the woman surely seemed to take more comfort in Roric's presence than in his own. Drawing a sharp breath, he dropped to his knees beside her, drawing away his foster-brother's attention with an ungentle nudge and loosing the woman's grasp on him.

"'Twould seem that I could see to her alone now, Roric Eirik's son." Vanaash kept his voice level but Roric raised an eyebrow at the coldness of the man's tone and the unwonted formal address, then shrugged and stood. Iseobel, eyes suddenly wide, begged him with a look not to leave, and Roric seemed to understand it. Dropping to one knee, he smiled and touched a finger to her cheek.

"I will return with your clothing when it has dried, lady," he whispered in that breathy way that Vanaash had come to call the man's pillow voice. Somewhat roughly, Vanaash pulled his foster-brother away with one hand, shoving a bucket of slops at him with the other. He felt a twinge of guilt when he saw the swift look of scarce-disguised hurt that crossed the other's handsome face.

Roric forced a dim half-smile and shook his head knowingly. "Aye, best you tend her yourself, Vanaash, whether she wills it or not. I will bring you back a hairbrush, that you may see to her appearance. 'Twould hardly be fitting for the people of Sogn's harbor to see us disembark with a woman all disheveled. Most would suspect that she is ill, surely, but no sense tempting tales. Folk are apt to think the worst when Roric Grim-Kill takes hand of a woman's care."

Dismayed with himself, Vanaash swallowed back the answer he thought to toss at his foster-brother's back as the man took his leave. He bent solicitously, but when he sought to put a soothing hand to the woman's brow, she turned her head fiercely away.

\*           \*           \*

Closing the door behind him, Roric swallowed hard, wondering what had inspired Vanaash's sudden coldness. Couldn't be the man suspected him of having designs on that piteous holy woman? Then he shrugged; so what if he had? Vanaash was supposed to be betrothed to another and had no right to be jealous. Roric shook his head hard, as if to throw off unbidden emotions.

Nay, he must be mistaken! Vanaash could never feel passion for such a waif—though she *was* somehow hotly inspiring, he had decided whilst he daubed witch hazel and other cooling brews on her neck and bosom. Must be Vanaash was angry at the thought that Roric might somehow dishonor this hard-won holy woman. Surely that was it! Vanaash regarded her as his private Holy and was wroth that any might think of her otherwise. He can save himself the worry, Roric resolved. He was too strongly tied to his foster-brother to let such a thing come between them.

But try as he might to ignore it, Roric couldn't help reflecting on the jealousy in his foster-brother's tone. If the man truly was smitten with this new conquest, then a tempest loomed ahead certain with Beatta. Had he himself not spent nearly a lifetime avoiding the wrath of his fiery elder sister?

Beatta had largely ignored Roric as long as her twin brother Staag lived. Those two were inseparable, and when Staag received his death blow in battle, Roric's every attempt to comfort her was soundly rejected. "You have not the mettle to fill the gap which my twin has left me!" Beatta had said scornfully, time and again. Roric oft felt she meant to finish by adding "'twere better it had been Roric the Useless that had died by that clout."

Then Beatta had married Thran Mangler. What a pair! Those two lusted after raiding, gaming, mead drinking, and especially each another, but when Eirik Half-Dane died and left his estates to Beatta's able care, the marriage began to sour. Thran had no head for management, yet insisted that his wife take his advice. Each time one of his ventures went bad, which all inevitably did, Beatta paid for it in bruises.

It had saddened Roric to see his strong-willed sister thus ill-treated, yet he seldom interfered. In this, Vanaash had backed him. "Let the cooks themselves pull the bones from out the bubbling stew, brother," he had told Roric more than once. "That way, you are not the one to burn your fingers!"

Still, he could not but blame his own inaction when things

turned out as they did. The couple fought violently one night and Roric ignored it till Beatta fled to the byre. Then, hearing her scream, Roric followed, bursting through the door in time to see his sister, her face bloodied and her red locks singed, crash her battle axe down hard, severing her man's head from his shoulders.

From the moment Thran was buried, though, Beatta had concentrated on winning Vanaash. She had adored her foster-brother even in childhood. It was she who had coined the name "Vanaash" by which he was now known; his true name, Vanaav, had been too complex for her babyish tongue. And as custom implied that Vanaash should care for her now, she used this opinion hard to her advantage, wooing the man shamelessly.

"Be off with you, Jarl Roric!" A familiar voice broke off Roric's reflection. Roric came quickly to his feet, biting back a sad smile at the sight of Wulf Shin-Griever's handsomely embroidered tunic. He scarce ever looked at Wulf without thinking of Kirsten and he oft wondered why, for surely he himself was better off an unmarried man.

Wulf, half-a-head shorter and broader at the shoulders by one buckle-hole of the quiver-strap, did not seem to notice, as usual. "I am come to relieve you at the helm, as ordered," he explained, grinning as he shaded his wide-set gray eyes from the bright sun. "Have I timed my coming well?"

"Aye," Roric replied, looking past him. "Better than you could know!" Reckoning that the holy woman's clothing must be dry by now, he left to fetch it, grabbing a hairbrush from his chest of stores as he passed it.

Opening the closet, he saw that Vanaash slept anext the woman on the straw; her head was cradled tenderly on his foster-brother's arm. *By Odin and Freyja,* Roric declared silently, *you may rely upon me in any battle, my brother, but I fear I will be as helpless as you against Beatta in this.* Shaking his head in resignation, he stooped to jostle his foster-brother awake, then shook the woman's shoulder gently.

She sat up, regarded them both hazily, and haltingly took the bundle of clothing Roric handed her before he and Vanaash stepped outside to let her dress. Later, Roric dosed her again with fever remedy and dabbed at her brow, while Vanaash worked with the brush to fight the snarls out of her long, dark hair. "Not much longer," he kept saying, obviously uncomfortable with his task. "Only a short while more...."

His words doubtless meant little to the woman, but even in her near delirium, it seemed she found the tones soothing. She jerked away, however, when he lifted the hair at her nape and began to remove the neck thong which hindered him.

"No!" she cried pitifully, pulling weakly away, "Dorflin told me never to remove it!"

Roric laughed, apparently not realizing the depth of her distress. "My brother wants none of your jewelry!" he cried, working hard to still his mirth with both glaring at him. "'Tis not so great a treasure as those he is used to stealing!"

The Grim-Kill seemed to think his words clever till Vanaash stilled him with a swat of the boar-bristle brush, pushed him aside, then returned to his task with determination. He worked to soothe the woman, but she fidgeted and would not unloose the amulet from her grip. So it went for some minutes, Vanaash's fruitless attempts at grooming being met with a stubborn, if feeble, resistance.

At last, tired of watching Vanaash's strivings, Roric moved forward and put hands on the woman's shoulders, kneading them gently to soothe her. "Sit still," he chid softly, "'tis only the snarls he means to—"

He did not finish, though, for Vanaash let go an oath, and raised the brush as if to smite the other man with it again. Surprised, Roric jumped back, but his fingers had become tangled in the poorly tied ribbons that held Iseobel's shift to her, and the knots came undone, letting the shift drop open and fall to her waist. Both men reacted as entirely as they were formed to do until her cry of humiliation and despair finally drew their stares away and snapped them back to uncomfortable reality. Sobbing, she batted them both away and tried desperately to cover herself.

"Gods!" cried Roric, and he blushed like a callow youth.

"I will kill you, Roric!" hissed Vanaash, blaming his brother entirely for the painfully awkward state of affairs.

"Begone from me!" commanded Iseobel, trembling so mightily that each time she managed to pull the shift up to cover herself, it slipped out of her shaking fingers and fell again.

Eyes shut, Vanaash felt for and found the ribbons. Holding them away from the woman's body, refusing to let his hands light where they obviously would have loved to tarry, he tried clumsily to tie bows or knots while her cries turned to sobs.

"Hush. Take ease," he lulled. "... no more weeping!" His efforts proving futile, he did not argue when he felt Roric's sure touch take hold of the ribbons, but he opened an eye just enough to ensure that his foster-brother was not advantaging himself of another secret look.

Roric's hands were so deft and sure, his bows so comely that it could not fail to remind Vanaash that his foster-brother had practice in such things. Even as a meanness crossed Vanaash's face, the woman turned all at once and gazed at him accusingly. Squirming a little, Vanaash handed her the rest of her sun-warmed clothes, and she smiled at him appreciatively.

The men hurriedly left Iseobel to finish dressing, but as the *Windrider* made its slow way into the harbor, Vanaash returned to the closet. He lifted Iseobel to her feet and, supporting her well, led her to the small window and pointed out the busy harbor, back dropped by mountainous fjords. "See there? We are but minutes from Sogn."

Iseobel looked out, relief plain on her face. "Land," she whispered longingly. "Dry land!"

When Roric poked his head in the doorway to announce they were mooring, he stayed himself a moment and watched the two enjoying this easy moment. The sight of Iseobel's lush figure had made him suddenly forgetful of all he had vowed earlier. In fact, the sight of the maiden relaxing now in his foster-brother's hold provoked a surge of jealousy which entirely bewildered him in its intensity. He had never known Vanaash to be smitten with a woman before. Certain, the man needed a woman's soft touch, and why he should begrudge Vanaash this one, so obviously of the man's own choosing, Roric was loath to consider. Clearing his throat, he made his announcement quickly and took a swift leave before either could turn to look at him.

Later, ashore, he was musing on it still. When Vanaash bade him go fetch the waiting wagon and horses, while he, Vanaash, waited with Iseobel, Roric surprised even himself.

"'Tis heartening to see you do manage to trouble yourself after all with the lady's comfort," he snapped, eyes blazing. "Seemed to me you worked over-hard to discourage any from showing her kindnesses!"

He was not sure why, but it took all his effort to stride away without saying more.

# Chapter Five

*Windrider* at moor always attracted a large crowd. She was the largest, worthiest craft in the fjord, and her crew always returned with the richest of plunder. Knowing it useless to hope to sell their wares again until the ship was unladen, the merchants gave up mongering in favor of gossip. When a feeble-looking, hooded figure disembarked, wrapped in a cloak heavily decorated with runic markings and supported by the jarls themselves, there were tongues enough to carry tales to Jutland.

The cloaked woman seemed exhausted by her short walk from the ship, and those nearest the wagon said it was a wonder she could walk at all, considering the trouble she had drawing air. Word was that she was so ancient she was not likely to survive the journey.

Suspicious, Brynhild, the taverner's wife, remarked loud that it seemed odd that the jarls were so serious and close-mouthed of a sudden. A smug smile lit her ruddy face when a sudden gust blew Iseobel's hood off, and the crowed gasped to see that the woman was no ancientess at all, but a willowy, dark-haired beauty.

Loath to cause any more of a spectacle than they already had,

Vanaash bundled Iseobel into the wagon bed and then swiftly climbed up beside his foster-brother on the driver's seat. Roric snapped the reins smartly, and off they drove, Ivar and Wulf following astride. Eyes from every quarter were fixed on the wagon, and few observers missed how solicitously Jarl Roric glanced into the wagon bed, obviously much concerned for the lady's comfort. A titter of speculation burgeoned as the harbor folk went back to their customary chores.

The day was lustrous. As they drove, Vanaash alternated between worry for his sleeping charge and warm joy inspired by the familiar scenery. Pine-blanketed foothills rose sharply to his left; ahead, titanic clouds softened the brilliant blue sky. Terns and gulls swooped and soared in the sun.

They had just passed beneath the towering oak which marked the final leg of their journey, when the woman abruptly cried out, startling Vanaash to action. In a single, lithe movement he jumped from his seat to the wagon bed beside her. Something had horrified her or caused her some painful memory, and Vanaash reached instinctively to comfort her, but she pulled away, clasping her hand over her mouth to stifle her sobs. Even so, Vanaash heard her clearly as she cried out a single name in an agonized tone: "Dorflin!"

He stiffened at the sound of it and was simultaneously flooded with images from her thoughts: *An ancient oak ... a sacred grove ... a circle of giant stones ... a goblet of mead....* To a place holy indeed did her thoughts turn now—a place familiar and comforting. A place where she belonged.

Suddenly, Vanaash was afraid. If he had snatched her from her holy calling, he was doomed with the gods! Why had he let Lord Stranger inspire him to this mad task? He squinted hard, trying to focus himself, but he was interrupted by a sharp cry.

"Well met, brothers! I am come to meet you!"

"Well met, Rhus!" Roric called, immediately recognizing his younger brother's voice.

Seconds later, a heavy plough-horse plodded into view and the rider, a gangling, red-haired lad of some sixteen years, dismounted excitedly and ran the rest of the distance to the wagon. "I galloped soon as I heard you were come!"

Roric grinned, knowing it had been a decade or more since the mount in question had trotted, much less galloped. "All is well on the homestead?"

"Aye! Well as ever. But riders say you have come with some powerful ancient holy woman to bring us good fortune. Is't so?"

"Look at the old hag yourself, Rhus. Even now Vanaash tends her health."

Rhus, pulling himself up to look, smiled greetings to his foster-brother. "How fares it with the withered one, Vanaash?"

Vanaash, in turning, unblocked Rhus's view of a wan, but lovely maiden, cradled to his chest. Obviously startled by the woman's beauty and his foster-brother's tenderness toward her, Rhus opened his mouth to speak, but Roric stilled him with a look. There was total consternation in the boy's wide-eyed stare, and Wulf and Ivar burst into laughter.

"Just ride full speed," Roric instructed, "and bid mother to ready bed and linen and make a soup of mallow and wild hops."

Mounting, Rhus cast a last look over his shoulder, then headed into the field which cut a short way to the farmstead.

The rocky steeps gradually gave way to rolling hills, green and fertile. At length the wagon crested a high rise dotted with birch copse where a rock-strewn path branched off the rutted road. Reining their horses to the left, Wulf and Ivar took their leave. Soon after, the wagon made its way downhill and came to a halt in front of a large, earthen longhouse. The tidy skaale was reinforced with a high, stone foundation and boasted a timber-and-sod roof and many windows cut through the mounded turf and covered in panes of hide, oiled and stretched thin. The two long entry tunnels were fitted snugly with sturdy frames and heavy, wooden doors. Flanked by free-standing animal byres and several outbuildings, the pretty estate was impressive in its size and obvious wealth.

Roric and Vanaash were helping Iseobel out of the cart, when a comely matron rushed out of the garden and approached them apace. She was not so tall as any of the others, soft yet sturdy, with a gentle, but sun-hardened face and a dimpled smile which she could not quite quell despite the seriousness of the moment. Embracing first one and then the other of the men, she signaled everyone to action.

"I have hung a curtain for her privacy and made her up a couch. Pray help her in there!" The woman directed with the air of one used to being obeyed. "Roric, make some poultices, and Vanaash, fetch the broth from the kettle."

Iseobel, unaccustomed to the accent, was pleased to understand much of what the woman said. It grated her sorely to be so ill. Had she been stronger, she would have devised a way to fight and flee. Now, smiling weakly at her hostess, she merely leaned on her escorts and let herself be led.

"Well come to our home," said the woman, moving the hanging blanket aside to reveal a freshly made pallet. Then she turned to her sons. "By what name is she called that I might introduce myself, as neither of you has thought to do it for me?"

The brothers exchanged a look of surprised embarrassment, then shook their heads and shrugged. "In truth, foster-mother," Vanaash said, staring at his own boots to avoid her accusing gaze, "we do not know."

"Indeed you are a pretty pair. Four days in her company and ignorant of her name!" Aasa shook her head despairingly. "Well, I cannot say that I am surprised in the least."

"'Tis not that we were callous—" Vanaash began, but stilling him, she dismissed them both coolly. Then, obviously distraught at the ill manners of her brood, she worked brusquely to make her charge more comfortable.

Having taken in the scene and most of its meaning, Iseobel decided that she liked this woman with the winter-blue eyes immensely. So when the woman introduced herself as "Aasa," Iseobel did not hesitate to reply with her own name.

"Well, Iseobel, perhaps you would like to untie your cloak and lie down?" Satisfied the girl could understand her, Aasa arranged the bolsters. Then, waiting until her guest doffed her cloak, she took a cloth from a ready pile of linens, wet it and wrung it out, then handed it to Iseobel.

Iseobel gladly wiped the grime from her hands and face before climbing under the blankets. The room was wonderfully warm, and the bedding smelled of fresh herbs. Although she struggled to keep her eyes open, Iseobel could fight the comfort no longer and she drifted off to sleep in seconds.

Without the smallest notion of how long she'd slept, Iseobel wakened to find Aasa beside her with a bowl and spoon, and Vanaash beyond, leaning against the daub wall, observing intently. Now, my dear," encouraged Aasa, blowing on a spoonful of steaming broth, "try to eat a bit. Vanaash!" she said without even turning, "suit Iseobel's—that's I-zoh-bel's," she drew it out as if speaking to an idiot, "pillows that she may lie on her side and eat comfortably." Vanaash reddened, but did as he was bidden and returned to his place by the wall. Under his doting watch, Iseobel accepted the soup from Aasa hungrily. Could be, she told herself, that she would feel better once she had a meal in her. And so it must have been, for she soon afterwards fell again into deep and peaceful sleep.

Vanaash and Roric, banished from Iseobel's sickroom, headed outdoors and dumped their gear in the mossy shade of a huge willow that stood next to the narrow brook beyond the byre and loom-house. Peeling off their filthy clothing, they scrubbed and splashed themselves clean in the chill water and, after a brisk rub with rough toweling, outfitted themselves in fresh tunics and leggings.

No sooner did they bend to the task of unpacking their sea-chests, than Rhus reappeared. Behind him a pace followed a flaxen-haired woman, tall and of slim but able build, leading a small tow-headed boy by the hand. Roric glanced at the trio once, forcing a dim smile. Then, flushing, he turned to his younger brother. "Ah, 'tis bold Rhus Red-Hair that I see, is't not?" he teased, ignoring the others. "Help me to oil my weapons, and I will tell you about our latest adventure. In but a few months you will see your seventeenth summer and you must be well prepared for your first raid after harvest."

"Could be young Gard would be pleased to look upon those weapons, Roric—" Rhus began, but Roric silenced him.

"Young Gard can look upon his *own* father's weapons, methinks!" Coming to his feet, he eyed the woman haltingly. "Best greetings, Kirsten," he called, standing awkwardly with his hands on his hips. She nodded, and he cleared his throat. "Must be Wulf Shin-Griever has already brought the childling gifts and let him awe over his sword and such."

"Aye, he has, Jarl Roric," she replied. Her voice was small but her blue eyes glittered. "You know Wulf well enow to be sure he has made his visit, tousled the lad's hair and dropped him a present, then made his quick way back to the mead hall."

Sensing the tension, Vanaash rose, too, and shrugged. "The Shin-Griever is not a one to let weeds grow underfoot, is he, Kirsten Jonnsdätter?"

"Nay, Lord Vanaav," she answered stiffly. "That he is not."

"And yet he is the best of men, methinks." Vanaash smiled and, reaching into a pouch, pulled out a handful of dried plums and offered them to the boy, who took them with a cry of delight. "Think you not he is the best of men, Kirsten?"

"'Tis true, he has been most courteous with me," she answered levelly, "He is bold and handsome and has done naught else than try to please me." As she spoke, her eyes wandered back to Roric's sun-browned figure, but he had turned his back now, and busied himself more with his armaments. Vanaash put a finger to her chin and re-directed her gaze to meet his own.

"Must be you know Roric Grim-Kill counts Wulf Shin-Griever the best of all his men."

"Aye." Kirsten sounded miserable.

"'Twould be best to take the boy back to your own hearth, then," Vanaash told her, "and wait there for your husband."

Kirsten, looking rebuffed, made no answer but held her hand out. When the boy took it, she led him away, glancing only once over her shoulder to be satisfied by the sight of Roric staring after them both with a sad, lingering look.

For a while, there was silence under the willow tree. Then Roric came to his feet again and, with an unreadable grimace, kicked hard at a large stone three times till he dislodged it, then bent, picked it up, and threw it into the brook.

"Mayhap 'tis not the best time to bring this up, brothers," began Rhus, who had taken on the task of cleaning Roric's gear, "but you should know that rumor has it you have kidnapped this Anglish beauty for your own purposes. Folk say the reputation of Roric Grim-Kill is so widespread that the two of you had to kidnap a maid of the Danelaw to find one who would wed him!"

Vanaash spun with a frenzy. "She is not here as bride to Roric!" he burst out, "Iseobel is—"

"—here as personal holy woman to Vanaash," finished Roric levelly, smiling at his foster-brother to calm him. He had hoped Vanaash would have put some thought into reasons or excuses before he began bandying about his intent to break with custom and entirely disrupt any hope of a happy, peaceful homecoming.

Roric's interference came too late, though. Rhus had discerned the truth from Vanaash's look and voice. He ran fingers through his thick, red hair and stared menacingly at Vanaash. "What say you?" he cried hotly. "Beatta returns from the fair tomorrow. Do you expect our sister to take kindly to this chattel's presence, when she has long expected to wed you?"

Vanaash, suddenly morose, said nothing.

"Surely there are few who would not leap at the chance to be wed to our fair sister and access these estates in the bargain!" Rhus continued. "Of all eligible, you, foster-brother, stand foremost. So you tell me that, for this … this *priestess*, you would dash Beatta's hopes and a certain future in the bargain? You must be mad!"

"Beatta and I have never spoken on matrimony," Vanaash replied evenly, lifting his sea-chest onto his shoulder. "Mayhap you assume too much … on many counts."

Pointedly, Vanaash strode off toward the longhouse, ignoring the argument that ensued behind him as Roric berated the youngster for his sharp tongue. This, he knew, was but the beginning of much unrest and quarreling sure to follow. They were right; Beatta's reaction would surely rival the harshest storm at sea. Glumly, he stowed his trunk near his pallet under the loft and headed to check on Iseobel.

Sensing his presence, Aasa drew back the curtain and bade him enter, gently answering his unvoiced question. "'Tis still grave for her, yet if she continues to rest peacefully, as now she does, I think we may have much hope of her recovery."

"I have made her ill through my willfulness," he answered sadly. "I did not foresee that she would wilt so at my touch!"

Aasa studied his stricken face with surprise. "Surely you do not blame yourself, Vanaash!" she exclaimed. "Can't be you never have heard how magick ones cannot cross over water?"

"Aye, but I thought 'twas just a story to make little ones feel safe when playing in the forest. Is this the truth of't?"

"Mayhap. It is old enow wisdom that there may indeed be something to it…. In any wise, there was no evil in your intent. Could be you might have found a gentler way to coax her, but if she is holy as you say, she will read your heart when she is well, and mayhap forgive you."

Vanaash started an answer but, seeing Iseobel stir, Aasa put a finger to her lips and shushed him. They sat wordlessly a long while, and when Iseobel had settled once again into peaceful sleep, Aasa rose to leave.

Pulling aside the curtain, she looked back with a look of undisguised pride and affection. "Vanaash, your sight has led you well. I will help all that I can."

Grateful for the first words of encouragement, Vanaash continued his watch, sitting tense on the bedside bench, brow knit in concentration. Seeing Iseobel lying peacefully in a clean bed and wearing a fresh nightshift made him long to touch and comfort her, to hold her, to feel her next to him once again. He tried to anticipate her reaction should she wake and see him, the very cause of her sorrow and sickness. He knew, and his mother's comments confirmed it: this was most certainly the woman that the man he knew only as Lord Stranger had told him he was meant to claim. Yet how could it be that Iseobel knew nothing of him? Why had she not been forewarned of his coming? Surely, this poor creature had no reason ever to forgive him.

Each time she stirred in her sleep, Vanaash's eyes riveted on her. So fair her face, so lithesome her form—he felt compelled to win her and resolved to do it though the odds be stacked against him. Never before had he wanted a woman ... and now he wanted nothing more.

Iseobel! Eyes closed, he concentrated on the syllables of her name, saying it to himself over and over. Iseobel! Again and again, as if it were the most sacred of galdor chants, he mentally cried her name. His heart leapt when she suddenly reached out to him and haltingly answered.

"Why ... do you call me, Vanaash?"

Startled, Vanaash met her hand. She had heard his thoughts! What surer sign could he have sought to confirm his choice? Choking back unfamiliar emotions, he dropped to his knees at the bedside still clutching her frail hand firmly in his own.

"Iseobel, forgive me!" he stammered, speaking slowly and simply that she might understand him, "I pray that, in my mother's able care, you soon are well again. May Æsir and Vanir alike stand witness that never meant I to harm you."

"If you would help me" Iseobel, laboring to breathe, answered haltingly, "tell me to what purpose you take me."

Cursing himself for making her exert such effort, Vanaash put a gentle finger to her lips. "Rest now, Iseobel. Rest now."

In the dead of night, Vanaash awakened on the rush-strewn floor by Iseobel's bedside, just as Iseobel stole barefoot to the doorway. He saw her don her sparkling talismanic cloak, and slip outside. Curious, but not wanting to disturb her, he followed, using the back way.

Under the milky moon, she quickly made her way to a stand of paper birch and seated herself within the circle they described. Hiding himself, Vanaash watched, fascinated by her movements. He saw her withdraw three runes from a pouch and hold them high in her open palm. First she praised Odin, but then began reciting rhythmic chants to Freyr and Freyja before closing her fist around the stones and drawing them to her heart. Vanaash could sense as well as hear the powerful prayer she used to dedicate them for this night's magick to the power of the Vanir gods; his gods.

He followed the familiar ritual in his mind as she reverently placed the runes on the earth and bowed low, thanking Odin for allowing her private converse with the twins this night. That, he knew, was a boon that the All-Father was bound to grant. It was plain she was wise enough to know how Odin rewards those who pledge him their honor and show gratitude.

She stood after a while, and with a lithe swaying began to dance to the whirring, whistling music of her own chanting. She prayed to Freyr and Freyja, then threw off her cloak. Its bejeweled fancy work glinted in the moonlight, distracting him momentarily. When he looked again, he saw three beautifully formed rune shapes glowing in mid-air.

Iseobel dropped to her knees, arms raised in supplication. "Most blessed Vanir, ever two in one, knowingness embracing knowingness, light embracing light," she whispered, "Let my will be born of your consummation!" Taking shape more forcefully than the others, a diamond of green light began to pulsate in the air above, seemingly the outline of a window to some mystical corridor stretching away through the vastness of space. She trembled from the sudden and violent release of energy, and Vanaash felt its presence like a soundless rumble of thunder. A warm wind hushed through the night, stirring the long white limbs of the luminous birch trees.

Gracefully, Iseobel raised her arms to the runeforms to drink in their power. The shimmering shapes appeared to pass through her, then to dance and spin.

Vanaash watched with awe. Standing before the moon, Iseobel's thin shift was like gossamer caressing the outline of her body. He knew he should turn his eyes away, but was powerless to avert his gaze.

Then he heard it! A sound that started as a distant buzz, but which grew louder until he could distinguish two compelling voices, male and female, chanting in perfect unison. *You must go with her to the darkelf realm*, they told him, *and you must be swift*.

He shook his head twice, thrice, to be sure of his senses. There was no mistaking it, though, and the more he listened, the more he was flooded with understanding and resolve. Only when the runeforms faded did the voices cease their chant. By then, he knew what he had to do.

Gathering up her cloak, Iseobel let herself into the longhouse and crept quietly back behind her curtain. Unnoticed by her, Vanaash, too, went to his own bed. *Swartalfheim!* He had never been to any other of the Nine Worlds, though when he had dreamt the vision that led him to Iseobel it was so real he had wondered ever since whether it might have been a memory.

In that dream, he had been with his mysterious patron, Lord Stranger. Somehow, they had come to be in Æsgard, on the high hill where stood Hlidskjalf, the throne of Odin, chief of all the gods. Hlidskjalf was the Eye of Heaven, and, if one knew how to aim it, through this crystal could be seen any of the Nine Worlds, the whole of Creation, all held together in the shape of an invisible tree, the great ash Yggdrasil, which had one root in each world, and branches that lifted up and out into infinity.

Vanaash knew none could come to Hlidskjalf without Odin's permission, but somehow they stood there side by side, and the jarl he knew only as Lord Stranger had shown him marvels.

"There, far to the east, is Vanaheim," the golden-haired jarl had smiled. "'Twas my home, and home of all the Vana gods, who ruled the universe for eons before the great war between the Æsir and the Vanir. The chief of us live here in Æsgard now, hostages exchanged supposedly for our equals among the Æsir."

Vanaash had seen that twilit world only dimly, but remembered it as beautiful.

"Now look beyond Vanaheim to Jotunheim, the giant world. Once the tall folk were civilized and respected, but they have grown reprobate and now 'tis a fierce and warlike world."

In that vision, he had touched his boar-headed necklace and then put his fingers to the similar one Vanaash wore. Immediately, Vanaash saw shining Alfheim, land of the lightelves, then Nidavellir, the murky realm of the dwarves beneath it, and far below them all, Nif-Helheim.

"That land of haze is Hel's own realm, whence go the ghosts of all the inglorious dead," the jarl had told him. "Must be you know only those slain in battle come here to Æsgard and dwell forever in Odin's Valhalla, the Hall of Valor."

"The boldest, though, may claim a seat in Freyja's domain, in one of the nine halls of Folkvang," Vanaash had replied, "my brother Roric is forever boasting that he will be chosen by Freyja someday; 'tis his one conceit."

Lord Stranger, appearing pleased that Vanaash knew this, had laughed merrily and said it was not the worst a man could hope for.

Above Nif-Helheim, Vanaash had seen Swartalfheim, land of the darkelves, a world steeped in mystery and peopled only with the males of a race more ancient than memory. "The darkelves are makers of the most powerful magick; they are the smiths who forge enchanted treasure," Lord Stranger explained as Vanaash had squinted to see it. Then, his gaze was directed back to Midgard, Middle Earth, land of mortal men.

"Focus with all your power as I guide you," Lord Stranger had said, his tone grave. Touching Vanaash's boar amulet once again, he continued. "The woman that I show you is the one you must seek, and find her you must, for you shall never attain your destiny without her. Already her sacred bind-ring is being forged. When your search for the treasure of which we have spoken brings you there, order yours made, too. Your name will be the sign of your worthiness."

The clarity with which Vanaash now remembered it all astounded him. Too, he saw of a sudden a greater part of the plan and was amazed he had not realized it immediately. The darkelves worked in magick metals; it was in Swartalfheim that sacred bind rings were forged. *That* was why he'd been told to journey there. He was truly meant to wed Iseobel!

He would find a way to talk to her on the morrow; maybe she had heard the same words he had. For the first time, he felt as if things were on the verge of making sense; as if an understanding of all that had driven him so relentlessly these last few months hovered right next to him, like a vague shape seen but dimly out of the corner of one eye. If only he could clear his mind and focus!

Perhaps he could. There was a trick that Aasa had taught him in boyhood to ease his restlessness and he tried it now. Mentally, he drew the rune OTHILA, $\diamond$, in the air above himself, a doorway of brilliant white light. Relaxing every muscle, he visualized himself drifting through it until he truly was afloat far beyond it, detached from all that stirred him. Yes, now he should be able to think.

There had been many occasions over the years when visions had come to him as he lingered thusly; strange, wavering dreams made more of sounds and feelings than of scenes and action. Sometimes he heard words of caution, or warning, or comfort which lingered long after, though he never felt they were said to him directly. 'Twas more as if he eavesdropped on distant conversations, spoken in shadowy voices that waxed both foreign and familiar, homing in on a life lived by people far away and out of his reach.

As he relaxed into the delicious peace of the exercise, hovering far above his own body in the doorway between worlds, invisible in the night, he heard those haunting voices and the words chilled him, for he heard a name he now knew: Iseobel.

"'Tis not business of any mortal sort that takes him from Angland, Shiorvan. He has no interest in the affairs of his estate at Trondelag! One thing only draws him back to the Nor Way: Iseobel. Outside that sacred grove, all fenced with prayers and enchantments, she is fair game and he knows it!"

"Aye. Childish, unschooled, and useless, though. He cannot find much to want in Iseobel!"

"You were but childish when he craved you, my darling! In a short while he had you schooled well enow and has availed himself of your magick since. Why not the same with her?"

"I bore his son! Do not pretend that he would ignore that."

"Mayhap he hopes this one will do you better, and bear him a daughter that he can tame to his own ways and delight in."

The whispering ebbed and faded. Vanaash thought that he would hear no more that night. But he was wrong. He was assailed by the sound of his own heart, pounding hard and speaking to him with a vengeance: No one else shall have her.

# Chapter Six

There was no chance for Vanaash to speak to Iseobel the next day for, midst great shouting and much excitement, the throng returned from the market fair. The courtyard was a chaos of household men, wagons, livestock, and happy activity—until Beatta rode up. Like a storm scattering brightly colored leaves before it, the indefatigable mistress of the Skogskaale cantered into the midst of the confusion as if refreshed rather than wearied by the day's hard ride. Eyeing the commotion from horseback, she already had formed a plan of dispersal by the time she dismounted.

After taking a moment to smooth her skirts and hug Rhus while he held her horse for her, Beatta brusquely began to mete out tasks to all in the courtyard. She brushed the dust from her riding clothes as she passed her keen eye over the throng, looking pleased at the immediate obedience to her commands.

"My family's good thanks and mine to all!" she called out loudly, clapping her hands together to laud them. "'Twas your hard effort, one and all, that accounts for the success of our estates at the fair."

A resounding cheer went up as she announced a bonfire and barrels of ale to be set up for them that night in the meadow beyond the east palings. She stood a moment longer, hands on hips, making sure her householders started on the chores assigned. Only then did she turn to greet the rest of her family, who stood waiting near the doorway.

"Mother!" She hugged Aasa close and smoothed her graying hair fondly. "We have done exceptionally well this year! And I found many of the special herbs you wanted."

She stepped to Roric, eyeing his unkempt appearance with a hint of disdain. "I am honored that you deck yourself so faultlessly to greet me, brother," she said, forcing a smile which barely masked her sarcasm, "and more so that you have stayed your trip to the mead halls until my return."

She laughed, though, when Roric shrugged carelessly, and embraced her warmly. Then she turned to her foster-brother.

"And Vanaash," she whispered huskily, beaming a saucy, white-toothed smile, "you will no doubt be interested to see that, with the great treasure we acquired during the fair, I keep pace with your efforts of bounty at sea."

Unbidden, Roric lifted the heavy bundles from her horse's back, and Rhus led the mare to the stable. Then, taking Vanaash's arm with the demeanor of a wife long wedded, Beatta steered him into the longhouse as the others followed. Coy smiles riveted on her foster-brother, she made her way to the great table promising them gifts and tales from the fair.

"The harbor was a sight to behold," she began, sorting through her sacks. "Ships lined the wooden piers, carts jammed the roads, makeshift animal pens took up acre upon acre of open space. Tents and stalls flew up wherever there was room, and country folk thronged from dawn until dusk. The mixture of Eastern spices and heavy Turkish attars mingled with the smells of the sea and livestock like an exotic cloud over the whole fair. Folk thronged from dawn until dusk, and anything—*anything*—could be had for the right trade. Silks for furs; Venetian glass for walrus tusk; Frankish blades for Danish hilts. I tell you it was nearly as exciting as a raid!"

"And only slightly less bloody!" Roric winked.

Scowling at his remark, Beatta caught sight of the curtain which he seemed to be guarding. Rhus, having stabled his sister's horse, rushed in just as Beatta wondered aloud about the identity of their guest. Bursting to tell her and watch the commotion begin, he was surprised by Roric's speedy answer and speedier elbow catching him full in the ribs.

"'Tis the holy woman we brought back from the Danelaw. She

took ill on board and now we are tending to her."

"Well," said Beatta, assuaged for the moment, "then we must be hospitable until she is on her way." Seating herself commandingly at the head of the great table, she set down a large bundle and bade her servant Valka bring mead and cups.

Valka, a sturdy woman who short moments ago had been shaking off the dust of the journey in the courtyard, appeared from behind the kitchen with a skin of honeyed mead and five tankards. As she began to pour, Beatta, in high spirits, unwrapped her parcels with great ceremony, enjoying the attention and hoping Vanaash noticed that her flaming hair and moon-white skin looked uncommon well against her claret-colored riding dress.

Obviously having selected each gift with care, Beatta handed them out with a flourish: a dress brooch for Aasa; an amulet in the shape of Thor's hammer, Mjollnir, for Rhus; a paper twist of bone fishing hooks for Roric (should he ever find more time to idle away while pretending to be productive); and for Vanaash, a silver necklace to replace the leather thong from which he hung his boar amulet.

After a few more tales of the fair, many heartfelt thanks, and another mug of mead, Beatta was in mellow mood. She pushed to her feet and announced that, as a lady of the household, she must now introduce herself to their guest and inquire if there was aught more she could provide. Roric cleared his throat uncomfortably as she stood.

"Really, Beatta," he pounced, "I have seen to her just a few hours ago. She says she requires naught."

"You? *You* are tending to her?" snorted Beatta, not having missed the fact that Roric had downed four mugs of mead to all else's two. "In this case I must make all the more haste. What is the crone's name?"

"'Tis Iseobel," replied Roric hesitantly, unaware that he was cracking his knuckles in sudden nervousness.

Beatta pulled aside the curtain. The room was enveloped in a tense silence until Beatta cut through it in a spitting whisper. "Holy woman! Holy woman, indeed!"

Stomping back, she wrapped her fingers tight in Roric's unruly locks and ungently pulled him to his feet. "I would see you outside, brother dearest!"

Giving no thought as to whether it was in his best interests to heed her request or not, Roric obeyed without hesitation. Vanaash pushed himself roughly from the table and followed. Soon as he entered the yard he heard her.

"How dare you bring some shameless leman to our very skaale! Mayhap you mean to pay one of your men to wed with this one and act as father to your wee bastard, like last time? All we need is another useless brat about the place."

Roric hushed her with a bold smirk. "Iseobel is not expecting any more than you are, sister!" All knew that to take Beatta lightly was to madden her more, but Roric had ever been unable to resist an opportunity to goad her. Hazel eyes twinkling, he tossed her a careless grin.

"Must be you are obsessed with the thought of bratlings since you are so hungry to be wed again," he declared in a casual voice. It was obvious at once that she found no humor in his words. Sidestepping the furious kick he thought was coming, he oathed as Beatta connected his ear with her fist.

"Hold yourself, Beatta!" Vanaash stepped in, forcefully separating the two. "'Tis true that you hold sway in your own house. If you wish it, Roric and I will part tomorrow and take the holy woman away. You have but to give the order."

He looked her square on. Beatta paled. All manner of retorts played across her face, but she said nothing.

Without another word, Vanaash strode purposefully to the barn as if important business beckoned. Roric followed.

Beatta, unused to being left speechless and not quite sure whether she just had been bested or not, flounced her way back into the longhouse. Well aware that honey-laced bait works best, she straightened her dress, smoothed her hair, and pulled back the curtain. Iseobel struggled to sit up.

"Don't rise on my account," Beatta smiled smoothly. "I am only come to introduce myself and offer you any trifling thing you might need."

Could this be the same shrewish voice heard just minutes ago? Iseobel eyed Beatta with suspicion.

Beatta waxed sweeter yet. "I am Beatta, lady of the house. If there is anything at all you require, do let me know. Dearest Vanaash assures me that you are a worthy friend of Roric's and insists, quite rightly might I add, that we extend you every help before you are on your way."

Iseobel froze. What was she hearing? What could this woman mean, wondered Iseobel, unless.... Could it be? This was Vanaash's *wife*? With horror in her heart at the way she blithely had misinterpreted Vanaash's kind attentions, she tried to make reason of all she had seen and heard so far. Must be, it seemed now, she had been abducted for her powers, after all. Or was it possible she'd been stolen to be made wife to the one called Roric?

Realizing suddenly that this woman must know as little of the circumstances of her being there as she did herself, and having just been extended a most gracious invitation of hospitality, Iseobel felt a surge of kindredness. She marshaled her manners and smiled. "My thanks to you, Beatta," she whispered earnestly. "I shall soon be well enough to travel, I am sure. Lady Aasa has been most helpful in getting me well."

"I am glad!" chirped Beatta with a doe-eyed smile, "but mayhap I can offer you something?"

Certain that it would be rude to deny Beatta's hospitality, Iseobel quickly thought to ask for a basin of water and a glass of red wine. After all, she considered, she might find a chance to scry for Dorflin later.

"Fine, Iseobel dear, you shall have them forthwith."

Beatta bade Iseobel a pleasant afternoon before going in search of Valka. *A bowl of water and a glass of wine!* How sorely she undertaxed the household. *It was an insult!* she fumed as she strode away. Whatever it took, she would have that useless foreigner out and on her way—and soon!

Vanaash paced nervously, his footsteps echoing in the large room which was empty but for Iseobel and himself. He had been hovering near her all the morning, starting conversations on one thing and another in hope of bringing the subject to some point that would help him determine whether or not she was privy to the message he had received while she worked her magick in the moonlight. It was difficult for him to make small talk in the first place, the more so when he was terrified she would discover he had spied upon her.

Iseobel looked up, fighting to identify, if not control, the emotions that threatened to unhinge her every time she found herself in Vanaash's presence. His lean grace enticed her; his gentle worry almost mollified her; his hidden purpose terrified her. She spoke now in her best imitation of her father. "You are wasting much energy in that aimless circling. Were better, I think, to be outside in the fine weather, enjoying the beauty of the season."

Her words surprised him. Perhaps this was his chance! "Best I would permit you to go with me, then!" he exclaimed, sounding hopeful.

Mentally, Iseobel congratulated herself for having wrung from him the very words she wanted. She started to her feet.

"Could be that you are not yet strengthful enow to allow it, though," he hesitated, stooping to re-lace his boot.

"I am ready to go," she declared, heading out the door.

Though he could think of scarce else than beginning the prescribed trek to the realm of the darkelves, Vanaash followed Iseobel wordlessly as she headed down the hill. Doubtless she thought him a ridiculous pup who tagged along though she seemed more content to ponder pious thoughts alone. What a millstone of intrusion she must find him! A dozen times today he had tried to broach the subject of Swartalfheim with her; it now was obvious to him that Iseobel had been sent no inkling of their joint destiny. He had hoped she would have heard those words the same way he had: as a command linking them together to some lofty and wonderful purpose. It would have been so much easier!

Unaware of his turmoil, Iseobel curbed her inclination to walk briskly and instead stepped slowly and deliberately. She did not want to be forced to lean upon Vanaash later. She knew his nearness would bring a flush to her which she no longer could pass off as fever and any closeness was certain to inspire a wash of strange yearnings.

Choosing her way with care as she navigated the downhill path, Iseobel catalogued through habit of her training the multitude of wildflowers and free-growing herbs which dotted the lea. Despite this distraction, her thoughts continually turned to her present predicament and her enigmatic captor. Absently she turned to study him, feeling again that familiar wave of warmth. It was preposterous! she fumed, irked at herself, that she could long for one who had treated her so badly.

Until she could manage to escape, she had to convince him to let her live away from his presence. It would be certain torture to cross footsteps with him daily and see that thick tow hair yet be forbidden to touch it; watch those prismatic eyes yet leave their depths unfathomed; breathe in the scent of him yet leave its perfume untasted. No! She could not be hourly near while he belonged to another. She had to devise a plan....

Her strength, she decided, lay in her training. The chances were good that here in the Nor Way, the folk afforded their Holies a bit of privacy and even preferred to keep them a bit apart. If their purpose with her really was to ensconce her as holy woman, there was little reason to think that they would not honor her request to live away from the farm proper.

Yet, if circumstances showed that they meant her as wife to Roric, she could demand of him that they live in a cottage well away from Vanaash or ... her heart leapt in relief, she could protest that she was far too pious to become a wife, and they would have to let her go back.

No matter which tack she took to explore her dilemma, all winds blew her judgment to fetch up on the same shore. Her calling was her way out. If the attitudes of the people in her own village were any indication of how most folk regarded Holies, she had but to act the part to win respect and increase their nervousness about keeping her captive.

Since none, in her small experience, exuded charisma and commanded respect like Dorflin, she began to pick apart the elements of his manner that continually earned him such awed admiration. The way he drew himself up in his shaman's robes and suddenly appeared nearly a foot taller; fastened his eyes to another's as if seeing nothing in all the world but that person, yet appeared to be looking beyond them into another realm, as well. Yes, those were the traits she needed to adopt. It was time for her to start making Dorflin's ways her own.

Unmindful of how far she had walked while deliberating, Iseobel felt her energy flagging. "'Tis enough," she said, stopping, "I believe I would head back now, though, if you relish walking farther, certainly I am able to find my way."

"Nay, Lady!" Vanaash ignored the unstressed plea for solitude. "Your safety and comfort are important above all else to me. Gladly will I accompany you the whole length of your outing." *And revel in your presence until you absolutely forbid it*, he added without speaking.

Iseobel froze. She had received outside thoughts unbidden before and had always found it unsettling. But this had to be a phrase of her own conjuring. Her heart was fooling her head. There was no question, she decided. Her illness had weakened her focus and she now read her own mind's blurtings as if they were another's!

Alarmed, she hurried uphill. Cresting it, she was glad to see Aasa and Beatta approaching; they would distract Vanaash, she hoped, so she could have a moment alone to collect herself. She quickened her pace but had not the vigor to maintain it. As she ascended the steep rise to the yard, she grew suddenly dizzy and weak. For a moment she thought it would pass, then darkness seemed to push its way over her, descending from all directions at once. After that, she knew nothing until she blinked her eyes and found Vanaash and Lady Aasa hovering above her.

"Vanaash," Aasa was saying gently, "I think you may let go of poor Iseobel's hand now. Your heartfelt concern shall bruise her."

From beyond, Iseobel heard Beatta's sullen accusation. "If she is so miserably ill, why would she go out hiking? The woman has not the gift of sense!"

Then Aasa spoke again, smoothing the tangle of Iseobel's hair. "Vanaash can carry you easily to the house, my dear; you must not exert yourself right now."

Then she was in his strong arms, her head against his heart, her own beating so wildly she was sure he could hear it, feel it, and most certainly read it.

*Spit!* fumed Beatta, flinging her thick hair back as she watched Vanaash lift Iseobel effortlessly in his arms. That brazen woman had better not disgrace them by dying under her roof! The fool had brought it on herself, that was plain. Yet it seemed none could pander to her quick enough. Poor holy woman ... Pah! Priestess of deception, was more like it! She had bewitched them, and had them jumping to her bidding. Vanaash worst of all!

Pacing the yard and stripping the buds from a sapling in her fury, Beatta raged on, mauling the young grass in her path. By Vanaash's steady attentions, one would think that so-called holy woman was the goddess Freyja herself, and he her thrall. Surely, he had not a portion of shame. Could he but see himself snapping to her side like a dog to its mistress; it was sickening!

Were it Roric alone, one could understand it, his being so weak-willed where women were concerned. He was a stag always in season, it seemed. But Vanaash, whose blood ran cold as fresh molten snow in him.... Vanaash was spelled for sure. For if she herself could not fire the man, Beatta reasoned, no woman could. Not unaided.

Though as lady of the house Beatta could do Iseobel no direct mischief while she lingered under their roof, there was nothing to stop her from finding a way to bring unpleasantness the wench's way. Wedding Iseobel to Roric-the-Shiftless seemed a fitting meanness, she brightened. But nay, Roric never left Vanaash's side except to wench. Beatta—and Vanaash—would be ever flung together with that woman. Well, no matter, she shrugged, smoothing her skirts and stomping off to the house, something would occur to her.

Later, she and Rhus sat at supper talking of the new livestock while Iseobel slept, but when Vanaash emerged from the holy woman's side, Beatta was quick to turn her attentions to him. Jumping to her feet, she herself ladled lamb and barley into his waiting soup plate.

"Vanaash, sit and eat. Roric's friend Iseobel will be mended in a nonce. See you? Roric does not chafe, and he has the knowledge of healing!" She was overly-cheery, planning her words for effect. "He would know if 'twere grave."

It annoyed her that Vanaash made no answer and did little more than shuffle food about the bowl with a thick slice of bread. There was an unnaturalness in the way the man was smitten. It occurred to her she might send a lock of Iseobel's hair to the seers at Uppsala and pay them to tell if there was aught of evil in her. As she thought on this, though, Vanaash turned of a sudden and glared so hard at her that she misswallowed a chunk of the meat, causing a spasm of coughing that brought tears to her eyes. Then she waxed all the more angry, for not a one of the dullards rushed to aid and comfort her the way she knew they would if Iseobel had been the one doing the choking.

While Beatta was fuming, Aasa, the picture of serenity, emerged from behind the drapery. All eyes turned her way.

"It is well, children. Iseobel sleeps a healing sleep. This episode will barely set her back. In truth, she is much more mended from the time you first brought her here. More than my knowledge of healing can account for."

"What say you, mother?" challenged Beatta, seizing the observation like a terrier. "Has she only tricked us into believing her ill?"

"Nay, Beatta!" Aasa shook her head patiently. "The lady's health was in deep danger when first she arrived. I only say that she must needs be of uncommon mind and constitution. It appears that she has strong healing magick herself, for she helps herself mightily in her own remedy."

"It would seem to me, then," returned Beatta, with a happy note of gloating in her tone, "that she should be well enow to continue on her way soon." She wiped her bowl dry with a piece of bread before continuing. "Although I don't believe anyone has mentioned whither she is bound...?"

She stared hard at Vanaash as her voice trailed off and was surprised that, for once, he met her gaze and smiled.

"Methinks she is bound for Swartalfheim," he said coolly, coming to his feet. Beatta laughed at that, as Rhus and Roric did, though she did not quite get the joke. She had no way of knowing that Vanaash was serious.

# Chapter Seven

The next day, Roric sat on the bench in the sun, poring over the treasures he found in the hollowed endpost in Scarbyrig. Brows knit, he tried to estimate the obviously considerable worth of the ruby-red runestone which seemed to pulsate in his hand as he inspected it. He knew he had made a good find and it had been difficult to keep his secret hidden, especially since Beatta's return. She was ever so proud of the riches she brought to the skaale, and so endlessly flattering of Vanaash's contributions to the family's wealth while ignoring his own. In his heart, Roric knew he worked harder, was bolder, and took risks graver and more often than any other householder, his foster-brother included. Yet he was ignored, derided even, while Vanaash was ever hailed and aled for his great accomplishments. A sudden wave of jealousy swept him, but he choked it back and silently berated himself. Since Roric was a tot, his foster-brother had been closest of all kith and kin to him, and there was not a another man in all Midgard he more loved and appreciated.

Reflecting, though, Roric had to admit that even as a child Vanaav Komling had been a strange one. He was forever babbling prayers and incantations, or meditating on runes or rocks or crystals. More than once he had claimed to see lightelves when it was plain to Roric that his foster-brother was alone, and he disappeared now and then with no explanation, sometimes for days at a time.

It had caused an uproar the first time it happened. Roric could still clearly picture the handsome jarl who finally brought Vanaash home to them. His parents had laid a fine table and thanked the man with gold gifts. To all, it seemed that the imposing lord had been a stranger, but Roric remembered peering over the edge of the loft to witness an emotional conversation the man had with Aasa long after Eirik and the rest of the household were asleep. Something told him then those two were old friends, and that it was more than a coincidence that Vanaash had found his way to that man's side.

"Roric! Bestir yourself!" Aasa's voice jolted him. Jamming the treasures back into his pouch, he rose and spun to face her. His boyish look of remorse must have softened her for her tone gentled. "Be useful and entertain our guest until Vanaash comes back from Sogn. He is long gone, washed and dressed at dawn!"

Aasa scowled as she spoke. Never the most ambitious of the household, Roric knew that his curls were matted and he was still shabbily attired in yesterday's linen sark, rumpled from sleep.

Unconcerned, Roric rose and stretched. Ambling into the house, he carefully hid the bag of treasure under the eiderdown on his sleeping pallet, stopping just long enough to run fingers through his hair, slip a clean jerkin over his shirt, and wonder what errand had drawn Vanaash away so early. Then, crossing to Iseobel's private alcove, he ruffled the curtain, listening appreciatively to the jangling of his many silver bands and bracelets, and asked Iseobel if a stroll would suit.

"Very much so!" Iseobel replied eagerly, drawing the drapery aside. Her dark, glossy hair was neatly braided, her linen blouse freshly laundered, and her woolen kirtle aired and brushed. Well recovered from yesterday's relapse, she looked lovely, and Roric felt a surge of pleasure at the sight of her.

"Then grab you your cloak and let us go!"

"My cloak? On such a fine day as this!" Iseobel balked, but noting his concern, thought it best to comply. She smiled when Roric bent solicitously to help fasten her brooch.

"Thank you, nurse!" She grinned mischievously.

"Nurse!" Roric grimaced, then burst out laughing. "Right! You are under my care. Now, would you like to see our horses?"

"Oh, yes—" Iseobel began, excited.

But she broke off suddenly. The thought of her own mare had swelled memories that panged her, but she shook them away, determined not to give Roric any excuse to deny her the outing. With effort, she brightened, and they stepped out into the day.

They had barely started their walk, when Iseobel felt Roric's hand on her arm. "Slower, Iseobel," he admonished gently, surprised by her brisk pace. "You will be winded 'ere we reach the byre."

Pausing, Iseobel considered and then agreed with his advice. "You are right. It is only that I am used to walking quickly to a place and only slowing when I reach it." Then suddenly thinking of a way to learn how much this man and his brother knew of her she stopped of a sudden and, emulating Dorflin's manner as best she could, looked deep into Roric's hazel eyes, gauging him. "But surely you know that. You and Vanaash already know everything about me."

Noting his startled look, Iseobel believed him when he protested that it was really Vanaash who seemed to know of her and that he had but followed his brother.

"Thing is, I expected an old hag of a seeress—" he began, but stopped himself, blushing.

"Be honest, Roric! What is his purpose with me?"

"In truth," Roric replied running his fingers through his unkempt, sun-streaked hair, "I know not! Vanaash does not always tell me the whole of his plan."

Though disappointed, Iseobel thanked him for his honest words and resumed her pace, drinking in the signs of spring. Tiny blossoms poked from the thickening grasses, sunning their bright yellow faces. Papery birch and deep emerald pine cast black-edged shadows along the edges of the stone fencing. A chill breeze blew a shivery gust which the sun obligingly warmed up.

Roric, slightly shaken by the feeling that she knew by more than his words that he told the truth, followed her, musing. A fine woman was this Iseobel, but capable as she seemed, he sensed that she would not be able to defy Vanaash's plans to keep her ... *whatever* his purpose.

Off in the distance, workers made themselves busy with repairing the sheep pens. Shepherds had already taken their flocks to graze in the hills, and now that the enclosures were empty, rocks that had worked free from the walls during the spring thaws were being patiently refitted. Pole fences that had been worked loose by one crowding too many were being anchored sturdily once more.

Iseobel and Roric climbed the flagstones to the stables with its agreeable scent of sawdust and leather. Roric held the heavy door for her to enter, then led her along the hard-packed flooring from one stall to the next, naming for her each horse.

"Ivar Half-Hand's red stallion, Baltha ... Wulf Shin-Griever's big Shimmel ... and here is my old mare, Wren," he said fondly, opening the gate. "A valiant mount in her day, 'twas she who trained us all for battle, dear girl."

Wren nickered softly and dropped her head to Roric's chest in greeting. He fondled her ears and patted her cheek.

Iseobel drew the mare's huge face to her own, nostril to nostril. Roric stepped back, puzzled. Suddenly, as if nodding assent, Wren lowered her head and nudged Iseobel, whereupon Iseobel moved her shoulder under the high arch of the horse's chin and began to stroke her neck and chest.

Roric was impressed. "This lets you speak to horses?"

"Aye," Iseobel turned her back to Wren's broad chest and arched slightly to reach the crest, "when you share breath with them, they know you for who you are and then are friendly."

"Such as this have I never heard," replied Roric. "But can you do the like with a more spirited steed? Certain my Beobald would not harm you, for he's not skittish, but I would find it queer if he let you pat him so."

"I am curious myself!" she laughed. "Let me meet him."

Roric led Iseobel to a second row of boxes. "Here," he opened the latch, "is Beobald."

The enormous gray stallion, almost two heads taller at the shoulder than Iseobel, flashed Roric a look of recognition, then turned a suspicious gaze on Iseobel. Iseobel, with no hesitation, walked directly to him. Briefly touching her cat amulet and looking Beobald straight in the eyes, she reached up with impressive confidence and pulled his head to hers, breathing into his nostrils as she had done with Wren.

Roric, happy that his horse had not backed himself into a corner to avoid her, was speechless with surprise as Beobald whinnied her a greeting, then insistently worked his head under her arm in complete surrender.

"You see?" She patted Beobald's cheek. "He is a well humored horse. Let me ride him and I shall show you more."

"I am fair astonished already," Roric smiled sincerely, and haltering Beobald, he led him out.

Pleased with the opportunity to fix her status even more firmly in Roric's mind, Iseobel continued, "Now here is a talent which you may not even know Beobald had, unless," she faltered a bit, wondering why she had thought it necessary to expound, and then hit suddenly on the perfect insinuation, "unless you have had a priestess here before...?"

"Nay, Iseobel!" Roric laughed with such openness it nearly panged Iseobel to act so arrogantly. "Save for Aasa's oak-stump harrow and Vanaash's magick mumblings now and then, this is not the holiest of households."

Holding the horse, Roric waited as Iseobel removed her cloak and laid it over the pen wall, then watched as she approached Beobald, who nuzzled her affectionately. She stroked the horse's neck and rumpled its forelock. Then, grasping his ear, she whispered to him and leaned into his shoulder.

Roric was astounded to see Beobald cock his head, then drop his entire front half in a kneel to her as if so trained from a foal. But when Iseobel tucked the hem of her kirtle into her waistband, baring her legs, to climb first on the bended knee and then up onto Beobald's back, Roric felt a sudden flush.

He hoisted himself up to the wall, his fervent gaze locked to the sight of her hips shifting to and fro with Beobald's powerful rolling walk. The innocence of his look as he watched masked a tumult of emotions akin to passion, though he was wroth to admit it. Roric took a deep breath and tried to distract himself.

There was little good in doubting any more that she was one of the Holies. Her illness upon the water, once explained by Aasa, and now her way with the horses had convinced him of that beyond contradiction. Must be, though, that even Holies married, unless their particular service strictly forbade it.... Roric took a deep breath and tried to distract himself, but the thought had come to him and would not go away: 'twould please him well to have her for his own. Before he could stop himself, his mind had wandered to a vivid imagining of the pleasures that would be his when she came to love him in return.

Iseobel rode close and invited Roric to sit behind her. Even picturing it, he found it hard to muster a semblance of self-control. "Nay!" he replied with what he hoped was a jaunty air, "You have had exercise enow for one day. As you and Beobald are such good friends, perhaps you would see him to his stall."

Truth was, Roric hard craved a moment to cool himself; strong desire had come on him unbidden, and he felt a sort of shame in it. He walked quickly to the trough and dunked his head. As he had hoped, his desire subsided somewhat and he felt able at last to join Iseobel again without the uncomfortable burning inside him which he feared she might come to fathom.

She greeted him in the doorway, a halo of swirling, sunlit dust dancing about her.

"Your cloak!" He held it forward but had trouble meeting her gaze.

"Aye, nurse!" She laughed teasingly, tugging on his dripping locks. "You make me cover myself even when you yourself wax so hot you need to dunk your head to cool yourself!"

Roric trembled, hoping she did not know exactly how hot he had been or how sorely he had needed cooling. Uncanny how she seemed to read his thoughts. It minded him of Vanaash, and for the first time he could remember, he purposely, willfully, brushed the thought of his foster-brother from his mind.

Iseobel walked slowly but easily. The day had passed happily and wisps of roseate gold had just begun to kiss the mountaintops beyond the high woods. She had been so happily distracted by Roric and the horses that the trials of her capture and her half-formed plans for escape remained tucked away in the back of her mind for the entire day. There might they stay, too, she decided, until she determined her next course.

Aasa, she felt, already suspected that she had exceptional powers. Her speedy healing would not go unrecognized as gods-aided by someone who had the skill and touch. Roric was now most assuredly convinced that she was of a higher order, and would undoubtedly gossip it about with Rhus and the townsmen at the mead hall. That left only Beatta to be convinced, and though that would demand unflagging diligence, it was not impossible.

Feeling as if, at last, she could draw painless breath, Iseobel paused, threw her head back, spread her arms wide, and pulled deeply on the fresh, spring air.

Roric, two gaits ahead for he dare not look on her as she walked, turned back. Seeing her stand, arms aloft, face to the golden sun, drinking in the sky glow, affected him strangely. For the first time, he saw beyond her appearance and gazed in appreciation at the able, mysterious woman that she was. Such a one as this, he thought, should not be subject to careless attentions. She deserved the caring, steadfast company of a devoted man. Tremendous riches he had not, yet certainly had he enough to begin a house-holding. He vowed to speak on it with Aasa that very evening, for suddenly he found that he could easily consider spending a lifetime with Iseobel at his side.

Iseobel, sighing happily, lowered her arms and opened her eyes to find Roric gazing at her. "You needn't have waited on me, Roric. We are but steps from the house."

"Aye, Iseobel, but it did my heart good to see you in health and free of misery, if even for a moment."

"You are a dear man, Roric Grim-Kill!" Iseobel clasped his arm, stood tip-toe and, passing up his scruffy, unshaven cheek, reached up slightly to settle a benevolent kiss on his brow.

Roric worked hard to keep his composure, cursing himself for feeling a rush of yearning at this innocent gesture. Without speaking more, he held the door and followed her into the house.

As they entered, Beatta emerged from behind the drapery that shielded Iseobel's quarters. The sight did not sit well with Roric and he eyed his sister suspiciously. Before he could question her, though, Beatta outmaneuvered him. Leveling a gaze directly below his belt, she pretended a look of modest shock.

"I see you have been enjoying Iseobel's company, brother..." she began with mock sincerity, then paused, looking smugly past him to Iseobel, who, to Roric's relief, seemed to be ignorant of the other woman's meaning.

Roric glowered and, without a word, strode to the shadow of the loft and lay down on his pallet to compose himself. "Fenris take her!" he seethed under his breath. "She has no scruple whatsoever when it comes to gaining the upper hand."

Miserably, he flung his head down on the pillow only to encounter something lumpy and foreign there. His treasure pouch! Surely, he had tucked it as always under the foot of the coverlet! Must be the ever-fastidious Valka had aired the bedclothes and moved it, he reasoned, tucking it into its usual spot. Then, somewhat more collected, he brushed past the women without a word and left to seek his mother.

Beatta turned to Iseobel in mock wonder at Roric's sudden haste. "Never mind—it is well we are alone, Beatta," Iseobel replied levelly. "I have wanted to speak to you in private, and this seems a good time to do it."

Knowing Beatta was bound to grant an interview at the behest of a guest, Iseobel settled herself at the table and lowered her gaze to Beatta's own. "I would have you learn a few things about me, Lady Beatta. For aside from your mother, you are the only one here who seems to have much good sense."

Iseobel pronounced the words in obvious sincerity, smiling a little. "I had hoped I might rely on you to fathom why I have been brought here and to what purpose. You need not pretend to care for my welfare, I know that you tolerate me out of custom."

Beatta, mindful of her duties, poured them each a mug of goat's milk and placed bread and honey on the board between them. Appeased by the other's recognition of her strengths and impressed with her frankness, she took a seat. She said little, and her face bore no hint, but she began to reassess her opinion of the woman as Iseobel recounted the story of her capture, sparing no detail regarding her anger, fury and resentment. She waxed furiously poetic, too, over the abhorrent treatment she received at sea, and her unwillingness to be here.

"I know that you deem me your rival for Vanaash's affections, unwilling and unwitting in that part as I am," Iseobel concluded earnestly, "but I think you can see that our immediate aim is the same: to get me from this place."

"Truly!" Beatta dipped a crust of bread. "If a ploy can be devised to do so, I will gladly aid in whatever measure I can."

Beatta bristled at the implication that Vanaash's actions were somehow less than worthy, but was genuine in her offer to help. Perhaps the huge red stone she had just stolen from Roric's pouch and planted in Iseobel's belongings would assist the woman out the door, for surely it was valuable. Or, could be Beatta would have no need to accuse the so-called holy woman of thievery, after all. Mayhap she would just leave on her own.

Iseobel now raised her palm as if to strike a bargain. "We are in this wise allied then, Lady Beatta, and so may be civil to one another with a reserve on the right to friendship?"

"Agreed," said Beatta, touching her own palm to Iseobel's. "Now," she added practically, "it would seem that even enemies under truce must eat real food. What else may I offer you?"

Iseobel, who had nibbled but little of the bread, replied formally, but with a smile. "Roric spoke of cold fowl and beer and, while surely your household could provide much lavishness, I trust I would be content with a cold sup."

"I will bargain with you, lady," Beatta straightened her sleeves and headed to the pantry, "we shall set a cold meal now, and have Valka start a warm dinner for later. It looked to me like Roric, at least, has worked himself up quite an appetite!"

"Again agreed," said Iseobel, entirely missing the nuances of Beatta's implication.

His sister's remark was completely understood by Roric, though, who had just re-entered and now scowled as he made his way in and sat down. Not having heard what went before, he was a little shaken by Iseobel's reply, so he squirmed a little when she turned a gaze on him. They sat wordlessly awhile.

"How fares the lady, your mother?" Iseobel asked him quietly after a time. "Was she able to answer your questions?"

Roric, certain that he had never voiced his intention of speaking with Aasa, was taken somewhat aback. He made no answer, though, for there was a sudden commotion in the court-yard, dogs barking and the cheerful shouting of greetings. Before any could comment on it, there came a noise at the door, and Vanaash entered, handsome in his cloak of midnight-blue wadmal.

Though he didn't mean to, Roric glared coldly at his foster-brother; he could not say why but it ever irked him when Vanaash disappeared any length of time with no word to him, his closest friend and chief of men. Vanaash didn't notice, though, for his eyes lit immediately upon Iseobel, who quickly lowered her gaze and flushed. He spoke to her warmly, as if his absence had bred a new familiarity between them. "Iseobel, how goes it with you?"

Choosing words and tone with care, Iseobel reached for her cat amulet and answered with as much control as possible, "Beatta has provided me all I wish for, and your mother and brother have great skill in healing. In fact, I feel myself quite hale."

At these last words, she fixed her eyes warmly on Roric. Vanaash, having hung his cloak on a peg near the hearth, turned just in time to see her do so. He hesitated, then said, "Indeed, you look much improved, lady!"

"I am indeed, sir. Roric seems to know just the remedies to lift my spirits and cure me!" A rustle at the door, and Aasa's quiet entrance caused Iseobel to pause, but she finished despite the inter-ruption. "In fact, your woman and I spoke only moments ago of my continuing on my way in just a few days more. Did we not, Beatta?"

Beatta, rather pleased at Iseobel's words and manner, nodded agreement and, mollified, went behind the hearth in search of more mugs and ale, which she brought out before she disappeared again to order the hot meal from Valka.

Vanaash, struck dumb by the same words, looked roughly at Roric. "*My woman?*" he asked in a growl, lifting his foster-brother by a fistful of jerkin. Unsmiling, he excused himself, and dragged Roric outside into the twilight.

In the shadows between house and byre, with Roric still in his grip, Vanaash demanded to know how Iseobel came by the notion that Beatta was his wife.

"How do you suppose I should know," answered Roric peevishly, irked by Vanaash's implication. "Do you suppose Beatta would waste a moment misleading her on that subject?"

Vanaash loosed his grip, and the two men stood eye to eye, glaring. Then they both broke into laughter and embraced.

"'Twas the only way I could think of to get you alone for a moment, brother!" Vanaash said apologetically after, wrapping his arms tight around himself, the night being uncommonly brisk. "Beatta will want me to account for each and every minute of my absence, no doubt, so there will be no breaking away from her later. There is a certain matter of import afoot."

Shivering, Roric scanned him quizzically. "Regarding?"

"Regarding Iseobel. 'Twill do you no good to argue with me now about duty to your sister and family and suchlike. I have been doled a quest and I need your help." Vanaash paused and gazed hard at his foster-brother. "I spent the day purchasing all we will need for a fortnight's journey. Now I must ask you to steal her away with me tonight."

Roric hesitated. "She will come to no evil in it, I trow!"

"Nay, brother. 'Tis an adventure to her betterment. When we reach our destination, she will be confirmed in her calling—" He stopped himself, turning the subject to something Roric could more easily grasp. "Make sure all are well armed."

"What think you?" Roric asked eagerly. "That there will be danger on the way?"

"Might be!" replied Vanaash truthfully. "Our destination is Swartalfheim and I have heard the way is perilous."

"Swartalfheim?" Roric was incredulous. "The realm of the dark-elves?" He gave a low whistle, visibly shaken.

"'Tis a lot to ask—" Vanaash began; Roric shook his head.

"Nay, brother! For adventure like this I am always game, as well you know!" Roric had never journeyed beyond the boundaries of Midgard, and the idea of experiencing another of the Nine Worlds was of vast intrigue to him. What is more, Iseobel would be with them! In his excitement, it did not occur to him to ask how or why Vanaash had been drawn into this adventure. 'Twas not as if humans were everyday granted leave to enter other worlds; rather, it was an honor of the highest order to be invited or compelled to journey there. He could scarce believe his luck!

"How many days is it there?" asked Roric, not stopping to wonder how the other could know.

Vanaash shrugged. "The thing on't is, Roric, that we can begin the way on horseback, but the end of the journey we must accomplish on foot. Wulf Shin-Griever, Ivar Half-Hand, and a few others need accompany us and then care for the horses when we take leave of them. Can you see to that without letting them know specifics other than their need for silence?"

"What mount shall I ready for Iseobel?" Roric wondered aloud, but even as the words escaped him, images of her long, bare legs wrapped about Beobald's wide back began to supercede his excitement about the upcoming journey. He swallowed hard to quell them, knowing Vanaash's power to read him, and not wanting to fuel the man's ire by untoward thoughts of the lady.

"Know you whether she can ride?" asked Vanaash casually.

"Aye," Roric's expression went vacant as now he pictured Iseobel's body swaying in rhythm to Beobald, "she can ride!" A sudden surge of longing ran through him but Vanaash, distracted by other things, happily failed to notice it.

Vanaash thought awhile. "Well, whether she is counted a fine horsewoman or not, I think 'twould be better that we ride Iseobel with one of us. Her small weight will matter not to either of our horses, and I think she would be safer, as well."

Roric straightened his jerkin nervously. He, for one, did not want to be the one tight in the saddle with that beauty. If he were to ride with her, he would suffer for sure, and he could scarce believe Vanaash would fail to pick up his imaginings then! Thinking on this, he did not realize how long he had been silent until the other loudly cleared his throat.

"On what think you, man?" Vanaash laughed, playfully clouting him on the shoulder. "We should go in and sup and jest awhile, but I warn you: keep your mind clear of this! Iseobel may read us and make our chore difficult, and a single slip of the tongue will have Beatta on us like Odin's snooping wolves!"

"Best you would pack a satchel for me then, Vanaash," rejoined Roric seriously, "and I will busy myself out here, and then be off to the mead hall, away from them all. Must be you know I have much the harder time keeping my thoughts in tow."

"Aye, openness is chief of all your virtues," agreed Vanaash, meaning no ill by it. So having said, he reached beneath his jerkin and pulled out the boar amulet which hung now from the silver chain his foster-sister brought him from the fair, and touched it first to Roric's brow and then to his own.

Then they went back in to their supper, arms around each others' shoulders like the brothers they were.

Roric, finding his retainers at the mead hall, bade Ivar ready the company and the horses. "I would, also," he added "that you saddle Effa the mare with the mane so black and bring her along with the rest."

"Is that mare not of your sister's stable?" Ivar scowled, finally allowing himself to be distracted from the merry harping and the dancing of two pretty maids. "Effa is no plodding nag that your sister is anxious to be rid of, Jarl Roric."

"'Tis not as if I mean to trade the horse away!" Roric, exclaimed, insulted.

Ivar shuffled his feet a little, and ran his oddly mangled left hand through his sand-colored hair. Knowing full well that Roric and his sister were not on the best of terms, he cocked an eyebrow. "You shall have trouble in this, I trow."

"Nay," replied Roric lifting his tankard and taking a deep draught, "I have a canny rider to put on her."

"'Twas not your rider's safety worried me Roric, but your own. Your sister will not be pleased to find one of her finest mares gone—and know 'tis you that has taken it!"

"I trow I have silver in plentitude to pay Beatta for the horse, and for money enow I can't think why she would not part with any of her goods."

"Mayhap you are right," sighed Ivar, stroking his bearded chin thoughtfully. "But I for one would not tangle with Beatta at any price. Give me better a field full of bold men and me unarmed. My chances at victory were tenfold greater."

Roric laughed good naturedly and slapped Ivar on the back. "In truth, Half-Hand, your odds would be better indeed! Besides, should you fall in battle to Beatta's tongue-lashing, I am not sure you would be rewarded in Valhalla though you well deserved it!" Still laughing, he drained his mug.

Searching the hall for a serving maid, Roric spied a trader, proudly telling the features of a fine sword which he was displaying to its best advantage near the fire.

"Ivar," Roric said abruptly, placing coin on the table, "order you for us!" Rising, he walked over to inspect the sword.

"... 'Tis Frankish and the golden cat embellishments on the hilt are wrought in Swedeland by the most skilled of craftsmen," heard Roric as he approached.

"Sir," interrupted Roric, "I would see your weapon. What price do you ask for it?"

"It is of Frankish make and—"

"Aye, but what price do you set?" asked Roric, thinking as he felt its heft and balance that the sword with cats so finely graven on it would make a fine and impressive gift to Iseobel. "Would ten Celtic golds be fair?"

"Oh aye," replied the merchant, knowing he could never strike a better deal, "your jarlship has a kenning eye."

"Save it!" laughed Roric wryly, slapping coins in the man's hand. "For the price, I trow this sheath is mine as well?"

"Aye, indeed! The sheath and the proud sash it hangs from!"

Roric returned to Ivar, who had watched the exchange with puzzlement. Placing the sword in front of his wondering friend, Roric instructed him to bring it with the horses when later they met. "For in truth, each who rides with us should have a weapon. And do me one favor more: see that the Shin-Griever leaves here in time to do some sobering."

Though Roric loved Wulf and counted him chief of his men, it ired him that the man was careless of his wife when drinking. Often he imagined that had he been allowed to wed Kirsten instead, ne'er would he have given her occasion to complain of his looseness as ever she did with Wulf. And she complained for good reason. Still, it was only a fancy he harbored for, in truth, Roric Grim-Kill was as dependent on wenching as some were on mead, and deep inside he knew it.

He thought about this and berated himself. How was it that he had dwelt so often of late on this well-nigh impossible dream of being true to only one? Striding hard down the trodden road, he recalled this morning's talk with Aasa. She had told him, in no uncertain terms, that Iseobel was not meant to be his.

"She is not for you, Roric! Surely you see she has the bearing of a holy one. Besides, how would you support her? Where would you live? You know as do I, my son, that you are not always of a practical mind."

"But I love her!"

"Think you not, Roric," Aasa had voiced matter-of-factly, "that I know not whereof I speak when I tell you to consider wisely how well you love and whom? Love, you will find, can be a far greater sorrow than it is a joy."

"There would be no sorrow with that one, mother!"

"You are wrong, Roric! There would be naught but sorrow if she is not meant for you. My advice I know shall displease you for a time and mayhap you will not heed it. You asked, though, and I answered, and that is ever the way with parents and children. I can but pray you take my words to heart."

Thinking back on it now, he felt both hurt and anger. He took a deep breath of the night air, savoring the chill that worked like a balm on his fevered brain. It was well that Aasa had such care for the matters of his heart. Now, though, if he were to have his way, he would be forced to act contrary to her advice and admonition, a thing which sat not well with him. Already he had been once robbed of a woman he loved by a parent's well-meant interference. Mayhap, if he thought Iseobel did not return his feeling, he would let the matter drop. Her touch had lingered on his arm though; her kiss on his brow—by Odin, he could feel it still—and her melodious voice had seemed to tremble when she had addressed him with that endearment.

*Kith and kin be damned!* Roric thought with a strength that surprised him. This thing was meant to be! He would have his way. He would find a way to make it happen!

# Chapter Eight

*"Iseobel. Iseobel!"*

The whisper came sharply to her ear, but before she could reply Iseobel felt a hand clasped over her mouth, preventing her from speaking. "Iseobel, 'tis Vanaash. We must make a journey, and speed is of the essence in't. Do not be afraid."

Strangely, Iseobel was not afraid; rather, she seemed to sense both the import and the urgency of the moment herself, almost as if it had been somehow revealed to her in a dream or vision. She shook her head hard, and Vanaash withdrew his hand.

"Your satchel and cloak are with the rest of the gear," he told her. "Ready yourself. I will carry you. You may don your dress and boots outside lest we waken the household. Do not argue—and be swift to waken."

"I am ready to travel even now," she pronounced firmly in her most confident tones, lifting herself on one elbow. She could sense that he was bewildered by her swift acquiescence, but heartily grateful for it.

In truth, she felt no reservations. If she had, what good would it have done to refuse? Probably none. Nevertheless, she felt no threat

now and was thankful for her strong intuition. It had served her
well in the past, and now it seemed to promise that this journey,
whatever it might be about and wherever it might take her, was
somehow meant to be. Perhaps they would be taking her home, she
hoped for a moment, then dismissed the idea swiftly as she unexpectedly honed in on Vanaash's thoughts, seeing that a long and
uncertain way loomed large before him.   Holding her eiderdown
close with one hand as she sought to settle her wild hair with the
other, she was surprised by Vanaash's grace as he lifted her. Feeling
oddly secure in his well-muscled arms, and picturing his placid face
in her mind, she found herself snuggling to him as they headed into
the chill night air.

Vanaash, already acutely aware of the feel of Iseobel's soft shape
beneath the coverlet and its effect on him, was glad of the darkness
when she nestled closer. Wishing that he might never have to put her
down, he was nevertheless glad when they reached the bench
outside whereon her clothing lay, for he felt his desire sapping the
energy from him.

Setting her down, he handed Iseobel first her stockings and
boots, then her kirtle and one of his woolen sarks to pull over her
nightshift. When she was dressed, he rolled the eiderdown and led
her down the incline to where the others waited.

Though she felt no fear or foreboding, she was disappointed
not to see Roric Grim-Kill amongst the small crowd. She recognized
Wulf and Ivar, Egil and Benne, and a few other of the household men
she now knew by name. Abject at leaving behind the one she most
counted on for friendship, she had just reached to climb into the
saddle behind Vanaash when she heard a familiar voice quietly call
her name.

Emerging from the trees, Roric, on Beobald, led behind him a
stunning mare, well-decked and saddled. "'Tis your own prancing
Effa," he announced gaily. Then he pulled forth a sword of such fine
workmanship that she caught her breath at the sight of it in the
moonlight. Leaning, he presented it to her with a smile so winning
and self-assured—so full of respect and admiration—that it seemed
to have etched itself upon her heart.

Hours later, she could recall that look still, in precise detail. It
had seemed stunningly perfect, she thought, that moment when the
Grim-Kill paid homage to her with these extravagant presents—a
moment marred in her eyes only by Vanaash's rudeness. He had
hissed at his foster-brother, shaking his fist and uttering oaths
beneath his breath. What a mystery was that white-haired one! They

were miles already into their mysterious journey and he was still sputtering and complaining just out of her hearing, no doubt jealous because Roric had shown the grace and manners to be kind to her, and he himself had not the gentle skills even to have thought of it.

She shifted in the fine saddle, wishing Vanaash would stop his tirade so she could fathom somewhat of his thoughts. It would be nice to know whither they traveled, although, since she was obviously bound to go, the destination probably made little matter. To while the time, she would have prayed or meditated, but the Shin-Griever, alongside, was too much of a distraction as he labored out loud to compose yet another grating verse of the hymn to Frigga which he was ever muttering as he rode or worked. Tired of it, Iseobel clenched her eyes tight and thought of Wulf's name long and hard until he suddenly stilled himself and spurred his horse to the front of the line, asking out loud who it was that had called him. Iseobel relaxed a little.

By the course of the moon, she knew the darkest part of night was long behind. Budding tree branches waved overhead, dispersing sweet scents of spring which, once marked in the chill wind, she could detect no more. Overwhelmed by Roric's gifts, the most important being his trust, she wondered now whether she could ever warm to his comely foster-brother whose demeanor was so icy. Strange she should be more attracted to that somber one who paid her no note more than to the blithe one who worked so hard to win her.


As night gave way to dawn, the skies darkened, then swelled with grey rain. Wet branches sagged thickly over the narrow trail, nearly obscuring it. Mud deepened; rocks teetered. No matter how carefully the horses stepped, their footing was unsure. The concentration required of the riders was constant.

The way grew worse as the day went on; at length the trail died into a scarce-marked path of sharp, pink rock which worked its way easily into tender hooves, threatening lameness. Vanaash marveled as twice Iseobel lithely dismounted to help her mare; the woman sang soothingly, and the horse willingly raised the injured foot and let her pull the crippling stone free. Not so with the other horses, already made skittish by the thunder, who pawed, whinnied, snorted and stomped throughout. Vanaash, thinking Iseobel had spelled the animal, found himself all the more taken with her powers. Still, she coughed now and again, so he kept watch for a clearing where the company might rest. Loath to slow their already impeded progress, he knew if Iseobel's health were to lapse, speed was for naught.

Noticing a steep rise, Vanaash lifted the edge of his hood and studied it. Soon his keen gaze lit on a grassy, tree-sheltered cranny above them. Though he had somehow known it would be there, he nevertheless took a moment to silently thank the gods as if finding it had been a turn of fate. In his forceful sea-master's voice he called for the men to pull together a camp at the top of the rise. Most scarce blinked at hearing Vanaash's orders, familiar with his second sight. Benne and other less seasoned retainers, however, exchanged looks of bewilderment as they climbed toward the hidden enclosure.

Still mounted, edged under a tree for shelter, Iseobel watched the men fall heartily to their tasks. In a little while, awnings had been raised, tarpaulins spread, horses rubbed and tethered, and Ivar Half-Hand had managed to coax a semblance of fire out of a hastily gathered pile of wet kindling.

Iseobel dismounted, and as she worked to make Effa comfortable under the makeshift stable awning, she found the steamy warmth among the horses agreeable. She craved the heat of the fire and picked her way to one of the ground furs, but the heavy smoke that hovered under the waxed-wool tent caused her great discomfort. Her eyes burned, her nose and throat stung, and soon, to her own great irritation, she began to cough. Vanaash, busy till then with concerns of the camp, was kneeling at her side in an instant, frantic. She bristled.

"My thanks for your concern, Vanaash, but a moment's warming by the fire is all I require." Her scowl was icy. She had not quite forgiven his shameless attitude toward Roric's gifts and, quite apart from that, there was something in his mewling paternalism that grated her.

Vanaash rose and turned to Roric with a helpless shrug. "Must be you are the one who should help her," he said miserably, "for from me she'll abide no show of concern."

"Despite that hacking, Iseobel is well on the mend, Vanaash," Roric smiled thinly, turning his back to Iseobel and speaking low so she would not hear him. "Methinks she would rather have you remark upon the stamina she has shown so far than to coddle and baby her as if she were strengthless."

Vanaash shifted uncomfortably. He *had* noticed her skill and determination; in truth it had held his attention the whole of the day. He hadn't thought to comment on it though.

"'Tis no easy thing to tumble into converse about a lady's accomplishments," he began. Roric threw his head back, laughing.

"Aye, but it is, brother!" So saying, Roric signaled Wulf, who was even now portioning out the honey mead, then loosed his drinking horn from the strap at his waist and bade the Shin-Griever fill it. Shaking his damp locks as if to present a more comely picture, Roric strode purposefully to Iseobel's side.

"Here is the reward for a day's work well done, lady!" he smiled, dropping gracefully beside her, handing her the horn. "You are ever an amazement, Iseobel! Your skill with horses is unsurpassed, I trow, and it gladdens me to see how that gentleness of yours belies such a strong and determined spirit!"

Vanaash noticed the fair blush that rose to Iseobel's cheek. He wanted to begrudge Roric the chivalrous words, but he knew they were true. She accepted the horn, her silver eyes shining, and took a sip, puckering. Roric laughed lightly.

"The taste is strong, but it will warm you! Taste more."

Iseobel took the requested sip and then another. "Beer, with its hops, would likely be the better cure," she commented.

"Beer is it? I'll not have my charges *liking* their medicine. 'Twould ruin my reputation as a healer."

"Could be the only aspect of your reputation left to ruin, Roric Grim-Kill!" she laughed. "Or so I have been told."

Roric laughed, too, then bit his lip as if deep in thought. "On the subject of cures, best you take this," he said seriously, loosing his neededs pouch and handing it to her unreservedly. "'Tis plain you have uncommon healing skills and I doubt there is a leaf or petal in here you do not know."

Speechless, she smiled at him appreciatively and took it. They sat awhile talking. Roric's hazel eyes twinkled and hers reflected affectionate fondness in return. Vanaash watched wordlessly as Roric worked his charm on the woman.

By the time Ivar's famous fire-burned fermedy was ready to eat, Iseobel had rid herself of her waterlogged boots and pulled her chilled feet under the furs. The smoke was still a bane, but she was resolved that Vanaash would hear her cough no more. She was tired, but none of the others seemed weary as yet, and after Roric's encouraging words she was wroth to appear a pampered babe. Though she yawned, she held her own, only half aware of the low converse. Exhausted, she scarce noticed when Vanaash sat himself beside her, and noticed less when she slipped into dreams with his arms wrapped tight around her.

Pale ribbons of silver streaked the mountains long before the sun climbed over the crests. Iseobel thought she was the first to waken, but was surprised to find all but Roric were already up and busy. Vanaash, Wulf told her, was repacking his horse. She had been waiting for an opportunity to question the man and, drawing a deep breath, decided now was as good a time as any.

Searching for him, she met his sleek black war-horse, Badger, instead. She shared breath with the stunning animal, then inspected his magnificence. She had seen a horse this handsome once. A bold black stallion had galloped to her father's doorstep, reined to a hard halt by a his commanding rider—a raven-haired warrior garbed in black and silver—who conversed tersely with Dorflin before galloping hard away. Unlike this one, though, that horse had a mean glint to its eye. She could remember praising the mount's beauty, and Dorflin in return admonishing her that the horse was enchanted—that she should never mount or ride it, even if it came bowing to her.

"I see you and Badger are become friends," Vanaash's voice surprised her so that she visibly trembled.

"Aye!" Iseobel backed quickly away and turned, making a pretense of working hard at a tangle in Badger's mane. When she was sure she had cleared her mind, she spoke again. "I have a great liking for horses. They are honest and straightforward."

Already unnerved at having gleaned from her thoughts that she dwelt once again on memories of this man Dorflin, Vanaash opened his hands in a gesture of helplessness.

"You seek to wound me with your comparison," he said, startling her with his frankness. "And could be I suffer by the match. You have no need to loathe or berate me, though. I know you want to know more of this journey and the necessity of it."

"If you can be open," Iseobel challenged, speaking to him underneath the arch of Badger's neck. "I would that you were. I am not a person who shrinks from horrors."

Vanaash gathered his composure. "By strict secrecy am I bound, but this much I can tell you. Our way lies in the darkelf realm of Swartalfheim."

Iseobel's hand flew to her mouth unbidden, as if to suppress an unwonted burst of emotion. It was not that the naming of the destination scared or amazed her, either. Vanaash could not know it, but his words had inspired one of those disquieting episodes of familiarity, the feeling that everything that occurred that very moment had happened to her once before and that every aspect of it—his earnest look, the bustling sounds around them, the scents on the wind—were identical. She swallowed hard, but answered him levelly, eye to eye.

"Oft have I heard how innocent maids are abducted and sold into evil service in Swartalfheim," she said daringly. "This then explains all, Jarl Vanaash! You stole me that my body might earn you coin in that lascivious land without women ... took me from my home that I might bed ugly darkelves for your profit!"

Vanaash stopped dead, his look of mortification so intense that she burst into laughter. When he realized she was joking, he relaxed and grinned, delivering a gentle mock blow to her shoulder. The effect of this was pleasing to her; she could not remember his ever acting so playful before. It changed his whole demeanor, she decided now, studying his fair face in the morning sun. He was more than comely.

Her direct gaze disconcerted him, and he cleared his throat. "We can only ride as far as the entrance on horse. From there, we complete the dark descent from Midgard on foot. The passage is, I am told, narrow, steep, and darker than moonless midnight."

"That it is, Vanaash! I have dreamt of it in detail. Once through the gates, though, methinks there are waterfalls that light the darkness with a glowing mist."

This startled him for he had been thinking often lately about Swartalfheim's phosphorescent waters. There was no telling whether his vague picturings of the place were real memories or imagined, though, so he answered carefully. "Mist-light or no, Iseobel, once there, we may be forced to rely much on your gods-powers, though this is an aspect of the undertaking not entirely clear to me."

He stopped, as if trying to remember something just out of his reach. Then he brightened. "I know little of what drives us, but I believe the answer lies in Swartalfheim."

When he trailed off into silence again. Iseobel wordlessly withdrew an apple from her pouch. Leaning against the trunk of a wide tree, she nibbled it, then offered him the rest. He took it absently with a nod of thanks, finished it in silence, then spoke again.

"I must beseech you, Iseobel, for your confederacy in the matter!" he said earnestly. "Unwilling and unwitting as you have been bound to this from the start, and as little as I can enlighten you now, please know that I pose no threat to you, lady. This is your destiny as it is my own, I am sure of it."

Iseobel, abashed by the scope of his plans and somewhat minded of Dorflin's more mysterious answers, which often left her bewildered, answered carefully. "Could be that a visit to the darkelf realm might be advantageous to me, as well."

"I hope—" Vanaash paused. "Nay! I am certain it will be!"

"So you say, and though you obviously would continue with or without my agreement, I swop you my hand that in this journey to Swartalfheim, your way is mine. Thereafter, I cannot say."

Vanaash was startled that his fervor had been so misconstrued, yet now he realized plainly how frightened she must have been— and still must be. He raised his hand to hers.

"A fair reply," he answered. Heartened, his hopes of having her as his own found rich tinder on which to kindle themselves. Even so, he smothered his own fires, as usual. Why encourage his desire until he was certain they could be wed? Then he flushed, realizing how hard he was working to hide his thoughts from her.

They saddled soon after and rode on. This day's travel was much as the last, though the rain had abated, making their progress easier and requiring fewer stops. The miles slipped by for the most part in uneventful silence. Iseobel herself felt remarkably clearheaded and hale. She had chosen freely of the remedies in Roric's pouch, many rare and potent. He was a good man, the Grim-Kill! It was a wonder that he remained unwed. So tall, so fair, with brilliant, deep set hazel eyes, his handsome mane of sun-streaked honey-colored hair, and that dazzling, open smile....

"What think you on so seriously?" Vanaash, who had trotted to her side unnoticed, startled her with his sudden question. She flushed. Maybe he had gleaned something from her thoughts, she grimaced, so she might as well be truthful.

"I was musing about Roric," she declared honestly, looking over her shoulder to ensure the Grim-Kill was out of earshot. "He seems so special."

Vanaash tensed. "Special? How so?"

"Few healers would ever think of handing over their store of cures. Yet Roric easily surrendered his neededs bag to me."

"Aye, that makes him a special one, certain!" Vanaash exclaimed sarcastically. Then he bit his tongue. "Mayhap it is you who are special, Iseobel, else why would the Grim-Kill have trusted you with it?"

She could not help smiling at Roric's fierce known-name. "'Grim-Kill' is so at odds with his easy manner!" she laughed. "Well, perhaps he is pitiless on the battle field, but off it he is another sort, sporting his winning ways and wearing more silver on him than most women have in their jewelry chests."

Vanaash, brows furrowed, wondered whether she viewed these as good points or bad.

"It is a wonder that one so fair remains unwed!" she added after, answering his unspoken question. "His healing skills and gentleness speak of a fine nature, and surely I am not the only woman who finds him pleasant to look upon."

Vanaash flinched. "Must be you know he has some faults that do not fit well with husbanding," he said, trying to hold his tone level. "He drinks and lounges! Too, he beds freely and seems to care little for those maids he woos and misuses."

"So Beatta has informed me!" Iseobel answered curtly. "Well, could be Roric does not give of his heart as lavishly as he does of gifts." So saying, she spurred Effa forward, leaving Vanaash to stare after her open-mouthed.

She was angry with herself. She had not meant to tease or rile Vanaash, but it ever irked her that he begrudged Roric's attentions to her, when he was so stingy with his own. Her calling as shamaness had taught her something of people, and 'twas plain that stern, handsome Vanaash was of a rare cut.

She could feel it when he gazed at her. As far as she could surmise, women appeared to have no draw to him at all. 'Twas strange to imagine his living so close with the beautiful Beatta, yet plainly unattracted to her. There must have been an odd rigidity and purpose in him that kept his eyes blind to the charms of that woman, and mayhap any other, herself included.

Thinking this, she suddenly pictured his eyes. She could never decide what color they were; they seemed to change with the hour: now green, now purple, now blue, now ice, now tourmaline. One could believe he had the weirding ways, but if so, how was it he crossed over the water so easily...?       Nevertheless, a power in him she surely sensed, and that a power far beyond his lifting of her against his well muscled chest; she blushed in memory of the strange effect he had more than once had on her. Well no matter! Whatever his plans for her were, they did not seem to include warmth and affection. He would obviously not give of that himself, nor would he allow her to enjoy such from any other.

Lost in these reflections, she had cantered past four of the men. When, distracted, she threatened to pass Roric at the very head of the party, he reached out laughingly to slow her, and they soon fell into step, happily talking together like friends of long standing.

Riding alone at the rear, Vanaash wrestled with bewilderment all the
rest of the day's journey, trying to distract himself from the sight of
Iseobel and Roric riding ahead side by side in constant and seemingly jovial converse. Seemed whenever he looked, Roric was tossing
his locks, or using his free hand to emphasize the telling of some
amusing adventure and Iseobel, ever gazing at the man, seemed rapt.
At one point, Vanaash was surprised by a prolonged musical chirping
and realized that the lady was near convulsed with laughter. In fact,
she had taken extreme merriment in whatever it was that had
affected her; Vanaash watched with detached wonder as she dabbed
at her eyes with her sleeve, literally crying from mirth. Later, when
they had dismounted to set the night's camp, Vanaash approached
his foster-brother on the subject. "Tell me, Roric, what it was you said
to Iseobel that caused her to laugh so hard?"

"I but said she was beautiful," Roric smiled innocently.

Vanaash raised an eyebrow. "And how did that come up?" He
hoped his tone spoke sternness, not jealousy.

"She said likely you and the others still did not trust her, else
why did everyone stare at her so," Roric's earnestness was plain. "I
told her 'twas only because of her beauty. How could men help but
stare when a creature of such uncommon shape rode before them,
I asked, and she fell to laughing."

Taken aback at Roric's frankness and a little uneasy that Roric
had used such an uncouth turn of phrase with Iseobel, Vanaash said
nothing. In a while, Roric spoke again.

"Seems it not strange, Vanaash, that she can be so comely and
not realize it?"

Vanaash, too, had wondered at Iseobel's seeming lack of awareness of her own beauty. Certainly, no other beautiful woman he
knew had any doubts as to her fine looks.

"Could be because she lived apart from the vill," he concluded,
watching with a wary eye as Roric slipped out of his heavy hauberk,
"and mayhap has no way of adjudging herself fair or otherwise.
Could be few ever gave her compliments."

Vanaash was displeased to have marked a familiar tone in
Roric's harmless conversation, a note of dreamy speculation which
always seemed to herald a new infatuation. He had need to watch
his foster-brother with keen attention, he thought grimly as the
other moved away. He was loath to picture Iseobel's falling prey to

the man's careless and seemingly innocent seductions.

Vanaash had little to say later as the band relaxed around a roaring fire, feasting on two hares young Benne Bjorn's son caught entirely by luck. Pretending fatigue, he ordered the party early to slumber, spreading Iseobel's bedroll well under the canopy and pointedly placing his own in such a way that Roric had no hope of resting near the woman. He would not be made privy to their useless whisperings all the night, he vowed. He tried hard to relax, but had grown so heart-cold thinking of the warmth fast growing between those two that he snapped a harsh reprimand when Wulf and Ivar began a low-voiced argument over whether venison was better steamed or roasted. After that, there was total silence in their camp but whether the others slept, or passed the night in restless speculation as he did, Vanaash was unable to guess.

"There! Yon ancient oak rent in half by Thor's bolt is the first sign that we near the entrance!" Vanaash cried loud, drawing the attention of Roric and Ivar ahead of him and pointing to a speck in the distance. "Soon the forest floor should turn to hard-trod lime, and last we look for a boulder so huge that this company could sup on its table."

Ivar, using his mangled hand to shield his eyes, searched the distance, but the blank look on his scarred, leathery face clearly spoke that he saw nothing. Roric, too, squinted in vain but, not about to be bested by Vanaash, expressed excitement as if the landmark were plain for all to see.

"This is a good place for a short and sheltered rest," Vanaash then announced, scouring their immediate environs. They had been riding hard since before dawn, and now the day was long. "Pull the men together, Grim-Kill; bid all dismount and stretch and such whilst I ride ahead to see our way sure."

Roric, glancing to Iseobel as his foster-brother trotted off, smiled, anticipating a moment alone with her, for Vanaash had busied himself with her to the exclusion of all others from the moment she woke. Then he turned back to the Half-Hand. "Set the horse to grazing there beyond those ash trees, and see if there is water to be had for refilling the skins."

As Ivar turned to this task, a sudden, thundering noise rent the still air around them. Their horses reared and whinnied, distraught; a cold wind blew suddenly, emanating in the shadowy woods behind them.

*"On them!"*

The cry echoed through the looming forest all around, and the air exploded with the din of a dozen mounted warriors galloping full upon them, spears and broad-swords hefted high. Fiercesomely armed, they were clad to a man in thick cloaks of hide over silvered mail. Roric drew a sharp breath at the sight of their helmets: snarling wolves heads, the eyes of which had been replaced by precious cabochon jewels which seemed to glare menacingly.

Though momentarily shaken, rarely had Vanaash or his men found themselves unprepared, and neither did they now. Vanaash at once galloped back, sword high. Roric, with a fierce war cry, urged the men, still mounted, into a stolid line. Their arms were at the ready even before the fury was full upon them.

Wulf Shin-Griever's battle-axe splintered the shield that rushed him and, whirling his mount, took a backswing that split his foe's skull in two. A long-spear bit into Ivar Half-Hand's shield. With a lunge of his steed he unhorsed the rider, bursting his sword point into the man's ribs.

A giant of a man came at Roric, who, war-plank ready, stopped the crush with a mighty cross-hold. Iseobel, spinning Effa, drove her shining new sword deep into the attacker's thigh, bathing herself in a spray of sticky blood. The war-hard wolf fighter turned to land his next blow on her, but Wulf was behind him, battle-axe whistling, and the man was lifted on axe-blade from his saddle and flung from the field.

These were no common warriors, Roric discerned with terror. In garb, they resembled Odin's bear-caped Berserkers, but as they wore wolf-helmets, those elite corps they could not be. They were vengeful and highly professional warriors, he knew, men no doubt bound by oath to some base jarl who served evil.

Hollering an unintelligible oath, he reined in close to Iseobel, sheathing his sword. In an unexpectedly swift motion, he ripped her from her horse's back and lifted her one-handed into his own saddle, crushing her to him with a ferocity that near robbed her of breath.

"Effa!" she screamed anxiously, as her prized horse shied away. Roric reassured her above the din that the animal would make a swift return once the commotion had died down.

"Think not I begrudge you thanks for your aid just now," he added gruffly as he jumped Beobald over a thick gorse hedge, then lowered Iseobel, against her squirming protests, to the ground behind it. "Methinks, somehow, 'tis imperative to keep you safe. So stay low here till you see how things fare."

He raised a hand staunchly to quell her arguments and reared his horse back to rejoin the fray. "Keep clutch on that pretty sword I gave you!" he commanded severely. "Since you obviously know well how to use the thing, be not shy in defending yourself if so you need!"

Iseobel melted into the brush. Assailed from all sides by the unwelcome clamor of the combat, she tried to distract herself with chants and meditations, but to no avail. She was steeped in sudden worry. If either Roric or Vanaash came to harm in this skirmish, she would feel it as a personal sorrow. Thus friendly had she become with her abductors!

A snapping of twigs jolted her to alertness. Approaching her was a towering black stallion, two hands taller than the average horse, taller even than Vanaash's Badger. Astride him sat a rider so striking she scarce could pull her gaze from his handsome, majestic form. Of a sudden, her heart gave a leap.

She knew both the horse and this man! 'Twas the pair she had so recently recalled! She had seen him then and again in her father's company, a mysterious visitor to their homestead whose presence had ever seemed shrouded in the same deep mystery that seemed to surround so much of Dorflin's life. Often she remembered being sent quickly away when this one approached.

But she had spied! Aye, enough to know that this was a magicker whose powers rivaled even her father's. Never had she been this close to him, however.

He was tall, powerfully lean and slender, raven-haired, and possessed of a regal bearing that demanded attention. Apart from his gleaming silver hauberk, he was dressed all in leather, dyed black and ornamented with silver brooches, rivets, and chains. All of these details Iseobel took in with a single glance, but his eyes—scintillating, black, emotionless—seemed to hold her in a spell. She could not look away, nor could she tell whether it was her will or his that deemed it so.

The rider drew near, wordlessly beckoning her with a black-and-silver gloved hand. "If you would be safe, as your father would have you be, Dorflin's daughter, then ride with me!"

So perfectly were the words enunciated, so awesome the deep and resonant voice, that it took her a moment to realize he had not spoken. Nay, his mouth had moved not at all! It was a thought he had sent her, and now, with just a narrowing of his glinting eyes, he emphasized it into a command which she had no mind to resist.

Moving forward a step, she reached to him and, in a single, lithe movement he leaned down and lifted her toward him, till they were eye to eye.

Ever after, Iseobel remembered it as a dream, unsure whether it was she who kissed him, or he who kissed her. One thing, though, she knew with certainty: 'twas an unearthly kiss, so smoldering with passion and desire that she was sure it had marked her lips forever. Suspended in his grip, the moment was at once fleeting and eternal. No sooner had she thought to mark the passing seconds than he loosed his hold on her and she felt herself float silently downward, until her feet once again touched the earth.

At that instant, the rider straightened, drawing his horse back a step. He glanced sharply behind, as if alerted by some sound or warning. His jaw tightened. Otherwise he gave no hint of emotion as he again leaned forward, locking his torrid gaze to hers.

"I will be back for you," he said, putting a gloved finger lightly to the hollow of her throat, trailing it, almost wistfully, down her breast-bone, in a manner both menacing and strangely assuasive. "'Tis a vow I have made your father, and I swear to you I shall keep it, else wreak death and destruction in the trying."

Iseobel quivered. It was a real whisper this time. She noted that his voice, deep and seductive, caused a tempest of emotion deep within herself, though she was helpless to say why, for there had been naught of boldness in his artless and spontaneous touch. Feeling weak, drained—aye, almost sleepy, she thought with a wonder—she buckled to the ground as he thundered swift away.

Private as Iseobel's meeting was with the lord who had so strangely stirred her, it did not go unwatched. Others had seen it. One, far away, in a high tower overlooking a grim wood in the Anglish Danelaw, sat gazing at the water in a huge bowl of remarkable and magickal workmanship. Obviously distressed, she sprinkled powdered henbane over the motionless surface.

Heavy curtains covered the wide casements, but a slit in the fabric allowed a single shaft of sunlight to permeate the room, and the dust that trailed from the woman's fingers glittered eerily as it wafted downward. She was tall, and marvelously formed, with a heavy cascade of white-blonde hair framing a beautiful face at once aristocratic and earthy; at once moon pale and sun brightened. On a choker round her neck, she wore a large moonstone of incredible depth; she put her hand to it as the last of the powder left her fingers.

Shiorvan Sunnivasdätter, though she had lived all but the tiniest slice of her life in that very tower, had seen more of the world than many ... all in the still waters of her talismanic bowl and enchanted scrying mirror. She had watched on uncounted friends and foes for her lord, read the inner workings of folk she had no dealings with, heard men's last words as they faced her lover's sword and made their final vows to Thor and Odin. She had seen many women— human, elf, and giantess—through his eyes; had felt his cold lust toward them before and his hot rage toward them during and after. She had borne it all unflinchingly, knowing he would search out her bed soon as he had finished servicing himself with their bodies.

This girl Iseobel's bewilderment was of no account to her; Shiorvan watched the woman only because her lord had instructed her to do so, and in all these long days of scrying she had scarce realized anything of note in the holy woman's mien or manner to impress her. Shiorvan wanted to know what he was thinking; what he was feeling when he touched Iseobel so intimately and made his vow to return and claim her.

She knew him better than any in the Nine Worlds did; knew his inner workings and every nuance of his restless, vehement spirit. She had given him a handsome boy-child, though none would ever have guessed it to look upon her lissome figure. Their son, Dahraag, was entering manhood now and was the very image of his black-haired, black-eyed father, but with a pretty boyishness she was sure the other had never possessed. True, that one had not been glad that the boy resembled him so thoroughly; he had hoped Shiorvan's Vanir blood would be more visible in their son so that he could taunt certain others with the fact that he, chief of the Æsir offspring, had sired him. 'Twas the physical likeness to her, Shiorvan Sunnivasdätter, that he had craved and, having not seen it, had never deigned to recognize the strength of the boy's magick or powers.

Even so, her lord loved Dahraag, and she knew it, in spite of the disinterest he pretended, just as she knew he loved her, and wanted her with the same hard passion that had smitten him when first he pulled her to his bed, a tender maid. In all these years, she had never feared another could cause him to burn more fiercely. Until this very moment....

Her fingers trembled as she held them to the magickal gemstone her mother had given her long ago. 'Twas the mirror to his elsewise unreadable heart. For the first time, Shiorvan felt something stirring hard within him that she had never felt before. It was a want and need more intense than any she had ever known to sweep him.

There was a strangeness to the whole affair that left her cold and bewildered. For so many years, Shiorvan had thought she knew what drove her lover ... what obsessed him ... but something about this holy woman burned him in a way she could not fathom.

Too, it intrigued her that this woman was so well protected. First by her father and now by an entire band of Norsemen, including one strange, and yet familiar warrior. She felt she knew him, yet he was unreadable. She could not focus on his face or his look. Mayhap, she hoped, he was a guardian steeped in magick, and placed there to protect Iseobel from Lodur's desire to have her. Shiorvan considered this awhile, fingers still tight around the stone, but naught came clear to her. Even were it so, she knew there had never been one yet who could outstrength or outsmart her lover; in the end, Lord Lodur, Jarl of Trondelag and Scarbyrig, would have his way.

Gritting her teeth, Shiorvan Sunnivasdätter pulled aside the curtain, lifted the heavy bowl and, though it took all her mortal strength to do it, emptied the water—thrice spelled and reliant—out the casement into the courtyard below. Dahraag, she knew, would be glad to draw her water afresh.

In the open lea beyond the sapling palings of the forbidding forest, out of Iseobel's sight and hearing, Vanaash, surrounded by a small but furious guard of his best men, waited for the man to appear. He could never explain it after but, somehow, in his mind's eye he had seen it all: the man's stealthy approach and Iseobel's obvious fascination with him. He had watched the passionate kiss with a tremble of revulsion, made the stronger by Iseobel's failure to fight it.

Vanaash did not know who the stranger was, but somehow sensing that the moment was dangerous, he himself had sent the mental summons that had alarmed the lordly warrior away from her. It was the defiant echoing of his own formal name, *Vanaav Komling*, which he broadcast upon the ether, that drew the baneful warrior forth. Must be it had worked like a madness in the dark-haired chieftain's brain, too, Vanaash realized with grim satisfaction as the man raged forward in awesome fury.

There was no time to savor his success, though, for in less than an instant, the fiercesome foe had sliced his way forward and descended directly upon Vanaash.

"I'll have your head for my own," bellowed Vanaash, and he set

Badger into full charge, broad-sword positioned to strike a death-blow. The dark-haired one stood firm, arms glinting. They came together with a thunderous crash, unhorsing both men. Scrambling to regain their feet, they switched to ground battle, evenly matched.

Hefting their blades, the fighters lunged viciously, each able to meet the other's ferocious blow with a staunch counter-swing until the dark one glanced his blade from Vanaash's thigh, causing him to stumble. Vanaash's men managed to keep the rest of the slaughter wolves at bay, but could not aid their own chief, though Vanaash's peril grew more apparent as he fended off each new gruesome blow. How it was that the dark lord taunted Vanaash, none could tell, but clearly Vanaash had grown suddenly bewildered. Then the evil one sprang forward, broad-sword poised as if for a final attack.

Of a sudden, a thrilling yell came from behind. Heads of both armies turned to see a sight most unexpected: flame-haired Beatta, dressed in full battle gear and wielding her double-axe, crashed into the fray. Leaning, she swung her weapon down like a pendulum, and a loathsome foe flew two man-lengths back, his chest-bone split asunder. Roric, well aware of his sister's battle might, wasted no time wondering how she came to be there, but took advantage of the new odds, goading Beobald to Vanaash's side as Beatta charged another of the warriors with a harsh battle-cry.

A wolf-caped warrior reared his horse to greet her, holding his seat as Beatta dealt him but a glancing blow. Rounding her mount, she galloped at him anew and, this time, brought him down, and herself with him.

The black-garbed chieftain unexpectedly raised a gloved hand, signaling his surviving henchmen to fall back. Dodging a blow from Vanaash's sword, he leapt astride his waiting horse and, as if finding new wind, disappeared swiftly into the wood.

Iseobel heard an unearthly scream and saw Beatta fall. Breaking from the fray with a final violent slash, Vanaash lunged his horse forward, reaching his foster-sister's side just as she stood staunchly, set the rim of her shield behind the spear-grip, and ripped a deeply buried spear-point from her own chest.

Having used her last strength to rid herself of the raider's insult, Beatta crumpled to the ground, face drained of color, eyes glazed. The shield fell from her hand. Vanaash, wasting no time, pulled her behind a gorse thicket, fastened his mouth to hers, and in a desperate attempt to save her, blew his own breath hard into her mouth.

Astonished, Iseobel, on the same side of the hedge, watched in horror. This was surely for naught! It had been a deathblow certain that scavenger dealt the woman; truly, valiant Beatta would sup among the glory-slain in Valhalla this night. Still, Vanaash mouthed silent chants, gazing into Beatta's eyes intently. Assailed by the strength of his forceful emotion, Iseobel trembled at the depth of Vanaash's feeling for this foster-sister. Haltingly, she moved to console him. He mustneeds accept now that nothing more could be done for the woman. She started forward, then stopped in her tracks.

Color almost instantaneously returned to Beatta's face and she stirred now. But the woman had been dead! As a healer, Iseobel knew enough to be convinced of it. Now, though, 'twas just as clear that the woman had somehow been hurried back to life. What kind of strange powers had this man?

More, Beatta was healing as she watched! Iseobel backed into the shadows, peering through the hedgerow until she spied Roric and the retainers galloping back from their chase.

"What magick has your foster-brother that he works such wonders?" she cried, exploding out of the brush in a flurry of emotion. "He has drawn Beatta back from death! She was felled by a long-spear, but now takes breath again!"

"Hold, lady, hold!" Roric demanded, dismounting. "Speak slower, for your words are suddenly atumble with accent and excitement and mean nothing to me."

Groping for control, Iseobel began more carefully, telling him all she had seen. Rubbing his chin, Roric tried to make sense of this while nodding knowingly. It alarmed him that the battle had brought Iseobel to such a state of shock.

"I have been on many a battlefield where a fallen warrior has but a bit of choke in his throat after a blow to the ribs and it takes but a small dislodging for him to draw breath once more. See you? Vanaash has no great power. Only good timing."

Iseobel did not answer. She was so distraught that Roric put an arm around her, and she did not fight it. "When I first witnessed this, I, too, thought it wondrous magick," he attempted to soothe her. "And seems to me that if we truly need a mystery to contemplate, we should wonder how Beatta came to be alongside our party like that when most we needed her aid!"

Having done his best to console Iseobel, Roric turned to his sister, surely in need of his healing skills. Dismounting, he went to Beatta. She was unconscious and, to best ensure her comfort, Vanaash had draped his cloak over her.

"Best we let her sleep for now," Roric told Vanaash, "until those unwounded can clear the fallen and pitch a camp."

Iseobel grimaced at the notion of bedding down in the midst of all that gore, but agreed that Beatta should not be moved far. There was nothing for it; she and Roric went back to the retainers and soon they had cleared the glen of the better part of the grue, tended to the horses, and started a fire.

When at last, water had been fetched and was on the boil, Iseobel and Roric fashioned a bed of sleeping furs, cushioned by a thick pile of sweet balsam bough. Vanaash lowered Beatta gently into it. Once Iseobel had bandaged the slice in his shoulder, Roric, with a resolve and efficiency not often displayed, tended his sister well into the night, until Iseobel commanded him to take some rest, saying she would keep vigil.

Tenderly folding back the coverings to dab the lesion with arnica, Iseobel gasped with wonder. The wound, though horribly bruised, now looked like a gash already three weeks healed! As Iseobel inspected it, Beatta fluttered to consciousness for the first time since falling to sleep in Vanaash's arms. Iseobel smiled her a greeting, but Beatta's reply was not cordial.

"Take your hands off of me right now!" she hissed hoarsely, lifting herself on one elbow and nudging Iseobel away. "I'll not have you play my nurse-maid after the treason you committed this day, with your comrades falling bloody all around you!

Iseobel trembled. Was the woman delirious? "I follow not your thoughts, Beatta!"

"I am no fool, Anglishwoman! Nor am I one of your mewling suitors, so there's no need to pretend. I saw you playing love games with our enemy in the woods, Iseobel! I saw you kiss him!"

Iseobel gasped. Beatta's words had caused a strange stirring; for an instant it seemed she remembered some distant dream of a long, yearning kiss. She recovered quickly though, and waxed indignant. "You are fevered," she said firmly.

Beatta gave a cold laugh. "Oh, you are a sly one, Iseobel! So well practiced in your deceit!"

Iseobel hushed her coldly and pushed her back down in the blankets. Beatta oathed and called her a conniving witch.

"Conniving is a strange word from one who hides in the bushes and spies on her kith and kin!" Iseobel snapped in return. "I would rather commend your courage than belittle you, but I'll not play foolish games, Beatta. Nor should you, I trust, for it will sap the energy you sore need for healing!"

She raised her voice more than she meant to, and not far away Roric stirred. "All is well?" he asked groggily.

Beatta spit. "Nay, all is not well when I am helpless, and our enemy's consort thinks to be my healer!" She tried to push Iseobel away but, weakened, her effort dwindled to nothing.

Roric stumbled over, rumpled and confused. "Idunne's apples! Mean you to rouse us all with a hen fight?" He tried to sound fierce but an unexpected yawn in the middle of his words gave them a comic effect.

Iseobel pushed him imperiously back towards his bedding. "Beatta has had some delirious dream," she began.

"No dream, Iseobel!" Beatta hissed. "I saw you reach to the man. I saw him lift and kiss you—and saw you revel in it!"

"Be still!" Iseobel's tone was uncommonly fierce. She would have said more but Roric hushed her. "Have a care for those who died here today," he told them both severely.

Then, taking Iseobel's arm and leading her away, he comforted her. "Pay no heed to Beatta's ramblings, Iseobel. Mayhap you do not know as I do from experience that a hard knock in battle can make it near impossible to tell truth from dream."

Iseobel thanked him. A bit uneasily, she straightened a pile of bedding for herself. It had been a strange and eventful day. She craved a dreamless sleep but, somehow, she knew that this night the forest would not afford her one.

# Chapter Nine

Though he would have scoffed at anyone who called him superstitious, Roric Grim-Kill had a healthy respect for the unfathomable. He was first to rise in the dawn that followed their skirmish in the woods, though he hardly considered it a waking for he scarce had slept all night. Ensuring the others still slumbered, he moved away into a dewy, sheltering copse and built a small circle of stones on the ground there. In the center of them he dug a shallow hole and placed in it a lock of his own hair, offering whispered chants of entreaty to Heimdall the watcher-god as the sun slowly rose. He was not sure what had happened to them yesterday or why a chance encounter should seem so ominous, but if anything like it were to occur again he would be glad for a premonition or warning from Æsgard.

A flicker of pain at the shoulder, where that chieftain's blade had grazed him, caused an instant of distress and he shivered, remembering the man's evil look when the blow was delivered. Seven of the attackers had already littered the forest floor when Roric, with Wulf, Ivar, and a handful of their best men, took off in pursuit of the three that fled galloping from the gruesome scene. Riding hard, Roric and his men separated as they came from the woods into another open field, each after his own chosen quarry.

It was the dread-inspiring leader of them whom Roric had marked as his own. Though he could not recall ever shrinking from battle, he had felt something strongly akin to terror at the moment that black-haired warrior turned to face him. Those dark eyes, glinting with rage and fury, had come near to paralyzing him. He'd scarce had the presence of mind to ward off that gleaming sword when it swung at him. It pained him to think he had only managed his escape by sinking his own sword deep into the neck of the other's horse: a fine, fiery black, taller and fiercer than any Roric had ever seen. The animal's snorting groan of agony was something he would not soon forget. He flinched, recalling the blood-chilling curses and taunts that followed as he fled trembling from the dark chieftain's gaze.

Aye, he had made light of it when he returned, jesting that the fray had been good sport long overdue and smiling as he listened to Iseobel babble her foolishnesses about Vanaash's magick powers. The confrontation had put him ill at his ease, though. They had fled the scene of the attack as swiftly as could be managed, bruised and aching. He wished they could have thundered further away from the cursed spot before setting camp for the night but Beatta could not be moved. They had dropped the dead attackers in the far-off woods, neither burned nor buried. Though the wolf-capes had fought boldly, Roric was certain it would not be the Valkyries who claimed them but the vilest and most wretched of the lower Hellions.

"'Tis early, brother, to muse on death!" Vanaash's terse voice cut through the scattering mist. Roric flew to his feet.

"By the gods! You'd do well not to make the mistake of coming on me unawares when I am fully armed and in a dread mood such as this!" Roric bit back the rest of his exclamation and, a little embarrassed, moved quickly away, hoping to divert his foster-brother's attention from the pile of offering stones he had earlier constructed. Vanaash had already spotted the small harrow, though, and he drew a sharp breath.

"Scarce can I believe that a small clash such as this one has put such fear into you—you who have boasted so often that the goddess Freyja herself would choose your ghost from the battlefield as worthy of even greater honor than Valhalla."

Roric turned on him, eyes burning. "Think not that I have turned timid, brother!"

His tone was so fierce that Vanaash backed away, hands raised in mock self defense. "'Twas not my thought, Grim-Kill! Must be you know that when every man in the hall is laughing, I am the one behind you imagining how Freyja will give her comeliest smile when she lifts you—"

His tone was earnest, but his eyes twinkled. They both laughed. Then Roric sobered. "I saw no harm in petitioning a forewarning. I am not minded to be surprised like so again."

"Soon we will be at the mouth of the Darkway and on our way down to Swartalfheim. 'Tis not likely we will come to any harm in that deep tunnel!"

Roric wrinkled his nose as if in distaste. "I have not heard the best of tales about the darkelf realm either, Vanaash. Men say their world is a pit of foulness. 'Tis known everywhere that darkelves must have been singled out by the gods for some retribution. There are no females amongst them, so they are ever on an edge—as we would be, think you not, under such a curse?"

"Aye, brother. You more than me, most like!" Vanaash countered. Roric went on.

"What is more, they may not step into daylight for fear of turning to stone. Must be you have heard horror stories of the darkness we will need pass through in order to reach the place."

"'Twould amaze me to think you would be more affrighted of the dark than of that eerie chieftain we encountered yesterday!" Vanaash leaned back against a wide tree and gazed at his foster-brother levelly. Roric sniffed but said nothing.

"He at least was a tangible enemy!" Vanaash added after a little while. Roric nodded.

"Aye! And formidable! I was minded to wonder how he came so hard upon us as if he knew where and why we wandered; as if he sought something that we carried."

"Mayhap that something of which you speak is Iseobel," Vanaash suggested in a tone so low that Roric scarcely heard him. Then he told him how it seemed he had seen them kissing, Iseobel and the dark warrior.

"Seemed?" Roric's voice was incredulous. "Either you saw them, Vanaash, or did not." Then he gave a hearty laugh, remembering the squabble that had wakened him in the night.

"Glad you find amusement in my distress!" Vanaash muttered miserably, and Roric laughed harder.

"This so-called vision came to you as you slept last night, Vanaash! Beatta and Iseobel had a spat in the midnight over some hot kiss Beatta pictured in her fever. Must be their talking loud about it forced its way into your dream."

Vanaash waved him impatiently to silence. "I saw it, surely enough. Not with my eyes, though. With my mind. I am minded to chase him down and repay him for so misusing her!"

Roric whistled. "Best you get your jealousy in rein, brother! Rather than an imaginary kiss, mayhap you could think about avenging the pain he put on you and me, and the gore his men laid on Wulf Shin-Griever, crashing into his shoulder and axe-arm so!"

Wulf and two other men had taken ugly woundings in the fray. Though all would heal, Roric grew angry thinking about it and kicked hard at a fallen tree limb which did not budge. "Beatta, too!" he added, grimacing at the additional pain he had now caused himself. "A strange one, my sister! Scarce can I believe she followed us all this way in secret! Iseobel told me how Beatta took a harsh hurting from the man."

Vanaash straightened. "All is well with Beatta," he said shortly. "The injury was not so great."

"Even so I would be pleased to seek the man out and repay him for his lack of couth! Would we knew of him...."

"No mystery—'twas Lord Lodur, Jarl of the Trondelag. I have passed him before, and heard men remark upon him."

Roric stepped back inspecting the other as if he were mad. He was glad Vanaash had lost interest in the dreamt-of kiss. Sometimes he got on a subject like that and Roric was forced to hear him toss his magickal theories back and forth endlessly. Now though, seemed he had just changed one strange speculation for another. "Mind you that the Jarl of the Trondelag was a great warrior when we were but babes, Vanaash! Did not our mother's brothers suffer harsh dealings with the man?"

"Aye," Vanaash mumbled, sounding unconvinced.

"And remember how father ever told us that Lodur had demanded a fully manned longship of him as payment of man-price for that servant of his who was killed in a brawl at the Skogskaale 'ere I even was born? Nay, *that* Lodur would be older now than Lady Aasa, and this one who drove himself upon us yesterday had but a few years on us!"

Vanaash shook his head though. "It was ever rumored that the same Lodur held some power that could not be reckoned! Scores of vast estates in the Nor Way and Dane Mark and even in Angland he lords. No man could amass such wealth in a single lifetime even though folk say he employs two powerful witches who keep magick eyes on his enemies at all times."

"Aye, I have heard somewhat of that story, Vanaash, though I scarce think it could be true."

"Why not, brother? One of them watches while the other sleeps, so Lodur ever knows when an opportunity exists to steal from his foes or smite them. Wulf Shin-Griever told me his father had kinsmen three generations who grew old in the man's service and never counted a grey hair amongst their lord's raven strands. Mayhap if you talked with men in the taverns, Roric, instead of lingering with wenches, you would have heard it surmised long ago that this lord was some great magicker, maybe even a god himself dressed in humanform!"

Roric gave a wry smile and shook his head as if to dismiss such speculation. "'Tis what I might expect to hear from one who thinks a journey to the darkelf realm is a normal piece of business," he said with exaggerated bewilderment.

They laughed and walked back to the little camp.

Later, though, when they had resumed their journey, Roric's uneasiness returned. From the first, he had wondered on the strangeness of Vanaash's quest. Though he could not help enjoying the adventure of a task that drew him for the first time from Midgard to one of the other worlds, he was wise enough to know that such commerce was far out of the ordinary, the sort reserved for those who dabbled in religion and wizardry. His foster-brother had ever been a strange bird, but till now Roric had not suspected the man might be subject to the dictates of magick or the whims of the gods. What this journey meant, he could only guess, but he suspected it had as much to do with the dark warrior whose forces had accosted them as it had to do with Iseobel, and, though he highly doubted the kiss reported by Vanaash was anything but fantasy, the thought gave him dread.

For a while Roric distracted himself by riding Beatta on Beobald with him, leading her empty mount behind. She was still weak and listless and complained of pain. Earlier, Roric had worked at applying rags and poultices to the men's wounds and had finally cajoled Beatta into letting him inspect her injury. He had discovered an unusual bruising there, pearly pink rather than black and blue, like the glaze of a piercing well healed over. The speed with which it seemed to heal had amazed him, but its obvious severity had caused a welling of pity for his sharp-tongued sister, not a little colored by the admiration he felt for the boldness she had shown.

Beatta had never been one to speak her heart with him, but as they rode she chatted ceaselessly, confiding all the fear and jealousy she had felt since Vanaash took his leave. Roric winced every time his sister referred to Iseobel as "the so-called holy woman," but it was not hard for him to understand the emotions that had driven Beatta to follow them secretly, and he had no choice but to marvel at her daring as she had traveled on her own alongside them in secret.

At first, her company soothed his troubled spirits, but in time she came round to the subject of his having misappropriated one of her finest mounts just to gift it recklessly away to that woman who had already so greatly infringed on their family's hospitality. Roric swore he had from the first determined to pay Beatta for the mare, soon as he had an opportunity to do so, but she would not let the subject lie.

After awhile, unable to bear her chiding any longer, Roric signaled Vanaash to take the shrew off his hands. He was amused to see how gentle and sweet his sister waxed with the other man as he helped her back into her own saddle. Relieved of her, Roric rode happily. Aye, he would have been happier yet flirting with Iseobel, but she seemed lost in thought, wearing a distant, unreadable look. Still, he rode a long while lighter of heart.

Soon as the huge, arching boulder came into sight, though, which marked the entrance to the Darkway, the dread was upon him again. The entire party dismounted in silence, eyeing with wary reverence this doorway to another world.

The stone itself was enormous, a hulking chunk of sparkling granite carved all over with short inscriptions by earlier travelers who had dared the treacherous downward journey. Some were magickers, intent upon testing their powers in the dark world of enchantment. Some were women, going thither to sell their services to a race that had no females of its own. Some were adventurers, lured by tales of great riches and debauched pleasures to be had below. Iseobel and Vanaash took great interest in reading and speculating on the cryptic messages. Wulf Shin-Griever, superstitious to an almost unbearable degree, parted himself a little way from the company, and began chanting his paean to Frigga, now a familiar symbol of his distress. Ivar Half-Hand mocked him silently with exaggerated grimaces of pretend aggravation while rubbing down the horses.

As for Roric, he busied himself giving orders to the men whose duty it would be to wait there for the return of Vanaash, Iseobel, Beatta, who now insisted on accompanying them all the way, and himself. His emotions fluctuated between curiosity about Swartalfheim itself and his fear of the Darkway, tales of which had frightened him from childhood on.

He had heard that the way was all blackness, so murky no torch could penetrate it. Ghosts, spirits, and renegade darkelves haunted the steep pit; any human without discretion could be irretrievably lost just by listening to their voices. Also, 'twas said the Darkway was a favorite haunt of shades, warriors brought back from the dead by magickal powers. Such folk as that lingered between mortal and immortal, forever fearing a second death blow, which would turn them into some creature unspeakable that fed upon human blood and flesh. These thoughts so haunted him that, when Roric made his farewells to Wulf and Ivar, he surprised both of them by embracing them long and hard, and slipping Wulf two valuable rings to pass on to Kirsten and young Gard in his own memory, should he fail to resurface from the netherworld.

"Best we hold on, one to the other," Vanaash had suggested glumly, when they could delay their start no longer. He did not look happy that Beatta had insisted on accompanying them, though to Roric, an extra hand and weapon seemed much welcome. Summoning all his will, Roric boldly took his place between the two women, especially glad for the comforting warmth he felt when he put his arm around Iseobel's tiny waist. Could be, he told himself hopefully, that in the darkness his touch might linger on her unchallenged, as would never be possible in the daylight.

The first few hours took them down broad steps carved in the rock of the underearth. For a while, they had the comfort of dim remnants of light from the opening above. After that, the passageway grew steeper, the darkness more stifling, and their descent more precarious. The dank smell and close, damp air waxed heavier as they made their way down.

In the pitch-black void, they clung to each other, pacing their slow way forward, so at one in mind and purpose as to seem like a single entity. "Much like Sleipnir, Odin's eight-legged horse," Roric pronounced solemnly, "save not so swift."

He had one arm around Iseobel's shoulder now and one around Beatta's, and was doing his utmost to hide his dread of the sodden, still darkness. No ghosts had materialized, neither shade nor specter had hindered their way. There was, in fact, no sight or sound of any kind. This was small comfort to Roric, though. The brutal blackness alone was enough to inspire in him an almost uncontrollable terror, and it took him tremendous effort to remain calm and steady.

"When we come to the gates, there will be light!" Vanaash sent the thought out with as much strength as he could muster, somehow surprised at the intensity of his foster-brother's fear. Thor as witness, he had seen that man laugh in the face of a bloodied she-bear; watched him fight off two Frisian battle-axes, himself weapon-less. Now, though the man put on a good show of iron-hard determination, tossing jests and words of encouragement with the women, Vanaash could feel plainly that deep within, bold Roric Grim-Kill trembled like a babe. Even Beatta, he noticed, was hard pressed. He sent the encouraging thought again, wishing he could think of a way to reassure them out loud without letting them know he had been here before.

The Lord Stranger had brought him, and then had made him vow he would never speak of it. Vanaash had been eight years old and had wandered away during the berry-picking. He was gone from the Skogskaale five full days and Jarl Eirik and Lady Aasa had given him up for dead. He remembered now how his foster-parents had given the Stranger a gold-gift and a silver-handled bodkin, richly scribed, to thank him for bringing their child safely to home. His step-mother, her face swollen with tears, had thrown herself before the visitor, sobbing litanies of thanks.

Aye, that sight had moved him, but of the journey itself, he remembered little, other than the strangeness of that place, deep under the ground, yet fairly lit by a strange and soothing gleam. *'Twas because Swartalfheim is built on one of the roots of the great ash, Yggdrasil,* Lord Stranger had told him, *and not really in the dark earth. The roots of the vast invisible tree pull nourishment from the infinity below, feeding them upward through the massive trunk wherein all knowledge runs like sap, free for the tapping, and out to the far most tips of the high branches, where they sway against the distant reaches of the cosmos. There, the leaves breathe in the Light of Eternity, and feed it back down. And that Light nurtures even the deepest roots, lighting Swartalfheim, Nif-Helheim, and Hel, even unto the lowest regions. This was the life cycle of foreverness....*

"Vanaash, I can see it!" Iseobel's voice, fraught with wonder, jarred him from his spiraling wave of deep thoughts.

"Mine are eyes accustomed to hunting, even at night!" Beatta snapped in belligerent response. "'Tis certain I would have spotted it first, were there aught to be seen!"

Iseobel gave a fleet, throaty laugh when Roric agreed with his sister that the gate lights of Swartalfheim were surely not yet visible. *'Twas not the darkelf city I saw, but the view of the heavens upward through the roots of the sacred ash just as Vanaash described them....*

Vanaash stopped dead so quickly that they all stumbled. Iseobel had not said the words, she had *thought* them! While he oft was able to fathom the minds of others, it was rare indeed to be so well read himself. Neither Roric nor Beatta, closest of all in the world to him, had ever done it save by chance. How could this woman have plucked so easily and so acutely from him?

He had no time to muse on it now, though. There was a scuffling in the darkness, and Roric muttered a low oath. He had hard tromped on Beatta's foot when they came to their sudden stop and now was warding off the blows she dealt him in her pain from it. Vanaash whispered a harsh reprimand. They grew still and clasped arms again, the four of them, then continued their halting move forward, enveloped now in silence.

There was an almost tangible surge of relief when Beatta finally spied a distant tower of flickering luminescence a scant way further. With that to focus on, their spirits lifted and their step quickened. In a little while, they had drawn near enough to realize that the glow which led them was a single crack of light, escaping from between two massive gates which loomed endlessly high in the darkness above them. As they approached, gate lights, one by one illuminated by some unseen power, began to emit a mellow blue-green gleam, exceedingly eerie, and yet encouraging after the many hours of blackness.

As their eyes adjusted, they came to an awed standstill. Now they could see that the massive gates were scaled with burnished trunks of ash and oak, carved everywhere with likenesses and runes, and studded with nails, rivets, and hinges of the finest workmanship, all wrought of precious metals.

Vanaash drew a sharp breath. He remembered how as a boy he had bent backwards, looking up far as he could, unable to see the tops of those gates. Feeling a flush, he darted Iseobel a glance, wondering suddenly if she might have heard his thought. Like the others, she was gazing upward, though, lost in silent awe. The magnificent disarray of her hair reflected the phosphorescent glow, as did those silver eyes, wide with wonder and pronounced against the fair paleness of her face. He was reminded of an image of a goddess he had seen at Uppsala long ago, four times man-size with an aureole of ocean green that burned round it, night and day.

Iseobel turned suddenly, and their gazes locked a moment until Vanaash shifted his uneasily away. It was a fair comparison, and he had no need to be ashamed of it, yet he felt relief that neither the woman's face nor mind showed evidence of having fathomed him.

As if to prevent himself from dwelling on it more, he turned swiftly and called the others to follow him.

"Best we search along the walls for a postern where we can enter," he said, laughing when Beatta expressed displeasure at having to walk further. She had expected they would enter the darkelf realm here through the enormous gates, she pouted.

"Even should they think to throw them open for a party as insignificant as ours," Vanaash told her solemnly, "still it could not be done without a roar greater than thunder, and a rumble that would shake the earth above."

That humbling thought served to still Beatta, but in the end Vanaash had to carry her till they finally found an iron-barred gateway where, for an exorbitant toll, they were allowed access. Beatta was entirely exhausted, she told Vanaash as he held her close, and still suffered that irksome throbbing in her ribcage. 'Twas well that he was so thoughtful of her discomfort.


The woman had pretty flaxen hair and was not entirely unattractive, despite overly-rouged cheeks and eyelids darkened with kohl. She moved with a suggestiveness that attracted and held Roric's attention; he could not remember ever having gone so long without a woman's comforts. Now, when she leaned over to refill his tankard, displaying herself to full advantage and studying him hopefully for a positive reaction, he felt his own yearning like the stab of a double-edged blade. Tora was the name she had given him when he asked earlier, after she snuck him a bold caress no decent woman would have dared. He bit his lip, stifling a sigh of resignation. He would be foolish not to advantage himself of her. She was not the finest of treasures, but she was the most promising thing about this day so far.

Exhausted, the four of them had made their way late to a travelers' hostel, overpriced and under-furnished, and visited the hall just long enough to take what food and drink they needed to steady themselves. Then they moved to the single available room, a veritable pit where they all collapsed immediately into sleep. Roric had wakened with a start in the dingy room to find four heavily armed darkelves standing over him. His fitful slumber had seemed only to have lasted a few minutes, so he was not well pleased to have been shaken so rudely awake. When he started to growl in protest, Vanaash, having obviously just been roused himself, signaled him to silence, indicating he might show deference to the two women who lay huddled under furs and coverlets a few paces away.

Groaning, Roric had come shakily to his feet. He'd been so weary the night before that he had fallen on his pallet fully clothed, and he roundly cursed himself for not having removed his weapons. He was sore all over, obviously affecting his usual merriness. When one of the darkelves flicked his sword impatiently on the way out, Roric had tossed him a gesture that no man in Midgard would have let slip by unnoticed.

Brooding here now, he was still stiff and aching, and this woman Tora had managed to add inestimably to his discomfort. His mood was not the best, either. To start with, he was famished and fatigued. He and Vanaash had been sitting wordlessly with two of their smug captors at a table in this damnable tavern long enough for him to down six full tankards, and he still had no idea why they had been summoned. Must be it was the wee small hours of the morning, too, though there was no way of telling by the unvarying light of the mist that passed for a sky here.

One of the guards, the one called Hvaam, turned and shot him an icy glare of disdain. "'Tis well past high noon in Midgard!" he growled, taking Roric somewhat aback. None of these elfmen were anything near to handsome, but this one was positively repulsive, with swarthy dark skin marked by pox and poorly healed scars. Roric took another long swallow.

He had known some dwarves but had never met with a darkelf before the iron bars of the Journeyer's Postern lifted to admit the four of them to Swartalfheim a few hours ago. Now, seeing them firsthand, he realized how wrong those men were who made no distinction between the two races. Aye, it was true they looked much alike, with stocky bodies, powerful and compact—darkelves being somewhat leaner and longer of limb than the bandy-legged dwarves, and clean-shaven where the others were bearded. Too, they had the same intense green eyes and odd voices.

But, apart from the occasional troublemakers common to all persuasions, dwarves were invariably civilized, thrifty, hardworking, loyal, and impeccably honest. The darkelves, on the other hand, exhibited a streak of perverseness that even a profligate like himself found reprehensible. Soon as they entered the hall of that hostel last night, he had noted it, and watching now further convinced him. Every one of the creatures had an evil look to him, and drunkenness, thievery, gambling, and foul-mouthed wantonness were everywhere in evidence. It was hard to tell who'd had the worst of it last night, Iseobel and Beatta fending off the rude advances of drunken wastrels, or the two men, who were continuously assaulted by whores.

The situation had not been without its temptations for him, either. He had been long without a woman, a problem painfully aggravated by Iseobel's constant and vexing nearness, and apart from a few dwarfwomen stolen from their home in Nidavellir, the prostitutes were all seductive human maids. Roric had always thought it unfair that the darkelves had no female of the species. In that, of all races, they were alone. Now he thought he understood why the gods had decreed it so: the beings were an abomination and not meant to procreate.

"Frigga's tit!" Roric barked the profanity without thinking, then flushed a deep red when he realized every eye in the place, which had grown unnaturally still, was upon him. Under the table, Vanaash had kicked him in the shin with as much force as could be mustered. Feeling it, Roric suddenly remembered his foster-brother warning him that these darkelves, for all their apparent worthlessness, were extremely skilled in the fathoming of minds. Hesitantly, Roric raised a glance to find Hvaam and the other guard, Wallin, staring daggers at him, sharp features lit with loathing. Managing a dim smile, he took another swig, trying desperately to keep from wondering if they had honed in on his thought. Could be they had just been insulted by his irreverent oath.

Thankfully, there was no time to muse on it. Just then a commotion arose. The outer doors swung open, admitting a dozen darkelves in battle gear. The one in their lead, two heads taller than the others and regally outfitted in finely linked silver mail, strode purposefully to their table. As he approached, Hvaam and Wallin sprang smartly to their feet.

"These are the journeyers, Lord Sivlir," the latter began. He was cut off with an authoritative wave of the hand.

"The women?"

"Safe at the hostel. We left two there to guard their sleep."

Vanaash had risen slowly, and now Roric followed his lead almost unconsciously, feeling the burning intensity of the darkelf's scrutiny. This Sivlir was clearly one to be reckoned with: lordly, autocratic, and formidable. Drawing near, the darkelf raised an arm as if in salute, then signaled wordlessly to his adjutants to clear the hall. When a murmur of discontent arose amongst the patrons, all it took was a single look from Lord Sivlir, and even the most brazen scurried out meekly. The tavern-keeper brought a pitcher and an extra tankard and, after depositing them on the table, took his own hurried leave, pulling the woman Tora by the arm up the stairs after him. She cast one last shameless look of interest over her shoulder as she disappeared, and Roric flushed with discomfort when he realized Sivlir had caught him returning it. The darkelf gave a snort of laughter and motioned both the men to sit.

"Best beware if you commerce with these women, Roric Grim-Kill," he said, pouring out a round of mead. "They are none of the cut of which you are used to fondling, but instead are hard and baneful."

"That one seemed not so base as many," Roric answered carefully, wondering how the other had known his name. "Could be she is a stolen maid."

Sivlir gave an easy laugh. "Still that is rumored in Midgard, then? That we steal innocent maids and force them here to do our bidding?" He laughed again. "Nay, Roric. Could be 'twas done in days of old, but now they come to us freely: loose women who are willing to trade a few years of hard work for a wealth in gems and metals!"

He took a long sip, then added darkly, in answer to Roric's unspoken bewilderment, that all four journeyers had stated their names at the hostelry, and the news had traveled fast to his ears. Roric shifted uncomfortably.

Vanaash, who had been silent till now, gazed at the darkelf over the rim of his cup, then lowered it. "Must be if you know *my* name, then you know what it is we are come for." Roric was surprised when his foster-brother said it, and even more surprised when the other nodded his assent.

"Aye. Soon as I heard one had come calling himself 'Vanaav Komling,' I made haste to petition the runes to prove whether it was true. Soon as I learned that in truth you were entitled to that name, I determined me to meet with you."

Now Sivlir was the one who looked uneasy. He settled far back in the carven chair and crossed his arms on his chest. "Seems we have been a long while awaiting this visit," he said low. "Mayhap too long."

Roric tossed his head; the warmth of the mead was inspiring him back to boldness. "Could be you might have afforded us a better welcome then!"

"Be thankful you were not greeted harsher!" Sivlir growled. "The last time we received humans here, a great wrong was done to us, one which it will take much to undo in the eyes of gods and men. Only since your arrival last night are we come to know how sorely we were robbed!" He paused, as if groping for words, then stared hard into Vanaash's eyes. To Roric, spinning a little from the strong drink, it seemed as if some kind of message passed silently between the two.

There was a long, uneasy silence; then Vanaash's look grew clouded. He pushed himself away from the table, stood, and began pacing back and forth nervously. Finally, he spoke.

"Are you not the Warden of the Gateway?" he asked the darkelf, obviously fighting to keep his voice level. "Are you not he who wields the most of all power in this realm?"

Coming staunchly to his feet, Sivlir replied that he was. Vanaash spun round in anger to face him. "Best you tell me then, how it happened that I have been so cheated!"

Sivlir tensed, and the line of his jaw hardened. "One came before you," he said simply, unflinching, "and claimed your prize for his own."

Vanaash bristled. "Yet I was told that my true name would be the token to you. The sign that I am he who was meant to claim it! That and the fact that I would order a sacred bind-ring to be cast!"

Sivlir shrugged miserably. "One came and said 'Forge me a ring fit to bind Vanaav Komling.' The same one carried a token that we knew to be of the Vanir, a ribbon that belonged to Freyja. 'Twas either coincidence or evil deception, but how could we know it then? Had you not come here now and pronounced that name a second time, ne'er would I have ever suspected it."

Vanaash slammed his fist down on the table so hard that mead splashed from the tankards. After pacing a while longer, he collapsed back into his chair and sat some time in a listless silence. "Since you were so careful to check my claim, I cannot help but wonder what the runes answered when you asked them to verify that other's right to take the treasure in the name of Vanaav Komling?" he asked finally.

Sivlir drew a deep breath. "Here is the mystery!" he exclaimed miserably. "They said that his right to the name was truth. Never have I known the runes to lie, and thus we trusted, and knew none the better till your arrival. Though later, when he had gone, I suspected it might have been trickery!"

"What mean you?"

Sivlir's look darkened. "The man who claimed it, seems he did not travel alone. Afterwards I learned that when he left, 'twas with another."

"With whom did he leave?"

"With someone powerful."

"Truly?" Vanaash spat bitterly. "Is there one powerful enough to make the runes lie?"

"Could be!" exclaimed Sivlir in a hoarse whisper. "He left here with Lord Lodur."

Despite his lightheadedness, Roric recognized the name and shot his foster-brother a grim look. Vanaash clenched and unclenched his fists so hard the knuckles showed white. When he finally spoke, his voice was hard but calm.

"'Tis a great wrong that has been done to me," he said slowly, "and I swear I will avenge it. First, though, I mustneeds order me my own bind-ring made immediately, Lord Sivlir, and claim the one already forged for Lady Iseobel so we can be wed. Then I will have you detail this man to me, if you will, and we will do what we must do to repay him."

"Must be you do not know what you say, brother!" cried Roric now, thickly and with much effort, as he sprang to his feet. "She is not the one you are meant to wed!" He had been confused almost since the start of all this, and his foster-brother's rage and harshness had bewildered him all the more. On this point, though, he was certain.

But when Vanaash stilled him with an ungentle gesture, Roric sat back down in utter consternation and took another swallow to clear his thoughts. It was the darkelf chieftain who spoke next, telling Vanaash it was not quite so easy as that.

"I do not have her bind-ring to give you."

"What mean you?" Vanaash trembled, clutching hard to the table as if to steady himself as he rose.

A shadow darkened Sivlir's face. "Her ring is gone from here," he answered in a husky whisper. "Borne away by the same hand that snatched your appointed treasure."

Fast growing faint and dizzy from the combined effects of hunger, sleeplessness, and strong drink, Roric grasped only snatches of what passed next.

"It was a magicker named Dorflin who helped Lord Lodur with the thievery," the darkelf said, "a strong magicker stolid in his powers, a human of great mystery. I mentored him in his youth; ne'er would it have occurred to me he would have so changed his allegiances in the long years since we have met."

"By the gods, I will smite him!" Vanaash was saying as Roric crossed his arms on the table and lowered his head. "By the gods, I will smite the man who stole her bind-ring! From this moment, he is doomed!"

It was a splash of water that finally wakened Roric Grim-Kill, and it must not have been the first, for his long hair was already matted and dripping. He shook his head forcefully, sending off a spray that made Vanaash take two steps backward.

Lord Sivlir was gone, the hall was full again, and the table had been laid with food. As he heaped a wooden planch with bread and chunks of dry-looking meat, Vanaash glared at Roric.

"Best you keep a level head about you from now on," he said shortly, shoving the food in front of his foster-brother with an angry flourish, then sitting down. "Must be you can tell from our converse that things have taken a turn that will demand of you a certain amount of discipline."

Biting off a chunk of bread, Roric eyed him disdainfully. "Could be I am not minded to follow you any more, Vanaash, when you hide from me your purposes and feed me lies for fodder!"

"What mean you?" Vanaash glowered.

"Seems you told me a certain cause for our coming hither, and 'twas none of the reasons I heard you speaking of today."

"Do not be jealous of the treasure he spoke of, brother. 'Tis not what you think. I would have told you of it were you not so loose-tongued always. Besides, it did not involve you!"

"Enow it did for me to risk death fighting at your side against this Lord Lodur! A like-brother and chief of all your men I am, yet you kept it secret that such a great warrior had sworn against us and let me think 'twas a chance encounter!"

Vanaash shook his head. "I have been warned against that man, as many have, but until this day I knew not that he had a personal feud with me."

Quelled by his foster-brother's earnest tone, Roric ate a few more mouthfuls in silence, eyes fixed on the stairway where the wench named Tora had reappeared suddenly, arm in arm with a besotted-looking darkelf wearing a fortune in golden trinkets. She winked, and Roric pulled his gaze away. As if recalling something painful, he turned back to Vanaash with an angry look.

"You lied to me in your reasons for bringing Iseobel here," he said low. "You spoke me grave mistruths."

"Did I not say she would be confirmed in her calling?"

"Aye, calling to her craft, I thought, not to your bed!"

"You were the one with the dream of ensconcing her as the holy woman of Skog, Roric. Ne'er did I lie to you."

Roric gave a bitter snort. "Nor to Beatta, I trow!"

Vanaash flushed uncomfortably. "Never have I laid a claim to your sister," he said in a hard whisper. "Nor ever have I led her to believe that I would have her."

"Say you so?" Roric's voice was icy. "Must be you have forgotten how well you comforted her after Thran's passing, and how oft I interrupted you two in the byre and in the meadow."

"She was the one who came to me, brother! And never came aught of it!"

Roric gave a cold laugh and pushed the remnants of the meal away. "Seems a different impression has been made all over Skog and the countryside there. Surely Beatta believes you will hold to custom, else she would not have turned down so many other men, bold and wealthy alike."

"Mayhap 'tis you, Roric, who wants most that Beatta would wed with me. Could be you are worried that any man save I would flush you off that homestead when he took her!"

Vanaash said the words heedlessly, and when he saw the hurt in his foster-brother's eyes, he softened. "'Tis not your concern to worry about it, Grim-Kill. A person has the right to choose or refuse, and 'tis dishonorable to question him why."

Roric turned on him, nostrils flaring. "Dishonorable, too, for a man to force a mating against a woman's will, like you mean to do Iseobel! It cannot be a surprise that she fears and despises you!"

Vanaash faced him furiously. "You could never be a good enough reader of things to understand why that does not matter!" He stopped himself, shaking. The two lapsed into an uneasy silence, broken only by the jangling of Roric's heavy bracelets as he signaled for more mead.

When it came, he sipped it slowly. Remembering Vanaash's admonition to soberness, he took just enough to relieve the head pain that had come on him unawares, then pushed it away. Vanaash cast him a twisted smile as he did so and, by habit, Roric returned it.

"Aye," Vanaash said easily then, as if the other had spoken first. "'Twould be best to keep our brotherhood strong now. Soon enough we will be facing Lodur and this magick-man, Dorflin. Then will we have proper quarry for our rage and furor!"

Roric nodded absently, then drifted into thought again. After a long time, he swallowed hard and leaned far forward, drawing as near to the other as he could manage across the table. "Just tell me one thing, brother! Do you love the woman?"

Vanaash looked at him with surprise, then shook his head and laughed loud. "By the gods, you have a bold wonder! All the many maids and matrons you have fallen to the bed with, and never once did I think to ask such a thing of you!"

Roric bit his lip. Had Vanaash bothered to fathom him then, he would have discovered a churning multitude of feelings within the man's heart, deeper and more profound than ever he had sensed there before.

Vanaash's mind was on other things, though, and he stood and stretched. "Best you should make your way back to the hostel," he said casually. "Lord Sivlir says the women will be well attended, but could be they will be anxious if the night comes and goes with neither of us returning."

"You are heading elsewhere?" Roric eyed him curiously but against his own will, spoke with a note of accusation.

Vanaash shrugged. "I must claim a weapon fashioned for me at the forge."

Incredulous, Roric flew to his feet. "You?!"

He knew only the most powerful in all the Nine Worlds were marked to receive a magickal weapon forged by the mysterious dark-elves. Freyja of the Vanir had been gifted with the stunning necklace called Brisingamen by them, though some claimed she bought it by bartering her lusty charms away to four of their most powerful. Each stone of that necklace had a different and awesome ability. Legend told, too, that at that very forge the lightelf chieftain Ljus had claimed the silver shields and cloaks of gold which afforded his race invisibility in battle. Cunning Lokji of the Æsir had claimed prize after prize there, magick spears and armlets, and the enchanted sword and the wondrous flying ship, *Skidbladnir*, which he had in turn gifted away to the Vana god Freyr in hope of buying the favor of Freyja. That ship, it was said, could grow to sail an entire army through the air yet shrink to fit in the smallest of pouches. Only at the darkelves' forge could treasures of such power be fashioned.

Aye, mighty ones like these were those invited to choose weapons of the darkelves: gods, augurs, runemasters, high magickers, and Holies. That his foster-brother could lay claim to a weapon indicated a past steeped in strong divination—a secret past. Apart from acknowledging Vanaash's second sight, Roric had never suspected this. He gave a low whistle and sat back down. He should have wondered when he learned that Vanaash was worthy of a bind-ring. That was a thing not ordained for ordinary mortals, either, but for those specially marked. Men powerful in their own right, or those....

Roric leaned back heavily, casting a troubled glance at his foster-brother as the man settled accounts with the tavern-keeper. There were others who were pledged with sacred bind-rings: those who would wed to tap and drain the magick of another, and use it to consolidate their own power, good or evil. And the weapons made on the forge of Swartalfheim, he knew, served darkness as oft as light, and mayhap more so.

Throwing back a huge draught of mead, Roric wiped his mouth hard and shuddered. He was still clutching the tankard tight in his hand when Vanaash walked by and chid him gently.

"Stay not overlong in this den, brother. I would be wroth to learn you came to robbery or harm here while you lingered half-conscious with drink."

Roric rose, somewhat numbly, and they took each other's shoulders in their usual brotherly farewell. Soon as the man was gone, though, Roric finished off his cup and called for another. When Tora brought it, she noticed immediately how tensed he had become, and when she suggested a good way of relaxing him, he followed her obediently up the steep staircase.

# Chapter Ten

Heavy of heart, Roric returned to the hostel. Two darkelves, ordered to stand guard until Roric or Vanaash returned, hissed a weary greeting and relayed the news that Beatta, grown tired of confinement, had haughtily demanded a tour of the city. She had left some time ago, they said, with five darkelf guardsmen who had eagerly volunteered to entertain and protect her.

Closing the heavy door behind him as he entered, Roric leaned back against it awhile, trying to collect his thoughts. He was maddeningly distracted by the knowledge that Iseobel was bathing behind the heavy curtain that separated the room into two compartments. She called him a greeting and, answering, he had realized that if he stared hard enough, her shape was just barely visible through the heavy cloth, outlined by the flickering light of the hearth fire she had lit behind there for warmth. With very little effort, his mind's eye could fill in the details of that slender form, perched precariously in the round tub, and the feelings his imagination aroused in him caused a torture unlike any he had ever known.

It was as if Iseobel had been calling his name, such was the strength of the need to see her that had drawn him, still unsatisfied, away from that Tora's willing body. Soon as the wench had bared her breasts and wrapped her arms around him, he had felt a shame that ravaged through him like a storm at sea. All the savage fury of his want and need was as nothing compared to the aching tenderness he felt for Iseobel, the need to see her, savor her innocence, and protect her from the loveless fate that loomed to swallow her. Aye, he would have wronged Iseobel had he let that other wench take him, and he was glad he had fled from Tora's lewd embrace. Yet, still he ached, and it seemed hopeless he would ever find release in this world again, unless this one were to draw him to her.

Worse, he realized with a sudden burning flush, his discomfort would be visible to her if she opened that curtain now and came to meet him. He had removed his heavy hauberk and his thin linen sark would do little to hide his distress. It was an abashment he could not hazard, not with all the important words he was resolved to share with her tonight. Groaning inwardly, he lowered himself to one of the pallets. Belly down, he crossed his arms and pillowed his head in them, working hard to tame himself before she found him. As if for strength, he gripped a tiny glass vial tightly in one hand. It was a magicker's potion bottle, filled with fragrant dried lavender which he had bought earlier for Iseobel. It had a metal loop over the top of its finely rounded stopper, so that it could be hung from a thong or string. He hoped she would agree to wear it alongside her amber cats, not only as token of his affection, but as assurance that, no matter what her fate, she might ever count him among those who would defend her. Holding it tightly, he was flooded with emotion. Though he grit his teeth and willed it hard away, he could not rid himself of the picture of her sweet, pensive smile and her languorous silver eyes the day she had stood on tip-toe to kiss him.

He could not have foreseen that when Iseobel saw him this way, she would take him for ill. Less had he anticipated that she would kneel anext him, wrap her fingers tight in his tangled hair, and lift his head, forcing him to look at her, which thing he had resolved not to do.

Her thin shift clung lightly to her damp skin, revealing her firm, well-formed shape. Her hand, grazing his unshaven cheek, caused him to shudder and, seeing this, she cried his name out in alarm. He trembled more. Roric Grim-Kill was not a praying man, but now, from his very depths, he cried silently to Freyja. She, if any, would understand his anguish and distract him from thoughts of dishonoring this blameless maiden. He gripped the lavender-filled bottle even harder:

*Freyja, help me. I am strengthless to resist her on my own.*

"Roric! What ails you that you pray so hard for relief!" Iseobel leaned close, frantically probing for signs of fever or pain. Amazingly, her sweet voice seemed to cure him—either the voice or the fear it inspired suddenly to realize how well she could read him. He let go a tortured breath. Aye, the goddess had a strange way of working things, but it was certain she had heard his plea. He tossed Iseobel a wan smile.

She eyed him suspiciously. "Have you dosed yourself in mead again?" she asked indignantly. He said nay, only that he had a head pain brought on by all the stresses of the day.

She softened. "Aye, your neck and back and shoulders are well tensed from it!" She began to knead and work his muscles in a soothing way. To his surprise, her touch, which moments earlier would have driven him to madness, now calmed him.

Relaxing to her ministrations, he drew a deep breath and, careful to formulate his words in the way that would frighten her least, he told her all: that the pretext for coming here had been a deceit; that Vanaash was resolved to have his way in wedding her, with her will or against it; and, in so doing, abandon Beatta, without a care for that woman's breaking heart or the vows that had Roric believed had passed between them.

"Despite all, I would back him even now if I believed he loved you," Roric finished in a weak and miserable tone. "He claims not to, though. Only that he mustneeds have hold of you in order to procure some thing which he feels by right is his."

At this last, Iseobel stifled a small cry of agony and Roric turned fast to face her. Sensing her tauten, he drew her close in a comforting embrace and she let herself be lowered to his side. She was trembling now, and he realized it was with anger. His voice grew solemn.

"Worse yet, Iseobel, there is some deception here I have not reckoned yet," he told her. "A prize awaited him in this place. Just what, he would not tell me. Seems it was stolen, though, by that same dark chieftain who waylaid us in the forest, working hand in hand with some magicker named Dorflin."

Iseobel stiffened, and Roric drew her closer yet. "This same Dorflin stole away a bind-ring meant for you that Vanaash had hoped to claim," he continued, unaware of her fast-rising terror. "Now Vanaash is sworn to slay the man at any cost."

Iseobel's mind raced frantically. Must be her father had foreseen all this! It could not be an accident that he had arrived here before them and spirited away that thing which Vanaash sought so desperately. Her bind-ring, too! Ever wise, Dorflin had known somehow that Vanaash would attempt to claim her, and had contrived to keep him from accomplishing it.

For reasons she could not know, her father had risked all to save her from Vanaash's clutches! *Hand-in-hand*, Roric had said, *with the lord who had attacked them in the forest.* She shivered. Dorflin must have sent that powerful, black-haired lord for her, just as the man had claimed! His appearance had caused her a tumult of emotion—the same sensations she had felt when, as a child, she hid and spied on his doings with Dorflin. Vanaash must have known the man had come for her, too, so harshly had he fought him. Suddenly, unbidden, she remembered how Vanaash had lifted Beatta's limp, lifeless body, kissing away her death wound with his awesome power....

Uttering a quick prayer in a language Roric did not understand, Iseobel shifted to face him, still wrapped in his strong arms. "By all the gods, I beg you help me, Roric Grim-Kill!" she cried desperately. "I am in need of a protector who will see me from this place back to my homestead. With all my heart, I would pray that man be you."

Roric felt a rush of love and warmth. "I had already resolved me to stand behind you, lady," he whispered huskily in reply. Lifting her chin with one hand, he locked her gaze into his own as he gently enfolded the little necklace into her hand with the other. So doing, he brought her mouth to his. She did not resist his courtly kiss, and her compliance flooded him with a burning fervor more sensual than any debauched pleasure he had ever known. It seemed to him like the innocent sealing of a vow. They were yet locked in embrace when the heavy door slammed, jolting them from the moment like a thunderbolt.

"You are vile, Roric Eirik's son!" Beatta's shrill voice ripped through the chamber. She kicked at something, and strode forward menacingly. Roric, certain he would have to fend off a thrashing before he could explain himself, sprang to his feet.

"Never any decency in you that I could see," she continued unquelled, "yet to think you could so misconduct yourself, and with *that* maid—" She stopped herself and raised a hand as if to slap him, but in an instant he had stopped the blow in midair, grabbing her wrist roughly and slamming it to her side.

"Aye, with Iseobel!" he growled ferociously, stepping his sister backwards without loosening his grip. Beatta, astounded by this show of fierceness, caught her breath, then laughed coldly.

"You are an amazement, brother!" she snarled, looking from one to the other accusingly. "To think you could seduce even this one, whose so-called holiness is of such great remark."

Roric tensed and drew himself to his full height, suddenly so formidable that Beatta, who had ever dismissed the tales of Roric's valor which carried from the battlefield, instinctively stepped back. Moving closer, he spoke in a hard whisper.

"I will bide no ill speech of her, sister! 'Tis not what you think, that I would advantage myself of her—"

But before he could finish, Iseobel came angrily to her feet and put herself between them. "I could say naught while a guest in your house, Beatta," she hissed, staring hard in the other woman's eyes, "though I was oft tempted. In my land, a woman would be called harridan who so meanly accosted any man, and most of all a kinsman! 'Tis despicable the way you taunt your brother with reproaches and recriminations, when he cares so for your heart and welfare! Even now, you accuse him, though 'tis for your sake that he has agreed to flee with me!"

Openmouthed, Beatta spun swiftly away, calculating with a frenzy. *Could it be?* She smoothed the wrinkles from her Loden wool bodice and pulled the sleeves of her shift straight. Scarce content with the spell she had cast on Vanaash, this vixen had now turned her enchantments on Roric, with obviously more gratifying results. Vanaash had withstood the witch's wily workings these many weeks, but Roric had tumbled with her at the first invitation! It was certain the foolish girl had no discernment of the worth of men to cast aside aspirations on one so noble as Vanaash just to frolic with this wastrel....

"Could be *you* are the one who blunders in your estimation, Lady Beatta!" Iseobel cried. "For all the faults you count in him, at least Roric is ever honest! The other has plied us all with deceit—" Iseobel broke off, flushing.

Subdued by being so keenly read, Beatta cast Roric a helpless glance. "What is she saying, brother? Best be frank!"

"The truth ..." Roric faltered an instant, as if weighing the wisdom of inspiring her ire by telling her more. Then he let go a deep breath and began.

All the while he spoke, Beatta paced nervously, listening and planning. In truth, it did not startle her to learn Vanaash wished to wed with the holy woman; she had known he was bewitched. What surprised her more was that these two, in turning their backs on Vanaash, were playing so neatly into her hands! Roric's motive was easy enough to discern. Any could see the lackwit had lusted after this foreign wench from the first, and no doubt the betrayal of his foster-brother was made easier by pretending he performed some noble purpose in saving her.

But Iseobel? Beatta wondered if her own jealousy caused her to read nonexistent affection into Iseobel's feelings for Vanaash? Could be the woman had never cared a mite for him. Iseobel would not be the first maid, either, to chase fair Roric until he fell to the bed with her.

Beatta swallowed hard. Vanaash, she knew, was sorely infatuated, and if these two lamebrains had devised a plan that might put an end to his foolishness, 'twould be best to further them in it. Who could tell? Perhaps Iseobel was only momentarily entranced by the heat of Roric's salacious embrace. Vanaash's return might snap her back to reality with entirely unwanted results. Beatta had waited long for Vanaash and he had never given her cause to doubt him— until this one arrived! Aye, it would be wise to see the two swiftly on their way!

Roric had stepped behind the curtain and was dousing and cleaning himself, while Iseobel scurried here and there, gathering things they both might need for their journey. Beatta bit the inside of her cheek, debating what to say.

After a while of silence, she cleared her throat. "Scarce can I believe that Vanaash would tell you we bore no claim one upon the other," she said, in a small and miserable voice addressing her unseen brother, "when even now I suspect I carry his child anext my heart."

She heard Iseobel gasp. Roric stepped out shirtless and dripping, in the process of refastening an ear-ring. Flushing belligerently, he spoke through clenched teeth. "Might of Thor's hammer! I should stay and smite him! More boldly has he lied to me than ever I suspected!"

Beatta jumped up, throwing him a fresh tunic. "Nay, brother! You do best by spiriting this poor lady away! I have forced my own fate by too easily assenting and … and—" she groped uneasily for words, "could be he will keep all the promises he made to me, once he comes aright!" Here she glanced quickly at Iseobel, with her best woebegone smile, but the other, distraught and agitated, did not see her.

Roric, still clad only in linen breeches, sat down heavily on the edge of a carven table. "This will likely burst into a longtime feud," he said to Beatta, watching as she dropped dried plums and bread into a burlap sack. "Could be I will never see you more, sister, nor my mother and hearth and homestead."

Made wary by the familiar tone of indecision which had crept unobtrusively into his speech and manner, Beatta straightened. "Put some clothes on you, Roric!" she growled low. "Surely you sense the wisdom of a swift escape."

The Grim-Kill stood reluctantly and pulled on a sark, still musing. "Best you should know I have always felt affection for you, sister. Aye, you were ever a maid of harsh words and mien, but methinks it was to be expected from the agonies of our childhood, and I have never marked that hard against you."

Something in his voice, grave and intense, made Beatta pause. He was tugging on his beltings and sword girth now, seemingly absorbed in the endeavor, but he raised his gaze and met hers with a flickering smile. Suddenly, and almost against her will, she was flooded with warm emotion. She remembered how he had oft sprung to her defense as a boy, taking the blame for her infractions, thus diverting their father's rage to himself.

It had been she and her twin Staag, not Roric, who trapped that stoat and hid it in the byre where it made an end of the new prize lamblings. Roric had taken the beating, too, when she accidentally loosed her father's peregrine falcon that long-ago market day, and she could not count the times he had hastened her away when her husband Thran came home drunken, then cooled the man's ire with his gay and carefree jests. As for Roric's killing of their kinsman, Haftor, she alone knew that Roric had dealt that blow in rage over their cousin's ill-usage of her, not in mindless drunkenness but so that *her* name would not be sullied. Nor had he complained when his rightful due, a rich and vast inheritance, had been gifted to her by the mad and fevered father who had despised him even as a tot. She swallowed hard.

"I *have* had a heavy hand with you, Roric," she whispered, struggling to keep a firm tone, "but you have ever been the sort who craved a stern guidance. And needed it, too, else you would have drifted even further asea than now you find yourself!"

He laughed. "As ever, you speak right! Still, you should know that you are the one I measure all women against...."

His voice trailed off, but the remark had returned Beatta to her more usual cynicism. She looked past him to Iseobel. Surely, he could not expect her to believe he had gauged *that* one to be of a like cut, she fumed. Apart from a certain skill with horses, the runeswoman showed no leaning at all to strength or valor. And if it were physical attributes he was talking about, there could scarce be a comparison.

Even so, there appeared to be a genuine tenderness between these two, she realized as she watched Roric help Iseobel with her mantle. Could be they would make a happy match. With luck, Iseobel would not come to resent Roric's aimless ways; he was handsome and had a good heart. If she did not expect too much of him, she would not be too terribly disappointed. As for her brother, he was plainly enamored. Too, it could do him no harm to settle finally with a single darling and stop his wenching.

Beatta tossed her flame-red hair to shake away the unwelcome bout of sentimentality. "Have you thought yet about how you will make your way out of this dungeon-world?" she asked coolly, looking from one to the other. They exchanged glances.

"I had half-forgotten about that long and awesome dark out there," Roric exclaimed with a note of consternation. "And mayhap we will not be allowed back through that gate."

Beatta cut him off with an impatient snort. "Any one of those armlets or rings you wear would buy your way through the postern, Roric," she said curtly, "and a second would purchase the gate-keeper's silence after he passed you through! As for the blackness, I may have a way of helping you."

"No torch in all the Nine Worlds will cut through that murk," Iseobel reminded her sharply, "not even a magick one."

"Nay, but I have learned a secret of one of the darkelf-warriors here," Beatta replied with a self-satisfied smile. "In his haste to make me promise I would revisit, Wallin showed me the passage upwards through the root. 'Tis a steeper ascent and smoother, but lighted all the way to Midgard by a sheen like that of gray dawning. All you need do is show this token to the gatekeeper, and he will direct you thither!"

She held up a pendant of scribed silver, which glinted in the flickering firelight. "Consider well, though, before you decide! You will surface at some unknown point and will have by-passed Wulf and Ivar and the others who wait at the mouth of the Darkway. You will be on your own then, the two of you. No horses, no provisions, and no guard to protect you."

"Seems a small price for avoiding that evil darkness," Roric muttered nervously. "What think you, Iseobel?"

"It would save us many hours," Iseobel replied after considering, "but must be you know I am wroth to part with Effa. Such a fine horse she is that you gave me, Roric!"

It took Beatta singular effort to subdue an angry jibe, but she managed it, handing the token to Iseobel. "You should hold onto this, lady, lest my brother mislay it. Oft he is careless of objects—and other things."

She smiled when Iseobel took it, kept smiling as they hugged and said swift good-byes, and after the two scurried, smiled still. Surely the lie that she was with child by Vanaash had turned Iseobel's heart against the man forever! 'Twas good work, for now the vixen was gone, Roric was suddenly gladsome and firm of purpose, and Vanaash was hers again. He would be happy that the sneaking pair were gone, too! Aye, she would see to that....


"I am worried for Iseobel!" Vanaash frowned to Sivlir as they hurried back toward the realm proper through the twisting labyrinth that guarded the cavernous sacred center of Swartalfheim. Sivlir laughed at his discomfiture.

"Do not bother to mentally search for her, Vanaash! This maze is constructed to block all thoughts, both to and from, as a safeguard to those who come here for holy purposes—to claim weapons from the magick forge or to be tested in the great hollow stone. This was so decreed by those who built it."

"Aye. 'Twas surely built with a wisdom!" Glad for a moment's distraction from his churning thoughts, Vanaash slowed his long-legged stride to match the other's pace. "Men say 'twas Dvalin, oldest and wisest of all the darkelves who chanced upon that opening to Mimir's Well, and diverted those waters to flow and tumble all around this sacred cavern, shielding it. I thought 'twas mere legend before this night!"

"'Tis truth, indeed," Sivlir replied solemnly, gesturing to the wide trough that ran beside their path. It was built so that the glowing water danced and gurgled, cascading down carven falls, rushing up steep sloped aqueducts, then bubbling down again with a soothing, musical life of its own. They let themselves be lulled by it a moment before Sivlir spoke again.

"To say he chanced upon it, though, is misleading. The well springs up once in each of the Nine Worlds, you know. Dvalin and his three brothers devoted years to the search before finding the fountains in Swartalfheim, Midgard, and Jotunheim, the giant world. They well hid the entrances in two of the worlds, for fear that unworthies might make access; and this one, as you see, is guarded by all the power at their disposal."

"No small amount, that," Vanaash added thoughtfully.

Sivlir readily agreed. "Remember they are the same four who fashioned the magick spear Gungnir for Odin All-Father, and Brisingamen, Freyja's charmed necklace, and other weapons for the gods, including the magick ship, *Skidbladnir* which Lokji gifted to Freyr. Mortals, halflings, humans, and humanforms, too, have claimed valuables made by their hands: a mirror that spies on all who stand before it, a scrying bowl of unsurpassed vision, a silver flask with eight drops of magick brew, seven that heal all, and one which restores life. And your handsome bracelet!"

Vanaash looked wonderingly at the exquisite golden band which now adorned his right wrist. In his anticipation, he had forgotten that a magick weapon was not certain to be a sword, axe or dagger, and so had been surprised tonight when, in the midst of a long and trancing ceremony, two darkelf smiths had come forward with a piece of jewelry balanced on a glowing tray.

"Most powerful of all mortals, this Dvalin," he murmured knowingly. "So Lord Stranger told me. None could ever know him, thus is he named Dvalin, "Deluder" in his own tongue."

"Rightly said, though his brothers, Alfrigg, Berling, and Grerr, stand near his equal. The years of men are as hours to darkelves. We were created all at the beginning of time, males only, and though no more will ever be born, we will live each one endlessly, unless purposefully slain. Think what can be accomplished in a lifetime that spans countless of human generations! Perhaps a godsire, a halfling, could attain to something like that might, if one of them were to earn and keep a portion of the godliness to which he was entitled. A mere man has no true share of immortality in the physical body, though, only his questionable power of procreation, and even that...."

But their converse had brought them to the end of the maze, and soon as they stepped out of it, Vanaash raised a hand sharply, stopping his companion in the middle of a sentence.

Something was amiss! Vanaash, his inner sight finely honed by this night's happenings, was sure of it. Nor did he need to speak a word of his worry aloud to the other. Exchanging a mute and meaningful glance, the two hurried down the twisted streets, desolate now and eerie, making their way silently to the darkened hostel.

As Vanaash threw open the heavy door to their room, Beatta sprang from her pallet and tumbled immediately into her frantic tale, following behind as her foster-brother paced the length and breadth of the chamber, his tall frame tensed with anxiety. Twice she

told the details of Roric and Iseobel's flight in a strangled tone
before he even seemed to take notice of her; then, he sat down
heavily on the edge of the table, and turned piercing eyes on her in
the dim firelight as she began the telling for the third time.

"Iseobel is gone, Vanaash. She and Roric are flown away
together! There was naught I could do to stop them!"

Vanaash drew a deep and tortured breath. "How comes this to
happen?" he asked low after awhile.

Beatta lit a pitch-torch in the dying embers of the hearth fire,
set it into a holder gouged deep in the stone wall, and faced him,
crossing her arms defiantly. "It lies not easy on me to tell this tale,
brother!" she breathed. "Less easy yet with another here to witness
your pain!"

She gestured toward Sivlir, and the darkelf stiffened, eyes glittering in the half-light. Vanaash shook his head. "Speak now!" he
said sharply. "I need hide nothing from this one!"

Sivlir stood up, though, as if sensing the woman's reluctance.
"The hour is late, and you will know where to find me on the
morrow, Lord Vanaash." He made his way across the room. "Must be
you know I am committed to helping you in this," he added quietly,
turning a strange look to Beatta as he pulled the door open. "Best as
I can, I will do what you require."

His footsteps died away. Seeming to relax a little, Beatta lifted a
heavy jug of water from the table where Vanaash was sitting, took a
deep swig, then replaced it noiselessly. "They were lying there
together, tight in each other's arms, scarce at all dressed and
sheened all over with the sweat of their exertions," she recounted,
gesturing over her shoulder to the unmade pallet where Roric and
Iseobel had lingered earlier. "I could tell the woman was sore vexed
that I had come in unexpectedly and caught them in such obvious
circumstance."

Vanaash waxed uneasy but his voice was stoic. "Said you aught
to them?"

"Oh, aye! I bade Roric dress himself and I tongue-lashed him
some, best as I could for my shock and shame at seeing them. Then
Iseobel called me 'harridan' and berated me for it, defending him.
They were already minded to fly off together. I remember Roric's
flinging harsh oaths in Thor's name, and saying he was minded to
stay and slay you first. Could be the maid had worked some of her
magick on him, for he was bolder and more insolent than ever I
have seen him yet." Pursing her full lips, Beatta paused, as if
expecting him to make an answer.

Vanaash said nothing, though. So well Beatta believed her own version that he read from her mind the story as truth, even sensing her fear at the memory of Roric's behavior. She moved closer, speaking in a cold whisper. "How well she tricked us all with that mock innocence of hers! Yet she was quick to seduce him, soon as they found an hour alone."

Vanaash's voice was a bitter hiss. "Think hard, sister! 'Tis impossible to picture one like Roric pushed unwillingly to the bed."

"Aye, he is weak willed and women sense it, but that does not lessen *her* guilt, Vanaash!"

"More likely the fault is his. You yourself remarked on the boldness of his mood. Must be he forced her!"

Beatta, striving for composure, resisted the urge to spit. "If so, seems she well appreciated his rough and ungentle embraces, to agree so readily to flee with him."

Vanaash flew to his feet, trembling with anger. "Has it not occurred to you that perhaps she flees in shame, broken by his vicious recklessness? Think you she would be the first maid ever ruined by his selfish wantonness? I will find Roric Grim-Kill and smite him!"

Furious herself now, Beatta spun to face him, quivering. "You flatter the bitch, Vanaash! Can't be she has put enchantments on you, too, that would make you swear blood against one you have known and loved since babyhood! Could be she is not so blameless as you think!"

"She is, though!" Almost as if for support, Vanaash put a strong hand on Beatta's shoulder, drawing her close in a sudden motion and lifting her troubled gaze to his. "Iseobel is holy!"

With the blood draining rapidly from her face, Beatta pulled herself away. "I know what I saw, Vanaash."

"Aye, I do not doubt it! 'Tis proof to me that the makebate has insinuated himself on one who should never have suffered his hurtful touch. With all the Æsir and Vanir gods as witness, I vow I will slay him for the ruining of her!"

As he said the words, Beatta crumpled, sliding to her knees in a lithely spontaneous movement. She stayed there, motionless, staring into the flickering fire while Vanaash paced like a caged cat, raging threats in a strangled half whisper, barely audible. Beatta made no sound at all, save when he asked her something directly. *Did she know whither they had fled?* Aye, they had decided Iseobel's homestead in the Danelaw would be the safest spot for their trysting. *Was there mention of the route they hoped to take?* Roric had cajoled from her a token that would let them forego the Darkway. By now, they had a full night's long head start.

Scarce could Beatta remember ever weeping for her own sake, but she felt tears now, and it was hard to hold them back. She only half-listened as Vanaash made his plans: first thing in the morning, he would take his leave of Lord Sivlir. They would reclaim their men and horses at the mouth of the Darkway, then make haste for the *Windrider*. Four days' sail would bring them to Scarbyrig.

Before all else, he would put death on the Grim-Kill, then he would find and succor the lady. If there was anything to be salvaged of her honor, they would make it up to her in gold gifts, even if it meant gifting away the Skogskaale, they would do it! He was bounden by the words of the heavens to do what he could for the maid. If Beatta wanted to make herself of use in the endeavor, she was welcome to come, but he would bide not her arguments. Roric Grim-Kill had sore tempted the ire of the gods by his willful heedlessness, and it was sure to take a great deal of effort to right things now.

Listening, Beatta took heart, and for hours after Vanaash had slipped into sleep, she thought about it. There was nothing in this that could not be remedied. She would sail with Vanaash. A good bribe slipped to one of his men would get her to Roric with a warning before ever Vanaash realized she was gone. If anyone was to taste of the wrath that had permeated this chamber tonight, it would be that foreign magicker woman! There was something unnatural about having the power to blind a man so cruelly to the truth, and making him believe the heavens backed such a one in her efforts seemed nothing but ominous trickery! The woman would soon be leveled, there could be no doubt of it.

Taking a deep breath, Beatta wiped her eyes with the hemmed sleeve of her linen sark. Vanaash had not reacted against the woman in the way she had hoped he would. Even so, the plan had not exactly gone awry. Now that he knew hot-headed Roric had managed to dishonor Iseobel, not once in all this long and feeling-filled night had Vanaash again mentioned wedding himself to that shrewd little charmer! Must be the wench had slipped a far peg in his estimation since her ill-timed little romp on the pallet. Biting back a smile, Beatta felt a surge of satisfaction. Despite the empty feeling in the pit of her stomach inspired by the night's events, she was gloating. When she finally tumbled into slumber it was deep and restful.

Even before he sensed dawn—for that was the most one could do in a world where the lighting never varied—Vanaash roused himself and descended the steep steps hewn into the exterior rock of the hostel. At their foot he met Lord Sivlir on his way up. It was as if the two had risen and rushed to meet on a given signal. For a while, they meandered silently through the narrow, twisting streets, the shadows lit here and there by small pools of hazy phosphorescence.

It was the total absence of vegetation of any kind, Vanaash had decided, that gave the realm its perpetually forbidding look. Even the abundance of precious metals wrought into every feature of the architecture could do nothing to relieve this starkness. At first, it had been disturbing to him. Now, it so perfectly suited his mood that he scarce gave it a thought.

Far in the distance, the pounding throb of the forge hammers, which worked day and night, reminded Vanaash of the bind-ring he had ordered with such high hopes so recently. He fought a rush of misery. Fathoming it, Sivlir turned, his fierce, dark features lit with determination. "Must be you know you need put yourself to the task of reclaiming her," he said sternly. "'Tis far more than just the matter of your heart and pride, Vanaash. If you cast her aside now, you look away while she unwittingly weaves her own doom. Maybe yours, as well."

Vanaash looked troubled. "I am not sure I understand you."

"You want the maid for your own reasons. Love is chief among them, but at the first, 'twas not a consideration. It was the recognition of her otherness that led you to her. Surely you realize that there are others who would seek her for the same."

Vanaash laughed bitterly. "You know little enough of Roric Grim-Kill if you suspect that such would be of matter to him!"

"Your foster-brother is not your worry!" Sivlir's look, already stern, darkened more. "Does it not fright you to know that a link exists between this girl and the Dark Lord, Lodur?"

"She has no association with him, I am certain."

"I do not accuse her! Even so, in some way, a connection exists. Along with that other powerful magicker, Dorflin, Lodur came here, steeped in dealings and arrangements that somehow touch upon her fate! 'Tis a fact that bears no denial!"

His tall frame slumping a little, Vanaash nodded glum agreement. Sivlir went on. "Your own strength provided her a protection which the Grim-Kill cannot hope to offer. Should she fall into Lodur's clutches, there may be no saving her. Others of great power, far more fully developed, have been lost to him in likewise. He spirits them away and envelopes them in a magick so stalwart that no searching spell can find them, ever. Some he keeps, slaves to his own ill-usage; others he but drains, then casts away like empty shells."

"A curse on my foster-brother for so heedlessly leading her into such danger!" Vanaash stormed, a little surprised to find that his hand had come to rest menacingly on his sword hilt. Rage welled in him so fast that it threatened his control.

He berated himself now for turning a blind eye to Roric's womanizing in the past so that it seemed like he condoned it, virtually granting permission for this cruel seduction. Speed was of the essence! If it meant abandoning the rest of the business which had brought him here, then so be it.

Reading these thoughts, Sivlir gave a satisfied grunt and slapped him on the back. "I will see to the forging of your bind-ring and such."

"And I will thank you for it, my lord! The urge for swiftness is upon me like a dread!" They had come a ways out of the darkelf city with their walking, and a droning roar, once vague and distant, had grown to a thunderous crashing. Now, Vanaash could clearly see the source of it, and he stared with wonder at a torrential column of frothing, glowing water, crashing down from an indiscernible point high in the creviced rock ceiling above them. Not far ahead, the road they had been treading ended abruptly, becoming a jagged cliff that overlooked a chasm of inestimable depth, carved by the shimmering waters as they blasted wildly into the solid stone below. For a moment the two friends studied the majestic falls in quietude and awe, then Vanaash vowed aloud that this would be the very spot where he would be made hand-fast to Iseobel.

Though the caverns of the darkelf realm were windless, a steady spray of mist blew at them from out of the turbulence and soon both were wet with the glowing drizzle. As if on signal, they turned, both at the same instant, and began their way back.

"Last night, I offered you my aid in this endeavor," Sivlir said after a while, when they had come far enough from the falls to speak in a normal tone and be heard. "Now I am going to do something out of the ordinary to prove my pledge."

As he spoke, he put a meaningful touch to Vanaash's golden armlet, and Vanaash studied it again. It was scribed all over with

Runic symbols of beautiful workmanship, only some of which Vanaash recognized. "Do you recall what we apprised you of the conditions accompanying magick weapons?" the darkelf asked solemnly. "First, that if you gift or lend one, do so carefully for 'tis a thing coveted and you may never be able to reclaim it. This is something that Lokji learned the hard way and it caused him much grief. What else?"

Vanaash did not need to think long. "That every weapon has many magickal properties, but knowledge of each must be earned by the owner, through prayer, meditation, dream, study or trial."

Sivlir looked pleased. "Last night's unexpected turn of events makes it imperative that I hurry you, Vana Avkomling! So I will tell you one of the properties of your weapon now. You need but touch it to your brow and think me a summons. I will be certain to hear it."

Vanaash looked from the armlet to the darkelf with awe.

"But remember there is an injunction on all my race," Sivlir continued. "We cannot be touched by sunlight lest we turn to stone and crumble. Powerful spells can be invoked to put an armor of protection on us, or cloak us in our fetch-forms so we appear as harts and are immune to the sun. They take long to work, though— half a day by Midgard reckoning. Give me time to perform these enchantments, and I can serve you up to the space of a fortnight 'ere they wear off. Elsewise, I can join you only from sundown to sunup, but can carry as many of my warriors with me as are wont to follow for the space of a night."

They rounded a dusky corner just then and were startled by the sudden appearance of a tall figure, hooded and cloaked in black. Vanaash hesitated, but Sivlir seemed to recognize the featureless form immediately. His leathery face erupted into a crooked grin. "My lord Freyr!" he cried heartily. Stunned, Vanaash dropped to his knees.

'Twas a name carried by only one, he knew—the chief god of the Vanir! He trembled now, not daring to lift his eyes as the newcomer spoke. "Thank you for your summons, bold chieftain!" He addressed the darkelf in a strong but hauntingly melodious tone. Vanaash stiffened.

"I dare not be seen here," the tall one continued, "but the Eye of Heaven is unattended, and I am strictly swathed in this enchanted cloak your brother made for me. I felt that happenstance merited the risk."

Vanaash was shaking so hard now he barely heard Sivlir bid the other well come. He knew that voice! As the import came clear to him, the others laughed at the same moment, and the dark, commanding figure reached a hand to lift him.

"Aye, 'tis I, Vanaash!"

Lord Stranger! Vanaash dared a gaze as the tall one drew back his hood, seeming to emit light along with recognition: the same fair and lordly features, the brilliant sapphire eyes, and flaxen hair held in place by a gleaming silver fillet, the center of which was designed as a finely wrought boar's head, tiny but perfect in every detail. Swallowing hard, Vanaash pulled himself to his full height and looked from Sivlir to Freyr, his brow wrinkled in confusion.

"So you never suspected your mentor was one of the Vanir, Vanaash?" Sivlir pursed his lips and cast them each a glance of satisfaction. "'Twas meant to be so! Now, however, the events of which we just spoke demand that your teacher come forward. This, above all, should convince you of the grave importance of finding Iseobel!"

"I cannot linger, Vanaash," Freyr added quietly, loosing his golden fillet. "This sacred toy can assist you, but none must know how you came by it."

Vanaash took it with trembling hands. "Its power?" he asked.

"You will know as soon as you wear it!"

Vanaash placed it carefully on his head and was immediately washed by a sensation akin to the wave of dizziness suffered on a long-ship during the season's first sea-storm. It fled fast, and once gone, he became aware of a low hum of voices. He reached up to pull it back off.

"Nay!" Sivlir told him sharply. "Those are thoughts you hear! This 'toy' as Lord Freyr calls it will help you read the thoughts of others, and will help to hide your own."

"Remember though. There may be some skilled enough to hide from it," Freyr added. "And mayhap some powerful enough to read through it, too! None knows for sure."

"And a warning: whilst you wear it, it will hamper your own ability to send thoughts to any others—" the darkelf began.

"Save one!" Freyr finished for him with finality. "'Twas first fashioned to be the link between twin-lovers, but mayhap it will further a mental bond with the one chosen for you."

Chosen? Vanaash stiffened. Then, distracted by the drone of far-away thoughts he felt no urge to read, he snatched the thing swiftly from his head and pouched it. Sivlir commended him.

"Best hide it till you need it," he said gravely, "Some may recognize it, or at the least question it."

Pulling up his hood again, and shrouding his face in shadow,

Freyr clapped his hand to Vanaash's shoulder, anxious to be on his way before his presence could be noted. It was a hasty and unfulfilling leave-taking for Vanaash, who was flooded with questions. He and Sivlir strode in silence the rest of the way to the hostel, where they found Beatta waiting, impatient to be gone. There they parted company, still unspeaking, gripping each other's shoulders in the manner of warriors stepping away into the thick of hardened battle.

# Chapter Eleven

From her snug bed of moss under a sheltering chestnut tree, Iseobel wakened to see the moon emerge in the night sky from its pillow of clouds. Slowly, quietly, she extracted herself from Roric's tender embrace, so as not to disturb his sleep. She stretched before turning to look fondly at her companion.

Though rumpled with sleeping, he still cut a dashing figure, sitting upright, back against the wide tree, hand on his drawn sword as if ready to defend her. In the moonlight, he looked bold yet boyish, and Iseobel flushed with tenderness for him.

He was handsome, without question, and gentle with his charming combination of boldness and merriment. Even so, no matter how good-naturedly he jested or ably kept them from harm, he could do nothing to make the Grey Sea vanish ... and they would reach its shore the next day, with no way to cross over.

Rather than worry, Iseobel determined to consult her runes! She knelt to her satchel and, quietly as possible, withdrew the well-worn pouch. Walking to a clearing, she spread her mantle on the ground. Kneeling in its center, she raised her arms to Æsgard, chanting. In short time, four runeforms shivered with light in the air around her. She reached to her cat amulet and, clutching it in both hands, began her supplication to the gods, ending with a special plea to Freyja. In an instant, she was lost in the magick of her own chanting. It began as a pulsing rhythm in her heart; coursed in wild echoes through her head; whispered from out her lips in strange release:

"OTHILA ... KENAZ ... THURIAZ ... RAIDO ... Vana ... Avkomling ... Vana Av ... Komling ... Vana Avkomling...."

The air around her crackled. Her fingers, unbidden, opened the pouch and withdraw a single stone, which immediately began to glow red, banishing the night mists in its halo of light.

Suddenly, a silent whirlwind lifted tendrils of hair back from her face. Spinning faster and faster, the brightness swirled around her, thinning and elongating until it seemed a single, flaming beam poised above the radiant rune. Slowly, Iseobel struggled to raise the gleaming stone to the brightness.

The highly charged atmosphere wakened Roric. Holding his breath, he watched her through an opening in the thicket, hearing but a whisper of her magickal chant. Fascinated by her beauty in the dappled light of the glowing runeforms, he felt an overwhelming awe and drew nearer through the mist, surprised to feel the air spark with the energy of her power. She was swaying in rhythm to her words, and Roric stared transfixed on the gleaming object in her hands—the strange carven stone he found in the Danelaw. How, he wondered, had Iseobel come by it?

A fiery ball leapt in an arc to circle the stone, leaving behind it a wake of thunderous rushing. Two times round ... three.... A mighty charge exploded, the dervish light vanished, and with it the hovering runeforms. Iseobel, trance broken by the sudden blast, looked down to her hands in bewilderment.

Never before had the runes behaved like this! They might settle her mind or put a sign in her way, but now, perched atop the strange runestone, sat a tiny wooden ship, perfect in every detail, right down to the threadlike ladder which hung over its side. Shields no bigger than her fingertip lined its wales, fiercesome boars' heads perched on its stems fore and aft, and the likeness of a golden-bristled boar graced the miniature sail. She was examining both the ship and the runestone more closely, when she sensed Roric's presence.

Roric had hesitated, awed by Iseobel's aura of magick, but his curiosity at length had propelled him forward. He cared not a whit that Iseobel now held the valuable runestone he had once called his own. He needed an explanation for what he had just seen. Despite all that had transpired of late, he was stunned.

"There is a runestone in my pouch I never saw before, Roric, and it conjured this!" Iseobel held up the tiny ship and then showed him the runestone. "Where could it have come from?".

" 'Twas in your own vill that I found it, stashed in a rampart post made hollow," Roric surprised her by saying. "I found a pouch and therein was much fine jewelry and this stone."

Then, considering, he added, "I looked through that bag the day I showed you our horses. The stone was there then...." He squinted in concentration which rapidly faded to comprehension.

"Beatta!" he cried aloud as the pieces fell into place for him. "I saw her skulking by your belongings, and later I noticed that my bag had been moved! I gave it little thought at the time, yet it had to be Beatta who did this trickery. But why?"

"I don't know why! Nor can I imagine why this powerful rune would lie hidden in a hollowed-out post near my home!"

More closely this time, Iseobel studied the miniature ship. It was too fine, too richly appointed and perfectly formed, to be a mere plaything. Roric whistled low as he inspected it.

In his travels, Roric Grim-Kill had heard tell of many legends, and there was something familiar about this fine-carven craft. As he inspected its incredible detailing, he was reminded of a tale he had oft heard told. "Mayhap," he said with awe, watching for her reaction, " 'tis the magick ship, *Skidbladnir!*"

Addled from her exertions, Iseobel eyed him blankly.

"Have you never heard tell of *Skidbladnir?* 'Tis the magick ship built in the darkelf realm for Lokji, and given by him to Freyr in hopes of impressing Freyja and winning her love. They say 'tis small enow to hold in the palm of one's hand, just like this, but is enchanted and can grow to hold the persons meant to sail it." He stopped short, blushing, for he caught her staring at him as if he were mad. "Mayhap we could ride in it to your very home," he added a second later, in a small and timid voice.

"I think you are muddled with sleep, Roric!" she laughed.

He was firm. "If we knew how to grow it, we could sail it."

Iseobel cut him off, worried for him now. "Do you say we could travel across the Grey Sea in such a wee toy as this?"

"Laugh if you like, but think on't, Iseobel," he protested. "Would a toy be so carefully hidden with such strong magick?"

Realizing he was serious, Iseobel scrutinized the tiny ship again, more reverently this time, and considered.

"When first in hiding from you and your raiders, I had a strange dream of ships. One small, one life-sized. After I was captured, I recognized the larger as the *Windrider*. Perhaps this, then, is the smaller ship my dream spoke of to me."

"Then how can you not know this is meant to be?"

Iseobel felt silly for pretending to lend credence to Roric's belief, but she enjoyed his boyish wonder. "So tell me then, Roric. How can we know if this truly is *Skidbladnir?*"

"Well, in the tales, Freyr had but to pass his hand over the prow and tell the ship of his destination. *Skidbladnir* would grow large enow to hold him and whoever was with him—even all the gods in battle gear if that was his desire! On his word, 'twould sail through the air direct to whatever place he named."

"Fine," laughed Iseobel, "so we shall try. Wouldn't it be better for me to place it on the ground, though, so that my hand is not soon crushed by this wee ship?"

It was ludicrous, but even so, it was with a stir of excitement that Iseobel placed the little craft down in the center of the clearing. Concentrating and grasping her amulet, she passed her hand over the ship's bow and intoned two words, picturing her destination in detail and wishing hard.

"To Scarbyrig!" she commanded.


Like the undulating ripple of heat above a fire, the air around the ship wavered and danced, and the ship itself began to grow, boards and planking groaning with such force that Roric and Iseobel stepped back, gazing in wonderment. Suddenly, all sound and motion stopped. *Skidbladnir* had reached its full size.

"Thor's hammer!" Roric gaped at the towering craft. "She is yet finer and grander then our *Windrider!*"

Iseobel, awed, wasted no time in reply, but grabbed her satchel and cloak and clambered round to hoist herself aboard by the rope ladder, which had grown stout along with the ship. As she climbed, she reached out in disbelief to touch the solid planking, running her fingers along the magnificent carvings.

Hastily, Roric gathered his own belongings and swung up after Iseobel. His hands shook so mightily that his grip was unsure, but he relaxed as soon as he landed on board.

The air around the ship was dead still. Sound had ceased: no rustle of leaves, no birdsong. The absolute silence was awesome, quivering with expectation. Then, suddenly, a twinkling wall of dust arose from the shielded wales, growing in height and spreading until it formed a vast rainbow-hued canopy of starry netting about the ship. The eyes in the boar's head glowed, awash with milky color. The golden fittings and brightwork gleamed with ethereal polish. The stately square sail billowed itself full of a dreamlike wind. With an eerie rushing at the hull, the huge craft lifted forward through the air.

Iseobel held one tusk of the boar's head bow with a white-knuckled grip. Hair streaming like a banner in a high wind, she gasped for breath, coursing with excitement. Standing at the fore, as easily as an old sea raider, she threw wide her arms and began to take in the fast-flying landscape.

Roric, amazed, rushed to the railing. Five, six, seven trees passed with each beat of his fast-pounding heart! Throwing his head back, he let go a resounding shout of victory, then made his way fore to partner Iseobel in a reel of childlike joy.

He spun her in a wild embrace, stopping all at once to pull her close in his strong arms. "Seems our excursion mustneeds be backed by the very gods themselves—else why this boon?"

Pressed tight against Roric's chest, Iseobel mused. She had the use of *Skidbladnir* and bold Roric Grim-Kill to keep trouble from her. Surely, Roric must be the man she was fated for, else why would the rune of Freyr's ship have been put in his way? If so, though, why the nagging doubt rising uninvited from her inner mind? Was she not meant to be this happy? Of a sudden the wind seemed to speak a name to her: Vanaash.

She shivered and tried to shake her doubts away. Praying silently, she reached back around Roric's waist and pulled herself to him all the harder, startling Roric with the ferocity of her movement. She loved the Grim-Kill and would be wroth to let him go. Her prayer was that she could stay as thus forever: relaxed against his sheltering warmth while all the world flew by.

In breathless time, *Skidbladnir* approached the Anglish coast. From her vantage point, Iseobel saw her village below, scarred and blackened by the recent invasion. Charred posts and scorched grass described the outlines of former dwellings. Abandoned fields and deserted pathways lent a ghostly air to the remains. Anxiously scanning the cliff for her home, Iseobel was relieved to see its sheltering grove still green and lush.

"Scarce can I believe that to your foster-brother I was worth this destruction," she whispered hoarsely.

"'Tis a vill wholly wasted, to be sure! Look, though, Iseobel!" Roric pointed out a bustle of activity far below. "The folk are well about mending things!"

Iseobel gazed down on a small group of men working busily at thatching a roof. She knew the man who shaded his eyes now and lifted a puzzled gaze, hair astream on a sudden wind. Her childhood friend, Geir! She felt a surge of joy at the realization he was alive and well, and as she enjoyed the sensation she began to recognize others down there, one at a time. With a prayer of thanks for the good folk who had been spared, she rushed to the starboard side, waving frantically to the men below. They seemed oblivious, though, and once the wind of the ship's presence had passed, they went back to their work as if nothing had occurred to disturb them.

Soon, the swooshing of the air died, the glittering of the starry veil dimmed. *Skidbladnir* slowed and began to descend, lightly as a bubble on the sand. Gently bumping on the beach, it settled in position and let itself down with a sigh. Instinctively, Iseobel strode to the prow and, wrapping her hands around the curving keel, pulled with all her might. With a groan, the huge ship lurched. Iseobel and Roric scampered down the rope ladder. Soon as their feet touched ground, *Skidbladnir* began to pleat itself first bow to stern, next mast to keel. In a scant moment, the ship was folded up and tucked safely in Iseobel's draw-string pocket.

Iseobel watched the men of Scarbyrig make their way down the switchbacked paths from the high cliff. Never had Geir's gaunt, handsome face been so welcome to her sight; nor had he ever seen so puzzled, his deep-set eyes so wary. Too, she was fascinated by the way his look relaxed all at once into one of bewildered joy when he recognized her. "By Odin!" he swore low, grasping her shoulders in a brotherly embrace. "My dream was true! Iseobel has returned! But how?"

Thrilled, Iseobel planted a kiss firm on his sun-weathered cheek. "We were working," Geir told her, holding her at arm's length as if to inspect her for bruises. "Of a sudden, 'twas as if the wind whispered to me that you had returned!"

"Aye," chimed in a powerfully built, craggy-faced man with massy black ringlets. "So strong was his intuition that he made us drop forks and tools and hurry here."

"Thank you, Wenthur Crow-Hair," Iseobel smiled, "for not calling him 'wild madman' as you used to do of old."

Wenthur grinned knowingly. "I have not called him that since he earned the known-name of Death-Crooner in battle! I would not risk irking him with a childish insult!"

Iseobel laughed at that, and reached high to hug the dark-haired man warmly. Then she embraced each of the others in turn—Arkill, Edwy, Geir's brother Cynedom, and Still the Simpleton, called more so for his frequent ale-induced stupors than for any lack of smartness. Spirits were so high in the little group that the very air seemed to shine with gladness as they babbled gaily. When the greetings and jests had dwindled a bit, though, Geir spoke again, more seriously.

"How came you here, Iseobel? You have not the look of hard journeying on you. Have you been back a while, yet not told—"

Iseobel cut him off with a wave of her hand. "My tale is an amazement," she told him earnestly, "but it must wait. Of more importance is the state of things here, in our homeplace."

Geir followed her sorrowful glance to the destruction that loomed high above them, then nodded glumly. "It's true, there have been many sorrows these last days. The Norsemen wreaked a havoc, to be sure, and since their coming, more have fled to serve that lord who occupies the manor north of here. Seems they must exchange their freedom for the safety of his staunch walls, for those who go are scarce seen here again, as well you know."

Iseobel shivered, though she could not see from there the sprawling, dark estate that bordered Dorflin's grove. All had heard tell of the wealth and power of the one who lorded the enigmatic shadow-manor, but few knew him. His factors emerged every so often to barter with the village folk—an imperious lot! No one would have dealt with them at all but for the quality and amount of gold that they offered.

Since she could remember, Dorflin had forbidden her to look on the place, wander near it, or even think of it. "Still a mystery!" she murmured, forcing her gaze away.

"Aye! Still it is as it was before!" Geir answered, thinking she was speaking to him. "Few see him save when he gallops his army past or boards his war-ship far down the distant coast. All know his lands are haunted and would scarce go there anyway, so what's the use of such a strong fortress?"

Wenthur Crow-Hair glanced uneasily in the direction being described. "Folk were well-angered that he did not lend his warriors to help quell the invaders," he reported with a shrug. "Could be he hopes to conquer us all for his own uses now that your father is no longer here to keep him in tow."

Disappointed they had no news of Dorflin, Iseobel considered carefully how much she should tell the townsmen, and decided discretion was likely to serve her best. She fielded their questions artfully. "It's best to say only that I am returned," she shared carefully with her childhood friends. "But could be that, like many of you, I have no home left standing."

"Nay, Iseobel," Geir shook his shaggy head, "the fires did not reach as far as your byre before a blessed, drenching rain fell. Your home and hut still stand and your livestock is well taken care of by Arkill and his family, who have stayed there while we rebuild their house. We will gladly help you settle in if need be!"

"Thanks to you all," Iseobel smiled warmly, "but Roric Grim-Kill and I will be able to set the holy hut aright."

At the first mention of her companion's name, the other men appraised the one by her side, bold-looking if unkempt. His was a Norse name, and a warrior's one at that, but Iseobel had pronounced it with a gentleness that bespoke love and affection. In deference to her, they held their questions, though it was hard for Geir, who had long nurtured the dream of courting Iseobel himself. In a while, seeing she was weary, the townsmen took their leave. Hand in hand, Roric and Iseobel started for the hut, he with both satchels slung over his strong shoulder.

A short walk brought them up the steep cliff to the trail, quite hidden now with lush new growth. Having known the way since babyhood, Iseobel spotted the path quickly and picked her way easily through the thick foliage. At last she saw it, sheltered under its protective fir boughs: the goddess hut.

Iseobel unlatched the door. It felt like she had been gone a lifetime! A thin layer of dust covered the table and chairs, and a musty smell hovered. The grate was cold with old ashes, and one or two clumps of mud still lingered on the rush-strewn floor. No one had been home to do the springtime cleaning and freshening, but the tiny hut was nothing less than inviting to her. She set to tidying, and sent Roric for kindling and water.

Later, after they had baked some bread and eaten a much-needed meal of dried fruit, nuts, and grain from the store-boxes, they relaxed lazily by the fire. Tickling the back of Roric's neck while he lay on the floor at her feet, Iseobel broke a long and easy silence. "I have been meaning to thank you for helping me, Roric," she told him seriously. "Truly, I am grateful!"

Surprised that she did not know he would brave the agonies of Hel's own domain for her, Roric sat up in disbelief. "Iseobel, the last few days are but a feeble sample of what I would endure for you!" he heard himself blurt to his own dismay. "Find me enemies to slay or what have you! I would brave Thor, Tyr, or even Lokji himself, to keep you safe. If any deed will keep you near me, you have but to bid me do it."

Sure he sounded foolish, he bit his tongue. What was it about this woman that had made him wax poetic like a harping skald in a hall full of drunken warriors? He felt himself redden. Confused, he searched for a phrase that would turn this moment to one of jesting, but his reason challenged him. He had meant every word; why should he not have voiced it?

Reversing himself once again, he reached for her hand, cradled it between his own and looked lovingly into the mercury depths of her eyes. "Will you hear that I adore you, Iseobel? Could you love one like me? For truly, I would cherish you!"

Iseobel, trembling, pretended to be busy with something entirely insignificant. Though flooded with warmth at his frank profession of love and his proposal, she hesitated.

"Roric, even were my powers greater, I could conjure no better man and I would gladly wed you. But as shamaness, I have responsibilities. The choice cannot be entirely my own."

Roric's wide hazel eyes visibly dimmed with disappointment. Iseobel found it took her a few moments to continue, and when she did, she picked her words carefully.

"I have promised my father that I would be married to no man unless somehow confirmed in the choosing."

Roric rose, trembling. "Can't be you would trust your future and mine to the Norns?" he cried miserably.

Iseobel flinched, feeling his distress, but warded off his protests, "You know that my way is with the gods. How can I do otherwise than to secure their assurance in this?"

Roric was forced to consent, though he knew not by what means such a nod of approval could be accomplished. He pulled her down to the floor and wrapped his arms around her, luxuriating in the satiny tangle of her hair, and swelling with affection as she nestled tight against him. Nearly overwhelmed, he clutched at the moment of closeness, seizing it like an invisible talisman of luck against some future verdict.

Whether they lingered thus for minutes or hours, neither knew. But a tickling movement at her ankle caused Iseobel to look down, and the spell was gone. "Machthild!" she cried in delight. Nuzzling the purring animal, Iseobel now felt her homecoming complete. Except for Dorflin.

Waking early on separate cots, the two rose and set to the spring cleaning, Iseobel somewhat more eagerly than Roric. He was amazed there was so much to dust, shake, and polish in the tiny house. Dishes, jars and pottery, furs and coverlets, clothing, burlap, leather leggings, and a large chest of fancy silks, sturdy woolens, and linens of every order. It seemed to Roric that he had been laboring for hours, but he was resolved not to complain or seem like an unworthy husbander to Iseobel.

"It seems strange to me," he said after awhile, as he and Iseobel worked together to shake the bedclothes, "that you and your father would have two dwellings less than a furlong apart."

"Though it's fully stocked, we have never used this hut but for retreat and meditation," Iseobel answered. "Because of the story connected with the place we have always set it apart."

Roric had never had lost his childlike love for stories and now, hoping for at least a short respite from these lowly labors, he begged her eagerly to share the tale.

Sensing his motive, Iseobel laughed. "A story it is then! And, having trained as a Druid, I am well aware a story must be enjoyed while relaxing!"

She handed him a skin of honey-mead. "Hold, Iseobel," he asked as he filled two mugs, "what is a 'Druid'?"

"They are the Wise Ones from Eire and the Cymry, whence comes my father. They serve the White Goddess, she who is nameless or has too many names to know. Druids speak to the spirits of the trees and the waters, understand the mysteries of death and re-birth, and hold the sacred songs. My father is an ovate, healer and magicker. I was reared in this ancient gentle wisdom as well as in the Vana ways."

In mid-sip, strong worry crept over Roric. No wonder she was such a powerful magicker! Mayhap his prospects of claiming her were hopeless. In an effort to banish his darkening mood, he took a long sip and bade her tell him the story of the cottage.

"Once," she began, "there was a young Cymrian priest who roved about, earning his keep with remedies and potions. In time he learned about the gods of Æsgard and became devoted to Freyja. He prayed nightly to Freyja that she would send him a woman to love— one with Freyja's strength, beauty and goodness. In return, he promised to settle down and become shaman to one, single vill, saying he would dedicate himself and the folk in his care to the cause of the

Vanir.

"Near here, he at last encountered the woman of his prayers. Though he glimpsed her rarely and seldom had the chance to speak with her, he fell in love. Wanting to be near her, he took this small abandoned hut for his own. He lived only to please her. The notion of day upon day of living wrapped in her love overwhelmed him. He could think of nothing else."

Roric sighed, understanding this entirely; Iseobel went on.

"'But my love,' the woman had finally confessed, 'I am the goddess Freyja, beloved of my twin Freyr. I want not for protection and care. However, through your sweet petitions, I have come to love you, and will stay with you for a time.'"

"Certain it could not be Freyja, though," Roric interrupted with a troubled frown, "for 'tis said she craves bold warriors, and so might scarce take interest in a priest or scholar."

*"It was she, Roric!"*

"How could he know of certain, though?"

"Because they made their way to this very hut, and when she cast off her dark mantle, revealing her kirtle spun of gold and cloth-of-attar, he could see the glow of her immortality through its sheer folds."

"Oh, aye!" said Roric dreamily, picturing it himself. "That would be a sign for sure!"

Iseobel smiled. "For that night and many after, she slept here with him. Then, she rose of a sudden from his warm embrace. Before she parted, she left him a ribbon from her kirtle, as a token that she would keep good to her word to return to him. They burnt together dried mullein and ivy and dawn-glory to bolster their concentration and meditated together in the smoke to bind their troth. Then she gave him some precious magickal toys, bidding him keep them hidden for ten score of waning moons."

"And he did?"

"Aye!"

"And she returned here?"

"Indeed! Good to her word, she returned each summer."

"Comes she still?" Roric leaned forward with interest. Iseobel shook her head, "Nay! Methinks this must have been long ago, Roric. I suppose she came until the man died or she had need of the toys once again. In any case," Iseobel refilled their tankards, "now you know the story of the goddess hut."

"'Tis no wonder, then, that Holies would keep this place to their use!" Roric mused, oddly moved by the tale of the brief, intense love affair.

"My father says Freyja still has a special care for this hut. That is why he took it for his own use. He says she can look here when she wants and read the hearts of those within!"

At this, Roric quieted. Privately, it unnerved him to think the goddess kept watch there. Late that night, after much tossing, he picked up his coverlets and headed out into the chill air. Wakened, Iseobel asked uneasily why he was leaving.

"'Tis only you I am protecting," he joked as he departed. "What if Freyja chose this very night to return to her hut? She would be strengthless to resist my comely look and charm. Then I would have to swear myself to her, rather than to you."

But the truth was, Roric did not think he could spend another night alone with Iseobel without claiming her, and this was a weakness he wanted no one to suspect. Not even Freyja.

# Chapter Twelve

At dawn, though both quite exhausted from their flight and the exhilaration of riding in Freyr's magickal ship, neither Roric nor Iseobel stayed asleep one moment longer than necessary. With the tension of the day's importance full upon them, they found that they dared not stand idle for fear of the somber thoughts which might creep up on them unawares.

Iseobel plucked errands both necessary and trivial from her mind to busy them both through the hours of daylight. They visited the village and found Geir Death-Crooner and Wenthur Crow-Foot, who warned the couple that they were the force behind every wagging tongue that morning. Not that the townsfolk were unkind, but they were full of curiosity. Surely Roric and Iseobel would have no peace.

Iseobel's friends had told the truth of it. Everywhere she and Roric appeared, folk stopped them for an interview. Most had heard rumor of her misadventures, but knew little detail. Indeed, too, what they had surmised of her abduction was placed in general doubt now by her apparent friendship with the comely and good-natured Norseman who kept her company.

Roric, for his part, spared no effort in winning the hearts of the villagers. 'Twas an ill-fortuned mistake, he told them, that the *Windrider* had wreaked havoc here—something not meant to happen and now of great regret. To prove his sincerity, he insisted upon doing what he could to make amends. To the miller and the cooper, whose large buildings were now rubble, he gave his prized ruby armlet, the sale of which in London or Eorforwic would finance the rebuilding twice over. To each of the six women made widows went one of his costly rings. And when his personal treasures were exhausted, all else were gifted with promises of recompense when the *Windrider* came again.

Iseobel and Roric threw themselves whole-heartedly into the vill's efforts. They drove posts, wove wattle, hauled stone, mixed daub, and carried timber. As she worked, Iseobel answered the questions heaped on her as patiently as she could. She made sure to ask after everyone's health and reassure them that indeed she meant to stay on as their shamaness if they so wished it. And so the long day passed.

Laden with the staples the townsfolk had pressed them to take, Roric followed Iseobel up the rise to the goddess hut. He had been pleased to learn how well regarded Iseobel was by all who knew her. He found it remarkable, too, how easily welcomed he had been. It never occurred to him his own merriness, care for Iseobel, and willingness to make amends had won them. As far as he could tell, simply being in Iseobel's presence was enough to grant him acceptance. These Anglish were so warm and open. No wonder their coast was such an easy target for sea raiders!

After eating, Roric, whom Iseobel had set to chopping wood while she fashioned a waxed-wool awning to shelter the goats she had by then retrieved, chafed that he had to keep his eye keen on his work. Much rather had he found a chore which would give him leave to watch Iseobel as she moved ably at her task with her kirtle hem tucked up about her waist to free her legs.

Grown warm with his efforts, Roric put down his hatchet and removed his tunic. He strode to the cottage to pour out a cooling drink of beer and fetched a mug for Iseobel, as well. Rounding the corner on his way back, he stopped to admire the view Iseobel presented. She stood tiptoe on a stool and stretched up to fasten a corner of the stiff cloth to the cottage eaves. With her bare legs at his eye level, Roric had to marshal every ounce of control not to reach out and run his finger down the dimple in the back of her knee.

Swigging fully half the contents of his tankard to calm himself, he reached the other mug up to her. Startled by his sudden appearance, she yelped as she dropped her hold on the cloth. Accepting the beer from him, she marveled at his handsome face glistening in the sunlight. The combination of his fine features and sweat-sheened muscles sent that same unfamiliar thrill through her that she had felt on board *Windrider* when Vanaash had cuddled her in his wolf-fur mantle, seemingly so long ago. Impatiently brushing the association away, she let Roric help her down from her perch.

Combing dampened strands of hair away from her blushing cheek, Iseobel raised the beer to her lips. "Thank you, Roric," she breathed, after coming up for air from a long pull, "I had not noticed how warm and thirsty I'd grown."

Roric had noted the strange way she'd looked at him, but resolved not to remark on it. Could be she felt the same trepidation about tonight as he did. Wishing he could give time's creeping pace a firm tug that they might be past this evening's judgment and the sacred spells favorable, he tossed off the rest of his beer and helped Iseobel tie the awning.

Near sunset, Iseobel excused herself. Gathering towels, and attar, and a white gauze shift, she set down the winding path to the stream, explaining to Roric that she needed to bathe and ready herself for the evening's ceremony. In truth, though, she also needed time undistracted to meditate; she had never performed a seith ritual of proving before. Once immersed in the fresh and vibrant waters undisturbed, she relaxed and prayed. Her mind, like a hawk swooping towards a fish, dove to remember every nuance of chant and staving. She could not make a mistake tonight—there was too much at stake!

Roric, having cleaned and decked himself finely in a carefully chosen sark and deerskin leggings, was napping when she returned. She did not waken him right away, but sat anext him on the pallet and combed out her damp hair, still thinking. She felt more confidence now, she realized, caressing both the little vial of lavender and her amulet fondly, knowing her amber cats would lend her strength.

Noting by the rising moon that it was time to start for the grove, Iseobel went to the secret panel behind the harrow and, pulling it back, withdrew her birken-cape. Unlike her sturdy dark woolen one, this cloak was finewove of linen, white as birch, and fashioned like Freyja's own. From hood to hem, it boasted gems, crystals, and feathers sewn to it in nettings of delicate twist. Along the cavernous sleeves and copious yoke, dangled strand after strand of freshwater pearls, mounted to swing in clacking rhythm to her movements. The entire border of bleached moreen was embroidered with cats and tied with hammered silver disks hung so to reflect light whenever she moved.

Undressing down to her thin shift, she sang a soft prayer, kissed the birken-cape and donned it, mind focused on the solemnity of the occasion. So steadily had Dorflin schooled her in the Vanir ways, that they seemed like second nature to her. She took comfort, too, in knowing that Freyja watched nearby. The gentle wisdom of the Vanir gave a center to her power and heart. Their purposes need not be hers to understand; simply hers to hold sacred. And so she would honor the ritual she knew they expected of her, despite her inclination to give herself fully to the Grim-Kill, with or without their consent.

"Roric," she bent softly to kiss him. "I am ready. 'Tis time that we were away."

"Aye!" Roric returned, instantly shaking off his drowse and opening his eyes. He swung his legs off the pallet and was in mid rise when he caught sight of Iseobel, glorious in her cloak. His eyes opened wide, his knees gave, and he rocked backwards sitting hard on the bed.

"By Freyja, Iseobel!" his hazel eyes blinked hard, "from ever I first saw you, would I have said that you were the fairest mortal woman I had seen. Now I think you may prove comelier than any goddess of Æsgard."

Shushing him for blasphemy, Iseobel urged him to abandon his foolish flattery and ready himself that they might lose no more time. Roric quickly bound his long curling locks in a leather thong and then, of habit, re-knotted his napped neededs pouch around his neck and tucked it inside his jerkin. Soon they were out in the freshness of the night air, walking in the early moonlight to the sacred grove. Breezes whispered through the leafy canopy, and the scent of loam mixed agreeably with the salt sea air. Though to Roric the tangle of new growth underfoot evidenced no footpath, Iseobel stepped easily, apparently sure of her way. By the time all of the stars in the great sky bear shone bright, Iseobel and Roric were at the foot of the ancient oak in the center of the grove.

Iseobel raised her hood and gestured Roric to sit a slight way apart from her. Tense, anxious, he did as she bade him, leaning uneasily against a massive, carven stone, wondering what oddities might lay within the many grotesque shadows that formed in the moonlight. Of habit, now, he kept his eyes on Iseobel, finding that her beauty and grace banished all unwelcome thoughts. She was an unending pleasure for him to contemplate and enjoy. With growing fascination he watched as she sat herself on a stone platform and began her spell.

Iseobel raised her arms and stretched out her fingers, moving gracefully so that the pearl strands on her sleeves swayed rhythmically. The silver disks that hung from her hem, reflecting the moonlight, seemed to dance.

She began to hum; when she bowed her head, the hood hid her face completely, but the humming grew ever louder. Her lilting melody gave way to chanting.

Then, Iseobel turned her cupped palms to the sky. Glinting slivers of light hovered above her hands, dancing like dust in the moonlight. Faster and faster the sparkles appeared. Milky white opals of flashing, the shapes coalesced, merged and settled, melted and formed.

When she raised her arms in silent speech, her gauzy shift floated about her, seeming to Roric like whispering cobwebs. The pale skin of her neck and arms shone pearl-like in the moonlight, and he could not help but imagine the silken feel of them beneath the touch of his lips.

Lowering his gaze to the outline of her long legs, he was flooded with desire. If he could but slide his hands along her skin, kiss the softness of her, and, finally, lose himself in the comfort of being engulfed by her, all the debauched entertainments he had ever enjoyed would seem as nothing.

Iseobel was too wrapped in the moment to give heed to his wandering thoughts. The moonlit night lurched before her and the very ground seemed to tilt. Visions filled her sight; voices her hearing. Out of the chaos, a single tone reverberated, gradually taking on the characteristics of a thrilling feminine voice. It was soon entwined with another, a hauntingly clear tenor—two voices, then, in unison chanting meaningless sounds and melody which swiftly coalesced into words: *Roric is not the man for you.* The shapeless stream of a feathery whirlwind encircled her head and deafened her with the chant. *Not the one! Not the one! Not the one!* Frenzied, Iseobel clutched at her ears, trying to drown out the sound, but the riot continued to echo within until, exhausted, she fought her way out of the trance.

Far above the grove, a light manifested, and drew closer. Roric jumped to his feet, ready to face it and, if need be, to defend Iseobel. The sparkling light grew brighter, the pulsating more intense, the particles of brilliance swirling and building until they formed a golden boar-drawn chariot. Two forms took shape within the blazing vision: a man and woman clothed in a fiery aura, glowing with translucence against the blinding illumination that surrounded them. Their voices were clear and sounded as one: *She is not for you, Midgarder, but for your defense of her, we gift you with a portion of our wisdom and poetry.* So saying, the blinding apparitions pulled their aureate brightness in around them like cloaks of glory. Then, they were no more, but as they vanished, a shower of multi-colored light drops fell from the spot where, seconds ago, they had lingered, spraying Roric with a visible and highly charged wash of glowing dampness.

His legs buckled and, stupefied, Roric fell to his knees, trembling, dazed, and somehow saddened. By degrees, he eventually grew aware of Iseobel anext him, clasping his trembling form to hers. He buried his head against her waist, groaning as in pain, in an attempt to succor his dissolving soul. Iseobel, too, had heard the dire pronouncement, yet felt compelled to hear him acquiesce to it, despite the agony it caused them both. She gulped his name.

Roric could not look at her. His mind roiled in unbelief that he must speak that which would put her from him forever. "My Iseobel, my own…." his voice, most-times so strong, trailed off in childlike misery. She twined her fingers in his massy hair, and lifted his head. He was stunningly handsome, she thought, despite his pallor and his tears.

He gazed at her questioningly. Had she seen them, too—the twins of the Vanir, Freyr and Freyja—or had it been some trickery of her seith trance? If the last, he thought hopefully, mayhap their message meant naught or was just an evil dream. Reading him, though, Iseobel shook her head gently, sadly.

"'Tis not my due to have you?" He asked it like a question, but he knew the answer even before she dropped to her own knees and reached her arms around him, cradling him like a babe. He clutched her hard to him, trembling. Kneeling thusly, face to face, they rocked together in the moonlight. Even in the depths of her grief, it was an exquisite moment to Iseobel. She mourned the stillborn passion they would never share, but she had tasted of it well enough to remember it a lifetime.


Roric had wakened to the first light of lilac dawn. Seeing Iseobel, fair and sensuously sweet in sleep, he had been reluctant to wake her. He wrapped her up in his cloak and lifted her gently out of the dew-kissed lawn, crushing her tight to his heart as he strode to the hut. Savoring her closeness now, he breathed in the perfume of her tousled hair and delighted in the softness of her cheek against him. He scarcely could believe they had passed the entire night together in the grove, locked in an embrace which would have trembled any man to madness, and yet had not partaken of each other in the way that had been forbidden.

More astounding, he thought with total bewilderment, was the fact that it had mattered not. He had been overcome with feelings, strong and vivid as visions, and with the urge to express them. The poetry which had escaped him in such graceful, easy phrases had given them both as much pleasure as a full night of lovemaking would have done.

As they approached the hut, Iseobel wakened, smiling tenderly. He set her down, and they walked the rest of the way, hand-in-hand, in gentle converse.

Opening the door, they were momentarily blinded by the dimness within. Then a shadow of movement in the corner caused Iseobel to stiffen. Sensing her distress, Roric drew his sword and pushed past her into the cottage. "Show yourself swiftly!" he cried in a menacing tone. "By what right do you trespass?"

The figure did not cower, but stepped boldly forward. It was a tall man in a grey cloak. He lifted his hand to push back his hood, but even before his face was revealed, Iseobel recognized him and ran to embrace him. "Dorflin!"

Roric's eyes widened in alarm. *Dorflin?* Could this be the same man Vanaash had sworn against? The snake who had stolen the mysterious treasure in Swartalfheim? If so, he was loath to consider what dealings Iseobel could have had with him.

Before Roric could ponder, Iseobel turned, relief visible on her face. The man fixed a look of expectant wonder on Roric. "Father, here is Roric Grim-Kill, who has been best of all friends and protectors to me in these many days of distress."

Her father? *Oh Frigga!* Roric cringed inwardly. How much more complicated could the Norns possibly make his life? Iseobel certainly appeared comfortable enough introducing them. Then again, there was much that she, mayhap, did not anticipate in a father's reaction. He himself had more often than not been less than cordially greeted by maidens' fathers. Yet now, when there was no question of the maid's honor or his own; when he had acted always with the utmost propriety, now was when he, the Grim-Kill, felt like a mouse trapped under the cat's paw.

If there were any way to have avoided meeting this particular father, Roric would have grasped at it. But here in Scarbyrig? There was nowhere for him to escape to. He sheathed his sword and, with incredible trepidation, found himself reaching a hand to the man with the wolf-grey beard and commanding gaze. The grip was strong; the imperious look unwavering. And as soon as their hands touched, Roric felt an affinity which both mystified and reassured him.

Dorflin gave a quiet laugh. "It is a deep comfort to me that you have seen to my daughter's safety, and for that, thanks to you, Roric Grim-Kill."

Dorflin smiled sagely, and then in answer to Roric's obvious bewilderment, added, "Aye, there has been much confounding in the last moon times. Well that we have a chance now to sort things out and form ourselves a plan."

The shaman removed his cloak and hung it over the back of a chair before sitting at the table. "But I would recommend that first we break our fast."

Agreeing wholeheartedly with Dorflin's practical suggestion, Roric and Iseobel eagerly busied themselves with finding the makings of a meal. As they went about setting the trestle with cold pottage and dried barley cakes, Iseobel animatedly recounted for Dorflin her adventures of the last weeks. Now and then, she would stop mid-sentence, beam at her father anew, and rush over to give him a hug.

Dorflin's reaction to her account was largely impassive, though he could scarce hide amazement at the scope of the adventures which had taken her to sea and to the shores of the distant Nor Way. That she had risen from captivity to favor by her own wiles and talents did not surprise him, for he knew she was both special and blessed. When he learned her wanderings had brought her to the darkest depths of Swartalfheim, though, a realm few mortals ever found it in their fate to visit or cared to, he felt a surge of dread. 'Twas a place he scarce would have condoned her going under any circumstances, and it occurred to him now that the days he had long dreaded were finally upon him: he could no longer dictate her safety.

She had been irrevocably drawn now into the events for which the gods had fashioned her, and henceforth he could but hope that the training he had labored to provide her would be adequate for all she was slated to face. As he struggled to suppress his sudden sadness, he fastened a fond gaze on his daughter, admiring her new-found womanly grace and strength.

Roric, for the most part, listened silently, occupying himself with small chores. Convinced there was naught the girl told her father that the man did not somehow know already, he felt a flush of discomfiture. It occurred to him that Iseobel was an admirable creature, indeed. The trials she now related with such detached stoicism would have doubtless been unbearable to a lesser woman, or man, for that matter. Though his own part had seemed dishonorable, in the beginning at least, he could content himself with the thought that since her abduction he had shown her every respect. Even so, he worried that the lustful feelings he had worked so hard to suppress might have eked their way into her father's awareness.

"Could not have been easy for you, my son." Dorflin turned toward him, arching a brow. Roric, unused as ever to someone keening his thoughts, gulped. Yet when he turned to face the man, he read not a particle of censure in the look. Feeling a surge of relief, he fell to eating hungrily, only half listening to the conversation of the other two, until Iseobel posed a question that perked his curiosity.

"Father," she asked as if suddenly reminded of it, "why do folk say that you are in league with this Lord Lodur of such ill-repute, one who some say is Lokji himself, the god of treachery, dressed in humanform?"

"Who says this of me, that I could be sworn to such a one as that?" Dorflin asked in wonderment.

"The darkelves in Swartalfheim professed to your alliance!" Iseobel shrugged apologetically before sitting on the bench anext her father. "Tales of your appearing together there on some errand of thievery are now told in that realm, and it seems many have sworn against you for whatever part you played in the deception that was made."

Dorflin scowled. "The lack-wits take coincidence for conspiracy! Of necessity you know little of my recent movements and reasons. Now the involvement is upon you both."

Brows furrowed sternly, he turned to make sure that Roric was listening, though his sudden change of tone ensured it. "You will need to know as much as I can tell in order to plan wisely and ensure your own safety."

Setting down his bowl, Dorflin helped himself to a barley cake. "Your eighteenth birthday was nearing, and I was committed to seeing to the forging of your bind-ring. When, at Beltane Eve, I descended to Swartalfheim to procure it, seems that Lodur's infantry of spies warned him of my going, and he followed me."

"Hold, father. Why would Lodur spy on *you*?"

Dorflin drew a deep breath. "I guess it is best to tell you all the tale at once, for the time has come that these secrets should be hidden from you no longer." He pursed his lips, then went on. "Men who see Lodur as Lokji see truth."

Dorflin ignored Iseobel's and Roric's predictable looks of astonishment, and poured himself a mug of water. "Through the trickery of angry gods, Odin All-Father has been made to believe that Lokji has possession of some things exceeding precious that were stolen from him. He has barred his makebate son from Æsgard until the items are returned. Elsewhere than Æsgard, Lokji calls himself Lodur and pretends to be other than the god of trouble, the better to embroil himself in the affairs of mortals and reap more power and riches for himself. He thinks himself superior to all other gods, even Odin All-Father, and would rather be supreme amongst mortals here in Midgard than be forced to do homage and bend to his father's will in Æsgard. He is sly, crafty, and powerful!"

Suddenly agitated, Iseobel clenched her fists. "Still, father, I do not see how he comes to have a quarrel with you or why he would choose to spy upon your doings!"

"He strives against any here in Midgard who are devoted to those gods he has sworn against; any who have found special favor with them. For me, he bears a greater enmity on several accounts, not the least of which is the fact that he suspects I hold the key to his eventual return to Æsgard. He keeps his agents watching me, therefore. And I, because I would know his movements as well, in turn keep my spies near him."

"Your spies?" Iseobel stammered. "Scarce ever have I seen you close with any! Couldn't be Geir Death-Crooner or Wenthur—"

"Nay, daughter!" Dorflin laughed heartily. "Ease your mind on that account, and look closer to home!"

"There is none but the two of us here, father!" she exclaimed, pouting as she considered. "Aye, Sire Yulk, comes of a time to aid you at harvest and busy times, and Mistress Ridi sometimes helps us with nutting and brewing."

"Yulk and Ridi?" Roric broke in quizzically. "Those are elven names, are they not?"

"Aye! They are long-standing friends of my father's and mine, lightelves who live deep in our grove. Father gave them a plot there, and a wee cottage."

"Lightelves ..." Roric repeated. He hoped he was not as wide-eyed with wonder as he felt himself to be. After all that had occurred in the last days, he was not sure why the fact that Iseobel counted lightelves amongst her acquaintances should surprise him, but it did.

"Must be you know lightelves hide themselves well," Iseobel added, as if Roric himself commerced with such creatures on an everyday basis. "We scarce ever see them!"

"But think when it is that you *have* seen them, daughter!" Dorflin smiled, eyes twinkling.

"Oh, it's true you ever set them after me when I disobeyed you, father!" Iseobel reddened, staring at her own feet.

Dorflin broke into hearty laughter and leaned closer to Roric as if to impart a confidence. "Since babyhood she has had but one injunction, and that to stay far away from the ditch that divides our grove from the dark manor yonder, and never to look upon or think about that place!"

"Surely you can forgive that I was curious, father!" Iseobel shuffled a little nervously and smiled wanly at Roric, as if petitioning his support.

"And who was it managed to waylay you each time you waxed curious, daughter?"

"Every time I came close to the edge of the grove, I met with Sire Yulk, and he fetched me home to you...." her voice trailed off.

"And if you recall, every time a certain visitor made his way here, Sire Yulk and Mistress Ridi arrived beforehand, and helped me hide you."

"Yes! They hid me every time that dark-haired magicker came!" She stopped, suddenly agitated, and walked a little ways away. "Was that their charge, father? To hide me from that man?"

"It was, indeed, Iseobel!" Coming swiftly to his feet, Dorflin strode to his daughter's side and put his hands on her shoulders as if to steady her. "Chief of all their duties was to closet you when I agreed to let him come here, or stop you if wandered too near his domain."

"Too near his—?" Iseobel stiffened with sudden realization and a look of dread crossed her face so intense that Roric, too, flew to her side. "Do you mean to say that the dark-haired magicker is the very lord who lives anext us? Father!"

Dorflin tweaked her hair as if to offer comfort. "All those of us concerned with your welfare thought it best you never know the man's name, lest you think of it unbidden and call his attention. Now, too, you can understand my sternness at your disobedience when you traipsed near that cursed place!"

Iseobel, now drained of color and trembling, spoke in a strangled tone. "That magicker accosted us, father, on the road to Swartalfheim! He spoke to me and tried to persuade me—"

Shaken, Dorflin glanced worriedly to Roric. "This is true?" he asked, and when Roric confirmed it, Dorflin let go a sharp exclamation of anger.

Roric did not hear it, though. His hand had gone to his sword unbidden at the sound of Iseobel's words and now he trembled, suddenly chilled. "Someone told us that the chieftain in the woods was Lodur," he declared levelly, searching Dorflin's eyes with his own. "Best you would tell me the truth of all this!"

Dorflin did not flinch. "You were told aright!" he murmured low. "'Tis an amazement to me that you were strong enough to withstand his cajolings, my Iseobel. He has a magick way of clouding memories and intuitions when it so suits him!"

Iseobel spun away, only half stifling a cry of distress. The other two watched wordlessly as she paced a while, deep in tumultuous thoughts. Ever she had known her father was a powerful magicker but now, thinking back on times she had seen him deep in converse with the ominous dark-haired one, the two addressing each other with grudging honor and speaking almost as equals, she realized for the first time how singular Dorflin must be among men. No mere mortal, he trafficked with the very gods, shared confidences with them, and was party to their doings. Thinking on this, she was assailed with the suspicion that perhaps her own destiny might be far, far more than she hitherto had imagined. Might even be all that had befallen her of late was no accident, but part of some well laid plan.

Dorflin coughed, interrupting her thoughts, and Iseobel turned to face him. "Let me continue my tale," he said, his gentle smile a recognition of her inner turmoil. "Where was I?"

"My bind-ring." Iseobel swallowed hard.

"Ah, yes." Dorflin gently took his daughter's hand and fondly traced the length of her fingers with the tips of his own. "I needed to have your bind-ring forged, so I conjured a bifrost bridge to Swartalfheim, intending to speak to the chief of that realm, Lord Sivlir. Instead, I was led to make my petition of his chief man, a gruff fellow named Hvaam. When I made my request and produced a token that identified your rights to a bind-ring, Hvaam cast runes to substantiate my claim. It was of course, legitimate, and he immediately ordered the sacred ring forged. But, apparently, the token I presented and the phrases I used inadvertently were the key to something more. Without hesitation, Lord Sivlir surrendered to me Boat-Beckoner, the long-lost runestone that controls *Skidbladnir*, as if it had been prearranged that I should claim it. I expected it not, certainly, but I recognized it at once and accepted it as if it were indeed my due. Must be Lodur had been made aware of my descent. Before your ring was forged, he appeared in Swartalfheim and attached himself to my company."

"He learned naught from us!" exclaimed Roric staunchly, moving boldly to Iseobel's side. "For all his trying!"

"I am sure of that, Roric Grim-Kill!" Dorflin assured him. Pausing thoughtfully, he sipped from his mug. "Truly I think not that he knew my reasons for being among the darkelves, but my presence there was strange enough to alert him. He has lived anext us many years in expectation of this time, with his heart set on claiming your bind-ring. Because he had arrived in time to ask questions, he knew that I had ordered its forging, therefore I considered it already lost to him. Lodur craved it not for its intrinsic value, you understand, but as a bargaining device. Lodur is Lokji, a skilled trickster, and uses every advantage he can, fairly gained or not."

"What of the red runestone, though?" Roric asked hesitantly. He was most interested in the magickal rune, for he felt that it was his personal link to this adventure, though his part in the whole affair—stealing it and hiding it as he had—was one he was not proud of.

"Oh, aye! The runestone!" Dorflin's eyes flickered. "Needless to say, I did not want him to know that I had the long-lost and price-less Boat-Beckoner as well. So when he accompanied me to fetch the ring from the forge, I displayed the band easily on my own finger, nearly flaunting it. I assumed that when he waylaid me, as I was certain he would, he would simply rob me of the ring and search my person no further."

Iseobel blinked. "And this ploy worked?" She was imagining the tremendous stoicism it must have taken her father to hide his thoughts from an enemy so strong.

"It worked!" Dorflin's sea-blue eyes turned stormy. "Nevertheless, I sped home, but instead of magickally hiding the stone in the grove, I stashed it, safely swaddled in my pouch of common jewelry, in a hollowed postern near the shore. For had Lodur or his spies sensed magick emanations, he would have suspected that I held yet more treasure."

Roric reddened and nervously ran his fingers through his tangled curls, remembering how he had come across the pouch while the crew of the *Windrider* laid waste to Scarbyrig. How long ago that seemed! How ignorant he had been! With no clue as to the rune's worth, by his wrongful actions he had meddled in important sacred affairs.

Then it began to occur to him that not only Dorflin, but even the gods might rightfully be ired with him! Squirming a little, Roric tried hard to hide the memories of his actions, but a swift glance at Dorflin told him it was too late: the shaman had read the entire episode as Roric remembered it. Crossing his arms on the table, the Grim-Kill put his head down as if to hide. Never had he felt as helpless!

"Never mind what you were led to do of old, Roric!" Iseobel said sharply, and he winced, knowing that she, too, had read him. "It worked out well in the end, for if you had not taken that runestone, had Beatta not in turn stolen it from you and put it amongst my things, we would never have gotten ourselves here! Sometimes, actions that were not imagined in the planning can prove to be for the good."

"Though it helps if we keep our actions honorable!" Dorflin added, eyes twinkling. Roric shifted uncomfortably, and Dorflin laughed aloud, sorry for the good-hearted warrior's discomfort but amused at his misery nonetheless.

Iseobel planted a kiss on the back of Roric's head, then turned to her father again. "Why does Lodur crave the rune? Is that what guarantees his admittance to Æsgard?"

"Nay, daughter." Dorflin shook his head, realizing how confusing his tale had become. "You yourself have invoked the stone, so you know it conjures Freyr's own ship, the very ship Odin chastised him for losing so carelessly. You also know that whoever commands the ship can guide it by merely voicing the desired destination. It can find anything in the Nine Worlds. That is why Lodur seeks it so desperately. In addition to the glory that would be awarded him for the finding of the magickal ship, he believes that *Skidbladnir* can take him directly to the objects he needs to re-enter Odin's realm. Little has Lodur suspected that it's not the *means* to the tokens which I have held for these many years, but the tokens themselves."

"You?" Iseobel cried in terror for him.

"Aye, daughter. I have in my possession two thralls from Odin's favorite chess set, forged for him by Dvalin the Deluder, and carved from the precious stone that forms the foundation of Vanaheim. Lokji, ever wont to make mischief, stole them from the All-Father. Naturally, when Odin missed them he decreed that Lokji, assuredly the thief, would be barred from Æsgard until the thralls were returned. But when Lokji went to retrieve them, he found that the thralls, in turn, had been stolen from him! 'Twas others of Æsgard, craving the peace and harmony only to be had when Lokji was gone, who hid them so he could not return them and make peace with Odin. Thus was the troublemaker cast into Midgard and forced into his mortal guise as Lord Lodur."

Astonished at this last, Iseobel and Roric exchanged a look of wonder, and Iseobel voiced their question. "You stole the chess-pieces from Lokji?"

"Flattered though I am at your appraisal of my powers, no. Rather, the thief charged me to safe-keep them." Reaching for a piece of barley cake, he waited for his daughter to absorb this last twist. "But, since the time of their hiding is over, now I may use them to barter for your bind-ring."

"Dorflin," Roric broke in, greatly impressed with the shaman's story, "if you relinquish the pieces, how can you be sure he will give back the ring?"

"We still have the *Skidbladnir* rune, if need be."

Dorflin's voice trailed off. Only with the strongest exertion was he able to suppress another fear that now plagued him: that Lodur, in the end, would not be cajoled to hand over the bind-ring, but that the darklord had determined that no one but himself should wed with Iseobel and share in her powers.

Dorflin trembled involuntarily, then raised a warning finger as if to fend off Iseobel's worried reaction. "Mind you, Geir's brother Cynedom keeps ready a pair of horses south of here, in the old Roman watchtower on the bluff. Tomorrow, make ready for a journey. Then go to Cynedom for the mounts and flee west across the moors to the Cymry. I doubt that my name will be remembered after this long while, but you need only commend yourselves to those there who serve the White Goddess, and you will be afforded immediate protection. In the meantime, I must return to Swartalfheim. I cannot say how long I may be gone."

Considering a moment further, Dorflin added, "And for safety, Roric should be the one to carry the Boat-Beckoner on his person. Lodur would not suspect you. Should he come into possession of the chess pieces, we still will have the ship to trade him in order to re-claim Iseobel's ring, but should he procure both the rune and the thralls, we shall have no chit with which to barter. That is why I would not have you carry it on your person any longer, Iseobel!" The wizard's voice was suddenly stern and he fixed Iseobel's mercury gaze with his own sea-blue eyes. "Henceforth, Roric must be its bearer. For Lodur, merely having the rune will do him little, unless he has possession of Iseobel, too."

"Me?" Iseobel was obviously bewildered, and Roric with her.

"Aye! After Lokji gifted the ship to Freyr in hopes of winning the Vanir over to ally with him, Freyr enchanted the ship so that only one of the Vanir could invoke its rune. Lokji, being of the Æsir, can do naught with that rune himself."

Iseobel was still confused and said so. Dorflin continued.

"Remember that I mentioned my spies earlier? Well, I have one in Lodur's very household, who has promised me the rune will not be allowed to fall into the hands of the Vana halfling whom Lodur holds there prisoner. Therefore, only if he gains hold of you, Iseobel, will he have the means to invoke it."

Roric dropped both knife and cheese. Iseobel's eyes opened wide, and the color drained from her lips. "Mean you to say—?"

"Aye, my daughter. You are a child of the Vanir."

Dorflin pretended not to notice her open-mouthed amazement as he smoothed his cloak. Striding to the door, he stopped suddenly at the threshold and turned back to face her.

"Remember you not the story of the goddess hut?" he asked softly, smiling at the amazement of the two who stared at him so incredulously. Pulling his linen hood onto his head in a signal for silence, he reached for the staff leaning against the wall by the door, and walked out into the night.

# Chapter Thirteen

When he was a boy, Roric oft-times had roused himself from his pallet in the middle of the night, and slipped outside into the moonlit darkness to sort his thoughts. Those were times, he remembered now, when confusion had kept him from sleep, or when emotions had pressed hard upon his sensitive soul, causing him to toss and turn till he could stand it no more. 'Twas the way with him tonight, he admitted glumly as he made his silent way through the darkened hut, noiselessly unlatched the door, and closed it softly behind him. More had happened to unbalance him in the last few days, he sensed, than in all his life before. Yet all these events and circumstances paled to nothing when measured against the secret that had been revealed to him, in such seemingly casual manner, this very evening.

Iseobel was a halfling! She, the finest, most complete woman ever he had known, was born of the blood of the gods! She was, in some measure he could not even fathom, truly divine.

Outside, the balmy air insinuated itself upon him like a half-remembered dream. A soft wind, ruffling through his loose sark, stirred vague snatches of memories. Or were they newly imagined fantasies? Roric Grim-Kill could not quite tell, but in the pale blue moonglow it did not seem to matter. Everything had changed of a sudden, and that was all that was important.

"I hoped you would come, Roric!" The low voice made him jump. He turned, and caught his breath at the sight of Dorflin, in white robes embroidered over with crescents of moons which glowed eerily, reflecting the moonlight in milky white silver stitching. The man looked awesome, holding high a staff and gesturing with it, just enough to draw Roric's eye heavenward.

"Have you ever thought to count the stars, Roric?"

Looking, Roric gulped. "Would be impossible, methinks!"

"That is the truth," replied Dorflin with a short laugh. In the half-darkness, there was a strength and majesty about him that Roric had failed to notice before. Now he could see that the magicker was, in fact, broad of shoulder and comely in a rough-spun, mysterious way. Short hours ago, he had not thought it possible that a goddess would choose this man of all mortals to father a halfling child, but looking now, he could see Dorflin might once have been surpassing fair in the lean and learned way that women oft seemed to crave.

The magicker was saying something about the mysteries of life being more in number than the stars, but Roric was not up to understanding him right then. Other urgent questions crowded him, and he could scarce keep them unvoiced.

"I am pleased you share this moment with me, Roric," Dorflin was finishing. "I did not deign to waken Iseobel, for the less care for me on her mind, the safer she will be."

"How say?" Roric asked him.

"Even now, there are powerful magickers who cast nets on behalf of my enemy, hoping to find me. They find it easy enough to hone in on a name repeated over and over, whether in voice or mind, no difference to them."

"And you? Have you no fear for yourself, Dorflin?"

"I am one who grows stronger when pursued, stronger yet when captive. Iseobel is not that way yet. Her gentleness makes her wither from the chase and wilt in a tight hold."

Now Roric was glad for the darkness that hid his flush of shame, for he was certain Dorflin spoke of the coarse way he had connived with Vanaash to steal and hold her against her will. Before Roric spoke, though, Dorflin laughed and reassured him.

"You have done her no harm, Grim-Kill! Think on it: Had you not spirited her away, she would already be in the grasp of the evil one who seeks her. He has long been devising spells and enchantments to allow him to swoop down on this homestead in my absence, just as you did, and take her. Such was his plan, and his motives would not have been honorable, I assure you, nor his care of her as gentle as yours has been."

Roric swallowed hard but said nothing.

"I bear you no grudge," Dorflin added after a little while. "Nor she does, I trust. On the contrary, I am certain your movements were fully dictated by the gods who guard her."

"'Tis Lodur of the Trondelag you speak of, is it not, who would take her?" asked Roric haltingly when he had thought on Dorflin's words awhile. Recalling the dark lord's menacing presence, he shivered. "'Twas no accident we met the man in the woodlands, was it? Must be he followed her even then. We thought 'twas my brother he was after."

Dorflin shook his head. "Nay! Iseobel was his mark, of certain. Since she was born, he has skulked in his grim manor north of here, waiting for a chance to pounce. He hates me unceasingly, for the one he desired most spurned him and turned to me. Iseobel he wants for the same reasons he wanted her mother—unholy ones. He would be pleased to destroy her just for the joy it would wreak him to gain revenge on me and Fre—"

But Dorflin stopped suddenly, as if he dared not voice the name. The two stood silently awhile. There was a sense of kinship that had somehow grown between them this night, and Roric felt of it deeply. He was musing on it, when Dorflin at length spoke again, almost loath to break the incredible calm.

"Lodur must never claim her, Roric. Nothing could be more dire than that for her or for the future of the Vana gods. Can you understand what I am saying?"

Roric nodded, though he doubted that he understood even a portion of what was imminent in the magicker's troubled tone. "Could be this Lodur wants Iseobel for other reasons instead," he replied gruffly. "Surely she is lissome and easily can inspire a man to passion." He flushed again in the darkness, scarce believing he spoke so frankly to Iseobel's own father.

"Aye, she is fair, I know," Dorflin gave an uneasy laugh. "and Lodur has a perverse streak of wantonness that is sure to make him sorely crave her in that way. What draws him so hard to her, though, is the fact that she is Vana Avkomling."

Roric straightened, not sure he had heard the man right. "Vanaav Komling?" he questioned haltingly, wondering how the Danelaw magicker had come to know his foster-brother's true name. "Say you

Iseobel belongs to this man, Vanaav?"

Now it was Dorflin's turn to be confused. "I do not understand what you ask, Roric. Must be you know that in the ancient tongue of your own homeland, 'Vana Avkomling' means 'descendant of the Vanir.' It is the name by which halflings such as Iseobel are called here in the Anglish Danelaw."

Once, Roric had held and fondled a huge shell brought by his cousin Haftor from the shores of the Mediterranean, and when he put the thing to his ear, he heard the roaring of that great ocean, seemingly far away. That same sound enveloped him now as uncounted mysteries fell into place like the painted wooden pieces of the toy puzzle he had oft worked at as a boy with Vanaash, the foster-brother who, he had just learned, was a descendant of the Vanir. Without even knowing it, he gave a low whistle, then felt Dorflin's hand on his shoulder.

"Can it be you know someone else who goes by this name?" the magicker asked low. Roric could tell the man fought to keep his voice level. He nodded.

"My foster-brother. The one who contrived to steal Iseobel away in the first place."

Dorflin's grip loosened, and he leaned back all at once against the trunk of a sturdy hazel. For a long time, he said nothing, but Roric could sense the tumult of his thoughts. Somehow, he seemed to share them. The moon had lapsed behind a giant cloud now. The night seemed to have grown exceedingly dark all at once and a multitude of stars, faint and hazy just minutes ago, now burned with an unmatched intensity. 'Twas much like his own life, Roric mused with a wonder, so much of it having flared into focus for him this very night. He could find no words to express what he felt, so deep ran his feelings.

One thing he knew with certainty, though. 'Twas no accident he had been chosen Iseobel's protector and Vanaash's chief man. As Dorflin had said earlier, his part in this must have been dictated by the gods who guarded Iseobel. 'Twas a momentous calling for one who had oft times shunned his responsibilities.

He was such a one, Roric woefully admitted now. He was flooded with sudden resolve. He would send a fine gift to Kirsten and young Gard on the morrow. Once home, he would build his mother that wintering house she had hinted she craved. He would pay Beatta for the horse so shamefully misappropriated. And he would make amends with Vanaash; he would swear himself to the man and serve him and Iseobel with a ferocity that would inspire awe! These were no idle vows. Roric placed a fist on his heart, then fell to one knee, crying silently to Freyja. She would know his commitment was firm. She had blessed him beyond imagining by entrusting him with the care of her daughter; he would repay that with a life of valiant service. He swore it out loud—amazed at how his voice, fraught with purpose, resonated in the still night air. Remembering the magicker, he felt himself redden a little for his childlike enthusiasm, but when he turned to look, he discovered Dorflin had slipped away, silent as a fleeting thought, into the arms of the dusky grove.

# Chapter Fourteen

The men of the *Windrider* could scarce believe their leader's haste when he and his foster-sister emerged from the darkelf realm. They had enjoyed three long days of rest, but the woundings they had taken in the forest skirmish had only just begun to heal. They had learned not to question Vanaash's ways, but even the most devoted among them seemed startled when given the order to ride, not to Skog, but straight away to Sogn's Harbor. To a man they wondered why Roric Grim-Kill and the Anglish holy woman were not with the two who emerged.

No easy pace was set. From sun-up to sun-down they rode hard. Had it not been for the horses, they would have pushed on without sup or rest, so determinedly Vanaash pressed. June was in full splendor. Her warm breezes brought heady scents; her clear nights scarce darkened this far north, now that the solstice was near. Yet Vanaash's retainers marked not the gifts of the season, only the urgency and the relentless riding. There was a marked dejection among them, for without Roric's merry presence, Vanaash seemed to them more terse and unyielding. Too, the men felt a dull sense of foreboding, for it became clear to them as they traveled that their jarls had quarreled, and this dread was proven aright on the last night of their ride.

Tired and grumbling, the force made camp a little ways from the town, not far from the sea, readying themselves for the morrow's journey to Angland. That night, Vanaash addressed the whole company at once, saying he was forced to make a confrontation now that it grieved him sorely to do, but Jarl Roric had done him a great dishonor and it needed to be avenged.

"You know me well enough," he said grimly, "to realize I would not make such a fight without the gods behind me!"

Glum and heavy with the responsibility of the choice they were being forced to make, the men whispered dejectedly among themselves. In low tones, they argued this point and that as Vanaash, Beatta silent by his side, called them forward one by one to voice their decisions in private.

Vanaash knew better than to ask these men to raise arms against Roric; to a man they loved that one and would have shirked the duty put on them by their chieftain if it came to spilling the Grim-Kill's blood. "All I ask is that no effort be spared in returning the holy woman to me," Vanaash assuaged them, "and I will gift half a hide of good Skog land, three smallholders, and an iron plough to any man who leads me to my foster-brother or brings him to me— triple that plus a hound's weight in silver to share if it takes a company to do it!"

Though this rich offer made quite a stir, there were still some who asked outright to be excused from this duty. Their fortunes, their lives, were tied to Skogskaale, but the Grim-Kill was a man all of them had come to love and honor, and many said rightfully they could not swear that they could be sure to do their best if it meant betraying him. Vanaash did not berate those who confessed this, but thanked them for their honesty and sent them off to other tasks at the Skogskaale until the outcome of the quarrel should be decided. Others chose to stay. Seeing clearly that Beatta had sided with Vanaash, they suspected Roric's cause could not be won. Not a one among them felt anything other than anguish, and many lay awake long hours despite their exhaustion.

So greatly had the *Windrider's* reputation swelled in the preceding years of raiding and accumulating, that eager replacements to man the ship could have been had for the asking, but Vanaash did not allow any outright recruiting. He would rather sail with a small crew, tested and faithful, he said, than with a full one of untried loyalty. And so, the next morning he sent the company to scour for provisions.

Beatta, too, felt the wisdom of this. It was no easy chore Vanaash had set for himself, and it did not seem fair to draw unsworn men into a fight between brothers. She herself had artfully dodged Vanaash's question of her loyalty to him. She was determined not to be left behind and could not help feeling that, deep in his heart, Vanaash was hoping she would either carry Roric a warning, or serve in some way to reconcile the two men. Vanaash had confessed to her that, despite his assurances to their household men, nothing would satisfy him but a deadly reckoning. She knew his love for Roric would make it a fearful trial for him to wreak the vengeance he had sworn so firmly, and she held fast to the conviction that she was meant somehow to help avert it.

The *Windrider*, without a hand to spare, set sail for Scarbyrig before mid-day next, with Vanaash at the tiller. Standing at the helm, he seemed the complement to the fierce wooden stem ornaments, rigid and staunch. Though his singlet was grimy, his sleeves tattered, he gave little notice to the linen shreds as they flapped about him in the breeze. His stare was hard on the west, as if he could pull the far shore of the Grey Sea to himself for the wishing of it.

He mulled ceaselessly. Roric's blood he would have ... how dared his oathed brother tumble with Iseobel as if she were a serving wench? Had he not made it clear, even the question of his love for her aside, that this was the woman he was bound—by a force and will greater than any in Midgard—to wed? But nay, Roric, ever yearning for a conquest, in battle or in bed, would see to it that he had his spoils.

Fuming at this last thought, Vanaash redoubled his resolve to repay the churl for this gross betrayal. He narrowed his eyes as he played the scene out in his mind. *I will walk in. Roric, like a mindless pup, shall be wearing a detestable grin—*

"Jarl Vanaav! 'Tis a full day since you left your post." Ivar Half-Hand interrupted, using his jarl's proper name as most often he did. "Mayhap you marked it not for all the heaviness in your mind last night. Let me relieve you now so you can sup and rest. Our leader must be hale and bold when we land!"

Still lost in unrelenting thought, it took Vanaash a moment to grasp the man's words. Then, having considered the sense of the man's pleas, he nodded and headed for the food chests. A moment's rummaging yielded up a mead skin and a parcel of victuals. After taking a long draught, Vanaash helped himself listlessly to his ration of salted fish and oatcakes and, speaking to no one, shut himself in the forward closet.

Beatta, glad to see that Vanaash was at last coming to reason about Iseobel's shortcomings, began to hope that his determination had changed. After her watch at the oars, she went to the closet wherein he had taken himself, first freeing her long hair and tousling it as she knew best suited her and pinching her cheeks a bit for luscious color. "Vanaash," she whispered, knocking gently, "'tis I, Beatta."

Receiving no answer, she cracked the door. Sprawled on the bed of straw, his thick hair matted with sweat, Vanaash lay oblivious of the Nine Worlds in a deep sleep of exhaustion. Admiring him as he slumbered, and sorely tempted to lay herself next to him in hopes he would waken too weak to refuse her, Beatta gazed on him long minutes more. Something held her desire in restraint, though— whether a true respect for the man's emotions or a fear of harsh rejection, she could not say. Maybe she just wanted so fiercely for him to be the one to come to her. That would be a moment worth waiting for! Swallowing hard, she finally closed the door and turned to see to her own bedding, while a tumult of vivid emotions churned inside her.

On the bow deck, she made herself a bed of canvas awning, folded thrice to afford more comfort. Knowing she scarce could sleep, she rested regardless, flat on her back, hands behind her head, fully intending to study the stars until sunrise.

A bit away, Wulf Shin-Griever labored at the ropes, having agreed with Ivar and Egil to share the night shift. Against her will and angry at the heat that drove her, Beatta studied his sturdy form in the darkness. He was shirtless now; his strong chest and well-muscled arms, decorated by runic symbols of victory and honor burned into the skin, gleamed in the summer moonlight. His yellow hair shined like a beckoning light and, resist though she might, Beatta was drawn to the sight of him like a moth to a candle. Groaning, she tried to look away, but found she could not.

*Curse Vanaash!* 'Twas unfair that he should be able to inspire her to such discomfort, and less fair yet that she could not claim him for her own, while a man like Wulf, pleasant but inherently weak-willed and pliable, she could have had for the smallest of efforts.

Beatta had no desire to see harm come to Roric. The idea that Vanaash would fight him for possession of Iseobel had never occurred to her. "Out of sight, out of mind" was the attitude she had assumed Vanaash would have exhibited. Now, proven wrong, she was in the grimmest dilemma of her life.

First and foremost, she did not want the holy woman to cross Vanaash's path again. In the last few days, she herself had grown greatly in Vanaash's esteem; indeed, she was sure she had almost regained the place in his affections that she had held before Iseobel had made her regrettable appearance in their lives. It had been imperative that Roric be made to spirit Iseobel away. On the other hand, she realized now, it was just as imperative that Vanaash never know that she, Beatta, had assisted the two in any way. Whatever it took, she needed to get to Iseobel and Roric before Vanaash found them ... get Roric to speed the damnable Anglishwoman far, far away from Vanaash. If doing so saved Roric from death or injury, that would be a good thing, too.

Genial Wulf could be her much-needed ally, she knew. Though she had never before considered it much to his advantage, he had both a loose tongue and the annoying habit of going out of his way to speak well of others. She could wrestle information from him now to aid her in her plan. At the same time, she could plant in his mind an eagerness to defend her to Vanaash, should her sneaking off to visit with Roric and Iseobel be discovered, gods forbid!

With an eye for his untamed handsomeness, Beatta had always found pleasure in teasing Wulf, though the man's ridiculous devotion to his low-born slattern of a wife had ever come in the way of brewing anything between them. She could use him now, though, and so she lifted herself to one elbow so that her coverings fell slightly away and tossed back her luxurious hair. Then, she made a small whistling sound through her teeth, enjoying the sight of him as he stopped, tensed, and looked around.

When Wulf realized it was Beatta calling him, he stiffened more. Even in the darkness she was sure she could see him flush as he made his way over, uncomfortably aware that she wore only the scantiest of night dress. He fell to his knees at her side, looking this way and that as if he knew they were about something furtive.

Keeping her voice low, Beatta began her proposition, "I count you firmest of my friends, Wulf Shin-Griever, and I need you to help me. Like you, I know 'tis honorable to give my allegiance to Vanaash, but I must do something to save my dearest brother Roric, else my heart—"

Here, Beatta broke off, making a face of such extreme anguish that Wulf was quick to put a defending arm around her shoulder, whispering. "What can I do to help you, lady?"

"When we land, after tomorrow, I must find Roric. 'Tis imperative that I do so before Vanaash discovers him. You, I know, were among those who knew how they made their way to that holy woman's hut, and that is where Roric is sure to be. Think you that, for a consideration, you can tell me where I might find him swiftly?"

Wulf, pretending to be distracted a moment, considered carefully. It had happened before that Lady Beatta sought to embroil him in some plot or another and it always made him uneasy. At sea, Wulf followed Vanaash's orders, but the lady had oft reminded him that it was she who ruled the homestead. Wulf, along with his wedded woman Kirsten and the child he'd been paid to raise as his own, was her tenant, and it would be wise for him to prioritize his allegiances, she had pointed out. That had been the deciding factor for him the day before, when he had vowed to stay with the *Windrider,* declaring stolidly nevertheless that speaking those words of commitment felt to him like plunging a knife not only into Roric's heart, but into his own. The Shin-Griever, whose honor was as sturdy as his frame, held Beatta in no particular awe and never hesitated to speak his mind with her, but he had an innocent streak about him (Beatta called it simple) that made it impossible for him ever to see below the surface of anything she, or any others, ever said to him.

"I will do what I can, though I know only the direction of her dwelling, and not the way to it," Wulf replied at length, adding, "but I must have your assurance that 'twill not cross me with Jarl Vanaav."

"In no wise," Beatta vowed emphatically. "The two have quarreled bitterly, and I only mean to warn Roric 'ere Vanaash kills him!"

Beatta paused for effect, then carefully chose words she imagined would impress Vanaash the most were he to hear them from Wulf later. "You know I love both of them, closest of my kin. I see now how wrong Roric was to steal the maiden Vanaash intended for his own bride, and I would do anything to help right Roric's wrong. Even so, must be you know I would die before letting them come to blood."

"Then gladly will I help you find him." Wulf raised a hand to seal his word.

Though she was careful to make no sign of it, Beatta was greatly amused at how quickly Wulf had changed direction at her bidding. Only hours ago he had sworn loyalty to Vanaash's plan and none other. Now, his vow seemingly forgotten, he easily offered her assistance in thwarting the very same plan. 'Twas the man's weak-willed way.

In truth, though, Wulf had come to share a special brotherhood with the Grim-Kill. He appreciated him above all other men, despite the fact that he had often waxed jealous at Kirsten's undying love for the man who had so dishonorably fathered her son. As did many of the others—and Beatta not the least, he thought—Wulf fervently hoped a healing could be made between the two before a death blow separated them.

"Like you, I would see no feud between the pair," he told Beatta firmly. "If the consideration you mention means silver or gold, then none need I take from you. This I will do for the debt I owe Roric Grim-Kill."

Beatta, who did not see the gaining of a spoiled wife and the gift of another man's bastard as much of an honor, could not quite understand Wulf's devotion to her wastrel brother. Nevertheless, she was in need of the man's aid now, and grateful for his willingness to give it. She bit her tongue and said no more when he rose and strode away, but she took even a bit more pleasure watching him as he completed his tasks in the moonlight and, eventually, she fell into a fitful but lasting slumber that saw her to the morning.

On the fourth day, *Windrider* landed in the southern cove of Scarbyrig. True to his word, Wulf carefully outlined to Beatta the way Vanaash and Roric had taken when they first had come, but he refused to accompany her for fear of Vanaash's wrath.

"Should Vanaash come to miss me, do not give him clue of where I've gone!" Beatta reminded him sharply, then added in an earnest tone, "but if he comes to learn that I've gone to Roric, I only pray he will understand."

Wulf smiled knowingly, and Beatta, with some satisfaction, sensed that the man had already determined to quote her in the most flattering fashion. "You can trust me to uphold your courageous choice, lady—"

Beatta cut him off, eager to be on her way, and pushed him toward Vanaash who was at the prow, gruffly barking orders. "... every man to carry a cask of ale, held high, so they can see it is a peace offering!" he was saying. "We mustneeds let them know we are not here to wreak havoc again!"

The first three men had already leapt into the shoulder-deep water, barrels held aloft. Satisfied that Vanaash was preoccupied with ambassadorship, Beatta followed, only slightly distracted by the townsmen straggling onto the ridge overlooking the beach. It surely did not seem they were attempting to mass a force to meet the warriors of the *Windrider.* Still smarting from the looting wreaked on them by the same Norsemen but a short time ago, the folk should have been preparing themselves to make a stand, but as far as Beatta could see they were scarcely armed at all, and their gestures seemed to be of greeting rather than aggression. Was it possible that they already knew Vanaash had resolved to deal with them peacefully, even apologetically, this time? Mayhap they were *all* witches like that smug Iseobel....

Well, none of it mattered to her. She could think of one thing only: forcing Roric to spirit that damnable woman away before Vanaash had a chance to lay eyes on her and be reinspired to his childish passion.

She reached the shore with the three ahead of her but, once there, headed in an entirely different direction, glad that none had noticed her when she dashed into the shadows of a brushy copse. Keeping cover, she headed up the craggy coast, increasing her pace. Fighting her way along the overgrown path, she finally pulled her axe and began slashing at the tangles. So occupied was she, she did not hear the rider behind her until he spoke.

"Hold!" he cried gruffly, holding the point of his sword to her back. "Whither think you that you are going?"

"Take your sword from me!" She spun to see an Anglishman, lean and hard-looking, staring daggers at her. He was dressed in a worn hauberk, hung here and there with bits of mail, probably confiscated in battle. She nailed him with her coldest gaze. "I have crucial business here," she said icily. "Let me pass."

Geir Death-Crooner, who himself had been attempting to reach Iseobel and spirit her to safety before the invaders made shore, betrayed no friendliness as he sized this unexpected situation.

"Name for me this crucial business."

Beatta, wanting to make certain this Anglishman understood her well, shouted loud enough to drown out thunder. "I mustneeds find a holy woman hereabouts and warn her, for the one who carried her here to safety, Roric Grim-Kill, is in grave danger. The jarl he crossed to bring the woman back to her homeland has landed there below, and comes forth armed to kill him."

Despite her resolve to be amiable, Beatta crossed her arms defiantly. Geir bit his cheek in amusement. She was imperious, but uncommonly beautiful, and he had never seen a woman quite like her before. Still, he scowled as he considered her words.

It made sense to think the Grim-Kill was a man hunted by his former comrades now; he had surely put his life on the line to help Iseobel escape. What Geir knew of Vikings told him they would exact a terrifying revenge on such a traitor. Must be this woman—Roric's jilted lover, perhaps—was even now risking all to save the man. Could be also, if what he knew of the Norse, that her greatest concern was that Roric's former comrades would strike the man down before she had the chance to personally deal him his death-blow herself with the battle axe she carried.

He would not be unhappy to see Roric take a hurried leave. In his estimation, Iseobel had grown far too fond of the foreigner. But a shameless murdering of the man he would not allow. If indeed Roric Grim-Kill was sworn to Iseobel as it seemed, Geir could not in good conscience allow harm to come to the man. However, he was also forced to consider the possibility that this flame-haired hellion spoke falsely: that Roric Grim-Kill was not at odds with the others at all but was in league with the warriors now sloshing ashore, making a huge show of the gifts that Roric had promised would be forthcoming. Mayhap the Grim-Kill had been ordered to keep Iseobel complacent so he could hand her over when the others arrived. Geir shook his head hard, fighting away a fast-encroaching confusion.

His head was swimming, but one thing was clear. Whatever was going on, it was imperative that he get to Iseobel with news of the ship—and swiftly.

Angered by his slowness, Beatta stomped her foot. "We have no time to sit here musing, Anglish!" She bit off the words, losing her civility almost completely, "I must warn Roric, and you must take me to him!"

Geir's sharp cheekbones and shaggy brows framed a suspicious stare, but he had already made his determination. "I shall take you," he told her staunchly, "but under my own terms. Should you be telling me false, you shall be dealt with in no small time." Steely eyed, he looked down his straight nose at Beatta, in a way that made it clear he was finished bargaining. "The first of my terms is that you surrender your axe."

"'Tis well," she agreed, handing over her weapon impatiently. Anxious to be on her way, she tried to step past him, but Geir reined his horse hard to block her and, in one swift movement, leaned down, wrapped his arm around her waist, and hoisted her to his side. She protested, but he growlingly hushed her. "We do this my way, lady! Else you see the man not!"

Indignantly Beatta resigned herself to being carried. She must get to Roric before Vanaash did! If this was the quickest way, then so be it! Besides, she reflected, this man who held her close was strapping and attractive. It was not strictly horrid to feel the strength of his arms about her as he rode. In truth, she was ever attracted to any man who waxed more forceful than herself, and despite the embarrassment of her situation, she found some pleasure in this one's hard grip.

Shortly, they reached a small clearing hidden deep within an overgrown grove of oak near the north cove. When Geir called out for Iseobel, Beatta realized that they had reached their destination, and began to kick and fight for her footing, but Geir was a good match for her and held her fast.

Iseobel and Roric emerged from the cottage which stood well hidden in the shelter of an enormous pine. They seemed relaxed and easy, Geir thought, as if they had been enjoying a pleasant moment. Dismissing his earlier suspicion that perhaps Roric was other than he appeared to be, Geir held the squirming, flame-haired vixen up as if she were a trophy.

Amazed and obviously distraught at the sight of Beatta, Roric and Iseobel exchanged a glance that seemed to speak their thoughts: how had she arrived here and what news did she carry? Even so, seeing Beatta thus held, like a child on the way to a whipping, Roric found he had to bite his cheeks to hold from laughing. "By the gods, our Beatta looks fiercesomely hot, does she not, Iseobel? Methinks you had best drop her, Death-Crooner, else she will burn your hands and fingers!"

Roric's friendly tones signaled to Geir that he might loose his cargo. After his questioning look concerning the woman's axe was afforded with assent, Geir handed the weapon back to her. For his efforts, Beatta wanted to deliver him a feisty kick, but thought better of it, so urgent was her news. She needed to speak fast, so she leapt forward, grabbing Roric's sark and pulling him close.

"Vanaash is more wroth about your running away with Iseobel than ever we could have imagined, Roric!" The depth of her emotion immediately dispelled the last vestiges of Geir's suspicions and Roric's good-natured smile alike. "He means to deal you a death-blow this very day, wergild be damned! 'Tis far worse than a feud. He will have your blood and nothing less."

With this, Beatta shook her brother hard by the shoulders that he might grasp the import of the threat and, weaving her way into her well laid plan, continued more breathless than before. "Your only chance for safety and happiness with Iseobel is to take her now and flee. Go! Pack! Be on your way! Vanaash will be after you in the blinking of an eye."

Roric warmly clasped his sister to him for an instant, admiration for her courage plain on his face. He was about to speak when, suddenly, a thunderous roar arose behind them, accompanied by a wretchedly mournful shrieking. Unbidden, Iseobel's hands flew to cover her ears, and Geir, bold and hale looking just seconds before, paled and began to tremble.

"Odin's eye!" he oathed, loud enough to be heard above the terrifying din. "War—"

"Nay!" Beatta, who retained her composure though not without effort, shook her head sharply. "Our men made no overture of battle or harrying, but went ashore with peace offerings and the like! And scarce did it seem the vill had armed itself. Their greeting looked cordial."

"Aye! Roric had assured the *Windrider* an amicable welcome by earning the vill's friendship and forgiveness," Geir began emphatically, only half noting Beatta's amazed reaction. "'Twill not be Norse and Anglish lunging at each other today!"

"Who, then?" Roric's tone was more level. The thundering had subsided a little, as with a widening distance, and the din of the battle horn had lessened, though not its effect on them. It was Iseobel who answered.

"I know that dreadful noise," she declared somberly, "and Geir does, too, I trow. 'Tis the war trumpet of the darklord, and the sound of his mounts rushing to battle." She trembled. "'Tis Lord Lodur whom Vanaash must face this day!"

The name Lodur, once voiced, seemed to work a sudden spell of dread. Beatta's hand went instinctively to her axe. Roric and Iseobel reached one for the other, looking for all the world like children trying to brave their way through the telling of a nightmarish tale. Geir gazed hard into the distance, as if to ascertain how long it would take him to get to the place of battle, riding hard. The thundering of hooves, more distant now, was joined by battle cries, the shrieks of horses, and the ringing of iron on iron.

A scant moment passed, then Roric sprang into action, putting a hand to Iseobel's arm as if to still an expected protest. "Beatta! Past the wood to the south there is an aged watchtower, ruined but sturdy. Iseobel knows where it stands out between the coves. Move her there swiftly and guard her with a will. Let no harm come to her!"

Before Beatta could answer, Roric turned to Iseobel. "If you conjure a spell of protection, you will be safe there until I can send Dorflin ... or Vanaash."

"But I would rather—"

"Still!" Roric growled with unwonted fierceness. "I will hear no argument!"

Amazed at this show of boldness from one she had so often chid for hesitation, Beatta stared open-mouthed as Roric embraced Iseobel passionately, smoothing her hair from her brow in a swift gesture of tenderness. He pulled himself away with obvious reluctance, gave Beatta a quick kiss, commanded her once more to keep a close guard, then made his way into the hut. In seconds, he re-emerged, more aptly garbed for battle. With a hard tug, he strapped on his sword before leaping up lithely behind Geir on the horse. Before Beatta could protest, the two were away to the battlefield, throwing up a cloud of dust that gave a misty look of dreaminess to the somber scene.

As they crested the high ridge road and began their steep descent, Roric's heart was clenched with cold fear. He could see that the fighting on the level stretch below them was already fierce, though only minutes into the fray. Lodur's immense black-clad army swept across the field on midnight-black mounts, looking for all the world like an evil fog. Trampling, hewing, slashing, they left a swath of terror in their wake. The Norse worked hard to dismount them and gain more equal footing.

Directly below, Roric spotted Wulf Shin-Griever, swinging his battle axe two handed at the breast of a great stallion, who pawed the air, wild with terror. The horse screamed a bone-chilling screech, then crashed over on his side, catapulting his dark rider directly into the path of Ivar Half-Hand's broad sword. A cloud of dust rose high, and Roric, angered that he could see no more, kicked hard into the flanks of Geir's mount, cursing under his breath.

Here and there, Roric spotted a man of Scarbyrig, but the ones he saw were ill armed and clearly no match for the foe. He was relieved to note a steady stream of villagers still poured down the ledges from the opposite hillside. There was a great clashing sound as they clove their way into the heat of the fight. Mayhap they were newcomers, newly alerted by the unmistakable scream of Lodur's battle horn, or could be many of the weaponless men had fled the field and were returning now, armed and dressed for war.

Roric and Geir had come half-way down the strand now. To

their right, horses screamed and reared, unable to gain sure footing on the rocks above the shore; to their left rose a raucous cry. Roric spun his head toward the sound and saw two of Lodur's warriors, cast simultaneously from their saddles. One crashed with a thud and was still; the other groveled helplessly while two men danced over him locked in combat until he convulsed no more.

A shift in the action afforded Roric a momentary glimpse of the one he sought. *Vana Avkomling.* He was surprised to find it was *that* name which came first to his mind. Struggling to keep Vanaash's position in his sight amidst the havoc, Roric yelled directions in Geir's ear as they galloped as near to the beach as they dared. When they were close, Roric leapt from the horse and bolted straight for his foster-brother.

Vanaash, his broad-sword in constant motion, kept the death wolves at bay. Seeing one of the black-clad warriors break past the circle defending Vanaash's back, Roric bellowed a curdling war cry. In an instant, he bore down on the opponent, hacking his blade through the man's skull, saving Vanaash from a mortal wounding. Three times he cried his foster-brother's name, shouting hoarsely to be heard above the din.

Vanaash, hardly knowing in that moment how to answer the man he had resolved to murder—the brother who had just saved his life—for once belied his confusion. His face hardened, froze, then relaxed. "Grim-Kill! I—"

Roric stopped him with a determined shake of the head. "No need, brother!" As if on unspoken command, the two pulled themselves back from the clamor. A short distance from the fray, they faced each other.

Raising his voice above the noise, Vanaash called Roric the best of men. He had seen it all in a rush of emotion, a dreamlike whirlwind of images that showed him all that had recently transpired between Roric and Iseobel—had shown him, most clearly of all, the beautiful innocence of a love beyond reckoning. Almost unconsciously, he raised hand as if in salute.

Accepting Vanaash's unspoken thanks, Roric forced a smile. "We have both realized each other's motives well enow to move past it all, I trow! Iseobel waits for you in the ancient Roman tower. Atop the cliff," he pointed north. Already tensing for battle, Roric readied his weapon as he barked short phrases to make himself heard. "Beatta defends her. Begone now. Get her to safety. 'Tis the thing of most importance, and well you know it. I will take care of the business here."

**The Vana Avkomling Saga**

Clasping shoulders in a brotherly embrace, a wealth of emotion passed between them, and both were made fully aware that theirs henceforth was a bond no work of the world could break. They pulled apart, and Vanaash watched a short while, swept with feeling, as Roric defiantly made his way back into the fight. Then he hied to the north and up the rocky path, unable to stop wondering at the judgments he had made and the bitter deeds he had resolved to commit for want of the exquisite Iseobel.

# Chapter Fifteen

"Lift your skirts and move swifter!" Beatta glared over her shoulder with exaggerated disdain.

In fact, Iseobel was no more than three steps behind and would no doubt easily have kept the same pace were she not forced to contend with the branches so heedlessly allowed to snap in her face. The woods were thick here; the going slow, and that more than anything else accounted for Beatta's implacable anger. She had hoped to sneak the warning to Roric quickly, then slide back to Vanaash's side in battle before her absence was noted. No chance for that now! In typical fashion, this damnable wench had managed to destroy her well laid plan. For her, Beatta of Skog, to be forced to play nursemaid to this detestable woman, while the men enjoyed the exhilaration of combat.... It maddened her just to think of it, and when Iseobel let go a small cry of pain after the particularly hard slap of a gorse bough, Beatta turned on her again, hissing with fury.

"Hold with your mewling, woman! Why not put on that false mask of mettle you always use to impress the menfolk?" Soon as the words escaped her, Beatta felt a surge of shame, and a glance at Iseobel's misery further abashed her. Never had she seen a harder parting than the one just witnessed; must be they were deep-smitten with each other, these two. Aye, it was seemly of Roric to be so concerned with his leman's safety, but that he had compromised his own sister in this way was an insult beyond bearing! Whatever had made her agree to it, anyway? Remembering, Beatta hesitated an instant, almost stumbling.

It had never crossed her mind to refuse when Roric ordered it. It was almost as if she had been in awe of him, his manner waxed so commanding. Well, could be there, at least, was something to this maid's credit: she had managed to inspire that hopelessly carefree lackard to a semblance of manliness, no small feat! Swallowing hard, Beatta tried to formulate a gentle phrase or two with which to assuage the other. She was entering a clearing now, and there, not too far ahead, lay the rotting ruins of a lookout tower, no doubt the place of safety Roric had described. That should prove a consolation.

Turning, though, she bristled, feeling her ire rise again. The girl had dropped behind a full twelve paces and was standing, stock still, with her hands over her ears, as if warding off some evil sound. *Cup of the Valkyries!* Beatta thought with irritation. *Was there no end to this one's mysterious foolishnesses?* She cleared her throat.

"Best hurry, Iseobel! The tower is but over yon ridge."

"Nay!" Iseobel's clear voice was adamant "I am not meant to continue." The wench had drawn her pretty sword now, after knotting back her hair, and for all the world it looked like she was preparing herself for battle!

"What madness is this?" Hands on hips, Beatta appraised her with a severe look of condescension.

Turning slowly, Iseobel returned a level gaze. "Someone calls me."

"Is't so?" Beatta's tone was slightly mocking. "How comes it that I hear nothing?"

"Could be the words are not meant for you!" Iseobel turned away again, seemingly straining to make out some distant sound.

Beatta laughed. "Who is it beckons you, holy woman? Frigga Cloud-Spinner?"

Heedless of her jeering, Iseobel replied seriously. "I scarce can make it out, Beatta. It is one who calls to me with great reluctance, as if both wanting and not wanting me to come. Could be it is Dorflin, else—" She stifled a gasp of horror. One hand flew to her breast where she felt for something and, finding it, grasped tightly the glass vial of lavender that hung from the silken cord round her neck.

Even at a distance, Beatta saw the color drain from Iseobel's face; there was no mistaking the terror which wrote itself over the woman's pale visage. "Find yourself safety in that tower, Beatta, and worry not for me!"

Though trembling, her voice was firm with resolution, and before an answer could be made, Iseobel had turned. Mouth wide with utter astonishment, Beatta stared after her as, with a lithe swiftness unhampered even by the choking forest growth, Iseobel forced a path through the trees with her Frankish sword, heading through more of the grueling growth they had just come through.

For a moment, Beatta was tempted to follow, then thought the better of it. She did not know these dreadful woods and would not hazard losing herself in them. 'Twas plain they were peopled with shades and wights of the most mischievous kind.

Heart beating frantically, Iseobel panted with exertion and slowed her pace, allowing her eyes to adjust to the brightness of the cloud-layered sky which assailed her soon as she came clear of the trees. Haste was of such import that she had cut crosswise through the forest, traversing the shortest but densest stretch, feeling each passing minute as a pain more intolerable than the lashing of branches and biting of thorns as she slashed her way through. She had come out south of the promontory, near the rushing meadow rill, where the hard ground began its steep rocky slope to the shore; a hundred fevered paces more took her over the crown of the last low ridge.

Staring down, a spasm of dread coursed through her. She had never seen the wake of a battle before, and her heart almost failed her. She had thought to find something like the aftermath of that skirmish they had suffered on the road to Swartalfheim. Horror and carnage enough, she remembered thinking then, when she had gazed on those corpses. Now, on a craggy lea some two furlongs straight and narrow, near two score were littered in the gruesome disarray of death, an indistinct mass of leather and metal and gore. Numb, Iseobel tried to clear her mind, then shaded her eyes, hoping that from this vantage point her eye might light on the one she sought. It was useless. She had no choice but to step into that blood-stained field.

Knowing that it would take a greater strength than her own to find the cursed spot from which that desperate voice beckoned her, she silently besought the gods for guidance. Clutching at her amulet as if it alone had the power to keep her on her feet, she shut her eyes tightly and stepped gingerly forward, reeling against the strong odor of sweat and blood which permeated even the salt wind as it rode in off the sea.

Apart from that one voice, fast dimming now, there was no sound save the droning dirge of the waves. She shuddered to think that these men had fallen in a clash so bitter that it had taken less than an hour to be resolved. Those who had been wounded had already crawled away; those unscathed had fled the beach. Now there was no motion at all and the dreadful silence waxed, unbroken by moan, cry, or thrashing.

Still not daring to look, she forced her way forward, led by some unseen hand so that her foot touched nothing but the sandy earth and her hem remained unstained by the horror close surrounding her. The pace though, was maddeningly slow, and with each step, her nerves tautened more, till she was certain she could go no further. Then, finally, she knew she was near him, and she dropped to her knees, choking back a horrified gasp.

Four wolf-cloaked warriors surrounded him, awkward in the grasp of a bloody death they had fought hard to elude. One languished with a fighting hand raised high, stiff now and motionless, bereft of a weapon. It was that man's silver broad-sword, she somehow knew, that had passed clean through Roric Grim-Kill's breast and started the gnawing of his death-throes before he found a final burst of strength to pull it from himself and cast it hard away.

Roric's hazel eyes, though glazed, were open wide and full upon her; he mouthed her name and forced a dim smile when she cradled his head and wrapped her fingers deep in his tangled hair. "Scarce ever could I have wished for a comfort fine as this one, Iseobel," he found breath to whisper, "that you should hold and brace me for my dying."

She shushed him, wiping a trickle of blood from the corner of his mouth. "Speak not so, Roric. All will be well."

"Nay, already I feel the trembling. 'Tis a death-wound, certain." He shivered and grew even paler. Her heart sank.

"If you can but hold to me a while longer, Vanaash will be here!" Her voice was wild now with desperation. Nothing in all her knowledge of healing could save Roric now. "He will help you, Roric! He has a power—"

"Aye ... Vanaash." In the grip of an intense stab of agony, Roric stiffened, nostrils flaring. "'Tis truth that he has a way with him," he went on when the spasm had passed, "and since I was blessed by the Vanir, methinks I have come to know him better than ever I did before. Can see his very heart, it seems. Can see how it aches with love for you, Iseobel."

His voice trailed off, and he winced again, biting into his underlip so hard that he drew more blood. Sobbing, Iseobel clasped him tight: when her tears splashed on his upturned face, she dabbed at them with her linen sleeve. Roric forced a wan smile. "When he comes for you, I would bid you cling to him, trust him, let all your boundless love be his."

Clenching his teeth, Roric closed his eyes and threw his head back, exhaling short and shallow breaths as if to pant away his anguish. This quickened breathing filled Iseobel's heart with a sorrowful dread; he was fading now, she knew, and fast growing cold. Stroking his brow, she bade him save his strength, but against all her admonitions, he drew himself up. With great effort, he grabbed hard onto the thongs that held her sacred amulet and the glass vial he had given her, filled with lavender. He pulled her face close to his, and kissed her with a strength that bordered on ferocity. Iseobel was loath to loose herself from his insistent grip, but soon as he began a fiercesome shuddering, she pulled herself away, her necklace breaking its knot with the force.

When she looked on him next, he wore a faint but satisfied smile, and it seemed a new light had come into his glazen eyes. Fast, fast, it faded, though, into the sightless stare of death. She clutched him helplessly to her as he labored through four more tortured attempts at drawing breath. Then his tall frame relaxed, all at once, cold and still.

How long she held him thusly, Iseobel could not say. It was as if she lingered in a dream, unaware of time's passing, and if the last patches of brilliant blue sky had surrendered all at once to molten purple, or dallied long in the changing, one was the same as the other to her. The wind had been gradually picking up all the while she comforted him, but she had noticed it not until now, when its low and mournful wail rose from the rolling crags to engulf her. It was nearing dusk, and the rock-strewn ridges all around shone stern, silver and rugged; a veil of scudding mist encompassed the gloomy shore and now climbed fast toward the grim field of death.

Ever after, she believed it was the call of her name by a soft voice fraught with emotion, that finally pulled her gaze from Roric's peaceful, lifeless smile to that fast-whirling fog. It scarce surprised her to see the three figures who strode so purposefully forward. At first she took the two in full battle gear for Vanaash and Beatta, believing they had someone else in tow, a holy woman perhaps. It was in seeking the identity of that third one that she made the realization they were all of them women, strangers. And yet the one she mistook for the healer—aye, that one she felt she had seen before, if only in a dream. She was tall and lovely beyond imagining, with a profusion of sweet gold tresses and a finely chiseled face. Her gown, woven of glinting goldstuff, clung to a gracile form both lissome and powerful, and reflected with unearthly brilliance the last vestiges of daylight. Wracking her brain as the three drew near, Iseobel could grasp no tangible memory, though, and had almost made up her mind she was mistaken when the figure moved close, arm raised in salute.

Their eyes met, and as Iseobel gazed into the other's, the deep blue color of rare gemstones, she felt a surge of emotion so strong it urged her to lightheadedness. No word passed between them, and no signal; the moment seemed both fleeting and endless.

Then, at the urging of the battle-clad maidens, the fair visitor turned to Roric, dropping lithely to her knees and touching slender fingers to his cold cheek in a gesture of affection. Never loosening her hold on him, Iseobel watched in bewilderment as the fair one toyed momentarily with the man's sun-bleached locks, then deftly removed his earring, a wide crescent moon of hammered silver hung from a solid, finely crafted stud. Puzzled, she looked at the cord of amber cats scattered on the ground. Quietly gathering it up, she held the necklace and the earring out, wordlessly enjoining Iseobel to take them. Their fingers met only briefly in the handing over, but Iseobel imagined a wealth of communication in that touch.

Thereafter, though, it was as if Iseobel waxed invisible, for no more heed was paid to her. The three busied themselves with Roric, and Iseobel watched in amazement as they worked their enchantments. First, all three of them fingered his death-wound, finding some sort of delight in the gruesomeness of it which Iseobel could not fathom. Then, the fair one bent to kiss his lips, lifting his head a little from Iseobel's lap to accomplish it.

Exceeding strange was the way Roric Grim-Kill wakened quivering to that deep and passionate kiss! Iseobel scarce felt the motion as he sat up, letting his hands linger brazenly first on the fair one's bejeweled golden necklace, then on her firm breasts and white shoulders. These boldnesses flaunted so closely in front of her caused Iseobel a torrid blush. It seemed to her that the armed maidens, who had pulled Roric to his feet now and were assailing him with indecent caresses, found amusement in her discomfiture. But when the fair one chastised them both with a look, they laughed no more.

They were walking away now, the three of them, playfully leading Roric into the mists. Watching them, Iseobel was swept by a feeling of emptiness, devastating in its intensity. What cruel magick had they wreaked, these ones, to grant him back his life as she had so sorely pleaded only to steal him away for their own pleasures, after blinding him to her very existence? Catching back a sob, she started to her knees, attempting to rise. She found it impossible, for something weighted her to the ground. Glancing down, she did not have to feign awe. There, head in her lap as before, lay the broken body of Roric Grim-Kill—colder now and stiffer, and robbed of a silver earring, but otherwise unchanged.

Iseobel cringed and turned wildly, searching the mists for those shades that had just left her. Could it be she had looked on the Valkyries and lived? Never had she heard of such before, and the thought was so awesome that it caused her to tremble. Without even knowing what she meant to, she pushed the lifeless form away from her and sprang to her feet, screaming for Roric in a voice she was certain could summon Hel herself. In a very few seconds, the mist parted a bit and she realized he had answered her call.

She saw that he was whole again, tall and lean, comely and strong as ever. The wound had healed, leaving every trace of blood and gore with the corpse. At first he regarded her without expression; then recognition broke through the invisible veil that enshrouded him. He reached for her, silently mouthing her name, consternation and sorrow clouding his features. It took all her effort not to run to him, but a sudden fear had clenched her. Could be he would never be anything but a shade if he returned to her, lost forever between life and death. Yet still, she craved him fiercely and could feel the depth of his longing.

While Iseobel wrestled with herself, the fair one shone through the mist behind him, clenching and unclenching her hands in vexation. Her lips moved not, but her clear voice rang loud in Iseobel's mind. *"Release him, Vana Avkomling!"*

Iseobel could see, too, that the Valkyries had drawn gleaming swords, prepared to fight her for possession of him. Then, it was as if a spiraling madness descended harsh upon her. First, she laid hand on her own Frankish sword. Then it occurred to her she might pit her magick against them. Clutching the amber amulet in her fist, she let her mind race, aware of a welling immensity of power within herself. She was confident she could win, if only Freyja would hear her pleadings and stand behind her in this—

*Freyja!* Iseobel reeled, staggering against a flash of realization that nearly blinded her. How often had even she heard him boast of it, Roric Grim-Kill, that it would be Freyja herself who plucked him from the battle-field with a bold kiss? *The fair one, the one who gave her the earring and restored her amber cats, was Freyja!*

Shuddering to think how close she had come to unwitting rebellion against the gods, Iseobel fell to her knees, arms raised in a gesture of supplication. As if her very change of heart had been the signal, the Valkyries sheathed their weapons and began anew their cajoleries to the warrior so recently claimed, and he relaxed again to their jesting. They had only gone a little way when the goddess reappeared, slipping her hand into Roric's, thusly to lead him to the seat of honor in Folkvang that he had earned with his life's blood.

It was all as it should be, Iseobel thought, watching with an aching heart until they disappeared into the fast-fading fog. They were invisible to her now, and she clung ardently to the echo of Roric's voice: *when he comes for you, I would bid you cling to him, trust him, let all your boundless love be his.*

Against all her will to stifle them, her tears flowed now freely, washing from deep within her a thousand griefs and memories: some vague as the balmy brush of the mother's breast on a newborn's cheek, some vivid as the gleaming smile and careless laugh which had so swiftly earned bold Roric Grim-Kill an eternal portion of her heart.

Carefully and with trembling fingers, she nestled the silver earring, the vial of lavender, and her amber necklace together in the pouch along with her runes. Summoning all her strength and wisdom, Iseobel raised her tear-streaked face to the heavens and silently commended the man to Odin All-Father. Then she sought out Roric's lifeless frame in the darkness and fell beside it, weeping herself in and out of sleep till she no longer was able to judge aright which incidents of the long and tragic day had happened in dream, and which in fact.

The dull thud of hoof beats awakened her. As it had not yet crested the craggy ridge, she could not see the single horse with its well-decked rider. Rubbing her eyes, she glanced around. The moon had scarce begun its slow ascent, and a full half of the sky still glowed rich twilight purple, streaked by the last iridescent remainders of sunset. She thought she had been drifting in and out of sleep for hours but, in truth, only a handful of minutes had passed. The rider was moving closer now, at an unearthly pace. Could be it was Vanaash or Geir or Beatta, Iseobel thought in hope, but a welling sense of uncertainty from deep within told her no.

Next to her, Roric's vacant, faded eyes, once sparkling with warmth and life, stared aimlessly. Aghast at her own negligence, Iseobel sat bolt upright. In hoping against hope that someone would come to help, she had failed to perform even the simplest of courtesies for her dead friend and protector.

Quickly, she set to work, first closing the eyelids, only slightly marking the dewy chill of the skin. A quick inspection of his hands greatly eased her fears: they were clean, and the nails neatly trimmed, so she would not have to waste time cutting them. Naglefar, the dreamlike ship of death—constructed of the parings of dead men's nails—would in no wise be enlarged by this untimely death, and Roric's mortal remains would be spared the humiliation of further handling by the despicable outlaw darkelves who robbed grave-chambers to gather them.

Roric's glossy locks were matted and tangled as always. Frantically, she searched for a comb. Aye, it was like him not to keep one handy, she thought with fond crossness, searching here and there for the neededs-bag she knew he was wont to carry.

By the gods! She remembered all at once how Roric had assented to carry the special runestone at Dorflin's behest, tucking it into that velvet pouch! She could picture him, with his easy grin, throwing his hair back with a jaunty toss of the head as he tied the thing on a thong round his neck and tucked it into his hauberk. There it hung still, she thought with a shudder, anext that gory death wound.

Dorflin had well convinced her of the value of that rune, and she knew she must retrieve it, yet she was wroth to put touch to the grossness there. Not because she never had encountered such before—no, as healer, she had treated countless similar wound-ings—but because she recalled how only nights before she had traced her fingers along that chest, and felt his heart beat strong and sure, when he still had been her own dear Grim-Kill, warm with life and love.

A nearby sound made her stiffen. The rider had come to the edge of the battlefield now. Hard she hoped he was one who gave honor to the vestiges of mortal men, and so would not chance to step his horse over them; elsewise, he could be at her side in a twinkling.

*Haste!* Swallowing down a wave of sickness, Iseobel forced an unwilling hand under the hauberk and reached to unlace the blood-sopped under-tunic. Soon as her fingers wrapped around the pouch, she drew it forth, vainly trying to loosen it by unknotting the thong. Finally, in desperation, she snapped the thong asunder with a strength that astonished her. No sooner had it come free, than she felt a presence—sentient and powerful—behind her. Cramming the velvet bag into the rune purse she wore hidden in the folds of her shift, she turned, working hard to mask her thoughts and the sudden swell of emotion this frantic unpleasantness had produced.

Scarce could she believe, even considering her panic of the previous moments, that she had been so unaware of their close approach. The horse, an immense black stallion, loomed so near now that Iseobel could not see the rider. All at once, everything seemed vaguely familiar to her, and she was reminded of the magnificent black Roric had slain during the journey to the darkelf realm; she flinched as she heard the animal's dying scream again in her mind. Struggling to compose herself, she came to her feet. As she did, the man dismounted.

"I fain would speak with you a moment, Iseobel," he said with cool courtesy, looking down at her with a dim smile. Had it been the mid of night, had they stood thusly face to face in total darkness, still she would have recognized him by the gleam of those sultry, cherry-black eyes. He had looked at her just this way, that time in the forest on the way to Swartalfheim, and then, like now, she had not had the strength to tear her gaze away. Then, like now, she had found herself rooted, unable to escape the fascination of his presence. She shuddered.

"Begone from me, Lodur!" she hissed low. "You no longer fool me with your sweet words. I am one of those who know!"

He took a step backward and raised both his hands, palms outward, in mock defense. "So harsh with me, lady?" he asked with a wide-eyed look that he hoped would project innocence but did not. "What mean you, you are one of those who know?"

"I know now who you are!" she replied, eyes narrowed. She would have called him Lokji then, except she knew that even to voice the trouble god's name aloud could summon his denizens from afar, and so she was loath to do it. "I know what manner of being resides inside that handsome human-form you wear!"

Here Lodur laughed smoothly, as if her words had been spoken in jest. "Mayhap you have taken a head-blow, Iseobel, or have been running in the heat till it unstilled you!"

Iseobel glared but said nothing, uncomfortably wondering if she would have been wiser to have put her amulet back on.

"I know I startled you that last time, apprising you without words," he continued, as if she had given him leave to continue. "Ever have I conversed in suchwise with your father, and it did not occur to me you were not yet as comfortable in your powers as he."

Iseobel backed away haltingly as he reached forward without warning and held his hand to her brow as if searching for a fever. There was a strange, almost metallic coolness in the touch, and she felt a marked wave of dizziness.

Lodur backed away with a look of concern. "What is it you were you saying? What is it that you know of me?"

Iseobel opened her mouth to answer, but in the time it took to form her words, she grew distracted and confused. *There is something about him!* she told herself fiercely. *There is something I must make myself remember!*

Lodur laughed low and put a solicitous arm around her shoulder. "You must remember that Dorflin told you I would come to help you!" he said. His smile was dazzling. "You must remember that he bade you put yourself in my protection!"

Iseobel nodded, feeling suddenly weak. His sonorous voice seemed to entertain a power over her; she was not sure why. Certain, he was among the handsomest men she had ever seen. The sheen of his silky black hair, barely ruffled by the sea wind, and the glossy perfection of his look held her entranced. His comeliness was of a different sort than Roric's untamed charm. It was a polished attraction, in nowise subtle, that caused a churning deep within her. He reached out again, taking her hand in a gesture of familiarity that made her flush.

"Even so, in speaking words this way, we lose precious time!" he went on. "I promised Dorflin I would see you safely to the protection of my fortress, till he can claim you. We must be swift, though. There are untold dangers at our very heels."

Iseobel flickered a frantic glance past him to where Roric's corpse lay, but the man shook his head emphatically.

"Two follow who are intent on seeing their brother off with due honor," he said. "'Twill mean carrying him across the waterway to his home, though, and must be you know you are in no strength now to bear that. Ne'er will I force you, Iseobel; still it would be best that you accompany me as your father bids. He says there will be a means of taking you there swiftly, soon enow, and that you will know what he means by that."

Finally, Iseobel felt a measure of comfort, for it seemed to her addled wits that none could have worded that message but Dorflin. Besides herself, only two knew that she had access to *Skidbladnir*, and one of them was here beside her—dead. Dorflin alone could have sent this man after her with such a plan!

Finding voice at last, she besought the man for his indulgence. "Much grief have I seen this day, my lord, and if you and my father have devised a way to spare me more of it, I cannot help but advantage myself of your kindness."

It sat ill with her to leave Roric unattended, even for the shortest while, and she was somewhat surprised at her own words. Even so, there was a certain wisdom in fleeing now, and she considered it drowsily as the man lifted her gently to the high, silver saddle, then climbed up behind her. Many of the warriors in that field had died in the service of evil. Dark magick would run frenzied here tonight; drained as she was, she scarce could face that threat. This comely one made her feel safe from it all. It was as if he had stifled her pain with that one concerned touch and wrapped her in a shroud of forgetfulness.

As the horse picked a careful way back through the fallen—led, she was certain, by the same power that had brought her to Roric's side—Iseobel relaxed a little, nestling against her new-found protector, finding comfort in his iron-hard hold. By the time they topped the ridge, and the stallion had been kneed to a straining gallop, drowsiness had claimed her. She slept, oblivious of the rush of the wind, sound as a babe in quiet cradle. Her sleep was dreamless and deep.

# Chapter Sixteen

Dully aware of Beatta's hand on his arm and her voice at his ear, Vanaash silently watched the horizon shift and eclipse as the *Windrider* crashed through the sea. Three days now had they been underway to carry the body home to Skog. To Aasa. Three matchless nights, three brilliant days, three lifetimes of sorrow at the loss of Roric, and still Vanaash had yet to steel himself to greet his foster-mother's grief.

He could not say whether he appreciated or despised the way Beatta attended his comfort. Uncommonly quiet, she brought him food, helped him with his tasks, and stood watch with him. Evenings, when the busyness of the ship had quelled, she soothed him, even mourned with him. Even so, Vanaash was inconsolate; her very presence was a constant reminder of how grossly he had dealt with Roric. Wulf Shin-Griever had confided the selfless courage Beatta had shown, trying to save Roric from his own foster-brother's wrath, and the fact that she had treated Roric better than he himself had caused him all manner of self-reproach.

Thinking of it now, his throat tightened for the hundredth time in a rippling spasm: now the Grim-Kill lay dead....

How often Vanaash had replayed the events of Hel's own day, he could no longer count. So certain had he been of his own purpose, that he had paid little heed to the manner in which disaster unfolded like a poisonous flower.

He was barely holding off Lodur's advancing forces when Roric saved him from that death-blow. The instant they met, their brotherhood was restored and Vanaash's heart, after a long taste of ice, made warm. But it was a fleeting swig of happiness! A swift embrace, and they parted. He himself had quit the battlefield to pursue an elusive happiness earned at Roric's expense, and left Roric to face an undeserved death.

Hazily, Vanaash tried to reconstruct the events that had followed. Hurrying to find Iseobel, he had come upon Beatta, frightened and sobbing. Only once before had he seen his foster-sister terrified— five of them forced to camp of a harsh winter in the white wilderness, stalked by ravenous wolves. Even then, she had made a pretense of courage. In the haunted woods of Scarbyrig, she wept and trembled like a babe, and he had felt little patience to comfort her. Iseobel, Beatta sobbed, was gone, fled to the call of some magickal voice leaving her, Beatta, alone to fend off evil enchantments in those cursed woods! Beatta had not hesitated to confess her own confusion; she remembered little other than the terrifying blast of Lodur's war trumpet, and Roric's sending the two of them to seek safety, telling Iseobel to wait for a man named Dorflin.

*Dorflin?* A blow from Thor's hammer could not have hit Vanaash harder. How often had he heard that damnable name only to be left wondering how great a part the churl played in Iseobel's affections? He had collected himself and wrenched the news from Beatta that Iseobel was last headed for the shore.

"Why said you naught sooner!" he had bellowed, grabbing Beatta by the wrist and hauling her roughly through the tangled growth. They had reached the beach as the sun sank low, casting a pall of gold and purple over the field, strewn with bold men slain in battle but otherwise empty. Of habit, Vanaash had counted the fallen, ignoring the dreadful perfume of death that rose on the fog. He felt hope at first; it was plain to see that his warriors had chosen their stand well and Lodur's army had of necessity retreated. At length, though, Vanaash's heart was rent by the sight of Roric's broken, lifeless body.

He had known immediately 'twas hopeless to breathe life back into the cold form; Roric was dead—had even been groomed for the grave by one who obviously revered him, mayhap one of their own men, now dead himself. Lifting the lifeless shell to himself, Vanaash had wept, heaping curses on both Lodur and Dorflin. Silently, though, he berated himself most. He would never forgive himself for the part he played in Roric's demise.

He had been further shamed when Beatta, wild with grief, riled madly against the undeserving Iseobel instead of aiming the blast of her temper at him. He had been too shaken to follow her rantings closely, he recalled now, though in her recounting of the events of that day he had learned things that surprised him—that there, in the very vicinity of Iseobel's own home, was where the two powerful magickers, Lodur and Dorflin, resided, and that Iseobel had known them both since girlhood. He wished now that he had better concealed his reaction to that news, for it clearly had fired Beatta further against Iseobel. Anger had boiled inside him to hear her, and in the end, still and sullen, he brusquely ordered Beatta to remove herself from his sight while he and Ivar made a full accounting of their men.

A dozen were sore injured, Wulf among them. In agony after pulling a long spear from his own shoulder, the Shin-Griever had stunned them with his ferocious reaction to the news of Roric's death. He had thrown himself at Vanaash, swearing to smite him. Ivar and two others wrestled the wounded man to the ground and stilled him roughly, threatening the dire chastisement deserved by any man who railed against his chieftain.

Vanaash, blaming himself for the tragedy, said he could not fault the Shin-Griever for his grief and anger. He had reminded them that Wulf and Roric had been friends since babyhood, and said 'twas likely the man was out of his mind now with pain and sorrow. Privately, it troubled him that Wulf deemed him guilty and loudly accused him of having sworn to murder the Grim-Kill himself. He *had* sworn it, he realized now with a pang, though none but Beatta had heard him. Perhaps the Shin-Griever was a better reader of hearts than any had guessed.

Later, he and Ivar had returned with the others to the field and begun the bleak search for men still missing. After what seemed hours of pawing through the sticky gore, they finally found the lifeless bodies and helped carry them shipboard, while a few others stayed behind awhile, looting the enemy's dead to embellish the graves of their slain comrades. Finally, Vanaash built a harrow, censed it with burning lavender, and made supplications while a band of hand-chosen men bore Roric's body to the *Windrider;* he had neither the heart nor the strength to help with his foster-brother's final boarding.

Once asea, Vanaash spent the hours in icy silence. He had been harsh with Beatta, and he regretted that now, for she had not deserved such treatment. Her own brother was among those whom they solemnly carried back for burial, and though she ever waxed stern with Roric from babyhood on, it was no secret that she loved him well and often delighted in his happy company. More, it was a double grief for her, for Roric was the second of her brothers to be slain. He felt a sudden surge of pity for his foster-sister. Wrenching himself out of his deep sadness, he settled his arm about Beatta's shoulders in mute consolation. Thus sharing their grief, they arrived at Sogn Harbor.


Two silent maids with vacant stares lifted her over-robe, with its sleeves of jeweled brocade, and hurried it from the candle-lit chamber, while attendants emptied pitchers of perfumed water into the tub, then bowed and retired. When the last of them had gone, Lodur rose. He was resplendent in black robes of rich-woven wool, ornamented with embossed silver stars, and cut in a simple curtate fashion which perfectly suited his height and lean strength. Iseobel caught her breath as he moved lithely toward her. She was certain she had never seen a man more comely than this powerful black-haired lord, though it was hard for her to be sure. The very sight of him seemed to drive the thought and memory of all others from her fascinated mind.

He came behind her, taking her shoulders and turning her gently so that she faced the looking-glass with him. It was a magnificent mirror, the largest and clearest Iseobel had ever seen—though, in truth, she could not remember ever before seeing more than a hand-sized shard of the precious glass.

Seemed there was no end to the wonders in this wealthsome manse. In the last two days and nights, she had been dazzled more often than in all the rest of her years together.

"Are we two not fair to see?" he mused in a deep voice that thrilled her. "Are we not stunning beyond measure?"

Woodenly, Iseobel nodded. Her own figure, well defined in the shimmering gauze shift, captivated her, and his—

Swallowing back the flood of deep emotions that always threatened to engulf her when she was in his close presence, Iseobel studied her new mentor's imposing appearance. His mien was noble, imperious, almost haughty. His face, framed by sleek black hair faultlessly groomed, boasted even, finely chiseled features—arrogant in their perfection—and those enigmatic dark eyes, sometimes cherry black, sometimes midnight violet, but always afire with insolent passion and indomitability.

His outfitting boasted elegance; there was nothing gaudy or pretentious about the multitudinous tokens of wealth he wore with such style. His strong hands were heavily hung with jeweled rings and wristlets, and his right ear was studded with a cabochon ruby of enormous size. From a finely linked golden chain round his neck hung a magnificent pendant of rare and expert craftsmanship. Tilting her head to better view it, Iseobel was surprised to discover that it represented Jormungand, the Midgard Serpent.

She had seen this symbol before: a fiercesome snake wrapped around the mortal world, holding it in a deadly stranglehold by anchoring gruesome fangs hard into its own tail. It was an emblem worn by magickers who worshipped the Trouble-god, Lokji. She knew there were cults that gave credit to Lokji for fathering the Serpent, as well as the horrendous wolf Fenris, but Dorflin had long ago explained that such legends merely symbolized the origin of earthly evil and violence, both offspring of Lokji's cunning and vengefulness. Could be that was true, too, of the legend that he had sired Hel, ever-decaying keeper of the underworld, though there was no doubt that he had somehow created that awful being, and it mattered not much to her whether it was through procreation or magick.

Nevertheless, the sight of such an unexpected and mysterious amulet hanging close to his heart vaguely disturbed her. It seemed to betoken some secret, dark thing suspended just outside the realm of her memory, which she was somehow compelled to recall, but in vain. Could be it was just the puzzle of it. Why would one who seemed so steeped in the knowledge and wisdom of the Vanir give honor to the most untrustworthy of the violent Æsir gods? It was a thing she scarce could fathom.

"No need to waste thought on such matters, my Iseobel," he whispered huskily, his mouth dangerously near her ear. "Must be you, of all Holies, most know the wisdom of reverencing any power that can serve your purpose. For do you not entreat Freyja with your runestones, yet lag not to summon the White Goddess with strange and secret chantings?"

Iseobel stiffened, as if sensing a threat. "Is that what you would have of me, my lord?" she murmured, watching in the mirror as his hands slid slowly down her arms, then encircled her waist, drawing her tighter back against him. "Would you use me to gain understanding of the White One and her ways?"

He laughed a smooth and soothing laugh. "Be not foolish, my fairness! I would not so abuse you! Rather I would put all I have at *your* disposal—my own power, even—when we are finally conjoined, so that you may be allowed a share in them."

Moving lightly over her breasts, her throat, her shoulders, his hands at last came to rest, one on either side of her face, deeply entwined in her tresses.

"How is it you suppose you are meant to wed with me?" she inquired weakly, studying his proud reflection with a sort of wonder. "I had presaged myself a different fate."

"Wrongly, perhaps, lady!" His slightly mocking smile belied the cool courtesy of his voice. Lifting her hair, he twisted it deftly, pinning it with a stunning comb of elkhorn and emerald. Bending, he kissed her neck, then her ear. Although the touch of his lips stirred her, she stiffened a little, and pulled away.

"The lady fears me!" he exclaimed, looking wounded, and her feeble denial did little to convince either of them otherwise. His tone and manner seemed to soften all at once; he turned her to face him. "Surely you realize by now that the one you grieve for had not the power to make him fit for you!"

Iseobel lowered her lashes. "Aye. I had come to know it...." her voice trailed off miserably.

Taking her face again in his hands, he lifted her gaze to his. "Must be, too, that you realize I do have such power."

She arched away. "I have not thought upon it."

"'Tis not the truth of it, Iseobel! You have thought that mayhap 'twould be wise to work your seith charm on me, that you might be convinced."

Iseobel faced him again with a glance of astonishment. "You know of that?"

"Aye, of certain—"

"And you would be willing to be proven by it?"

"'Twould gladden me more than you can imagine...."

Whispering the words, he bent and lifted her, crushing her frame to his strong chest. His words seemed to echo in her brain as he carried her across the chamber.

If only Dorflin were here, she mused with bewilderment, shivering as the gauzy shift fell from her shoulders. She frowned, perplexed. Something was amiss! This man who knelt behind her now, kissing her back and shoulders so boldly had promised that her father would meet them here! Scarce could she count the hours that had fled from her in this enchanted house.

"Dorflin!" Suddenly anxious, Iseobel struggled to rise. The dark-haired one got up and walked over to a nearby coffer. Lifting a goblet of wine from the tray of refreshments, he put himself down anext her once more, and held the cup to her lips.

"A dram of wine to ease you, Iseobel!" The sonorous voice was assuaging beyond measure. "Be not addled, my beauty!"

She took a long swallow. The soothing was immediate. She took another and settled back in the cushions with a languorous sigh, watching through heavy-lidded eyes with a strangely tantalizing satisfaction as he pulled the black dalmatic over his head and unlaced his dark-dyed sark.

A flush of heat threatened to overtake her, whether inspired by the potent drink or by the sight of his finely muscled chest, gleaming in the flickering light, she could not say. When he bent to kiss her, forcing his mouth to hers with unnerving ardor, the room seemed to spin away. Scarce did she notice the warmth of his hands beneath her, the whisper of his breath at the hollow of her throat. By the time he lowered himself next to her and drew her close all was as a dream.

... and the dream was like dreams of her childhood, wherein time and space had no meaning, and chief of the players were strangers. She saw herself, stretched on a voluptuous bed of foreign fabrics, being rubbed with oils and perfumes by a maiden of rare beauty, with a heart-shaped face, unblemished skin, and a full, sensual mouth. Aye, she was a stranger, yet there was something eerily familiar about her tourmaline eyes and the confusion of moon-blonde hair that massed forward when she bent. Her voice, at once gentle and imperious, begged to be obeyed and, in the dream, even the black-haired magicker, whose power was great, seemed wont to give her sway.

"She was meant to bathe in those attars before I began this!" the maid exclaimed with a hint of annoyance. "When I heard you had sent her attendants away, so that you could toy with her thusly for your pleasure—"

"A moment's distraction, sweet! Scarce can I believe that my most natural shred of weakness could turn an exceptional one like you into a jealous chit! Seemed you would be above it."

"My lord, I beg you. You must not give in to this desire, else you will lose the chance to most fully possess her!"

A laugh followed, cold and emotionless. "'Tis a trial to hold myself from her; her very presence is an invitation!"

"So you said it was with me, when first you brought me here. Yet you held yourself back a full moon cycle, as the ritual prescribes, for anointings and drinking sacred brews. And is it not true that now all my powers are as your very own?"

"Aye. You well serve me yet!" Iseobel heard a rustling and knew they were embracing. She could feel their mounting passion.

"Use me then to avert your desire. Put her from your mind this fortnight more. Then she will be yours forever, and I will help you train her well."

Another cold laugh. "Scarce will I need assistance with that, fairest!"

There came a muffled cry of passion or delight, and a whisper. "Must hush, my lord, lest she wakens."

"Mind you not. 'Twill all seem as a dream to her, so deeply has she drunk of the brew."

"Kiss me then!"

"Aye! I will kiss you, sweet—and more...."

Stretching a little, Iseobel turned herself face down in the luxurious bedding, spiraling deeper into sleep. If there was more to the dream than this, she did not remember it after.

# Chapter Seventeen

The oaken ship stretched nearly five man-lengths. Next to it stones were piled so high that it had taken four teams of men a full day to cart them there. Closest to the vessel stood Aasa, Beatta, Vanaash, and Rhus. Just behind them, the Shin-Griever, gritting his teeth against the pain of his injuries, comforted his loudly grieving wife while he tried to hold young Gard in tow. Though he mourned hard as any man there, Wulf secretly fumed. That morning, after the ceremony to honor and bury the household men killed battle, Kirsten had asked Vanaash to grant the youngster the right to be called Roric's son. Wulf felt Vanaash's ready assent bode nothing but ill for any of them.

The Shin-Griever fought hard at Scarbyrig, and had taken harsh woundings in Roric's defense. Despite his pierced shoulder and shattered ribs, he was still swinging his axe savagely when he fell and was bodily dragged from the field. Had he been able to speak his own choice, he surely would have preferred to die rather than leave Roric's side, so great was his esteem of the man. Despite all that, though, he knew that Vanaash's decision today, absent-minded as it had been, had driven a wedge forever between Kirsten and himself. The woman had never much returned him the affection he'd showered on her. Now, flaunting her new-found status, she had begun already to refer to herself as Roric's leman rather than as Wulf's wife, making no effort to hide her satisfaction. Wulf's heart had already hardened toward Vanaash. He could not help but blame the man in some part for Roric's death, and this last insult had ripped it beyond repairing. Never again would he call Jarl Vanaav his friend or kithman. Despite his love of the homestead and his dedication to the *Windrider*, were it not for Beatta and Aasa, he would be gone from here forever, and with but small remorse.

Near him, the remaining men of the *Windrider*, battered from their recent ordeal, offered prayers and petitions for their favored jarl as they had for their fellow householders earlier that day. Behind them lined folk who came from beyond the homestead and the harbor, wishing to pay their respects to bold Roric Grim-Kill, blessed of the Valkyrie, chosen of Odin, champion of Freyja, now seated at the ready for his passage to Valhalla—or mayhap Folkvang.

After all had joined in chant to bless the final journey, Aasa reached into the boat and placed a comb of fish bone and a large box filled with fragrant herbs next to Roric's body. When she was finished, Vanaash made his halting approach, arranging a splendid helm of hammered bronze on his foster-brother's head. He fitted Roric's prized sword, now polished to perfection, to the lifeless hand, and, with a tear, placed his own Roman ring on his foster-brother's finger.

In turn, Beatta and Rhus made their offerings for a rich after-life. Then Wulf offered him the splendid gold ring he had worn since wedding Kirsten, knowing none but Roric would understand the import of it. Afterwards, the rest of the retainers filed by, each laying hoard silver by their chief's side. They made much note and praise of the wealth of the gifts, from Beatta's glass cups to Rhus's pewter tankard, and were proud that they often had fought by the side of this valiant warrior who was still surpassing fair in the pallor of death.

None spoke a word, and the silence prevailed a long while, until Vanaash walked over to the nearest pile of stones. All lined behind him and, taking their turns, picked up as many stones as they could carry and placed them one-by-one into the ship. In little more than an hour, the grave-boat was filled—then finally buried—by the stones. When the last stone was lowered into place they knew Roric no longer could hear them, and the wailing began. Where there had been unearthly stillness, there was now a crying and moaning loud enough to spread to the edges of land. Men and women alike mourned grief-stricken, finally turning their way home, mindful of the sorrow left to those in Midgard while bold fighters rejoiced in Æsgard.

The family started back to the skaale. Vanaash, who had begun the trek alone, made no protest when Beatta moved close to him, forcing herself under his arm, into his limp embrace. Aasa walked behind with Rhus and watched in dissatisfaction. Suddenly, she hastened her step and, catching up, placed herself between them, bringing the puzzled Rhus up beside her. Thus, four abreast, with Aasa and Rhus separating Beatta from Vanaash, they made their way back to the longhouse.

Despondently, the family sat at the great table and slumped wordlessly in their chairs. Her red-rimmed eyes betokening a day of extreme sorrow, Valka placed cheese, bread, and sausage before them. She was a shy woman, plump and plain, but Roric had always greeted her with the charming smile, the fond embrace, and the merry words that made her feel clever and pretty. Like many another woman that day, she was sure there was no one who could miss him more than she herself did.

Despite the fare, no one ate and no one spoke. Eventually, Vanaash fetched mead and cups to the table. He poured a round, drank his down in one steady draught, and refilled his cup. Then seeing all the cups were empty, he poured again. Rhus, unused to drink, broke the silence, raising a fond salute to Roric's memory. Soon they were all talking. The mead flowed steadily, and the mead-skin lost its fullness to the thirsty mourners.

Night fell. Aasa, Rhus and the others at the table had drooped to bed, one by one. Now, left alone with Vanaash, Beatta studied him by the flickering firelight. She could not remember his tall frame relaxing even once in the course of the day, and it was no different now. Tense and sullen, he emanated a strength that stirred desire in her beyond reckoning. His long, white-blond hair, loosed from its bindings, shimmered like cold frost at sunset, adding a cold and purposeful intensity to his unreadable gaze. His very silence spoke to her soul.

Now and again, she noted a sad smile or a tear, and at times he winced, as if steeped in guilt. The pain that crossed his finely carved features was, she knew, as close as ever his look would come to betraying what it was he felt inside; his was a coolness she found dizzyingly erotic. Still, she was anxious to make him speak to her. If she could but express the depth of her feelings for him, and remind him of Iseobel's hand in the tragedy which they now mourned together, mayhap he would somehow come to realize the happiness he was missing by spurning the love she was trying to offer. He made no move to break the stillness, though, and at last, despairing, she spoke.

"Must be you know, Vanaash, that we should be proudly rejoicing right now, not selfishly mourning. For though lost to us, Roric sups tonight with Staag in Valhalla—if not in Freyja's own Folkvang. At the very least he is honored as one of the valiant glory-slain."

Vanaash appraised her with an unreadable gaze; she did not know it, but he had been somewhat startled by the unfamiliar gentleness of her tone, and it moved him. Reaching across the table, he placed his hand on hers. She grew hopeful, but his words disappointed her.

"Do you know why it is, Beatta, that Iseobel found it easy to love Roric, but could not love me?"

Now it was Beatta who stiffened and grew cool. "There is much about the woman which makes little sense to me!" She mulled her answer carefully, hoping all was not yet lost. She refilled his cup. "Could be she found him easier to bewitch, is all."

"Nay!" Vanaash shook his head hard, as if he found her answer impossible to believe. "I know she found me less easy in her company than was our brother, but I am loath to believe that she would consider naught else than bearing, or that she would choose careless sport over my own deep regard for her. Can't be that she found me wholly to her disliking?"

"The wench was simple in her tastes, Vanaash!" Not caring at all for the subject of Vanaash's sorrows, Beatta itched to stir the coals of discontent. "More indignant against the woman I could not be. I saw early on how gallantly you displayed your interest and, to my mind, any woman would be flattered by notice from you. Yet she took no heed of your manly marks. 'Tis why I always doubted her much-remarked upon holiness."

Vanaash quickly downed the drink, then grew flushed with its heat. His face hardened with uncommon passion. "Could be you speak the truth! *Never* did she respond to me as a woman to a man. She was the first woman, the only woman, to have stirred me, and methinks I made no secret of it."

"That you did not." Beatta spoke honestly, silently fuming.

"I would think I had at least something to interest her."

"Yet she chose to ignore your virtues and reject you. I am sure she has hurt you deeply. Even more so as she has made so easy with others and made no secret of it, either."

She took a long swig and, studying Vanaash's stolid face, decided she could afford to say more. "In truth, brother, she taunted you. Not only with Roric, who at least had a stout heart to offer her, but with that churl Lodur. Roric and Iseobel may have conspired to say I was fevered that day, but I *know* what I saw! She kissed the man."

Vanaash's pale cheeks reddened as he considered these words. He had long tried to forget the vision of that passionate kiss, dismissing it as a strange mistake. His foster-sister's talk of late, though, had re-ignited his curiosity about Iseobel's connection with Lodur. He had not realized, until Beatta told him, that Iseobel had lived anext the darklord since her girlhood. Dorflin and Lodur were said to be in league, so it should have surprised him less that she had dealings with those two, powerful magickers both, than with Roric.

"And what about this mysterious Dorflin for whom she plays such a pitiful act of fidelity?" Beatta's timing, heretofore perfect, she thought, had begun to suffer because of his long, distracted silence, but she was not about to lose the moment. "Roric was the least of your troubles, brother!"

"Aye, Iseobel has played me like dice-bones!"

To her great satisfaction, Beatta's earnest tone and careful fanning finally had burst Vanaash's discontent into ire.

"She spurned me and caused me to swear vengeance against my own oathed brother."

"That she did."

"Now my future is forfeit."

Beatta impulsively kissed her own fingers then touched them gently to Vanaash's brow. He gave a dim smile. She whispered his name in a husky voice, and he raised his eyes to meet hers.

"Mayhap I could make for you another future," she said, in a voice that invited speculation. "Mayhap I could be for you all that you dreamed she might be!"

Shaking his head, Vanaash drained his cup and looked away, thereby missing a look of sorrow that shadowed Beatta's face a fleeting instant before hardening into a cold and bitter frown. A silence loomed, grew, and settled over the room like a cloud. Vanaash rubbed his temples, wondering what charms this Dorflin fellow had that the image of him could not be wiped from Iseobel's mind even though she had put herself, by her own choice, in Roric's willing arms. Laying his head on the table, he fell to sleeping until Beatta, sure that he would not take a turn at remorse as well, wakened him and sent him to bed.

*         *         *

"I trust you slept well?"

His voice stirred Iseobel from a flurry of indistinct thoughts. She rose from the stone bench where she sat in the cool morning shadows of the courtyard. He looked exceptionally fine today, his usual elegant black garb somewhat enlivened by a wide sash of madden brocade which matched the lining of his sleeves and cloak. As if acknowledging some unspoken admiration, he tossed back his glossy hair, a contrived but seemingly artless gesture which, for some reason, caused her to blush and stammer.

"Fairly. I—I suffered dreams...."

"Dreams?" he arched a single eyebrow, gesturing to a small, well laden table in the shade of a flowered trellis. Lifting her heavy skirts, Iseobel followed, allowing him to adjust her chair before he seated himself.

"Describe for me these dreams, fairest!" He said it absently, seemingly intent on filling her goblet with an uncommon-looking green nectar, but somehow she understood it as a command. He motioned for her to take a sip and that, too, she felt was a bidding not to be argued. Swallowing the sickly sweet brew, she cleared her throat.

"Seems to me I dreamt of one ... I scarce remember him. One who played me false, and so doing led my Roric to that bloodfield where you found us together."

He looked up with pointedly feigned interest, beckoning her to drink again. "Best not dwell on morbid thoughts, sweet! Did this bold forsaker have aught to say to you in your visions?"

"Nay. But there was one, somewhat like to him, who spoke." She broke off, as if suddenly reminded of a vital fact. "Seems to me you lingered in my dreaming, too, my lord!"

"'Tis so? And what part did I play in your imaginings?"

With a start, Iseobel remembered the fevered dream: his forceful kisses, the heat of his iron-hard body pressed tight against her, the willingness inspired by his strong hands. Her sudden flush and obvious discomfiture caused him delight.

He tossed his head and laughed. "Is't true then, that you are as eager as I am for the moment of our joining? Blush not. Oft I have dreamt of that myself!"

Abashed by his boldness, Iseobel lifted her cup. After the first disconcerting sip, the taste was strangely comforting. She was about to take another swallow when a figure caught her eye.

It was a willowy woman, tall and well formed, who approached by the garden way. The sight of her unbound hair, white-blond and billowing as if by a strident sea wind, awakened an image buried deep. Iseobel's heart leapt in consternation. A name occurred to her. *Vanaash.* And she repeated it silently in her mind two or three times, that it might linger in her memory when the moment had passed.

Alerted by this sudden surge of emotion, her companion rose. Following her gaze, his cherry-black eyes glinted angrily. When the woman came closer, he addressed her in a cool voice.

"'Tis a pleasure unlooked for, Lady Shiorvan, that you would seek to join us here. Seems I remember you had business to be about today, brewing attars and remedies and such."

"Aye, but I have come from the market, just, with word that I suppose will interest you." Iseobel watched as their eyes met, certain that an unspoken message passed between them. Then the woman tilted her head away, appraising Iseobel with a cold smile. Made uneasy by the palpable tension, Lodur cleared his throat and haltingly introduced the women to the other.

"Do I not recall that this is the daughter of the shaman who protects that forsaken vill beyond your leas, my lord?" Gathering her richly fashioned sky-blue skirts, the blonde one swept forward haughtily, offering a bejeweled and well groomed hand to Iseobel with obviously more formality than affection. Iseobel took it, then drew back quickly, staring with confusion while the other two moved away, arm in arm, out of her hearing.

The woman had pressed something into her hand! Now, inspecting it, Iseobel saw that it was a runestave. Squeezing it tight, she could feel the intensity of the power that had been worked into it through spells and chantings. It was the work of someone highly skilled in seith and galdor, she could have no doubt of it. Darting a quick glance, she assured herself the two were still occupied, then ran a finger into the deeply scribed symbols. On the one side, was carved PERTHO, ⚹, rune of fate and mystery. It was a symbol she had not much used, partly for fear of its strange power. She felt no ill will from the carving now, and somehow her thinking seemed to have cleared a bit. Turning the piece of wood, she inspected the other side. This mark was not of the FUTHARK, she knew. It was a special bindrune, and so must hold a special force all its own. Closing her eyes, Iseobel concentrated, and through her very flesh the rune spoke to her. *Guard your thoughts!* it cried in a silvery voice. *Mark well that you keep your mind empty, lest he read you and destroy you!*

A rustling warned of Lodur and Shiorvan's approach. Iseobel loosed her grip, hastily shoving the stave deep into her bodice.

Gulping a breath of air to help in regaining her composure, she swiftly emptied the remainder of the green nectar out of her goblet onto the mossy growth at the base of the twisted pomme-fruit tree. She was not sure what was happening, but knew she would be hard-pressed to marshal her will and memories and she felt certain these brews afforded her no help in doing it.

Vanaash tossed and thrashed. His brow streamed with sweat. "Iseobel!" he cried out from his sleep. "Iseobel!"

In a moment, Beatta was at his side, stroking his clammy brow. He sat up frantically, looking at her without recognition. His eyes were wild; his motions sudden. Beatta gently chafed his shoulder and soothed him. By steps, Vanaash's breath came more evenly; the panic abated.

Resting back against his bolster while Beatta tenderly swept the hair off his face, he noticed Aasa was watching. He read fleeting disapproval in her eyes and then saw resolve settle over her features as she readied herself for the day. She was determined about something. That he knew by the set of her jaw and the rough way she pinned the shoulders of her gray wool cloak over her undyed shift, but his agitation was too great still for him to sift her thoughts for a clue.

Hours later, though Vanaash strove to keep the night's horrors from his mind, images from the nightmare still haunted him. To occupy himself, he walked to the stables and sought distraction with busywork. After oiling the leather tack, he decided to groom Beobald and Badger. He had just started to comb the tangles out of his own mount's mane, when a nicker from old Wren told him that someone had entered the byre. It was Aasa.

She greeted each horse warmly and then told Vanaash she would like to speak privately. He nodded, wondering what lay so heavily on her mind.

"Do you remember some years ago when you and Rhus went swimming?" Aasa abruptly began, leaning against the rough hewn wall as if for support. "He took on a great deal of water and you fished him out and breathed into his mouth to restore him."

As confused by her beginning as by the source of her knowledge, Vanaash nodded again, and she continued. "You know well that your breath carries unmeasured powers of healing, else we would not have Beatta with us now. You should also know that it imparts a measure of immortality. Rhus, and now Beatta as well, shall live for an uncommon long span."

Seeing that Vanaash meant to speak, she waved him to silence. "I know you think I am addled and I bid your patience. There is much you must know, and I can think of no good way to begin," she explained, pretending to examine a dusty leather bag draped carelessly over a nearby beam. "Too, there is my own shame in't, and the telling comes not easily. Short of revealing that which I am bound by oath not to speak, I will continue."

Vanaash, bemused, begged her to continue and resumed combing Badger's mane.

"Aside from that one rare strength, you have others, like your second-sight. Mayhap you discovered other talents in Swartalfheim, and more may come to fruition yet through study or by the blessing of the gods." She fixed her eyes on his. "At any rate, the short of it is that I see how close you have become with Beatta since your return, and now I must beg you to forego custom. You cannot marry Beatta."

"What would you have me do?" interrupted Vanaash, pacing, "I learned in Swartalfheim that 'twas Iseobel I should wed, but she refused me."

"*How* refused you?" Aasa chid him sharply. "Made you her *ever* any offer of explanation? Thought you that she simply and gladly would accept the will of a man who abducted her?"

Vanaash was brought up short. "But last night, Beatta said that Iseobel clearly had rejected me."

"*Beatta said!*" scoffed Aasa, slapping the leather bag hard so that the dust motes rose and glittered in the shaft of sunlight that surrounded her. "Think you Beatta would make the way to another woman easy for you when she is determined to have you for herself?"

"Even I could see Iseobel had set her heart on Roric, and she proved me right by running off with him," Vanaash's voice was cold, his look colder. "In any wise, she is now lost to me for all time, unless I should again abduct and force her to my will. Roric, my dearest like-brother, is dead because I insisted on tracking my own future with no thought to his own. 'Twould seem the price of my interests are too dear. Mayhap 'twill be better for all when I abandon my selfish cravings!"

"Nay!" Aasa was adamant, "No matter how comforting Beatta's company, you must not join yourself to her. Despite the trouble which has twained you and Iseobel for a time, I know beyond doubt she is indeed the woman for you. But there is more!" Here she stopped, moaning as with pain.

"Foster-mother?" Worried, Vanaash gathered Aasa in his arms, but she pulled back till she could look him in the eye.

"Beatta is your half-sister, Vanaash."

Vanaash eyed her blankly, then exploded with rage. "How can it be? Do you mean to tell me that I am some bastard brat, gotten in Eirik Half-Dane's wenchings?"

Aasa shook her head. "Nay, you are mine own child."

Vanaash stared in bewilderment as, trembling, she sagged onto a bundle of straw. "When I was but young, I happened on an injured hunter in the woods," she told him, wringing her hands like a nervous child. "I was skilled in healing, so I helped him to a small pilgrim's hut in the wild and tended him. In a short time we grew to love each other." She stopped, swallowed hard, then spoke again in a dull whisper. "Soon I was with child."

There was a long silence; Vanaash broke it. "Must be there is more to the story than this? Did you wed with this man?"

"Wed we could not, but when he learned of your coming, he was thrilled, and determined that he would take you off to raise you in his own land. This I would not hear of."

"So?" Against his will, Vanaash's voice turned harsh.

"So we compromised: I would spend my lying-in with a woman of his choosing, a woman of Uppsala with unusual skills and powers. She was a special one he told me. Rumor was that once she had been the beloved of the Vana-god, Freyr. Folk said he had come to Midgard especially to find her, for the power of her galdor and runemagick was so strong that she was known of and remarked upon everywhere, even in Æsgard."

Vanaash closed his eyes. There was something familiar to him in the story she told, but he could not place it.

"She had borne Freyr a girl-child, marvelous beautiful, but 'ere the maiden even came of age, she was stolen away. No one ever knew after whether the girl lived or died, though the mother's magick convinced her the child thrived, only fogged and bound by enchantments somewhere. Ever she was convinced 'twas Lord Lodur of the Trondelag who had taken the child. All knew he had a quarrel with Freyr and was watchful ever for a chance to put grief on the Vanir, and 'twas whispered ever after that he held a strong magicker in his service to do his will."

"I have heard somewhat of this!" Vanaash said low.

"Could be no one ever shall know the truth, but one thing is certain. The woman of whom I speak was most loving and solicitous of me then, and once you were birthed, she agreed to take on the care and rearing of you until you were six, and then contrive to return you to me."

Feeling caught in an uneasy dream, Vanaash sat down beside his mother, fighting to reclaim snatches of memory that hovered tantalizingly out of his reach. Aasa continued.

"Good to her word, she presented you in Skog as her sister's orphaned son who needed fostering. She offered a goodly gold-sum for the trouble. She told us your name was Vanaav Komling. Jarl Eirik and I took you in, each for our own reasons, and him never the wiser as to your parentage."

"My parentage?" Vanaash repeated her words softly, but there was no doubt as to the question he asked with them. Aasa shook her head.

"Your true father's name I cannot reveal to you, but you have met him. He is the man who returned you safe to us that time you wandered off into the wood at the berry-picking."

*Lord Stranger!* Vanaash sprang to his feet and paced furiously. How could he doubt her story? Yet the truth made him flushed and fevered; there was no comfort in it. Aasa's voice seemed to come from far away,

"Since then, I have not seen him ever ... but I trust that *you* have."

The anguish of her burden lifted, Aasa sighed and stood to face her son. "Now I must enjoin you to silence. For me, I would not have my shameful past visited upon any of my other children. For your true father? I can only say that he fears for your safety should his enemies learn that he has a son."

Though Aasa waited anxiously for his response—adjusting her brooches, smoothing her hair—Vanaash remained silent. When he spoke, his tone was flat, but his words uncensuring.

"I have always known that you stood behind me, closed though I have been about my purposes," he said, no hint of emotion in his icy eyes. "Never have I fathomed how you learn so much, yet patiently keep your council until we despair. In your ways there is much wisdom."

"'Tis because I love you." Her voice faltered.

"Then will you support me now when I sail again for Angland and try to find Iseobel. Or shall you scoff at my foolishness?"

"My dearest Vanaash, you have my blessing. From the first I met her, I knew that Iseobel had the powers and magick to take you to the greatness meant for you. Prepare your journey. Go find her.

Leave me to deal with Beatta."

Vanaash pulled his mother to him and kissed her before she left, then turned to saddle Badger. Even those of his men still fit to go adventuring, he knew, would not be eager to set sail so soon again. Many were wounded; all were heavy of heart and, besides, the last voyage had brought them nothing in the way of profit but the salary Vanaash had contracted with them to pay. Now, he had to set their sights on yet another journey that had no concrete promise of loot or treasure. It would take him longer than usual, and cost him more in coin and ale, to excite them to the prospect. Best he head now to the tavern and begin to cajole them. Too, had been a rare week, this one, and it seemed it had taken a lot out of him. It would do him well to enjoy a tankard or two with the men he called his friends.

Vanaash returned to the skaale before supper. Having rubbed Badger down and stabled him comfortably, he strolled to the stream where he and Roric had played as boys and allowed himself a quiet time with his memories. It was strange, but his foster-mother's convoluted tale had given him an unfamiliar sense of peace. As he walked back to the longhouse, he felt happier than he had in many days.

Beatta, who had been awaiting his return, ran to join him as he approached. She wore a long dress of fine spun green linen, cut in a style she would never have chosen for herself had she not seen Vanaash ogle Iseobel so shamelessly every time the woman wore one like it. He had been drunken the night before, she had told herself over and over during the course of the day, and that was the reason for his witless refusal of her proffered love. In fact, she was quite sure he remembered little of it, so unused was he to strong drink. Still, linking her arm through his, she was surprised that he seemed so stand-offish. Trying to lift his mood, she spoke light-heartedly of her day in town, all the while admiring the fineness of his look.

Aye, she considered, his handsome features and tanned chest causing her great distraction, he has been a long time coming around, this one. But now that the holy little minx is well lost in England, I think I may count on marrying him in one or two months' time. Oh, what a prize in the bed he will be, she day-dreamt, warming with anticipation. Day after day of romping with her. *That* should snap him back into this world for good!

Beatta called to Valka to bring the meal. Smiling in anticipation of Vanaash's reaction to the favorite dishes she had arranged for him—roast boar smothered in leeks and carrots, hard white cheese, goat's-milk whey, and fresh berries—she listened absently while Rhus talked about his day.

They passed the supper-time pleasantly, though Beatta would have been happier with a few more words from Vanaash, who seemed lost in thought, missing the point of every jest and ignoring the crux of every conversation. He had thanked her politely for the fine meal, but he waxed distant and cool, and it irked her. Still, she followed him about, telling details of this recipe and that so he might better appreciate her womanly talents. He cut her off with a wave of the hand.

"'Twas a tasty meal, Beatta, as I have said already," he said almost gruffly. Then, he added in a more kindly tone, "I will think of it fondly tomorrow when I break fast on dried fish and biscuits."

Beatta stiffened. "What mean you?" she challenged, narrowing her eyelids. "Why should you be eating from the winter stores in June?"

"I sail again for Angland, even as the sun rises." Vanaash's voice was firm, determined. "Dorflin or no, Lodur or no, I am determined to find Iseobel."

*"Iseobel!"* The color drained from Beatta's cheeks. She clenched her fists. "After all that has happened, how can you still be infatuated with this useless, trouble-mongering foreigner?"

Vanaash gave her no answer at all, but strode purposefully through the outer door and into the night. Rhus ducked quickly to avoid the beer mug Beatta threw when the man was gone. Seething, she spun on Rhus in anger.

"Why go you not, too, Rhus? For 'twould seem that every man of this family must have a try at that so-called holy woman!" Pulling her cloak from its hook and loading her pocket with coin from the mantel jar, she ducked through the passageway, flung the heavy door wide, and stormed out.

The crisp breeze did little to cool her. "I'll fix that wench once and for always," Beatta muttered as she strode to the horse stalls. "With silver enow I can buy a furnished sea-chest in Sogn, stow myself in *Windrider's* closet, and dare them to throw me overboard by mid-day."

Thus determined, Beatta mounted her mare and headed for the harbor.

# Chapter Eighteen

"That woman who came here this morning—where is she from?" Iseobel asked the question with calculated nonchalance. The night was chilly, and servants had lit a fire in the huge hearth of the great hall. Now, she reclined on a wolfskin rug with Lodur in front of it; they were alone in the massive room and its shadowy depths seemed somehow threatening to her. She snuggled against him as much for security as for the warmth of his body. He obviously delighted in this display of familiarity; he had grown so genial and relaxed that she was sure no other time would be better to ask. Even so, he hesitated a moment before he finally answered.

"She comes from the Nor Way."

"Strange, for she speaks not with their accents."

"She was young when she came hither, methinks some fourteen or fifteen years only."

"I was raised in this same vill and have never seen her 'ere today. Cannot be she lives roundabout?"

Rolling onto his back and putting his hands behind his head, the dark-haired one eyed her curiously. "Aye. She lives in this very house. High in the turret."

Eyes flashing, Iseobel drew herself to her knees. "Is she then your leman?"

Mistaking her carefully worded probe for a jealous woman's accusation, Lodur rose, too, and took her shoulders. "I will forsake her if you wish, precious. She scarce is of use to me now." He pulled her close, kissing her neck, her shoulders, the crevice between her breasts.

Iseobel fought the thrill of it and, in so doing, tensed. He pulled away, dark eyes glittering in the wavering light.

Recovering herself, Iseobel spoke quickly. "She was of use enough today, methinks!" Truth was, Shiorvan had come with the news that the men of Iseobel's vill, believing Dorflin's daughter to be held here against her will, had appeared at the marketplace to amass men for a confrontation. Even now, Iseobel shivered a little, remembering how things had been resolved.

"We scarce can allow them to think I hold you unwillingly, can we?" the dark-haired one had asked her musingly, and she had found herself having to agree.

"Ride with me, then, and convince them!" As usual, his words had come to her like an indisputable command; it was a gift he had of gazing deep with those haunting eyes when he said things, she had decided. It left one no will for argument.

So she had ridden, pressed hard against him, high astride his magnificent stallion. They had meandered all through the vill in a costly procession, making a great show of the many hardened warriors in his service, and a greater show of the affection between them—a thing which she no longer had the tenacity to doubt, so favored did she feel in his strong embrace. One thing only sat ill with her. Scanning the crowd for the almost hopeless chance of gleaning news of Dorflin, her gaze had fallen on her old friend, Geir.

"How is't you can ride smiling in the wicked embrace of Lord Lodur?" he had called—meanly, she thought, and with unwonted vengeance.

In truth, it had taken her aback, for it was the first she realized that her dark-haired one was so called, and it perplexed her, for the name sounded familiar, as if she had heard something of the man before, but could not remember it. She had tried to formulate an answer and wished she dared carry the mind-clearing runestave with her, but knew the gift was safer in its hiding place beneath her mattress. As the catcalls grew bolder, she felt the strong arms around her tighten, and she turned to look into her lordship's seething eyes.

*Kiss me now.* His lips had not moved, but she had heard the command, so forceful that it filled her with terror. Scarce could she pull her gaze away, drawn as she was to his sensuous mouth. She had parted her lips then, and received his deep and searching kiss with a welcome surge of pleasure. Aye, and she had let him touch her lewdly, too, right there, in front of all the villagers assembled.

"My love, you are trembling!" For an instant, the flash of his eyes minded her of a wild black he-cat she had once seen—a glimpse only in the misted moonlight of the grove before the creature bounded away. Seemed to her, just for that flickering moment Lodur regarded her like prey. Touching a finger to her brow, he emptied her mind, swiftly and smoothly.

"It has been a long day, is all." She forced a smile, trying not to look at him. He reached forward; the light touch of his fingers caused a wave of heat. Then he moved away, picking up a goblet and handing it forward.

"Here, sweetest. You've had naught but a sip of your wine. Drink of it now, and relax yourself."

She flushed, grateful for the darkness that concealed it. She had managed to spit only a scant mouthful away into the fire while he was dismissing the servants. Now she would be forced to drink the rest under his cautious gaze. She tried to word a protest, but he said the words again.

"Drink of it now."

She raised the cup to her lips. When she had drained it, she lay back down on the thick woolen rugs, and let him kiss her once more. Iseobel fought to keep her wits, but her attention wandered to the tapestry which hung from the high stone wall. The picture, a finely woven account of Odin All-Father and the Fenris wolf in battle, was intriguing to her. That there could be women with so few chores that they might simply work their needles and costly thread for the beauty of it ... unimaginable.

"Just think, sweet," the dark-haired lord said, fingering the collar of gold and gems she wore round her neck. "In less than a fortnight we shall be hand-fasted."

She arched her back. "I had hoped to wait for Dorflin...."

"Aye, but well you know how it goes with him—here, then gone, and only the gods know for how long."

"'Tis true," she agreed, purring. "Here, then gone...."

"No need to wait for Dorflin. I have your bind-ring."

She stirred a moment, half-grasping a thought that seemed of import. Then his hot hands at the small of her back, lifting her towards him, chased it away and it seemed she slept, while he toyed with her a while, till she dreamt the blond haired one made her way into the hall and chastised him harshly. Could it be, then, that they rubbed her with sweet-smelling oils while she slept? How chanced it that she felt no shame, displayed thusly before him while the woman touched her so?

Then the dark-eyed one seemed angry, stood and said the other one should not have come this morning; said he had read Iseobel's mind then and knew she had cried out to the Vanir. The woman called Shiorvan laughed, though, as the two fell together in a lascivious embrace, and said nay, the maid had but cried the name of another: "Vanaash."

*Vanaash!*

Even in the depths of this dream, the name had power to stir her. The pair had left the hall for a more private chamber, Iseobel knew, and lost to their debauchery would not hear her consider the sweet sound of that name in her restless mind. She reached under the mattress for the runestave. *Vanaash.*

She squeezed the wood, and her recollections encroached through the fog of her bewilderment. She could almost see his face, feel his presence. He would have wed her but her bind-ring had been stolen hard away. Aye! She remembered now that Dorflin had said the darklord had stolen it: Lodur. The evil one.

*Vanaash!* In her mind, that name had become more than a tenderly murmured memory.

**Vanaash!** It had become a desperate scream for help.

Standing at the prow, the salt wind buffeting his stony face and whipping his thick hair where it had come loose from its fillet, Vanaash looked as menacing as the *Windrider's* fierce figure-head. It had been four days since they set sail from Sogn, which made it three and one-half that he had been avoiding Beatta.

Barely had they lost sight of the Nor Way and recovered their sea-legs, when his foster-sister had emerged from the closet and truculently dared him to jettison her. "You scarce can afford to lose me! You will need my skills, foster-brother, since you have fewer hands in your service now."

Vanaash had paid scant attention to her carefully planned argument. As if she were elsewhere and could not hear him, he had called over his shoulder to Wulf Shin-Griever, commanding him to set Beatta to rowing at the afternoon watch, "same as any other mercenary or adventurer who might try to bargain for passage." She had stared daggers of hurt and resentment after him as he stalked to the bow.

By Thor, he had been angry with her then and he was irked still. To her credit, she did not act the wounded lover—a part he had seen too often played by wenches for Roric's benefit. Nevertheless, since sailing, he had simmered, stewed and stomped away at her approach. If she tendered her assistance as a ship's hand and warrior, then so be it. He would take her proffered service and allow her no more regard than that.

As if chastened, she had accepted every task, no matter how menial, with none of her usual complaining. She asked no favors, and conducted herself as one of the crew, setting to the required work wordlessly and with vigor. It was hard for him to avoid her in such close quarters but he managed it, insinuating himself into other men's conversations at her approach, ignoring her when she vied for his attention. He knew she desired private converse with him, but he stubbornly refused to grant it.

At length, though, the Anglish coast appeared, and Vanaash could no longer honorably avoid her. When Wulf Shin-Griever again urged him to receive Beatta, he agreed to meet her at the prow, away from the others' hearing. He waited uneasily, almost regretting his decision as she approached. He could not have been icier. A rich silver brooch in the likeness of Frigga's distaff gleamed at her throat. Had it been there before? Vanaash couldn't remember. And that gleaming amulet? Trying to pretty herself? Did she think a few domestic props would sway him?

"I give you thanks, foster-brother, for hearing me out, for I must-needs speak to you!" He had expected a tirade, but Beatta's smile was gentle and her tone softer than he could remember it ever sounding before. "What I have done to deserve your censure, I cannot think, unless it were to love you as a brother all the more, now that I have lost Roric. I exact no reply from you, but 'twould serve us both ill if I took my leave of you, perhaps forever, and did not make an apology for whatever it is that vexes you."

Vanaash was startled by this. As she spoke, against his own will, he found himself keening hard into her mind, looking for deceit and falsehood therein, but read nothing but an honest concern for him. Something like an apology began to form in the back of his mind but, suspicious of her motives and hardened by sleepless nights and sorrow, he kept silent.

Looking him in the eye with a frankness that struck him as forced, Beatta continued. "'Tis plain to me now that you will cast custom aside and have this Iseobel instead of the one to whom you are bound. Mayhap you think me some vengeful maiden who will come to arms rather than let you dishonor me by the breaking of your vow—"

Vanaash bit back an oath and turned a withering look on her. "I made no vow to you," he growled.

She smiled patronizingly and touched a finger to her lips as if to shush him. Before, it had always astonished Vanaash that such a pretty mouth as Beatta's could house such a sharp and lashing tongue. Now, he was just as surprised by the honeyed sweetness it pronounced.

"... Or mayhap you thought I could not bear the heartache of being forsaken and that is why you slunk about so in this endeavor. Had you been a staunch man, or even a caring brother, you would have imparted your resolve to me forthright, that I could loose myself of the obligation I feel to you, and be about my own life and pleasures again."

Vanaash felt a stirring of guilt, but his long-pent anger made him stifle it.

"That is why I travel with you to Angland, Vanaash—not to grovel like a pitiful maiden, but to be about my own pursuits again. You know there are none amongst the Skog men who are even near my equal, so 'tis useless for me to stay there searching while I grow older and less able to charm."

She was fishing for a compliment, Vanaash thought coolly, but she would not have it from him. He let her continue, despite his sense that her soft-voiced heart-baring was a charade.

"I have determined me to seek out the man Geir Death-Crooner again, for he seemed somewhat smitten with me and, though I might not love him, I apprised him as one strong and competent enow to do well by my holdings. He would work hard to keep me in comfort."

She paused as if expecting a reaction. When Vanaash showed none, she continued unbidden. "Could be you think me heartless, but 'tis not so. All I have ever cared about was your happiness, Vanaash, and if it is Iseobel that you will have, then I would do best to rejoice with you. In fact, I will drink to your happiness with her, for she has won your affection fairly, and I can do naught but love her for giving you the joy you deserve."

She paused, as if biting back a coy smile meant to melt him a little. Unable to contain his anger, he turned on her with a force that made her jump.

"Too bad you did not see the wisdom in removing your unwanted self from my path earlier, Beatta! Had you left me to my own devices, Iseobel would be safe with me now, and both our happiness assured."

Beatta pouted and started to speak, but he cut her off with a harsh gesture. "What is more, had you not brazenly meddled with circumstances entirely beyond your understanding, Roric would be alive even now!"

"Vanaash!" Beatta spun away from him, her voice trembling with pain and disbelief.

"We both know that is the truth of it! 'Twould have been gentler for me to have left it unsaid, but surely you cannot deny your guilt."

When he saw how she trembled at his words, Vanaash felt shame. He reached a hand to her shoulder as if to offer comfort. She growled, though, like a wounded animal, and batted his hand away. Before Vanaash could say more, she took a swift leave, jumping aft unbidden to help Wulf and Ivar lower the sail.

Astonished at the vehement emotions that had goaded him into lashing out at Beatta, Vanaash blanched and spun round again to face the bow. He gripped the upper planking at starboard and dug his fingernails into the caulking of tarred fur. It was incredible to him how enraged he felt. Had he been unfair? Perhaps. But who knew how much Beatta had meddled ... how much blame really could be placed at her feet.

As her brother, Vanaash had had no trouble understanding her. As the object of her desire ... laughable. He knew naught of women's ways. Roric had ever teased him upon that point. Knowing Beatta as he had in both babyhood and battle, though, swayed him to believe that she was ever on the lookout for an advantage, and where none revealed itself, it would be fashioned. For Beatta had always been determined to win.

Seeing the sweep of Scarbyrig's familiar cove should have made Vanaash's heart beat high. Instead, he found he could look no further than the ornate dragon's head that sprang menacingly from the *Windrider's* prow. So like Beatta that beast was. Beautiful in its curving lines and flawless symmetry, but fiercesome and deadly nonetheless

***"Vanaash!"*** A bellowing seized his brain.

***"Vanaash!"*** Whether a noise or a thought, he knew not, but it caused him an agony as tangible as any he had ever suffered. Fists clenched, he tore at his hair as if the pain of that might distract him from this other, more intense anguish—but to no avail. The torment held him in its fiery grip.

Then it stopped as suddenly as it had come. Vanaash squinted, as if against a great light, and gingerly lowered his hands from his ears. A picture had come to him, causing his heart to beat with panic. Concentrating, he sent one thundering thought: *"Iseobel, I come to you."*

But when the moment passed and he caught his breath again, he waxed anxious and felt a stir of fear. Try as he would, he could gain no sense of the direction in which to seek Iseobel. There were two things only that he knew with a certainty: she was not in the hut where first he had found her, and he would have no way of helping her unless he could first find and confront the man named Dorflin.

The *Windrider* was barely moored at Scarbyrig when Beatta jumped overboard, determined to reach Iseobel before Vanaash did. She hoisted her sea-chest onto her shoulder and slogged through the shallows while the men were still securing the ship. Knowing Vanaash would be busied with details of the disembarking, she scanned the small crowd who had run to line the bare coast. At length she spotted the gauntly handsome features of Geir Death-Crooner, breathing a sigh of relief at seeing his familiar face. His shaggy dark hair and beard were sun streaked now; his tanned skin almost Moorish. But his quiet gaze and serious expression assured her that this was the man she remembered.

Making a great show of it, she dropped the chest on the sand as if fatigued by its weight and collapsed on it. Sure Geir had noticed her, Beatta waved weakly to him. She made sure all could see her now on the open strand, flirting with the Anglishman, so it would not occur to any that she meant to visit Iseobel before her foster-brother had a chance to do the same.

Had Geir been watching the ship's crew, he might have noticed the longing looks that followed Beatta when she made her way forward. But when Beatta was near, few men noticed more than her lusty beauty, and to that Geir was no more immune than was any other man. When he came close enough to appreciate it, Beatta smiled and bit her lower lip while addressing him by name. He was almost immediately enslaved to her charms.

"Well met we are again, Geir Death-Crooner," she flashed her dimples and then raised one hand in greeting; the fingers of the other were wrapped tight around the chambered amulet that hung between her breasts. "Seems I am once more in need of your help finding someone. This time, 'tis Iseobel I seek, for my foster-brother is come once more with an aim to taking her, and I would counsel with her first to learn her heart's desire."

He made no reply, so she leaned a bit forward, showing her cleavage to advantage, and continued with her carefully planned script. "Surely you know by now they were joined in some holy quest, and mayhap she will be glad to know he comes for her. 'Tis well if that is what she desires and, if so, I will tell her where to find him; but if not, mayhap you will help me hide the helpless woman from him, for he has vowed to have her!"

Geir, a careful man, was still making sense of her odd accents and considering how to answer this when she continued. "Mayhap you know of her whereabouts and could direct me to her?" Prettily casting her curling lashes downward, Beatta stretched her legging-clad legs out in front of her and examined the toes of her sodden boots while she waited expectantly for an answer.

"Aye, Lady—" Geir seemed to have forgotten her name. He dismounted, held by the sight of her in clinging wet kidskin.

"Beatta," she reminded him, forcing a coy blush.

"Beatta," he repeated somewhat dreamily. Then, catching himself, he pulled his gaze from her figure and looked away a moment before meeting her eyes with his own. "As to Iseobel's desires, I cannot say. She has been distant of late to all who care for her, methinks. However, it does happen that I know where she stays these days. Seems she has made herself at home in the embrace of the great Lord Lodur."

Though adept at both feigning and caging emotion, this time Beatta could not disguise her shock. "Lodur?" She mouthed the name more than spoke it. Had she had heard aright? She recalled the passionate kiss she had witnessed between the two that day in the forest, and now felt a smug sense of vindication. She would have no need to devise Iseobel a compromising situation for Vanaash's behalf; the witch had managed to put herself in the worst possible light, all by her devious self!

Geir gave a thin-lipped sneer. "Aye, the same Lodur who put to grave those many men we brought against him, including your brother Roric, once her protector. Now she lingers with him of her own free will!" Geir, eyes narrowed with anger, seemed to bite back his own words, as though he had spoken a blasphemy.

Beatta eyed him sullenly; it was obvious that this one, too, was smitten with the worthless woman. By Freyja's hard-won necklace! The woman had led Roric to the grave with her conniving seductions and now she dallied with the man who had killed him! What in the Nine Worlds could valiants like Vanaash and Geir find to respect in one like that? Men! There was no understanding their witless whims!

Even so, Beatta was certain she might avail herself of Geir's untoward emotions, if careful not to rile him. Obviously, he did not want to hear ill of the vixen. She forced a smile.

"Ever I have shared a confidence with the lady," she said softly, brushing his arm and making him flush. "If you lead me to her, I know I can sort the problem out to satisfaction!"

"I would gladly show you the way there, but there is danger in it, lady, and it would guilt me to expose you to it."

Beatta thought quickly, and said words that perked his interest, danger or no. "Mayhap I can satisfy you that she is not a willing guest to the man. Surely a vix— I mean, a woman of her talents would only linger with that one if held hostage! We must get to her if we are to know the truth, and if ever there was one who might charm a way past that Lodur, that one is I."

Geir, ever more impressed by Beatta's boldness and willingness to risk unspeakable consequences on Iseobel's behalf, took her hand and pulled her to her feet. "It would not set well with me to let you go there alone. It is impossible to imagine what might befall you. You are right, though. Force is useless against the man, but a good tale might buy us a way in."

He looked at her admiringly now, and Beatta enjoyed it. But Geir's company in the handsome lord's house, she worried, might hinder a plan that was beginning to take shape of its own accord inside her, so she did not want to encourage him too well.

"Lodur has seen you and knows who you are. You would be hard put to devise a way to make your visit seem innocent. But I" Here she broke off, biting the inside of her cheek and making another show of dimple, for the plan had begun to crystallize, and she realized that she might be able to effectively wreak a double revenge: on Iseobel *and* on Vanaash. She toyed again with her amulet.

Must be the holy woman had set her heart on having that comely, powerful lord all to her own! Recalling Lodur's stunningly sensuous look, Beatta vowed that, before she lifted Iseobel the poisoned cup, she would find an opportunity to steal the man's attentions to herself. Certainly he looked like a hot-blooded one who might be seduced by parted lips and a tempting embrace. She would enjoy falling to the bed with that comely one herself, too! As for Vanaash, what greater pain for him than the realization that his spotless, holy would-be bride had lingered for weeks in the bed of his enemy? 'Twould pay him well for his cold-heartedness to be so leveled, and she herself could not but gain from an alliance with one so wealthy and influential.

"Could be you are right," Geir's voice, seeming to come from far away, interrupted a chain of thought which had taken on a measure of urgency for her. "If we devised a way that you could signal me should you need help, perhaps I would be minded to hide myself nearby and let you try your hand with the man."

"'Tis not a worry. My foster-brother follows me soon with a mass of men, ready to tackle this Lodur if such need be. I will be safe enow."

"Let me at least accompany you there," Geir replied seriously. "I can stand guard till others come to join you."

"Aye," Beatta brightened, hopeful again for the first time in a while. "I will be glad of your assistance, Geir. You are one who most impressed me with your valor!" She spoke earnestly, laying her hand on his arm and happily noticing the little shudder her touch caused him. "I can't imagine how ever I could make my thanks known! To think that just moments ago I was so desperate and now, thanks to your kindness—" She had no need to say more. It was obvious that the man was already intrigued by vague visions of the compensation he imagined she was wont to offer.

Bidding her permission, Geir hefted her trunk atop his mount and, leading his horse, beckoned her to accompany him up the coastal path. Working out details of a plot that Geir believed they had hatched together, Beatta, despite the weariness that plagued her a short while earlier, kept admirable pace next to him all the way to Lodur's manor, though she made certain to find an opportunity or two to stumble and lean demurely on her companion for support.

# Chapter Nineteen

Despite Beatta's hopes, Vanaash missed his foster-sister's fine performance. His thoughts lay elsewhere, and as soon as he had left instructions for his retainers, he headed for the vill.

At the top of the rise where, only weeks before, Roric had fallen to Lodur's marauders, Vanaash peered into the afternoon sun and made his way west along a small rill that babbled its way eastward to the sea. The broad path, rutted and worn from generations of use, led easily to a pretty clearing where sounds of carpentry and smells of freshly hewn wood mingled in the early summer air.

Suspicion greeted him as he approached a group of men, rebuilding a wasted byre. They kept a jealous care of the huts so newly wrought, and Vanaash realized it was because of him and his raiders. Even the few children backed away from their work on a wattle fence and retreated to the far side of the yard.

The men set down the enormous timber that they had been trying to maneuver into place. Their expressions approximated a mix of staunch resignation and mild curiosity. Finally, one of the workers stepped forward and said loud, "It were some men of your ship who beat back Lodur's forces when they lay in wait for you but half a moon ago, was it not?"

"Aye," chimed another, "love have we none lost on such a one as that!" Squinting to peer at Vanaash, he added, "Word has it that he holds our priestess in his house. Could it be that you and your bold men are come to help Dorflin free her?"

Cringing inwardly at the name that had plagued him this month or more, Vanaash made no answer. Holding his urgency in check, for he knew that the less interested he appeared, the more gabble he would hear, he took off his leather hauberk and laid it on a nearby bench before striding over to stand beside the huge timber they held. Indicating that he wished to make himself useful, Vanaash waited for the command to hoist.

"Who is this Dorflin?" he asked casually as they worked.

"You know not of Dorflin?" the man across the timber from him asked, lifting his brows in surprise.

Vanaash strained with effort as he helped heave the column upright. "Could be I know him by another title," countered Vanaash, hoping to finagle the answer by thickening his own accent and feigning poor understanding of theirs.

"Oh, aye," said the other, slower and distinctly louder, "you would know him as the shaman, the priest, the girl's father, perhaps...."

*Her father! Dorflin was Iseobel's father!* A surge of relief swept Vanaash.

"Aye," he answered quickly, his urgency again upon him, "Dorflin! I should meet him at his homestead."

"I would have thought he would meet you there," the man gestured, "near Lord Lodur's grounds!"

Vanaash grabbed an image from the man's mind and saw the path to the manor he sought. "Only if Dorflin has not waited upon my arrival," he replied casually, hoping to imply that the meeting had been predetermined. Casting his gaze as if to mark the sun's course, he added hastily, "and if I am but in time!"

It took all of them, but they managed to set the support in place with a shout. The two strongest held the piece upright while Vanaash and the other four shored up the posthole. When it finally was secure, the householders thanked him for his help and he bid them good day. While still in their view and hearing, he trotted up the northern coastal path until he was under cover of the thickening forest. Then he veered northwest. At length, he knew the manor was near. Then, he carefully loosed his fillet from its pack and placed it on his head.

\*               \*               \*

***"Vanaash!"*** The shriek pierced his thoughts with such force that he fell to his knees for the pain. Vanaash gripped his boar necklace with both hands and, finding small enough strength in its talismanic charms, waited for the inescapable torment in his head to stop. Unable to stand, he clenched the carpet of undergrowth to keep the ground from reeling. Runnels of hot sweat dripped from his face, while a wash of guilt swept over him. If only he had clasped Iseobel to himself half as tightly!

When the cries subsided and he again felt the damp grass between his fingers and heard his own heart pounding, he knew he had come back to himself. He channeled his thoughts and sent as before, *"Iseobel, I come!"*

"'Twill do you no good," came a deep voice from behind him. Vanaash rose; his sword came swiftly to his hand. He spun to face a tall man with a grizzled beard, sheathing his own sword.

"What mean you?" Vanaash asked, backing as he rose, shaken that he could read nothing from this one's mind.

"Sending to her while wearing the boar-headed fillet."

"Why say you such?" Vanaash asked, fingering the handle of his weapon. That the man knew this astounded him yet, oddly, he did not feel threatened. He studied the man at length. Thick hair, once gleaming brown, now streaked with silver, framed a face that showed less age than wisdom, less emotion than spirit. The man's angular build and strangely musical way of moving seemed familiar in some way; his eyes seemed endlessly deep and dreamy. Like hers.... It had to be. Vanaash swallowed. "You are Dorflin," he said, almost with awe.

"And you are Vana Avkomling."

"How know you me and my name?" challenged Vanaash, unconsciously playing with the balance of his sword.

"It is not you I recognize, but Freyr's magick fillet."

Surely few in Midgard ever wore the god's headband, Vanaash admitted to himself, and the headpiece, as far as he knew, had no power to broadcast his name. How much else did this man know? Did this Dorflin realize that he now stood eye to eye with the man meant by the gods to be bound to his daughter?

"If I cannot be read while I wear this fillet, how is't you can glean from my mind what I am here to do?" Vanaash stepped slightly forward, surprised that he did not quite tower over Dorflin as he had hoped he might. Still, he held his voice remarkably steady considering that he now faced the man he had been imagining in his mind for many days as a dire enemy.

"Nay, I cannot read you," Dorflin answered without stepping back. "That is one gift of that head-band. However, I may guess by your stance and your presence that you mean to deliver my daughter from Lodur's company, and I will tell you what you may see for yourself in little time: force shall be feckless."

Vanaash's looked away, and began to lift the fillet from his head. Dorflin stopped him.

"If you do not think that any call you make to Iseobel will be heard, and louder, by Lodur, then you do not know how powerful he is, or how dedicated the witches who work at his bidding, watching and listening day and night for anything that might bode their master ill." The merest wince passed over the man's face. "Sore at heart am I, as well, not to be able to comfort my daughter, but to toss her thoughts of reassurance now would certain her demise."

He stroked his beard, saying no more, but released his hard hold on his private thoughts so that Vanaash was able to glean that the man had a plan in mind. He asked him to describe it.

"Aye," Dorflin replied, apprising him with more respect now. "I do have the means to another way, though it shall tax your powers more sorely than ever did the most lopsided raid."

Vanaash blinked. Questions rose to his lips and died before he asked them. He needed a moment to sort them before he could make sense of half of what this magicker told him. He sheathed his sword and, staving his flood of thoughts, elected first to know more of Lodur and why Iseobel now was at his mercy.

"Perhaps you already know that Lodur is the trickster-god Lokji in his mortal form," Dorflin said. This did not surprise Vanaash, but shored up a suspicion that had come to him often in thoughts and dreams. He nodded, and Dorflin continued. "Having lusted after Iseobel's mother to no satisfaction, he now seems to have settled on Iseobel in her mother's stead." A gleam rose in his eye. "The Norns of fate, however, have smiled upon us."

Vanaash sniffed in spite of himself. The Norns' favor! Well, if the weird sisters who wove the tapestry of life were being kind, he himself had seen no indication of it. Where his future with Iseobel was concerned, the weave of his life's threads seemed to run only tangled and fouled. And now they were knotted up with the villainous Lokji? Oh, yes, the Norns were smiling.

Vanaash frowned. He would listen to Dorflin, but reluctantly. Too many schemes already had gone awry; too many plots had come to naught. This was a time for action, not dreaming. The man was addled if he thought they could count on the good will of Æsgard to save Iseobel from Lokji! He turned his attention back to the manor's structure and grounds.

"It happens that I possess some things Lokji wants even more than he wants Iseobel." Dorflin lowered his voice in a way that lured Vanaash's focus from the estate and enticed him to listen more closely. "To secure these objects, I am certain he would leave Iseobel unguarded. If I can tempt him out with the promise of these prizes, you may be able to enter the manor and guide Iseobel to safety while he is distracted with me."

Vanaash allowed his hope to rise, then remembered the wards that guarded the manor. "What of those witches who scry and do his searching? Will they not raise an alarm?"

Dorflin laughed, and placed a hand on Vanaash's shoulder in fatherly fashion. "Lodur is a powerful adversary and exerts such a strong control that he might cause me to worry for you. As for those who serve him, though, even this short time in your presence convinces me that you might well prove near enough their match. What is more, you wear Freyr's fillet and that is your key."

Dorflin lifted the branch of a nearby bush and swiftly picked a handful of berries, half of which he pressed on Vanaash before eating the others. They were walking together at a leisurely pace now, and both were silent a spell before Dorflin spoke again. "Blocking your thoughts to the seeresses of Lodur is an advantage, however small," he mused. "Your—our—chances of freeing Iseobel will depend as much, though, on courage and planning. Let us sit down together and make a plan."

Vanaash was not in the mood now to be treated like a callow youngster. "Time is not our ally in this, Dorflin," he snapped. "I have a bold army with me! In the space of an hour we can breach that fortress well enough to find her!"

Dorflin scowled petulantly. "You forget that I, too, concern myself foremost with my daughter's safety. Do you think you alone worry for her?" His jaw became rigid. He stroked his bearded cheek as if to hold his tension in check before stopping suddenly. Then, shutting his eyes, he stood silently, his leathery face softened by a dreamy smile.

Vanaash, inexplicably overcome with a sense of calm, was surprised to realize that Dorflin afforded him a new sending.

Unbidden, a scene began to play out in his mind, wherein a figure, shrouded in shadow but for the gleam of a silver-wrought band on his brow, moved unseen among men. The figure hurried not, and had but the most moderate sense of urgency about him. Throughout, a message echoed in his mind: *Bide your time!*

When the sights and sounds had faded somewhat, Vanaash eased his stance and faced Dorflin with a look of consternation. "Can't be you mean to wait ... to leave her there until ..." His voice trailed rather than speak the thought that terrorized him.

Dorflin put an arm around the other's shoulder, an artless gesture at once brotherly and paternal. "Must be you know I would take no chance if I feared that! I have some intelligence of Lodur's purpose, though, and it is reliable. Of necessity, he performs a binding ritual upon Iseobel that requires a full moon cycle. If interrupted, her presence cannot profit him unless he begins again. Were we to stay our movements even a full fortnight, she would be in no more danger than she is now, yet the advantage would be ours. A mighty force will not daunt him nearly as well as two who wield magick with their weapons."

How hard Vanaash found it to even consider the notion of inaction! The man made sense, though. Surely he didn't waste his breath simply for the joy of victory in argument. He was her father and doubtless found as much concern for his daughter's safety as did Vanaash. Too, Dorflin's wisdom made the air fairly sing with its power. Wherefore he surmised Lodur's purpose for Iseobel, Vanaash could not guess, but the man's assumption sounded so certain, Vanaash never thought to question it.

Still, no matter how trustworthy Dorflin seemed, Vanaash could not let himself be persuaded simply by his reassuring manner. The man might be a brilliant magicker, but he certainly didn't look as if he oft swung a sword, and he favored one arm as if it ailed him. Vanaash remained cynical. "So you tell me that the successful entering of this great house is not to be accomplished by force but with this fillet?"

Dorflin nodded. "Cunning you will need as well, and in good measure. But Freyr's boar will wall your mind to all but the most expert probings. So unless you move direct along a sight path, none will mark your presence. Leaving shall be more challenging, I warrant, for Iseobel is spelled, and her groggy mind, as well you realize, runs time to time unbridled. I doubt you will accomplish her release without using sword as well."

In short time, they came to the goddess hut which Dorflin now called home. The shaman lifted the latch and glided across the threshold, his cloak barely stirring when he stooped to pass under the lintel. Vanaash ducked in after him. His nostrils flared involuntarily at the vague herbal attar that permeated the air—the same gentle perfume that had always enwreathed Iseobel. A warm shiver danced down the back of his neck and across his shoulders while the memory of her scent tickled its way into his consciousness.

Filtered sunlight spewed in at the unshuttered casement making the small hut airy and light, far different from the close sod longhouses of the Nor Way with their skin-covered windows and perpetual smokiness. He looked along the rows of drying herbs that hung from the thatched roof framework and again breathed in the heady mixture of smells that mingled lavender with bergamot; roses with yarrow.

"Son."

The gentle word startled Vanaash back to himself.

"Of what use is your fillet when you take no care to erase your thoughts from your face, where any might plainly read them?" Dorflin doffed his cloak and hung it from a peg near the door, then gestured for Vanaash to do the same.

Vanaash teetered between astonishment and frustration. He unfastened his sword belt and looped it over a free peg, then jerked the lacing loose from his hauberk and pulled it off before taking a chair. Must he always appear as stony-faced and humorless as the magickers he had known, even among friends?

The leather-slung chair felt so comfortable that he made a note to build one for Aasa. She would like that. He ran fingers though his hair, tickling it from his face, smiling fondly at a memory of Iseobel, whose hair never could stay neatly bound, but always snaked out about her face and neck in little tendrils.

Dorflin knelt by the hearth and struck a fire in a mound of fresh-laid tinder. "Advantages are few in this world, Vanaash. It is wise to use the ones afforded you." He rose and walked to the kitchening. Selecting two onions, Dorflin set to peeling. "Ask yourself this, then," he said, dropping the paper skins into the growling fire. "Is it not better to keep your thoughts your own until you wish to share them? Or is it in your favor to couch your ways only when you deem you must?"

Vanaash watched the man cross to the planked table and slice the onion. What was it about this Dorflin that made him feel so inadequate? So unprepared? He had been more successful than any raider out of Sogn's harbor, mastered the ways of persuasion, and inspired his men to devotion. How was it that this simple shaman could make him feel as if he had accomplished naught in his life, and yet evince no resentment from him?

Dorflin tested the tuning of every string upon which Vanaash had played his life. These were not trifling observations the man made. He was boring his attention into Vanaash's very nature. Vanaash watched him and waited until the placid eternity behind a pair of sea blue eyes met his gaze.

"What is it about you, Dorflin that clears my vision without drawing my anger?"

"I need make no secret of it to you," Dorflin replied softly as he finished slicing the onion with steady strokes. "I was taught by the White Lady's druids in the Cymry. They believe that the nature of the world is to present its truths openly. Those who study the patterns find wisdom reveals itself. It is the druids' way to be no more obtrusive in their teaching than the lessons taught by the sun, the trees, or the rocks. What the druids have to teach may be painful, but there's no use in being angry with the stones or the oak or the moon."

While Vanaash mutely wondered whether his question had been answered, Dorflin scooped some fat into a shallow iron pot and set it near the fire. When it melted, he added the onions and salted them as he stirred. They sizzled and spat in the heat, turning quickly from white to clear. Just as the pieces started to shrivel and brown, Dorflin moved the pot onto a flat rock near the hearth, and sliced some slabs of bread. Scooping the onions into the trenchers, he gestured Vanaash to eat. Realizing there was nothing to drink, he reached back to fetch a pair of tankards and a wineskin of mead.

"Fresh bread and onions is most welcome after the dried fish I've been eating. Thank you." Vanaash hoped he wasn't wolfing his food too hungrily.

A twinkle sparked briefly in Dorflin's eye. "After lutfisk, moldy cow dung would taste good."

Vanaash snapped his gaze to Dorflin; it had never occurred to him that a Holy might possess a sense of humor. He grinned. "Aye, even green cheese from Jutland tastes good after lutfisk!"

They sat in easy silence, enjoying their meal until Dorflin turned expectantly toward the open door. Vanaash's gaze followed Dorflin's. He saw nothing but the thick fringe of pine boughs shading the doorway; heard nothing but the trill of a lark nearby. He turned questioningly to Dorflin, who merely pointed to the center of his forehead and turned back to watch the door.

The fillet? Hesitantly, Vanaash opened his awareness to the ether. *"For Iseobel alone, I'll do this. For Iseobel alone."* A strange chant; an unfamiliar cadence. Startled to think that these were Dorflin's thoughts, Vanaash let go the thread of them. But of course, Dorflin's thoughts they were not; the shaman heard them, too, and clearly recognized their bearer. *"Her perfection alone makes me worthy."*

Who…? Vanaash started to his feet, but a raised eyebrow from Dorflin sat him back down and reminded him to turn his face to stone. He calmed the blaze in his tourmaline eyes and forced his shoulders down. By the time he slowed his heart to a steady pace, he heard the step of a man along the path.

"Well come, Geir Death-Crooner," Dorflin called out gently before anyone even brushed aside the canopy of pine, then turned to give a wink to Vanaash. "If early on you unsettle one thus determined, it is easier to redirect him should you have need."

Geir's tall frame blocked nearly all the filtered light in the doorway. "Dorflin!" he bowed slightly, but did not otherwise move until the shaman invited him in. With a grace seemingly incompatible with his powerful build, Geir ducked into the hut and removed his sword belt, hanging it near the door. Mutely, he sat where Dorflin indicated he should. He raised his head to look at his host, but did not quite meet the man's eyes. Something about his demeanor cried out to be asked the nature of his errand there.

Though he felt like an intruder, Vanaash focused his attention on the murmurings brought to him by the fillet. By the gods, the poor man was a jumble of emotion with a tenderly cushioned pack of sorrows at the base of them all. Fleeting images of children at play … of Dorflin and Iseobel robed in white … of a tiny hut … of Lodur's manor … *and of Beatta?*

Vanaash lost his concentration. What commonality could these images share? He looked hard at Geir's face. It revealed little, as little as he hoped his own did. How could turmoil and pain of such intensity be masked so well by a simple townsman? There clearly was more to this Geir than Vanaash had measured.

Feeling almost criminal, Vanaash turned his attention to Dorflin's thoughts. Aye. The shaman read Geir's pain plainly and considered how to persuade the man to open up without exploding entirely. Dorflin's marked kindness and gentle patience impressed Vanaash deeply. No doubt there was much to be learned from the man. The wisdom Vanaash sensed set up a craving to acquire of it all that he could.

"You bring news from Lodur's manor, but not exactly of Iseobel, I think."

If Geir were startled by the statement, and Vanaash was sure he must have been, it showed in nothing but a more intense look on the man's face—a stare that gave way in only the smallest degree to relaxation. Vanaash worked quickly to transfer the boar's focus again.

This was more work than he had imagined. All his years of sensing thoughts that came to him unbidden only served to assure him that he read the thoughts borne to him on the boar aright. Those few times he actually tried to command his second sight into seeking had drained him sorely. This was easier to search with, yet far more exhausting. Vanaash channeled into Geir's foremost thoughts again. *Beatta!*

"There is a warrior woman come with this man, I think," Geir started, nodding ever so slightly in Vanaash's direction, "who sought your daughter, Dorflin. I found her on her way to Lodur's manor and promised that I would wait for her to have her way inside safely or conduct her from there to find lodgings." For the first time, confusion showed on his face.

"Yet you have left your watch, Geir," Dorflin said, somewhat accusingly, though mildness shone in his eyes. The magicker scraped his chair back and fetched a tankard, which he placed in front of the Death-Crooner before sitting again.

"Because I was bidden to do so by the very woman!" Geir poured himself some mead and took a long pull, his look of uncertainty growing, as if he could not help but doubt his own words as he spoke them. "She now stays at Lodur's willingly, she says, and assures me that Iseobel does, as well."

By now, the other two were painfully aware of their companion's bewilderment, for Geir's unspoken thoughts showed him unable to reconcile himself to the fact that he had allowed Beatta to enter there, and they saw that he suffered as he silently lashed himself for doing so. The private agony of the man's self-accusation was too painful for Vanaash; as if in concession to the other's discomfort, he unceremoniously lifted the fillet from his head and placed it on the table.

"What was I thinking?" Geir muttered under his breath as if aghast at his own distraction.

"Must be he was spelled!" both Dorflin and Vanaash thought at the same instant and, jarred by the unison of their unexpected mental chorus, they exchanged a swift, surprised look. Dorflin cleared his throat.

"Vanaash, do you know this woman of whom Geir speaks?"

"Oh aye," Vanaash mumbled miserably. 'Tis Beatta, my foster-sister."

Geir looked up quickly at this last. "And this foster-sister of yours. Do you suppose she thinks to spirit Iseobel away from Lodur?"

"Beatta is a woman hard to fathom," Vanaash replied guardedly, trying to hide his thoughts from Dorflin as he reflected bitterly on those things which he knew best served as motivation for his strong-willed foster-sister: jealousy, revenge, and a comely warrior. A stony look settled over his features, for it occurred to him that perhaps Beatta's truer purpose was to spirit Lodur away from Iseobel. He tensed, wishing he hadn't removed the fillet after all, then tried to banish the unwanted thought. Without meaning to, he snuck a worried glance at Dorflin.

Dorflin's face remained impassive and the man said not a word. However, in Vanaash's brief, meandering thoughts, Dorflin had read much of the history that had passed between Beatta and his daughter, and he scarce felt that the Norsewoman's current doings could bode well for Iseobel's plight.

Oblivious of the turn which the other men's thoughts had taken, Geir tapped the side of his tankard, steeped in remorse for his own stupidity, and wondering what could have caused him to abandon Beatta to a fate which he now knew could only prove unfortunate. He pinched a tuft of his beard and twisted it slightly. He lifted his eyes; lowered them; raised them again.

"Seems odd to send a sister to the likes of that lord," he accused tentatively, hoping for another to share, however slightly, in his unwitting sense of guilt.

Vanaash's reply disappointed him. "Few send Beatta where she will not go. Certainly, I have no such influence."

A memory of carrying a kicking, biting hellion crossed Geir's thoughts, but did little to assuage him. "In truth, I do not believe that Iseobel stays willingly there!" he exclaimed forcefully, jumping to his feet and rubbing his temples hard as if to massage away a pain. "I saw her ride out with Lodur one morning, sitting tight against him in the saddle, and she appeared dazzled. The man handled her roughly … and…." He choked a bit and squeezed his eyes shut in sudden revulsion. "She can't be willingly with that man," he repeated dolefully. "And now I have led yet another one straight into Lodur's evil clutches. By the gods, what have I done?"

Moved by Geir's obvious misery, Dorflin reached to touch the man's shoulder. "You have done naught but what you were forced to do by the enchanted atmosphere of that wicked place."

The effect of Dorflin's touch paired with his compassionate whisper caused the blood to rush angrily to Geir's head. Assured now beyond a shadow of a doubt that Iseobel was indeed the dark-lord's captive, he was spurred to rescue her the best way he knew how: by force. He muttered a low oath, shaking. His hand went unbidden to his sword. Then, realizing the weapon was hung near the door, Geir crossed to it. It was Dorflin's voice, stern and domineering in the sudden silence, that stopped him.

"The force that caused you to abandon the woman on Lodur's doorstep is stronger than your will, Geir Death-Crooner. It is far stronger than your sword, also."

As if to emphasize his point, Dorflin leveled an accusing gaze at Geir, who quivered momentarily before releasing his hold on the sword belt. Looking somewhat surprised by his own actions, he turned woodenly from the doorway, returned to the bench near the table, and sat down heavily, still shaking. Vanaash drew a deep breath, admiring the shaman's obvious power.

Anyone passing the open door of that hut an hour later would have seen three men, obviously single-minded in purpose, conversing low, debating, drawing maps in the hearth-ashes, then scattering and redrawing them again. Late in the night, Geir Death-Crooner took his leave, weighted with the responsibility of the charge given him by Dorflin—to secretly alert each and every man of the vill to the probability of a battle-muster before the moon's cycle ended.

Soon after, Dorflin led Vanaash the short way from the hut into the depths of the grove, where enchantments hung heavy in darkness which was only now and again relieved by the snatches of silver moonlight that threaded their way through the thick, shielding boughs. There, in the confines of a huge tree, both hollowed and hallowed, Dorflin seated his student on a stone bench carved by skilled and magickal hands in the depths of Swartalfheim and blessed by Freyja herself.

In the air before the young man's eyes, Dorflin cast a rune of pure blue-white light. To Vanaash, its form at the same time resembled the moon and an eye of astounding depth and brilliance. Could be it would inspire him with a better understanding of Lodur's strengths and weaknesses. In any case, it could not fail to build Vanaash's strength, courage, and inner power for his impending ordeal. Leaving him only a bucket of water, for food would hamper the meditation while water enriched it, Dorflin bade Vanaash to let the light teach him.

For Vanaash, whose soul drank deeply of the light's proffered power, the rush of inspired wisdom was almost tangible, and under the influence of its soothing balm the hours passed like minutes.

Vanaash was not the only one for whom time ceased to exist in the days which followed. Beatta stood now at a dusky thick-paned window, looking down on the somber courtyard below and the seemingly endless purple forest that stretched beyond it, misty in the dawn light. There was a sullen beauty in the grimness of this place, inside and out, and Beatta long ago realized that it mirrored the heart of the handsome warrior who lorded it.

... Or *was* it long ago? Maybe she had only come to that realization in the last few minutes; she wasn't sure. To shake away a threatening sense of confusion, Beatta shut her eyes and tossed her flame-hued hair. Unbound, it reached well past her waist, and it enveloped her now with an unfamiliar sweetness for, by his very own hand, that comely black-haired lord had bathed her last night in perfumed waters, and had worked attars of rare blossoms into her tresses while he whispered to her.

Beatta shook her head again, vehemently this time, for she could not quite recall his promises. Thus it had been since she arrived: a continuous, comforting aura of delicious dreaminess. She knew why, too. Beatta Eiriksdätter, who prided herself on her abilities as huntress and warrior and who had long ago earned herself the known-name of Hard-Axer, was in love.

She had known it the moment she crossed the threshold— whether weeks ago or days ago, she couldn't quite say. Her heart had given itself to him when he greeted her at the looming hearth. The look of the man had entranced her: tall and dark, with sleek hair and glittering eyes of inestimable depth. His splendid manner and conduct had held her transfixed.

They were like-minded, too! Where she had come foolishly supposing this great lord had been taken in by the charms of Iseobel, she had been delighted to learn that he loathed the woman. Though Iseobel had thrown herself into his arms and his bed, he had recognized her for the witch she was. Even now, he held her prisoner to prevent her further poisoning the hearts, minds, and souls of others who might fall prey to her spells.

No, Lodur (Beatta trembled as she silently voiced his name) was far too shrewd to be fooled by the holy woman. There never was a man fashioned as strong and striking as this one! The intensity of his presence was overwhelming. His look, his voice, his touch all bespoke an intermingling of power and beauty that begged to be obeyed. She had waited all her life for a man like this, and the moment he first crushed her in that hard and passionate embrace (last night? last month?) she knew beyond a shadow of a doubt that she was totally, eternally his.

Recalling his arms hot around her caused Beatta to twirl in an uncharacteristically spontaneous dance of delight. As she whirled, she caught sight of her own reflection in the tall, curved looking glass. Quickly, she checked herself with a sharp reprimand. *"Silly as a low-born, lovesick slattern!"* she cried inwardly, assailed by a dim memory of herself hissing those very words at a byre-maid named Kirsten who danced thusly in the barn of the Skogskaale after a kiss from Roric. Beatta frowned momentarily, desperately trying to focus on the vague, half-formed recollection, but in an instant it had all fled: golden-haired Kirsten, her brother's carefree smile, the long ago kiss, and the faraway homestead that had once meant everything to her.

All that remained was her reflection in the priceless glass, and Beatta could not help admiring her own voluptuous figure, displayed to best advantage in the gown of white muslin he had tossed her when he took his leave of her in the midnight.

In the chamber above, Lodur, staring into a small glass ball which rested now in the empty eye socket of a skull that adorned his window sill, was able to admire Beatta, too. Both the mirror and the ball, fashioned in Swartalfheim, had magickal qualities he was careful to keep secret from his guests. He did not watch her long, though. Shiorvan, on the huge bed behind him, was sure to grow wroth if he showed more than a romping interest in the red-headed bitch. He slid his hand inside his linen sark and wrapped his fingers tight around the pendant that hung there—the Midgard Serpent made for him by the darkelves—knowing his hard touch on the thing caused his thoughts to be cloaked beyond fathoming. Even his powerful leman and her witch crone of a mother could not read him when he grasped it. It was all that afforded him precious moments of respite from their constant probings.

Beatta, lusty and responsive, had provided him pleasant entertainment since her arrival, a welcome distraction from the aching desire he suffered for Iseobel ... desire he was forced against his will to keep at bay. Beatta rated highly amongst his countless toys and conquests but, in truth, he already found it tiresome to pretend that he loved and adored her, which play-acting seemed integral to their shared enjoyment and pleasure.

No matter. He would soon have excuse enough to avoid her. Though no one knew as yet, he had planted the seed of a boy-child in her womb the third time he tried her. Mayhap this half-human child would prove to his liking if the boy inherited the brash force-fulness of the mother. Of course, it could not hope to be as perfect as the child Iseobel would bear him—another powerful intermin-gling of Æsir, Vanir, and mortal blood. Shiorvan, though dear to him, had produced a man-child wholly inferior because her claim to Vana-blood was through her despicable weakling of a father, the prettified, hopelessly impotent Lord Freyr. Lodur's own Æsir blood had entirely dominated the boy, the perfect image of his father. Dahraag showed no hint of Vana power, no force or power, and was therefore next to useless as far as Lodur was concerned.

Iseobel, though! Hers was the blood of Freyja herself! His child by her would surely boast the power necessary to fulfill the destiny he envisioned: the groveling subjugation of both the Vanir and Æsir, the birth of a new race of superior Immortals who would rule Midgard with himself as chief of their gods!

Hearing Shiorvan stir, Lodur turned. "Get up!" he told her. His tone was neither cruel nor gentle, but one she had come to know well. "I have need for your magick today, sweetest. 'Twould be best if you would conjure for me a vision of wraiths … several hours worth, at least."

Not wanting to let himself be stirred again by her nakedness as she rose, he turned away and made a pretense of choosing armlets for himself while she put on her shift.

"For Beatta?" Shiorvan's voice sounded hopeful. Indeed, she would scarce be surprised to know that the loud-mouthed vixen had already inspired Lodur's wrath.

"Nay. There is one in the vill who has been speaking bitter-nesses. It seems he is urging the men there to make their weapons ready and be prepared to rise against me."

Shiorvan nodded knowingly. "Geir, the man is called. He is the same makebate who raised a hue and cry when you rode with Iseobel in the village."

"Aye. He is a trouble-maker! Package the spell in a luscious pear or a cold horn of ale—something he'll be unable to resist. Let it take effect in the midnight, when it is dark and he is most likely to cringe in fear."

Lodur slipped a tunic over his sark, cinched it at the waist with a belt of silver, then narrowed his eyes and faced her with a cold smile. "Make sure there is at least a modicum of pain to accompany the vision. In fact, let him writhe."

Shiorvan smiled inwardly as Lodur strode from the room. Oft she resented being forced to put discomfort on those with whom she had no personal quarrel; it seemed to her a sad misuse of power. She had a bone to pick with this Geir Death-Crooner, though. 'Twas he who had led Beatta here. For that, she would not forgive him until Lodur grew tired of the lusty wench and banned her from his bed. In the meantime, she would be glad to cause the man nightmares and agonies.

# Chapter Twenty

The massive stable door slammed shut behind Lodur's stallion. He paused. Abruptly, as a hound regaining the scent, he mounted and quit the courtyard, then cantered to the woods' edge. Peering into the gloom of the thick forest, his wary motion belied a readiness to spring free from unseen snares. He had brought but ten Helsmen with him. More would have cost him precious concentration.

*"Lodur."*

He whirled at the voice which sounded in his head.

*"Lodur. South."*

Lodur signaled to the ten, and they quickly and quietly broke ranks with him, disappearing along with their mounts into the forest shadow. Stepping from his mount carefully, Lodur turned and followed along the rim of the clearing. When he came to a sturdy chestnut tree, Dorflin emerged from its shadow.

"Ah, priest, 'twas you after all," said Lodur without a hint of surprise in his voice. "What bargain will you strike?"

"I would have back a certain bind-ring."

"And not your daughter?" Lodur queried, arching a single eyebrow. "How you surprise me! Can't be you care more for objects of darkelf magick than for your own wench?"

"Odd that you should concern yourself for mortal motives with you so nearly back in Æsgard," countered Dorflin cagily. He narrowed his eyes. "Aye, my daughter I will have also."

Dark eyes glowered. "Your trade will I make, wizard. But how then will I know the pieces are truly in your keeping?"

Reaching up his billowing sleeve, Dorflin withdrew an alabaster thrall. "This I present to you now. Once the ring and Iseobel are safely under my protection in my own grove, then shall I reveal the mate to this thrall."

"You cajole the White Bitch of the Cymry to serve you?!" Lodur spat. A look of rage played across his tensing features.

By way of answer, Dorflin turned toward his grove. "If you would have a matched pair, Lodur, 'tis best you follow."

Waiting for Dorflin to draw Lodur away, Vanaash stopped to cast his mental net. With the skill of a driver playing the reins of a team of twelve, he singled out the one he sought the most. Honing in, he was disturbed that Iseobel seemed so muddled—no image took full shape before replaced by another hazy shadow—but he took no alarm, for he sensed also that she felt safe.

Concealed in a thicket of hazel, he stared at the high stone wall surrounding the manor. The runlets of ivy that crept up its walls were near fully green, but the leaves had not thickened so much yet that they obscured the many symbols and pictures incised there. Gripping beasts, holding their own necks as firmly as they held helpless creatures, made a graceful design, broken now and then by an image of a warrior. Along the top of the wall, the undulating body of a double-headed dragon looped so that, as far as Vanaash could tell, each passageway was protected by a snarling head coming round from either side.

The courtyard did not look wide. Crossing it might be less trouble than he had feared, especially if he entered where there looked to be a small orchard between the outer wall and the manor. He hoped that a doorway lay near the cover of the trees.

He set to watching for a pattern in the sentry. Guards came into view now and then at the gateway, but patrolled in only one direction. None ever crossed the sentries' path from Vanaash's left. How complacent they had grown in the service of one so feared! They scarce cast a glance in any direction.

*Checkmate.*

Vanaash stiffened as the sound of the word surrounded him, certain from the clarity of it that Dorflin must be nearby and shouting. A moment's concentration convinced him otherwise. Though a furlong away, Vanaash heard the enticing call to Lodur exactly as Dorflin had told him he would. Lodur, he knew, would follow, fully distracted by the magicker's promise. It was time.

Marveling once more at the strength of Dorflin's powers, Vanaash drew a deep breath, then darted furtively toward the eastern wall. Timing his way through a service gate so as to miss the patrol, he moved swiftly under the canopy of crabapple and cherry blossoms. Once in their shadow, he paused. In a calculated attempt to calm his racing thoughts, he leaned against the trunk of a sheltering tree, and waited for the pounding of his heart to subside. He needed to rely less on his eyes, he reminded himself, and a week's training and meditation had thoroughly convinced him that this headband was far more than an adornment. It was a worthy piece of battle gear. Of fine-wrought filigree, it was fragile, yet it served as weapon and shield alike. Now more than ever he had need to trust to his gods-given talents and assume his mortal senses to be inadequate.

Combing the atmosphere once again, he found the air awash in indistinct noise. He tightened his headband and gripped his boar amulet. Still, the manor was unreadable. He inched forward. Scanning the second story casements, he noticed that one, mostly hidden by a sweeping bough, stood ajar. He made straight for the foot of a tree which seemed the perfect ladder to the window.

He was mere steps from its mossy trunk when he sensed motion. Catching his breath, he froze alongside a twisting crabapple, scarce daring to look but unable to stop himself.

In a blue and white frock so subtly woven that it looked like cloudy skies, a woman stood by the garden door. The first sight of her tall, willowy form, the cascade of moon-blonde hair, the pale, perfectly sculpted face, caused in him a trembling of emotion almost unmatched in his history. He was flooded with feelings akin to old memories for which he could find no reasonable explanation. Was it her beauty? The artless grace of her movements? For a moment he stood paralyzed. Then his wits returned and he realized his danger.

His mouth went dry; his mind raced. If he drew his sword, her screams would alert the household to his presence. Yet he had been seen and could not well proceed without in some wise waylaying the woman. Unless he could silence her long enough to use the fillet, flight seemed the only other choice—but a choice he would not make, not while Iseobel....

*Calm yourself, Vanaav Komling! Must be you know there is no time for hesitation now! For Iseobel's sake you must not falter.*

Stunned by the soundless sending, Vanaash began to form an answer, but the woman motioned him to silence, then stepped back into the dark doorway, beckoning him to follow. Suspicious, his sword at the ready, his energy channeling into the fillet, Vanaash inched forward, wondering how it was she knew his name and mission. Wordlessly, she pointed to her brow.

As if in echo, he touched his finger to his own forehead. Ah yes, the boar-fillet! Shedding his doubts, Vanaash pushed himself close to the woman in the safety of the dark entryway. His fillet-enhanced powers had convinced him all at once that she meant him no harm, and he was thoroughly confused. As if sensing his welling questions, she placed one finger gently to his lips, cautioning him not to speak, but he ignored her.

"How is it you mean to help me? 'Tis plain that you are one of the witches who serve him!"

She gave a whisper of lilting laugh. "Witch I may be, Vanaash, but no matter what you or any in the Nine Worlds may think, I serve no one. If the gods grant me a vision of how things are meant to be, I work for that purpose and care not at all who benefits and who suffers for my doing of it!"

She knew his familiar name, too! He quivered, but replied stolidly. "'Twas the very encouragement I needed at this time, lady, to know that my having Iseobel is a thing meant to be!"

"'Tis not what I said. Mayhap you toy with my words or know more than I. All I know with certainty is that she is not meant to be here, in his house."

Vanaash did not have to bend to hear for she was nigh as tall as he. Though anxious to be about his task, he felt a welcome warmth in her presence and was somewhat wroth to leave.

"Even so, you must be gone quickly," she admonished, as if hearing him. "You will find there is nothing in the way of safe or familiar in this place, so I shall provide you guidance."

"I would be glad for your company. Mayhap you can flee this odious place with us."

"Nay! You cannot succeed with me alongside. My place is here. 'Tis Sron who will go with you!"

While she spoke, Vanaash felt more than heard a rustling in the darkness beyond and was surprised by the appearance of a fierce-some warrior unlike any Vanaash had ever seen. Pale of visage, extremely comely, his long white hair was wrapped into a thousand tiny braids, tucked here and there with feathers, ties, and tokens. He was fully clad in battle gear of ancient make but of the finest workmanship—a gleaming hauberk of silver mail, a leathern jerkin laced with gold bosses and precious stones, and a sword inscribed with powerful runic symbols. The creature himself seemed to glow, in fact—not anything that would be noticed in the daylight, but there in the heavy shade he emitted a hint of phosphorescence that could not be ignored.

So impressive was the warrior, that it took Vanaash a while to realize he was small, his head not much higher than Vanaash's chest. His hands were small, too, but in no way maidenish. Diminutive, formidable, commanding: it could only be....

"Aye! Sron is a lightelf!" Shiorvan smiled as if pleased. "Rarest of creatures to be seen in Midgard, come from his home in Alfheim long years since."

Vanaash eyed the woman with renewed appreciation. Members of Alfheim's bold, ancient warrior race were wroth to let themselves be seen by many—yet these two were fond friends.

Once again, the woman cut off Vanaash's thoughts. "A fond friendship we do maintain, indeed, but Sron risks much for it!"

"How so?" Vanaash's eyes darted from one to the other. The woman tossed her head proudly and laughed.

"Must be you have not heard much of me, if you do not know that the Vanir most-times shun me. They lord the lightelves, as you know, and would be none too happy to know this one oft lingers and shares news and deep thoughts with me here!"

Vanaash cast her a wan grin. "'Keep a friend against the odds, but ne'er against the gods!'" He quoted the adage as if it were a question, and she nodded, looking glum.

"Aye. Sron has proven true to me, and will to you also. You could not ask for a better guide."

Vanaash shook his head insistently. "Nay, he is too visible! 'Twill be impossible to make my way unseen with this one glowing alongside me!"

"Can't be you are so ill-schooled! None can see a lightelf when he uses magick cloak and shield to make himself invisible. Only those of the Vana blood can see through those disguises."

"And other lightelves!" Sron added, tugging on the strap that held his long-shield. He pulled it in front of himself, as if ready for battle. "If I hide behind this, none else will see me, be they human, dwarf, giant, darkelf or Æsir."

Squinting, Vanaash noted that even to his own eyes, the elf seemed somewhat less tangible when it stood behind the shield, visible but difficult to discern. He cleared his throat. "I will be privileged to have you alongside me, Sron!" Then he looked back at the woman and asked what she was called.

"Shiorvan."

"As you are able to see your elf companion well enough, 'tis plain that you are of Vana blood yourself."

"I am."

This admission, so frank and artless, filled Vanaash with wonder. There was something nagging at him ... something he could not place: a story Aasa told him about Freyr's begetting a child who was stolen away and made to serve Lodur.

"Shhhh!" Shiorvan's hiss jarred him and made him jump. "Still your mind!" she demanded sharply. "Fillet or no, there are certain thoughts—certain names—that have a sacred power all their own. And if such can be fathomed by me, you mustneeds fear that he might be made aware of them, too!"

Vanaash swiftly began an apology, but she hushed him with a wave of her hand. "Best you should realize the danger we are in, is all. We have lingered long enough. To cover our meeting, another is engaged in littering the air with thought-noise. I must soon take over else my presence will be missed by—" here she stumbled, as if afraid to voice the name.

Vanaash nodded knowingly and was suddenly flustered to realize he was making a conscious effort not to think of Lodur's name. He shook his head hard, as if to banish his own thoughts. Shiorvan and Sron, watching him closely, laughed, amused by his struggle. Reddening, he drew a deep breath.

"I will be about my task now, lady! Tell me where I must go, and accept my thanks for the gift of your assistance!"

"Gift? I never offer gifts. I do but strike bargains."

Her voice was suddenly cool, the set of her mouth harder, though it scarce detracted from her beauty. He swallowed hard.

Shiorvan leaned forward nearly touching his fillet. "I can put two fingers to that ornament you wear, and you will know every door, hall, and closet in this cavernous place. You will see clearly where both of them are: your long-desired lovely and your stunt-brained sister. With Sron to work unseen against any guards who cross your path, you will have scant trouble finding them, and less trouble removing the one and restraining the other. Once you are out the door, your memories of the place will fade and all inside here will lapse foreign to you again. That will be of no matter, for by then you will have your lady in your arms and the both of you will be on your course away."

"And in return?"

"In return, you will burden yourself to rescue a hapless woman, weak and old in body but astonishing in spirit and power. One who has suffered much and must be moved from this place—" Her voice broke off with a sob, but she stifled it and faced him, eyes blazing. "That is my bargain. Agree to it, else you will stumble haplessly through these haunted halls in vain, until strong enchantments draw you deep into his maze of darkness. You will wander 'til you are entirely at his mercy."

Vanaash felt a shiver traverse the length of his frame. He bit his lip hard, considering. "How will I know 'tis not some trick that she is sent along with us," he asked carefully, "to weave a mental trail marking to wherever it is that we flee?"

"This is the bargain I offer. Weigh the risks yourself. That boar-headed fillet is both weapon and shield alike," she said. "Now more than ever, you must trust to your gods-given talents and assume your mortal senses to be inadequate."

Vanaash caught his breath. She had echoed in exact words the very admonition he had given himself earlier! Had she penetrated his thoughts through the barrier of the fillet? If so, what was the connection between them? He pondered on this fruitlessly a moment. Then, deciding to trust her, he asked how he might be expected to recognize the woman in question.

Shiorvan laughed. "You will know her, Vana Avkomling. She hides herself well, but Sron can lead you to her should you fail to find her after I put the promised touch to your fillet. She is the only other one in this house who will see the lightelf, save you, I and your lady."

She reached forward again, but Vanaash grabbed her wrist. "There is more to this than you tell me!" he growled. "I sense that you would spell me in some way if you put a hand to me!"

As if appraising him with more of a respect, Shiorvan lowered her hand, cheeks flushing. "You read me well, Vanaash!" She held her palm open to reveal a small golden rune. "'Tis naught but a rune I would have placed on your person for luck."

Warily, Vanaash took it from her hand and studied it. It was a well made rune of TEIWAZ, ↑, symbolizing justice through self-sacrifice. He was more familiar than most with the runes of the FUTHARK, and often had meditated on the ↑ rune, since it cropped up frequently in castings he had done for Aasa and for Wulf. He was not as highly schooled in the magickal arts as some, but his finely honed power of intuition told him that this particular rune was different. Eyes narrowed, he tried to fathom it and was rewarded with a revelation.

"You have spelled the thing!" he exclaimed. "Must be you are a doer of galdor-work!"

"Aye. I worked hard and furtively to fashion it."

"Its purpose?"

"The old woman ... she would have read it as my promise to join her in this escape. 'Tis certain she will not leave this place without me."

For a moment, Vanaash was confused, for he was certain that Shiorvan did mean to run away with them. Dropping the stave back into her hand, though, he recalled suddenly that the truth was just the opposite—she had stressed to him earlier that she would not leave. Fighting bewilderment, he eyed her accusingly. "That is the purpose of the stave's magick then? That others will read your intent falsely?"

"'Tis not that there are others," she whispered miserably. "Only one—one who must be free of this place but will linger as long as she thinks that I mean to stay."

Shiorvan averted her face, but Vanaash locked his fingers in her gleaming hair and gently turned her gaze to his. He was only slightly surprised by the tears that had welled in her eyes. "She is your mother?" he asked. Shiorvan nodded.

He loosed his hold and paced away, trying to collect his thoughts. Shiorvan, he could see, was a galdor-worker. Despite her Vana-blood she was skilled in the Æsir art of magick-speak. With incantations, she could reshape the power of the runes to fulfill her own objectives. 'Twas a dark and powerful skill, one oft frowned upon by those of Vana blood, much the way the Æsir resented the art few if any of them ever mastered: the Vanir ability to create and invoke runes that were not of the FUTHARK.

That the woman should have learned and excelled in this art did not surprise him, considering who had mentored her since her arrival in this grim place. Still, he felt not the dread he might have expected to feel in the presence of one powerful in the Æsir arts. No, what disturbed him more was that he felt a bond of kinship, as if they had shared a history or a secret past. It made him feel helpless. He wrestled with these thoughts for minutes that felt to him like hours before he spoke again.

"I am minded not to play this game with you," he said finally, his voice strained. "I do not know what power holds you to this place, or whether the aid you offer me is of a fashion good or totally unholy. Might be you are my enemy, or Iseobel's. On the other hand, might be, even though tightly bonded, that you are his enemy." He was careful not to voice the name.

Shiorvan swallowed back sobs. "The fact is," he continued, "I do not know you. Seems you have guarded yourself from being known by any—for good or ill, I cannot say. But I have come of late to understand the strength of love between child and mother, and have tasted myself of the devotion that it brews."

He had walked further into the darkness in the silence that followed his words, but now he spun to face her. "You said I should trust my powers, and my heart tells me you make this move in good stead, even in self-sacrifice, so I accept your bargain, and will help you as you have agreed to help us."

Shiorvan's fingers flew to her lips, only half stifling an exclamation of relief. She sprang forward lithely. Vanaash thought she meant to kiss him, but she stopped herself, and he became aware, all at once, that she feared she might not have time this day to perform the complicated enchantments that would keep him from knowing that another man had touched her.

"I beg you to take the runestave," she said, displaying it again. In the dimness it seemed to emanate a pale green light. "You must promise to hold tight to it all the while so that she thinks I will join with you, else she will refuse your help in leaving. Sron will bring it back to me once she is safely away. She will not be able to see him— she has no Vana blood in her. Only does her wayward daughter, who had no say in choosing it!" Her voice was strained and tortured.

"So 'tis certain you will not be joining us?"

She shook her head hard; the moon-blond hair shimmered in the half light. "You spoke before of a black power that holds me here. 'Tis not so grim as that. Only that I have a son. His son. That is my bond to this place. My mother so despises the father that she mistrusts and fears the boy. She would be glad to see me lose him. He is the curse, she thinks, of our existence."

"Can't be he is so terrible if you are the one who schooled him! Must be she can see that."

"He is comely and of uncommon powers, but the temper and arrogance of his Æsir blood will ever need much taming and a stern Vanir hand nearby. 'Tis only his Vana blood that keeps him from being the very image of his father in more ways than his look. How could I abandon him now, just as he comes to manhood? With me, he will grow to be a great boon to the Vanir, steeped strong in those of our ways which most desperately need preserving. Without me, though, he would grow more and more like ... him. At length, he would be a threat to us all ... might even fulfill the worst of my old mother's fears."

Vanaash felt a disconcerting warmth surge through him. It was strange not only to feel the strength of Shiorvan's emotion but to recognize it for what it was. Strange, too, that he somehow knew, despite her protestations, that her love was not lavished on her mother and son alone. There was a secret chamber in her heart, shadowed and sad, filled with desire for the dark one. Vanaash's heart was inexplicably pained by the realization that Shiorvan found something to adore in the perverse beauty of the man she knew to be her own mortal enemy. The thought sobered greatly him.

Shiorvan's brisk tone broke him from his thoughts. "As you surmised, Iseobel is bespelled. Her runes and amber cats have been taken from her, and her mind shall not clear until the amulet is restored. You will find her things in the garderobe by the bed. I will go now and help confound Lodur with mind-noise until Sron guides you safely to where my mother stays."

Vanaash thanked her earnestly. He did not word a farewell. Unspoken between them was the certainty that they would see each other again, when circumstances were not so crucial.

Shiorvan dropped the softly glowing rune into his waiting hand. Then, eyes clenched in concentration, she touched his fillet, infusing him with a tense desire to be on his way. As if in response to an unspoken command, Sron stepped forward boldly.

Vanaash turned and started hesitantly into the darkness. Strangely, Shiorvan was nowhere to be seen now but, close to where she had been standing, he saw the dim outline of a heavy door, and he knew that beyond it was a hall that led, with only three turns and a long trek up a winding staircase, to the room where Iseobel languished, listening to Beatta's tirade.

Lithely, Sron peered through the latch-hole. Apparently satisfied that the way was unobserved, he opened the door silently and signaled Vanaash to follow. There was no question but that the headstrong elf meant to take the lead, though Vanaash could picture their route and their destination quite clearly, and found the meandering passageways of the great manor as familiar as his own Skogskaale. Uneventfully, they reached the base of the dark stairway in little time.

Flat against the wall, they paused to listen. Vanaash heard no sound save that of his own pounding heart. Treading evenly, he followed Sron up and onto the landing. Pausing once more to coax a single distinct impression from the magickal humming that permeated the place, Vanaash perceived no wardens, only a sudden awareness of Iseobel and Beatta nearby.

Of Iseobel, his vision was vague. Beatta, though, he could sense with unwonted clarity. She was berating Iseobel, and Vanaash flinched at the despicable meannesses emanating from her. Rather than anger, he felt a tug of fear for his foster-sister, sensing a taint about her. She was different, he knew. Her time in this wretched house of darkness had changed her.

Vanaash shuddered and followed Sron into the hallway. The flickering torches set into wrought-iron sconces in the recessed alcoves of the enormous passageway cast peculiar shadows, effecting an eerie sense of animation to the scenes on the many tapestries. Yet Sron made his way forward quickly. Too quickly, thought Vanaash until he recalled no one else could see the elf.

Nevertheless, though Sron impatiently gestured him forward, Vanaash stopped at the next corner and reached out with his mind to probe for guards. Satisfied that the way was clear, he caught up just as the elf unlatched the far bedroom door and entered warily. With a last searching glance down the hallway, Vanaash shut the door silently behind them.

His heart lurched at the sight of Iseobel. Never had she seemed so frail and vulnerable. Folded miserably in a massive ebony bed that was carven over with mystic symbols, she leaned heavily into a pile of brocade polsters and richly sewn pillows. Near her feet, looking comfortable on an array of huge cushions, Beatta reclined, picking fruits and sweetmeats from a golden tray on a small table where also rested a silver-wrought wine flagon and goblets. His foster-sister had not heard them enter.

Vanaash, in the shadows near the doorway, stiffened when Sron leapt forward and stood, masked behind his cloak and shield, directly in front of Beatta. It was plain at once, though, that his foster-sister could neither sense nor see elf. Sron had seemingly drawn the attention of Iseobel, though. She turned lusterless eyes toward him, and squinted as if trying to discern something just beyond her line of sight.

Still unaware of the intruders, Beatta continued the thread of her discourse. "Aye, I know one at least of your discarded lovers who will be interested in learning how you put yourself into Lodur's bed in your vain attempt to suck away his powers in order to enhance your own!" she exclaimed, popping a grape into her mouth. "Roric is dead and Geir too simple to care, but Vanaash has not yet realized how you tried to seduce him for your own witchy purposes. He still believes you virginal and ... holy." Beatta spat the word as if with disgust.

"Foster-brother?" Iseobel lifted her eyes inquisitively, but seemed to exert much effort in forming the question.

""Aye! The one whose powers you wanted for your own! Had I not stepped in, you might have slipped next to him under the covers and tried to drain him as you tried with Lodur! Little fool, you never suspected that Lodur was so strong he could avail himself of you without passing you an ounce of his gods-given magick! Disappointed, were you? He feels nothing for you but disdain, and hence he keeps you here a prisoner."

Vanaash, silent in the gloom, heard these words with a clench of despair and they worked upon his heart like graters upon mace, numbing him.

Still, Beatta had not finished. She licked her lips, which Vanaash noticed were dyed obscenely red now, giving her the look of a harlot, pretty but false.

"Others might have been lost once entangled in your clutches," Beatta pronounced with a sniff. "Not a strong and gifted lord like Lodur, but lesser, unworldly men like Vanaash!"

"Vanaash?"

Iseobel spoke the name like a question, but Vanaash felt it in his head like a piercing, desperate scream. Unwilling to hold himself back any longer, he lunged forward with a harsh growl, drawing his sword at the same instant Sron did.

With a choking cry, Beatta flew to her feet, astonished. Iseobel, with obvious struggle, fought her languor and rose, nearly upsetting the little table. Beatta jumped to steady the refreshments then leapt to embrace her foster-brother.

"Vanaash!" a strange smile twisted her gaudy mouth. "At last you have come to see Iseobel get her due! Could be you have already realized what has been revealed to me by Lord Lodur—the magicker who is immune to her 'charms' and vows to hold her here, keeping her from poisoning the minds of men."

"Beatta ..." started Iseobel, fighting her torpor to comprehend. "Vanaash?"

"Come," Beatta patted the bed, encouraging Iseobel to sit again, "I think you shall find she has naught to say in her own defense." Barely pausing to take breath, she turned on Iseobel, "Tell him, holy-woman, why Lodur keeps you here!"

"Beatta,"Vanaash reddened in anger,"I scarce expect you understand the nature of Lodur—nor the danger you put yourself into as well by serving him!"

"I am able to look out for myself!" Beatta bristled."I have aligned myself with one who has the intellect and skill to repay this witch at last for all the pain she has afforded us?"

"What say you?" Vanaash was astonished, "Iseobel is no sorceress and she has dealt you no pain at all. And the only grief I have suffered was in the losing of her."

"Your brain is ever yet muddled with her spells." Beatta bit back, "This wench has served us platters full of hurt, beginning with the guiling of our brother Roric unto his death."

"I killed Roric not!" Iseobel cried out, lurching once more to her feet. Made dizzy by rising too fast, the color drained from her face. She shot out a hand to grab the sturdy bedstead, but missed her mark and reeled precariously. Anxiously, Vanaash dashed forward to steady her trembling form. With a solicitous touch, he tenderly brushed the wisps of dampened hair from off her brow, and the cool graze of the silver armlet given him by the darkelves served to revive her equanimity.

"Hush, you! Sit down and settle your nerves with a cup of mead," commanded Beatta, abruptly handing Iseobel the goblet which sat full on the table."You will hear yourself accused, though I doubt not you have already formulated a reasonable explanation for each of your atrocities."

There was something contrived about this invitation to drink, and it made Vanaash suspicious. True, Beatta missed no chance to remind others of their faults, but seeing to Iseobel's comfort while berating her...? Something was amiss. Vanaash watched as Beatta's eyes followed the cup which she so pointedly had thrust into Iseobel's hands. Alarmed, Vanaash moved toward his foster-sister, but Beatta snapped at him to be still. "I will have my say with her, and you. Put away that sword and hear of the sordid dealings of your precious priestess!"

Facing Iseobel again, Beatta raged on, "How long, reckon you, would Vanaash have suited your lustful sport, enchantress? My brother Roric was scarce cold 'ere you ran to the arms of the man called Dorflin. Hardly half a moon phase more passed and, already tiring of the last man you bespelled, you tried to become cozy at home with yet another—the very one you would conveniently blame for forcing Roric to his sorry grave! But this last one, clever Lodur, has seen past your wicked weavings and now, finally, here is an end to your wiles."

Iseobel set the goblet down and looked at Beatta without a single glimmer of comprehension registering on her face. "Beatta," Vanaash forced his tone to one of soothing as he crossed to Iseobel, "this outburst becomes you not. You scarce understand who this Dorflin is. And Lodur ... surely you can see he holds her here against her will for his own ill purposes."

Wishing he could snap Iseobel to her senses, Vanaash put his hand gently on her shoulder. Just the nearness of her brought Shiorvan's hurried message about the amulet back to him.

Glancing about the room, Vanaash spied the garderobe exactly where he had expected it to be. Sideling quietly toward it, he nudged open its door. There, as Shiorvan had said they would be, were Iseobel's things. He let Beatta rant on while she waved the goblet of mead under Iseobel's nose. Stealthily, he thrust Iseobel's Frankish sword, still in its fine-made sheath, into his own beltings and, fingering the cats and runepouch, pulled them unseen behind his back.

"I have seen her try to seduce Lodur," Beatta spat, "with my own eyes."

Vanaash casually fastened Iseobel's necklace around her throat. She gripped the amulet automatically, fingering the finely carven cats. Almost as soon as she clenched them to her, her eyes became more focused, her look more lucid. Vanaash could almost sense the fog begin to disperse from her mind.

Beatta strode purposefully to Iseobel and thrust the goblet back into her hands. "A choice will I give you now, holy woman. Either absent your sorcering self from our lives of your own accord by drinking that mead or I shall see to it another way!"

Sron's ephemeral hands flashed frantically around the goblet; Iseobel watched him with interest. Suddenly, Vanaash understood what Beatta was about. The capsuled amulet that she had worked so casually to hide from him on shipboard, he noticed, no longer hung from her neck.

Poison!

"No!" Vanaash knocked the cup from Iseobel's hand. He drew his weapon and smashed the goblet. "You shall not injure her!"

"We never will be free of this witch and her curses until she is poisoned or beheaded, you fool! At least, allow someone with courage to act!" Quickly, Beatta kicked the table over onto him. Vanaash leapt out of the way, but in so doing, turned his back on Beatta. She grabbed the Frankish sword from the sheath at his beltings. She swung it up to face him, but he blocked her with a hold so clashing that a spark flew off his blade. Leaning with a terrific force, Beatta forced their swords hilt to hilt. Vanaash wavered.

'Twould be next to impossible, Iseobel knew, for Vanaash to force himself to wound Beatta enough to stop her. Scurrying out of the way of the flashing metal, Sron pivoting to protect her, Iseobel ran around to the other side of the bed and dove her hand between the cushions, searching frantically for the rune gift from Shiorvan. Rife with power, PERTHO, ᛈ, would prove itself a match to any weapon! Willing herself to concentrate and gripping her cats tensely, she called upon the rune until it sizzled with vitality. With a life of its own, the rune's red light flashed high and vibrant. Beatta, startled, turned. In that instant, Sron, reaching high, raised his sword into the air behind her and brought the flat might of it down onto the back of her head. Stunned, Beatta crumpled to the ground.

# Chapter Twenty-one

Iseobel stared wide-eyed at the elf. "My friend!" she exclaimed, her voice soft with wonder.

Sron blushed visibly. "Aye!" he replied in a self-conscious whisper. "I am that presence you felt as a warm comfort when things were low with you here! 'Tis well you see me clearly now, for it means your senses have been somewhat restored to you!"

Vanaash shifted uneasily. "Let us be swift on our way!" he urged. He was anxious to complete his tasks and be gone, for the eeriness of the place had begun to encroach upon his senses in an uncomfortable way. Then, suddenly remembering it, he drew Iseobel's sword from Beatta's limp hand and thrust the hilt toward Iseobel.

Iseobel's reaction, one of hesitation and a wistful smile, confused him. He was too distracted to read that the sight of the sword had forcefully brought to mind a vivid picture of the one who had gifted it. It seemed she had not thought of Roric in ages, and the rush of fond memories threatened to engulf her.

"We must move swiftly, Iseobel!" Vanaash jarred her back to reality as he fastened the sword belt at her waist.

"A moment," whispered Iseobel, sheathing the weapon. She

glanced to Beatta's limp form, "I would leave a runeform to guard her, for she has played us false and will not be slow to do so again."

"Can't be you believe Beatta could be held fast by glowing light?" Vanaash's voice was skeptical.

"Aye, Vana Avkomling," broke in Sron, "Lady Iseobel well knows the power of her runemagick. She does well to fetter this treacherous one in such potent shackles."

Holding her necklace for another measure of strength, Iseobel blanked her gaze at the space over Beatta. "PERTHO," she invoked, her left hand describing the spilling-cup shape, "rune of mystery; rune of wyrd: I call upon you now to fasten the foot of all things past upon this beaten one. Let the next step she takes fate her to embark on the road to Hel's realm, else let her take no step at all."

A phosphorescent Ƿ appeared, large and carmine with jagged points turned downwards to hold Beatta captive like a nutshell might jail a beetle. Iseobel gave one more squeeze to her cats before she blinked to focus again on Sron and Vanaash.

"I sense you have business yet unfinished," she said levelly, looking from one to the other of them.

Vanaash nodded. Then, again as if thoroughly familiar with the layout, he moved to the huge tapestry which Iseobel so absently had studied these many long nights. Confidently pulling the hanging aside, he opened a small door which lay concealed behind it. Beckoning them to follow him to the hidden hallways, he took one last look at Beatta before pulling the door shut. Satisfied that she was dead to the world and had not observed them, he poked his fingers through the crack in the door to re-align the wall-hanging behind them.

The musty passageway was dim, and the stone walls damp and covered over with rime and cobwebs. The dust that rose with every footstep showed that few had trod these ways of late. Now and then, these halls, which extended around the entire span of the outside walls, opened onto outdoor catwalks leading to other portions of the manor. The three moved in line, whether walking the accessways or hunching down to pass the open walks unseen: Iseobel following Sron and leading Vanaash.

Crouching as they approached an outdoor balustrade and pointing furtively upwards, Sron turned and spoke to Vanaash. "'Tis in that high turret you shall find the old one."

Vanaash looked up with a surge of fear. The tower loomed high above them, grim and narrow with windows few and small. The exterior was honed smooth and slick with nary a crevice in which to fit a hand or foot. Vanaash swallowed hard. "'Tis from that place we must then make our escape…." he trailed in a miserable voice.

Following his gaze, Iseobel's heart filled with dread, but there was not a moment of hesitation in her resolve. "There is a woman there!" she exclaimed softly. "A woman old and wise. I have dreamt of her … dreamt that she danced in the moonlight in a meadow beyond the Skogskaale and that darkelves knelt to do her bidding for the Vana gods had put a mark upon her breast."

Vanaash stilled her, but he nodded for, of a sudden, it occurred to him that once, long ago, he had dreamt a similar dream. "She is our unfinished business, Iseobel!" he whispered. She squeezed his hand to let him know she understood.

Listening, sensing, at every turn, the three climbed unobserved to the unlocked door which stood, without benefit of a landing, at the stairwell's top, moving quickly until safely locked within the chamber. Vanaash approached the woman, who was crouched over a scrying bowl, and gently touched her shoulder. As the woman looked up, Vanaash gaped in recognition. Only a surge of self-control hindered the cry of *"Am-ma"* that pushed at his lips. This was the woman who had raised him from a babe! He stood speechless in the presence of Sunniva Baardsdätter, revered for her powers in all the Nine Worlds.

"My Vanaash! Shiorvan has apprised me you come. She works charms to furnish calming babble to Lodur's mind while she watches his movements," Sunniva said calmly, swiping her thick curtain of white hair behind her shoulders and lifting her frail-looking arms to hug Vanaash close.

Wholeheartedly, he returned the fervent gesture and bent to brush his face affectionately against her softly wrinkled cheek. "True. We mean to take you with us, and we must be swift."

Sunniva, her pinched face drawn with worry, squinted hard at him. "Shiorvan will meet us near the forest gate, or not?"

Her voice had an accusatory edge but Vanaash, squeezing the runestave given him earlier, found it easy to lie. "Aye. She provides us cover now and works enchantments to hide her own going." He did not feel guilty and knew it was thanks to the runestave's power.

Though Iseobel, not knowing why, raised an eyebrow at his words, Sunniva relaxed. "In that case, we have much to do. Iseobel, belay your puzzlement! You shall soon be satisfied with explanation. For now, rest and block your thoughts entirely. I have begun to fashion a special rune, and you must soon invoke it. But I didn't dare complete it, lest something go awry."

"Vanaash, dear one, take up your sword and guard the door. Unlock it again, that we may not alarm anyone by seeming to offer resistance—but without restraint, slaughter any one who enters!" Nodding, Vanaash did as she bade him.

Iseobel was glad of the chance of strengthening rest. Though she needed to stay alert to continue enforcing the runeform that held Beatta fast, it took but little of her concentration, so she sat herself where she could watch the old woman, of whom she was already in awe, work her magick.

Sunniva busily searched along the high shelves. From an apparent chaos of crocks, satchels, books, and stores, she pulled out a highly carved wooden box. Rummaging within, she pulled free an odd tool of bronze, then replaced the box.

Turning to Vanaash, she pointed at a muslin pouch attached to his belt near the sword girth. "Feel in that pouch for a powerful blank!" she ordered.

He found the strongest immediately and offered it, not bothering to wonder how she knew the muslin pouch held small rounds of apple branch, already blessed and kept close at hand for anytime the situation might demand an emergency rune-carving.

Touching the blank briefly to her brow, Sunniva gave a smile of satisfaction and darted lithely to a low table by the window. Kneeling on the floor with surprising grace for one her age and putting bronze to wood, she began to hum while carving the final staves.

Scarce mindful of joining in, Iseobel rocked gently to the quiet incantations. She knew that she was witnessing an uncommon art. Though she could invoke runes, and carve them of the FUTHARK as well, she as yet had not the skill to engrave one to special purpose. Only one strong and sure in the Vana arts could etch new work, yet even such a powerful one as that oft needed the skills of another to bring those same runes to speak.

A sudden sound caught Iseobel's attention. She looked around in time to see Vanaash dash behind the door, sword drawn. Sunniva never looked up from her work, but her voice sweetly granted entrance, even in advance of the impatient knock. A rough-looking guard entered but had scarce poked more than his face beyond the door, when Vanaash swung his blade, splitting the man's head-bone wide. The guard fell heavily to the floor, spraying a fizz of blood as he went down. Wiping his sticky sword on the man's sleeve before he resheathed it, Vanaash pulled the twitching body out of the doorway.

Iseobel leapt to her feet, shutting the door as soon as the way was clear. At the sound of Vanaash's startled cry, she spun around to see and smell a strange gray vapor rising from the corpse. With a disgusting sizzle, the body seemed to melt and, in seconds, there was nothing to be seen but a putrid skeleton, still garbed in sark, hauberk, and helmet.

Sron stepped forward defiantly, gave a disrespectful kick to the bones, then shrugged. "Must be you know the bulk of the darklord's henchmen are already dead when he recruits them," he whispered so that Sunniva could not hear. "Oft-times men who were cowardly in life will swear to serve darkness just for the chance to walk in Midgard again!"

Vanaash saw Iseobel pale as a wave of sickness came over her, but brighten again when Sunniva beckoned her over and held out the tiny round of fragrant apple wood, astonishing now in the beauty and detail of its carving. "'Tis ready and willing to work for us, dearie, and you are the one who must summon it."

Iseobel hesitated. Despite the long hours she had pored over her studies, despite countless lessons eagerly absorbed at Dorflin's side, she was yet unused to the notion that she might have such power as the one Sunniva now bade her use. Besides, she was still tired from her enchanted stupor. The cat amulet had restored much of her reason and some of her strength to her, but not all. She started to protest, but Sunniva stilled her with a look and dropped the carven token into her hand.

Iseobel looked closely at the newly wrought rune circle. The applewood blank now boasted a finely twined rope pattern carved and dyed in it. That such an exquisitely detailed design had been produced within so short a time filled her with new awe at the rune writing art. Though she had been but rudimentarily trained in the conventions, Iseobel asked with great ceremony "Lady Sunniva, how is this one named?"

Sunniva, responded just as formally, "I have charged it RÅP, the rope, and that is what it will form, as long as your will so impels it. It shall take no tying, for we need to bring it down with us, as there shall be none left above to unknot it. Shiorvan must stay ardent at her scrying until she follows by another route. Mark you, 'tis but your mind alone can command it. Neither I nor Vanaash can aid you."

"Aye, but I am weary and already holding another fast with a spelled rune: Vanaash's foster-sister, who seeks to harm me. If I concentrate on this rope, no longer will the other rune hold Beatta captive."

"On that we must take our chances, young one. I cannot hold her and neither can Shiorvan, for that runework is yours alone. We have sensed in the woman no especial powers, so she is not likely to find us. As for alerting the one we seek most to avoid? She is comely, and he has already pressed her into his service, so chances are he would listen to her." Sunniva shrugged. "First she must flee to find him, though."

Nodding, Iseobel crossed to where Vanaash stood listening at the door. "This is a rope rune which the lady your friend has contrived!" She held it in her open palm for him to inspect. "First I will invoke it and then we may climb down to safety. Have you any thought as to the order in which we should go? For it would be best if I had little distraction once I begin."

Vanaash needed but a moment. "To me, it seems you should go first. I will steady the rope from up here. Next, Sunniva can climb down, while you steady the rope from below, too. I shall come last so that my sword can stand ready until the last moment. Our friend," here he gestured to the lightelf, "can follow last if need be."

Vanaash bent his attention to the window—and to Iseobel. Surely few but he, who had studied her at every chance, would have marked how carefully she moved now. A strange frailty which spoke of the trials she recently had endured added a touch of feebleness to her gestures. Though she looked as lithe as ever when she opened the casement and knelt to the rune, Vanaash sensed her exhaustion. What would he not give to be able to lend her his strength? He was compelled to watch idly by, however, his heart swelling each time he noticed her clutch her cats and steel herself. Had it not been for Sron's hand on his arm, reminding him that he must not divert Iseobel, Vanaash would have leapt to her side in a eye-blink.

The thudding that had filled her ears had now nearly subsided. The woolen rug and scattered cushions beneath her were comfortable enough, but she was pinned under a red light so brilliant that it pained her eyes to look on it.

*The beasts!* Beatta cursed as she struggled fecklessly against the glowing shape, *offspring of the Fenris Wolf!* She would smite both of them now! That sorceress Iseobel, Hel's own bitch, would suffer the wrath of her hate—for Roric's demise, for the trickery she had wrought on Vanaash, and for trying to charm Lodur for her own pleasures.

Lodur might be hesitant to do more than keep Iseobel walled away, but she, Beatta Hard-Axer, had the courage to do what must be done. If Iseobel couldn't be poisoned, she must be beheaded. No other method would kill a witch with certainty. And nil-willed Vanaash, who trailed after her like a gormless wonder; for him, she found, she held no longer one single measure of desire. That he would play her false time and again for Iseobel's sake. It was a *man* she wanted, and Vanaash had proven himself none.

The carmine light wavered for a second. Beatta seethed and flailed, but could not work herself free, and the light recharged itself almost immediately. She toiled harder against it, waxing angrier. Bitterly she resolved through clenched teeth that she would broadcast the pair's escape to Lodur; surely he would crush Iseobel's wanton bid for freedom! The witch had toyed with Lodur in an attempt to avail herself of his power and had learned a hard lesson when he turned that very power against her!

Let her gloat that Vanaash had fallen prey to her seductions. Let Vanaash enjoy the fruits he had lusted for these many months ... had traded his dignity away to obtain! The two deserved each other. Let them share a soft pillow until the swift sword of Lodur's vengeance smote them both. Beatta cared nothing now for either of them and could scarce contain her glee that the undoing of the odious pair would soon be sealed!

Kicking at the magickal bars that bound her, Beatta plotted further. As soon as she fought her way loose, she would claim a swift mount from the stable and find Lodur. Surely he would leave off his business in that grove on her account once she told him Iseobel had fled. Ah, how she savored the sweet taste of revenge on Iseobel for her false ways and on Vanaash for his idiocy. And the promise of Lodur at the end of it all, there to soothe her ... 'twas richer than Norman wine!

Again the runeform flickered, then held. Now it dimmed and weakened. A triumphant smile lit Beatta's face and she braced herself to leap. When, with a hissing gasp, the light finally died, she launched herself into action, quitting the room even before the afterglow dispersed.


The stout rope poured out of the high turret window. Iseobel, determined not to let her concentration wander dangerously, resolved to block her anxiety about Beatta entirely and focus on the line. She reached out, held it tight, and, with a daring born of need, swung herself off the window ledge. Hand-span by hand-span, shoe-breadth by shoe-breadth, Iseobel shinnied her way downward, distracted only by Vanaash's nervous emanations and a pinpoint of light above her, the anxious Sron.

Despite a steady breeze, Iseobel's scalp ran with perspiration, and her head ached with the labor. She paused, panting, aching to relax. Knowing Vanaash and Sron gripped it sturdily from above, she nevertheless felt the rope shiver. Shocked back into focus, she yanked the slackened rope taut with her mind, then resumed her descent. Every muscle screamed for balm. Quake as they would when she finally reached the ground, Iseobel now fed them strength from every prayer to the gods she knew. When it seemed as though her will could hold the rope up no longer, she snatched at her amulet and shoved the cats between her teeth in a bid for renewed power.

The instant Iseobel's toe touched ground, her eyes wrenched open; she let go of the rope and steadied herself. Swiftly regaining her composure, she looked up to see Sunniva, clutching her heavy skirts close, lifting a frail leg over the sill. Iseobel caught the rope's tail and, with Vanaash and Sron's help, kept it rigid only by taxing both her hands and her mind.

Determined to see the old one safely to the ground, Iseobel spared not an ounce of her strength. She was tired, but each time she felt herself falter and the rope slacken, she forced herself to hold onto it just a few moments longer. At last, Sunniva's foot was on the firm ground. Iseobel let go an audible sigh of relief, Now, though the runecarver could finally take physical hold of the rope in Iseobel's stead, mental relief was not Iseobel's to enjoy, for there was still Vanaash's turn to endure. Though she strained to hold her focus, she could not shut out her awareness of him completely.

Swiftly Vanaash handed himself down with such litheness that the rope barely wavered. When he was all but to the ground, though, a sight in the distance made him pause. He was certain he saw a golden flash of fire from the direction of the grove. So, he realized, Dorflin had been right to prepare some magick. Well, Geir would see it and know to bring the retainers.

"Be swift!" Iseobel hissed, jarring him and, as he turned his gaze downward to acknowledge her, he fumbled somewhat, disrupting his own balance and nearly tumbling forward. He grasped wildly at the air to steady himself, then found his hold on the rope once more and slid quickly the rest of the way down. Something had fallen from his hand in that moment of panic, though, and now it lay in the grass near their feet, glittering in a way that drew the eyes of all three.

Vanaash jumped swiftly to retrieve it, but Sunniva lunged forward and kicked it away, glaring. "I will go no further with the two of you," she exclaimed staunchly, reaching for the rope as if to reclimb it. "There is no time now to sort out who is to blame for this trickery, but I am no longer fooled!"

"Be down from that rope, Am-ma!" Vanaash commanded, forcefully lifting the old woman and placing her back on the ground. "You and Iseobel make your way swift as you can into the shadowing wood. I will be the one to reclimb the tower, if Iseobel can hold it for just a little while more." Now that the spelled rune was out of his hand, he too felt that leaving Shiorvan behind had been a terrible mistake, and he was wroth with himself.

Iseobel was confused, but only for an instant, for it had occurred to her also, and with jarring swiftness, that there was someone left behind—someone who had helped her and should not be left.

Vanaash started his climb, moving quickly. "The two of you begone to the grove!" he called over his shoulder. "I will have no trouble finding you once I have Shiorvan!"

Iseobel, trembling, watched as he scurried upward, scarcely noticing how Sron struggled to keep his hold on the rope. Near her, Sunniva planted herself firmly at the rope's end and tugged it taut with a ferocity that belied her years and frailness. "They will have to haul the rope back up after themselves and find another way out, for we cannot linger here."

Vanaash and Sron had ducked into the tower window now and were out of sight. Watching them disappear, Iseobel was afraid. Eyes blazing, she sprang forward, grasping the rope with trembling hands and hoisted herself onto it. "Hide yourself in the copse there, lady, until we come back for you!" she cried over her shoulder without even looking at the bewildered Sunniva. "I *will* be at his side as I am meant to be!"

Before Sunniva had time to realize what Dorflin's daughter meant to do, Iseobel had pulled herself so high that she was well out of the old lady's reach.

# Chapter Twenty-two

Geir Death-Crooner, crouched behind a boulder above the cozy hut where Dorflin and Iseobel had often entertained him with savory soup and clever tales, was thoroughly confused. Dorflin had bade him make ready for battle against Lodur, and he had done so. Even now, a score of village men (and the two feisty daughters of Cought the Cooper, who could not be dissuaded) were gathered just behind him in the green wood, swords at the ready. At the magicker's bidding, he had told them to lie low till the signal came. Despite a clammy fever and a headache which had not left him since the night he'd been haunted by nightmarish shadows that howled through his cottage and heaved themselves against his gut, he had kept himself alert and anxious, watching.

So far, no clash of arms loomed. Lodur seemed to have come alone, fully armed and galloping like thunder on that beastly war-horse of his. Dorflin had stepped from the shadows; Lodur dismounted to meet him. The two had been standing face to face, a few yards apart, for half an hour now. Geir knew his eyes were raven-sharp but he was prepared to swear on Odin's eye patch that the two had not spoken a single word, though they gestured and scowled as if engaged in a heated quarrel.

Now, as if on a given signal, the two moved closer to Dorflin's holy meadow both at once. At its western entrance, Lodur drew up short, and a scowl passed over his face. Geir thought it looked as if the dark one simply could not enter the sacred place—as if he'd been physically barred. Must be what the townsfolk said was true after all: there was an evil in Lodur so vile that he could not even put himself into the presence of the fair White One's sanctuary.

Again Lodur's face took on a grim look. Dorflin, standing just within the grove, remained inscrutable. He turned to face Lodur, obviously waiting, until at last Lodur reached deep into a pocket and handed the shaman a small, glinting thing. With no reaction but to accept the prize, Dorflin entered the grove fully and made his way, Geir guessed, to the ancient oak.

The thick ring of trees surrounding the meadow obscured Geir's sightline, but Dorflin's ethereal chanting filtered through the leaves and reached across the leas and into the dense surrounding woodlands. Geir let its soothing cadence and rich baritone tambour float over him. A little dizzy, he pressed his forehead against the coolness of the rock that hid him, and, for what seemed only a moment, lost himself in the lilting song, forgetting his headpain. There was healing in the wizard's ways.

Feeling slightly better, he perused the situation. It would be good if they did not come to arms. There were but a score of fighting men left in the village, and each of them sorely needed to tend to ordinary affairs of living. Aye, they all would have been proud to fight for their shaman or his daughter, but the ferocity of Lodur's army was well known. The outcome of a battle between his force and theirs was fore-ordained, and they knew it. Swallowing back a wave of nausea, Geir groped in the grass for his wine-skin of healing barley water. Then he heard it.

"Make way! Make way!" It was a shrill voice, faint in the distance, and a rumbling, more sensed than heard, of a horse's hooves. Heart lurching, he shaded his eyes. It took a moment before he saw the charger breaking over the hills that separated Lodur's dark lea from Dorflin's meadow. Geir strained to watch the rider dismount and storm toward Lodur, obviously weighted with news.

"Dark tidings, my lord!" Geir was fully amazed when the figure pulled off its helmet to reveal a voluptuous length of flame red tresses. *Beatta!* Geir, who had not seen her once since the day he deposited her at Lodur's threshold, felt as if the wind had been knocked out of him. She had sworn to the darklord!

Beatta spoke, and Lodur smiled and kissed her fiercely. Wordlessly, she wheeled, mounted, and sped back toward Lodur's manor. Geir had no doubt she had been sent to rally warriors.

A rustle in the undergrowth behind Lodur caught Geir's attention. He squinted hard as he searched the dark forest that separated Lodur's manor from this lea. Sucking in his breath, he estimated there were dozens of Lodur's men hidden among the trees. They must have made the long way there silently while Lodur, in the open, rode to meet Dorflin.

Lodur's short, sharp whistle pulled Geir back to the moment. His gaze traveled to the western entrance where Lodur now paced. The riderless stallion headed briskly toward his master. Dorflin now stood once more at the arbored entrance, keeping himself just inside its protection, seeming to taunt his adversary with the grove's resolve not to allow the darklord passage. Over the threshold, he handed Lodur what looked to Geir like a toy. Grabbing the carving from the shaman, as if so much as putting his hand under the arbor caused him pain, Lodur mounted and turned his horse prettily toward his own manor. Geir sagged with relief. So it would not come to battle!

Lodur was near the grove when he stopped sharply and raised a clenched fist. Four of his men, still mounted, burst from the forest and, with well rehearsed movements, thundered toward the grove, hooves crashing in unison. Recognizing their gear, the snarling-wolf helmets and black steeds, Geir swallowed hard. They were armed, that was certain, but their approach was not the headlong rush to battle he might have expected.

At first Geir thought they meant to trample Dorflin; but the magicker lifted his arms high and let go a fireball that surged from deep within the earth and gained focus as it exploded with a blinding flash. The horses reared, throwing their riders, then pawed the air and pounded away in terror.

Lodur signaled again, and four others charged. This time, when Dorflin raised his arms, Lodur let go a terrifying oath. Ever after, Geir shuddered at the memory of that curse. Screamed in the Æsir tongue, it was an unholy screech of rage that gained in fury, echoing till it seemed the very earth shook from the force of it. Yet horse and rider stood an interminably long time while Lodur brought his arm slowly up, pointing all the while at the hapless Dorflin, who trembled and raised his hands to his face as if to shield himself from the barrage.

Then it seemed to Geir that Dorflin was hit by some violent, invisible force that wrenched him from consciousness. He slumped forward, but did not fall. Rather, he hovered where he had stood in the entryway, limp and seemingly lifeless, rising suspended just above the ground like a toy on a string.

Those warriors still horsed drew up in a line before Lodur and halted a respectful distance, as if now unsure of their course of action. Ever so slowly, the black steed turned, towering as it pawed the air upright on its rear hooves. Lodur's back was to Dorflin now, but still the wizard hung motionless. A look of satisfaction lit Lodur's face, and his voice, calmer now, but cold and rife with vengeance, rang out once more.

"Look upon Dorflin, the erstwhile purveyor of Vana magick, whilst I hold him here!" he cried arrogantly. "This man whom you take for holy and believe above reproach, has stolen my golden ring. The carven thralls of mine he has restored, but he means to keep the ring beyond price for himself. It is hidden somewhere in this grove or in the huts and cottages yonder."

Dazed and distraught, Geir heard a low commotion as the dark-lord's men jostled each other in an odd mixture of war-glee and disbelief. His heart froze when Lodur spoke again.

"Make ready to search. The grove before us is enchanted and promises us uncounted dangers, but you are commanded to find a way through it. Furthermore, I am told the wizard's daughter has fled my hold. Should you find her, bring her to me alive. Elsewise, spare nothing and no one in these environs," he demanded in an iron tone, "until you find my ring! The rest of our company rides now to join us, but you need not wait."

Exhaling so hard that his own whistling breath jarred him, Geir stiffened with resolve. Had Dorflin been able, he knew, surely he would have given the signal. Stealthily, the Death-Crooner crept through the copse to call his men to battle.

She could feel as much as hear Sunniva's violent protests, but Iseobel would heed none of the old one's arguments. Arms wrapped tight around the rope, she continued to climb despite her exhaustion. "I'll not let him go!" she vowed to herself as she scuttled upward, amazed at her own nimbleness.

Below, Sunniva, in exasperation, had freed her end of the rope. With no one now to steady it from below, Iseobel felt the untamed swaying as it whipped with her weight. Suddenly aware of her danger, for she had attained a goodly height in very little time, she froze, looking over the dense treetops to the meadow. Drawn by some commotion, she focused on its source. *Oh Freyja! Not the grove!* She ignored her fear when the rope wavered dangerously, and looked upon a scene that filled her with dread.

Though small in the distance, she knew Lodur at once, for her heart surged at the sight of him despite all her will to stop it. Mounted and armed, he was addressing a small group of his warriors as if to goad them. Could be all was lost!

To no avail, Iseobel tried to discern what was happening in the distance. Frustrated by distractions—the movement of the rope and the barrage of protests that Sunniva spewed—she was hindered in all attempts. Her eyes were keen, though, and when she saw Lodur direct the gaze of his men to a shapeless hovering form, she exerted every effort to concentrate.

*Dorflin! Captive!* A shriek escaped her, and, like the rope, she threatened to buckle. Adding to the intensity of the confusion, she was rocked by a thunderous noise, grating and harsh, filling the air from below. With horror, she glanced down. The massive gates of the courtyard had scraped opened, and a dark mass of fully armed warriors marched forward, led, it seemed, by Beatta herself. Their backs were to her and their faces hidden, but she had an instantaneous vision of their vicious resolve. Loosening her hold on the rope, Iseobel slid down at breakneck speed and, landing hard, drew her sword.

The Death-Crooner made his way down the short hill to where the handful of villagers waited. He was determined not to be intimidated by the weightiness of his task. Geir was by no means a ring-giver or thegn. This rugged length of coast knew no lord except for Lodur, but those of Scarbyrig who refused to serve the darklord trusted Geir to lead them when it came to protecting their own hearths and hides. Oh, how he had hated to lie to them! If he did not lie, though. If he told them that the ten men now there were expecting reinforcements, how could he expect them to muster even a shred of hope for protecting their shaman? Geir ground his teeth. The villagers were good folk. They deserved to know the truth of it.

"Mount up," he cried, his voice quiet but forceful. "Surely you have heard that there are not many warriors here now, but those half a score are wolf-brethren, to a man, and Lodur has sent for more. Surely we can expect his blood-thirsty housecarls as well as another score of wolf-fighters."

Urgith, the older and plainer of Cought the Cooper's two unruly daughters, broke in as she reined in her eager horse. "With Dorflin on our side, how can we lose?"

Geir winced. "Our shaman cannot help us in this, I fear. Lodur has bespelled him, and it is to his rescue we ride."

A hush of disbelief quieted them all, and the splintering sound of rending wood filled the air. Wenthur Crowfoot was the first to speak. "Then the man needs not our hesitation!" He mounted his gelding, reined hard, and stood his horse alongside Geir's. "Let us ride."

"I told you I will not go, Vanaash!" Shiorvan shook her moon-blond mane vehemently. "My place is here. Go rescue that fair young one and my mother, as you agreed. I am in no danger."

No danger, at least, that he could entice her from, Vanaash grimaced silently. Though his mental map of the manor had started to fade, he had found his way to Shiorvan despite Sron's urgings against trying.

It had been no easy task, noiselessly descending the winding stone stairs from the tower, sneaking down corridors and crawling through countless huge halls while staying hidden from Lodur's minions. He had found her on her knees before the hearth in the great room, burning a lock of her own hair. 'Twas the lock that Vanaash had wrapped round his fingers earlier while entreating her to leave with him, she told him ruefully, best destroyed before Lodur sensed the other man's touch on it. Now, Vanaash wasted precious minutes while the woman stubbornly held her ground, heedless of his cajoling. Setting his jaw, he gazed into her eyes and asked her one last time.

"Will you come or not, sister?" He stopped, flustered at the word which had flown so easily from his mouth, and noticed that she was trembling.

"You have felt it, too?"

He nodded numbly and when he spoke again his voice was weak. "There are horses in the stable. Ride with me. Please!"

But his sudden plaintiveness had made her stronger, and she tossed her head defiantly. "If there is any honor in you, you will bide by our agreement. Meddle with me more here and it tells me you are naught but a vain and foolish knave—one who would endanger the others in his care to follow a witless whim. Begone with you!"

Sron, impatient and wary, stepped forward staunchly. "'Tis not in your best interest to linger and argue, Vanaash. I will stay yet awhile in case there is aught she needs, but you had best take leave now to accomplish what it is you must!"

Vanaash shrugged helplessly. "If so be it."

"So be it!" Shiorvan answered sharply, pushing him back into the darkness of a cluttered hallway that led, he knew, to the orchard door where first he had seen her. Vanaash realized he could not win. What webs kept this woman bound so fast, he could not guess, but her obvious entanglement left him no alternative.

"By Tyr's good hand, I vow I will come to you again!" he cried breathlessly, but she shushed him.

"Speak no more. Just be about your business and be swift!"

When he was far enough down the hall that he no longer could hear her, she said two words more under her breath.

"Brother mine!"


Without stopping to formulate a plan, Iseobel turned to run. The rope, completely unheeded now, collapsed. Sunniva caught her by a fistful of hair. "Girl," she fairly shouted, "be sensible!"

Iseobel whirled on the old woman, frenzy in her eyes. "What do you deem more sensible than trying to help my father? Do you think I would leave him hostage to that villain?" she snapped as she struggled to tear her hair free. "Let *go!*"

"I said naught about leaving Dorflin to the mercies of Lodur—which he has none," Sunniva retorted, hauling Iseobel closer. "I merely bade you be sensible. You cannot overpower that one without a bit of planning. *Will you stand still?*"

Iseobel nodded, and Sunniva released the fistful of tresses. "Though you fight well, perhaps, with a pretty sword," Sunniva scolded, "your true advantage is in your strength of magick. I suggest you use it now."

Startled, for she never had considered her powers to be particularly potent, Iseobel hesitated to consider. "Whether my skills are as sufficient as you think, or no, I will take your advice—but only if you will help. I have no little chance with the might of the Vanir behind me." She squared her shoulders and smoothed the hair off her face. "Let's go, then. Perhaps between us we can lend a spell or two."

"Dorflin's daughter!" Sunniva barked sharply; Iseobel stiffened. "Set you no more store by your father than to wish to 'help'? If we had time for me to teach you patiently, I would do so. Now is not the time. Make a plan, girl! Think!"

Iseobel reddened, knowing the woman spoke aright. She gritted her teeth. "I never had to formulate an attack before. I have no idea what to do."

Sunniva softened, but barely. "Assess what you have at your disposal and decide how you can use that to advantage ... *before* you enter the fray." Looking quickly around, she indicated that they should move out of the open.

"Offense comes not easily to me," admitted Iseobel as she followed Sunniva to the cover of the woods. "My father trained me to be strong, but never taught me battle magick." Surely Dorflin would be safe by the time she and Sunniva reached the grove ... or maybe, she would lose him to Lodur, as she had lost Roric. Perhaps, and the thought chilled her, she would come under Lodur's irresistible spell again. This time, irrevocably.

"Maybe you could work harder at broadcasting those fears of yours wider, missy!" Sunniva snapped. "Some of Lodur's Hellions have rotten brains and don't pick up such subtle sendings."

"I try to school my emotions, but I have not yet mastered them," Iseobel mumbled shamefaced as she smoothed the falcon feathers on her cloak. "Shall we continue?"

Sunniva gave Iseobel an apprising look. She knew her own tongue to be sharp, and had half expected naught but an acid return like those Shiorvan flung back at her. Iseobel, though, was different from her own girl. She wished to learn, and faced up to her shortcomings. Well, Sunniva arranged her shawl around her ample bosom with a snap, that would be the difference in being raised by Dorflin rather than Lodur.

"Search your runes for direction," Sunniva ordered flatly.

Nervously, Iseobel dabbled her fingers among the runes in their pouch, hoping that one would insist she choose it.

"Hold your amber cats while you search your runes," prompted Sunniva. "They will lend clarity to your choosing."

Iseobel clenched her teeth in exasperation. "I do not see how the healing spells I know—"

"Don't fight *me!*" Sunniva flared. "Let me help you fight for your father."

Iseobel, shamed to realize she had been resisting Sunniva, suddenly felt a rune firmly lodged between her fingers. Closing her eyes in an attitude of quick prayer, she drew the stone forth. EIHWAZ, ↯, the trunk of the world-tree Yggdrasil, the numinous axis that connected Midgard to the heavens above and the underworld below. She showed it to Sunniva, whose quick nod affirmed her own interpretation.

The runes truly *were* helping her in this matter. EIHWAZ bade her choose another stone, confirming ahead of time that the wisdom she needed was indeed within her comprehension.

The sound of a shout and a skirmish blasted Iseobel's concentration. She froze and listened while searching the woods for a dense thicket that might hide them.

At the thud of galloping hooves, she steered Sunniva quickly into the underbrush. The old woman slipped deftly through a smooth opening among the brambles and crouched low in the shadows. Iseobel, hard behind, snagged her shoe binding on a woody vine and pitched forward against a sapling. Quickly, she dropped to all fours. From her crouch, she tried to reach back to free her shoe, but the horse and rider were nearly upon them, and she dared make no obvious movements.

"Like Machthild," she told herself, recalling her cat's surreptitious manner of movement. "Stay as still as Machthild when she's creeping up on a bird."

Iseobel bunched her muscles, tautened every one, and purposely steadied her breathing. From heels to head, she commanded an alertness into every inch of her being, forcing herself to stay still and unnoticed though the ground throbbed ever more violently as horse and rider thundered nearer. At the rush of their passing, she felt the down on her arms stir. She could smell the animal's lather, overpowering even the piney scent of the trees. And the warrior astride him! Hel-driven urgency screamed in his anxious sweat.

*Vanaash.* A swell of relief rushed through her. Then, Iseobel snapped out of her brief trance. It *was* Vanaash who headed so fast to meet Lodur. Fear for him clutched at her. She ripped the shoe lacing free with a ferocious tug. *Perhaps he could distract Lodur and his men to buy her time.*

As she climbed out of the thicket, Sunniva touched Iseobel's arm, a huge measure of excitement coloring her tone. "Can you project something more fiercesome than a cat?" Eagerness sparkled in her eyes. "A wolf perhaps?"

"I can only project runes, lady," Iseobel answered, "and then only with the greatest concentration—"

"No, not pictures in the air. I mean *yourself.* Can you project your *appearance* as anything but a cat?"

Iseobel was wholly bewildered. "I fear that is far beyond my training and requires a strength of magick as powerful as your daughter's at the least." Oh, she would disappoint this lady greatly, she could tell. Sunniva was used to having the incredible galdor magick of Shiorvan's to command. "I'm afraid that we must set our sight lower than you have reckoned. I am not a potent magicker who can shift shape at will."

"Aye, but you could, girl," came Sunniva's reply. "You may be trained in seith, not galdor, but you are already more capable than you know." Sunniva took a deep breath. "What is more, you can indeed change shapes."

She fixed Iseobel with a stern look to stop her from breaking in again. "No arguments! I just saw it. Scant moments ago, when you wished to be hidden from the rider's sight, you changed yourself into a cat. Not entirely … but a cat you would have seemed to all but the most careful of observers."

Unnerved a bit, Iseobel scanned the other's face for even the slightest uncertainty, but there was none. "'Tis strange," she murmured, shaking her head a little as with disbelief.

"Nay, Iseobel! Listen—" Sunniva steeled her gaze on Iseobel as if to impart the knowledge directly into her understanding. They had little time to waste before confronting Lodur, but she knew a few moments of explanation and practice might grant them an immense weapon. "My guess is that you imagined yourself as having the attributes of a cat, so that you would stay crouched and motion-less while the rider rushed by."

Iseobel nodded, and Sunniva continued. "That is the secret to shape-shifting, Iseobel. You must not only imagine yourself as that animal but project the belief, to the tiniest detail, on those around you. And of course," she glanced at Iseobel's necklace, "having such an amulet helps."

Iseobel did not hesitate. If Sunniva felt that she was capable of shape-shifting, then shape-shifter she would be! Though she had known the woman for scarce but an hour, Iseobel counted her already as a teacher of greatest merit. Anything seemed possible now! It was time to cast doubts aside.

At Sunniva's direction, Iseobel knelt, then reached in her pouch for URUZ, ᚢ, a rune she could count on to inspire the will's vital energy. After a few hurried moments of practice, she felt the surge of certainty that Sunniva had told her would come. Perfection was not paramount. Surprise and fear were the keys now. After asking Sunniva's counsel, Iseobel assembled a few choice runes in her pocket: ANSUZ, ᚨ, to lend energy to magick; HAGALAZ, ᚺ, to unify opposing forces into forces of potential; THURIAZ, ᚦ, for action, power, and protection.

Finally, with a silent prayer to Freyja for guidance, Iseobel moved her fingers gently through the pouch, till one last rune was chosen for her. She drew it forth with a small gasp of awe: BERKANO, ᛒ, the goddess's own birch rune, symbol of transformation, protection, and concealment!

Impulsively, she kissed it as it lay in her open palm. For that instant, it almost seemed she could feel Freyja's touch on her cheek. Breathless with a mixture of happiness and relief she flew to her feet and paced, meditating on the ᛒ rune that she clasped tightly as if to draw from its wisdom. Then, still clutching it, she and Sunniva made their wordless way east.

As the trees began to thin, signaling their nearness to the edge of the forest, Sunniva gently took Iseobel's elbow. She needed say nothing. Iseobel was as steady as a battle-steed—even when she caught sight of Dorflin hanging suspended and helpless, cocooned within the protecting incantations of the grove, but unable to touch the earth and draw from its strength. The thudding clashes of weapon upon shield and the sight of Lodur's men attempting to raze the trees that protected the grove's outer boundary arrested no more of her attention than did the chirping of the crickets or setting of the sun.

In the stables, where he had only narrowly missed the flood of Lodur's warriors as they mounted and charged off, Vanaash had chosen well from the handful of mounts he found. The silvery gray mare he rode now was an energetic animal, strong willed but sensible. Vanaash was pleased he had remembered Iseobel's trick; he had shared breath, just as she taught him, with the horse before leaping onto her back. Now the creature seemed alert to his every need. At his merest urging, she unleashed speed and willingness that caught Vanaash by surprise. Reining, he paused a moment, listening to establish in which direction Lodur's forces had gathered. Then he urged the horse a bit faster, easing her onto a woody path where he was less likely to be seen as he made his way along the outskirts of Dorflin's grove.

The troops' noise soon arose on his left, and stayed there as he moved from behind them to alongside them, finally passing them.

Seeing a brightening in the trees, Vanaash signaled the horse to slow, which she did reluctantly, then stopped while they still enjoyed cover at the forest's edge. From his hiding place, he could see little, but the sounds of edged metal and thunks of tearing wood assailed his ears.

Confident that the mare would stay still, Vanaash calmed himself and reached out with his fillet. Iseobel and Sunniva, he was sure, were still behind him. That was good. Lodur lay before him in the lea, and Vanaash could sense many men with him. Their essences seemed odd; inchoate; decayed. Dorflin, he sensed not at all. Vanaash's heart sank.

Quietly, he side-stepped the mare to the north, still careful to stay under cover of the foliage, out of the view of Lodur's men. Now he scanned for evidence of the wizard.

Ahhh ... there he was, hanging like some long-empty scabbard at the edge of the grove. Vanaash was sure from the look of him that the man was able to sense the chaos and the wanton destruction of the trees around him. Perhaps Vanaash simply fancied it, but Dorflin seemed to agonize as each tree and sapling crashed to the ground, and stiffen each time another axe stroke fell. Could be the shaman was in a protective cocoon of his own making, Vanaash thought at first, but the wizard's feet were not touching the earth. Lodur must have bound him somehow and removed him from the source of his power. At least, though, Vanaash thought grimly, the man was alive.

Now things happened with furious swiftness. Lodur's troops burst out of the forest and into the lea north of him; Geir and the defenders of Scarbyrig rushed in from the south, shouting boldly and radiating confidence and a stout will to win. A fierce war cry sounded, then another and another. The lines came together with a deafening roar of iron upon iron. Thunder rumbled somewhere in the distance, and the ominous clamor urged Vanaash forward. The lightest touch from his heels caused his mount to gallop, and he charged his way through a storm of arrows and stones, toward the huge, surging circle of shields that he knew surrounded Lodur. If only he could best the man, perhaps the rout would leave a few of the village defenders standing.

# Chapter Twenty-three

Geir Death-Crooner, sword in hand, only half noticed Vanaash's approach as the entire field exploded into a bellowing tempest of battle. Within seconds, all was frenzy. Horses screamed and shied, reared and plunged. Men bellowed oaths and curses. Lodur's Hellions fell, were crushed in the screaming press, and their places taken swiftly by others from behind.

Vanaash slashed his way closer. He and Geir exchanged a swift, desperate look, then worked together to spur the men of Scarbyrig to crush forward. Lodur's fiercesome warriors held—then wavered, broke their line and fell back. Some staggered, seemingly with death wounds, but the smitten wolf-brethren did not fall lifeless. Attacked by sudden and all-encroaching second-death, their flesh rotted instantly and their torsos writhed as they clawed with maggot-ridden fingers to keep from disappearing altogether.

A nauseating stench of weeks-old decay arose, permeating the air, and it was all Geir could do not to heave at the grue. He had heard it said before, that some of Lodur's army was built of men brought back from Nif-Helheim by spells and enchantments, but 'twas a sight he had never expected to look upon. Raising his sword, the Death-Crooner screamed a heartfelt prayer to Thor and reined his horse hard. He was too busy fighting to worry about it now and he knew that on the morrow, whether he dwelt still in Midgard or supped in Valhalla, this horror would seem but a distant nightmare.

With the BERKANO rune clenched between her teeth, Iseobel pressed her hands to the falcon feathers that dangled from her cloak. The air seemed to charge with dazzling energy. The cloud of pulsating light shifted. Its outline began to change shape and, pulling the woman's features irresistibly with it, illuminated Iseobel. The undulating glow rippled along her contour. What once was hair, became feathers. Her eyes became steely and nerveless; her mouth a flesh-tearing beak.

Behind her, Sunniva enveloped her with augmenting mind noise. *What comes then from the shadows of the trees?* it said, *Run!* **Run!!**

Fully man-sized, the terrible she-falcon emerged from the wood. A mighty flap of powerful wings carried her aloft on streams of air. In her beak she bore a radiant rune.

*Look, look and be frightened. This is the fearless falcon of Freyja come to rip into your hearts and souls, to swallow alive your spirit, to assail you without mercy.*

Circling high over the fighters, the raptor suddenly spit the ᛒ stone from its mouth. BERKANO, most often a gentle rune, was now made to represent the word, the will, the weapons, and the awesome abilities of the great goddesses. It hovered red ... menacing. Beneath it, Lord Lodur, steeped in venomous rage, felt the assault of its screaming heat and shuddered as with searing pain. Still, it hovered there, flaring.

*It comes for you ... it comes for you ... **it comes for you.***

With a piercing, predatory scream, the falcon dove at the assembled men, swooped over the minions of Hel, fixed its unforgiving eye on the black-clad lord as he raged—you are forbidden to interfere! The runeform careened angrily. The falcon plummeted away into the forest, but few noticed, for they were fixated on the cascade of tumultuous, unearthly light that poured like liquid fire from the runestone, marking Lord Lodur as evil and tainted; holding him captive in its horrible glow. Men rushed from the grove, as if forcefully expelled, and fell in the grasses outside it, cowering.

In the shelter of the grove, Iseobel fell to the ground, weak and dizzy, scarce hearing Sunniva's solicitous whispers. She was bewildered. It had happened so fast and left her so weak. She was unsure now of what had really transpired. Had she become a bird, or simply cast the startling vision of a one high over the battlefield? All she knew was that she was breathless, her heart pounding with unfamiliar ferocity as she struggled to her feet.

Mere yards away, the ongoing struggle still waxed. Men screamed and cursed; there was a merciless clamor, like the beating of heavy instruments on walls of iron. Against her will to look on it, Iseobel edged herself to the forest's rim and looked out again at the field. A dozen of his men at arms surrounded Lodur, slamming with their great pikes, swords and spears at a wall that must have surrounded the darklord—a wall that could not be seen but against which the heavy weapons flailed helplessly.

"Batter it down, you whoring sons of bitches!" Lodur shouted as he struggled to break free of the barrier that poured forth from the fiery runeform above him. His stallion reared and kicked against the invisible wall surrounding them, a snarling, snorting battle ram fired by madness and fear.

None who watched could doubt the sheer force of will it cost Lodur to fight the power of the rune that burned fiercely above him. He smoldered with rage. straining to defeat the spell that held him. One defiant Æsir oath after another broke from his grim lips, and his sword became a glowing firebrand. His terrified horse frothed and foamed at the mouth while the grass under its plunging hooves vanished with little bursts of flame.

The wall, at last, was growing weaker. Then and again a sword or spear penetrated it, so that Lodur now had to duck his own men's weapons as they worked to free him. Looking past the atrocious scene which she herself had ordered, Iseobel's eyes met those of her father, as he lingered yet, helpless, where the enchantments had hung him. Without a thought for her own safety, she started cross field, Frankish sword held high, a grim look of determination on her face that must have been fiercesome, for men, both friend and foe, parted to let her pass as if she had the power to disable them had they not.

"By Lord Freyr's stolen sword, child! Are you out of your wits?" Sunniva, red with fear and anger started after her but, by then, Iseobel had reached Dorflin's side. In one lithe movement she stood tip-toe to touch him and gripped a hand hard into his belt. "In Freyja's name—" she cried loud, and that was all she had to say.

Slowly, gently, Dorflin relaxed to his daughter's strong touch, and dropped gently earthward, like a fallen babe set back firmly on the ground by its mother to toddle safe again. Iseobel did not see her, nor did Dorflin, but there was no denying the goddess's presence; both smelled her gentle perfume and heard a distant whisper of delight. Whether any other sensed it, they would never know; it lasted but a scant instant and was gone.

All at once came the baleful scream of Lodur's battle mount as the darklord reached high with his sword, slamming the weapon over and over into the fast lowering runeform which, instead of dying, waxed brighter until at last it exploded into a shower of fragmented flame. Lodur's mount sprang forward frantically until horse and rider thundered to a halt inches from the three who stood fearlessly in mid-field. Glaring down at Iseobel, Dorflin, and Sunniva with tempestuous rage, Lodur glowered a command.

"Surround them!"

An instant later, the three were enclosed in a prison of gleaming swords as a dozen of Lodur's most fearless housecarls rushed forward to encircle them.

Vanaash had been in constant motion during all this, galloping from one end of the field to the other, hastening men back into formation and shouting commands to rebuild the lines that had broken during the first frenzied moments of battle. But now he saw Iseobel clearly through the surging wall of men, and he rushed forward. The vengeance he sensed in Iseobel's look filled him with dread. Watching with horror as Lodur leaned down, as if to lift her to him in the saddle, it turned to a swelling hatred. He fought to goad his wary steed to approach the seething dark lord.

"Halt *there*, Lodur!" he found himself bellowing in an iron tone. "Do not think to handle her more!"

"You shall not have her, Vana Avkomling!"

Vanaash stiffened at the man's harsh voice: the evil laugh that followed filled him with a rage beyond enduring. With a hasty plea to Freyr for guidance, he urged the mare forward until he could feel her tense. He waited for her to rear. When her fore hooves struck the ground once more and she rocked into a plunge, Vanaash threw himself forward with all his might, smashing into Lodur with a hatred that stunned them both.

The mare reared and screamed as the two men crashed to the ground, wrapped each in the other's stranglehold. There was a moment of vicious struggle and they were on their feet again, weapons ready. Vanaash only half heard Beatta's savage oath behind him when he lunged forward, fending off the other man's broadsword with his own. Twice more; thrice more iron harangued iron with a tolling clang that rent the now-still air like a shriek from Hel. Four, five times more, with both men gritting against the agony of the hard exertion, they met again. There was a moment of respite as a particularly violent thrust, equally met, sent them both reeling backwards, then Vanaash spun with a fury, goaded by the mad glitter of the other's eyes. He slashed savagely into Lodur's shoulder, stumbling himself as his blade glanced off the other's collarbone with horrific force.

Regaining himself, Vanaash raised his weapon preparing to advantage himself of his enemy's momentary pain. Heedless of Lodur's oaths of avengement, he charged forward but, before he could land his carefully aimed death blow, Beatta leapt from her saddle and threw herself before Lodur to shield him.

Vanaash went livid with rage. "Betake yourself away, Beatta, and swiftly. You know not what evil power you serve by placing yourself there!'

"Nay! Who are you to speak of evils? You who have harbored and helped that conniving sorceress."

"You know not what you speak!"

"Could be I do not care! Could be I care only to ensure that no more men die or suffer to fulfill that witch's aims. That this one comes not to greet a dire fate on her behalf!"

Before Vanaash could answer, Lodur reached forward, twining his hand in Beatta's thick locks and drawing her mouth to his own in a swift, passionate kiss. Then he loosed her, laughing. "Beyond measure I appreciate the boon you have offered me this day, lady, and soon will I prove this appreciation to you. Even so, you had no need to risk yourself for me."

He lifted her hand with his own and touched it to his vicious wounding which was already half healed and drying. Beatta jerked away with a cry of surprise. Laughing again, Lodur turned his back to her and moved close to Vanaash with a hiss.

"Must be you knew by now that you could not kill me, Vana Avkomling!"

"Aye, but 'twould have pleased me well to have put you from that humanform and left you to wander Midgard invisible and bodiless." Though shaking, Vanaash still held his sword firm and high, trying hard to ignore two-score of warriors who, silently massing behind Lodur, had finally decided that this was a threat to their master they could stave off.

Lodur's eyes narrowed to icy slits. "Little do you understand my might if you do not suppose I have a second form already at my disposal, and magickers in my power ready to weave me yet another!"

Now Lodur gestured to the two women who stood with Dorflin, held in tow by the crossed swords of the housecarls. Vanaash, his attention drawn to Iseobel once more, swallowed hard, made anxious by the sight of her. Keening in on his discomfiture, Lodur turned to him with a brazen smile

"'Twill avail you none to long for her, halfling," he whispered coldly. "I have already made her mine."

"Smite you, Lodur!" Vanaash growled, exerting every effort to hide the tumult the other's words caused in him, and grateful for the fillet which aided him in the task. "All the gods in Æsgard know you lie."

"'Tis so?" Tossing his black hair with a smug smile, Lodur turned to Iseobel, gesturing, and called her by name. "Come to me, sweet!" he cajoled, his cool tone of command only half disguised by his casual smile.

With a willingness that caused Vanaash agonies, Iseobel moved forward, looking suddenly confused. She placed her hand in Lodur's, standing on tip-toe to kiss his cheek. Lodur stroked her hair, her face, her neck in an overt display of affection, then put his hand under her chin, turning and raising her gaze to Vanaash's. "Your friend here waxes uncertain of the bond we have made between us, fairest," he said, looking from one to the other with a complacent smile. "Mayhap you can convince him of the affection we have shared these many nights."

Iseobel said nothing but looked at her dark-haired mentor with a flickering smile, nodding a little. Then Beatta, unable to hold her tongue any longer, darted forward, pulling Iseobel by the arm out of Lodur's grip and confronting her with a vicious glare. "Look at my foster-brother in the eye, won't you, holy woman?" she mocked in a voice charged with hatred. "Look straight at him who holds you in such an awed regard and deny that you have shared this other's bed!"

Trembling, Iseobel raised a miserable look, shrugging. With a plunging heart, Vanaash realized she could not negate the accusation. Scarce did she seem minded to, either, he thought bitterly, the way she had clung to the makebate. Lodur turned on him, eyes agleam with satisfaction.

"You see? She will never forsake me. Nor ever will she pretend that she has not given herself most fully unto me—" He was cut off by a wild, soul-shattering sound spiraling around them. An eerie screech pierced the air, like the unearthly scream of an animal in death throes.

Vanaash caught his breath as Sunniva, with an agility that belied her years, threw herself forward, arms raised ominously to the heavens. In that instant he realized somewhat of the awesome beauty she must have boasted in her youth. Day's end was rapidly approaching, and the last red rays of sunset reflected in her eyes and silver hair. The force was dazzling. She put herself directly in Lodur's way and spoke with a venomous hiss.

"'Tis truth the girl will not deny your falsehoods, for you have bewildered her with your potions and enchantments till she cannot rightly remember that naught has passed between you."

As she spoke, she pressed a hand to Iseobel's brow. The girl raised a hand to her lips, stifling a cry, then forced herself away from Lodur, looking as if Sunniva's touch had finally banished the dark enchantment from her heart entirely.

Lodur seethed, "How dare you to betray me, crone, when I have cared so long and well for you and yours?" He raised his hand as if to ward against her magick. His face was a mask of rage. "You are mad to suppose you even know."

Sunniva glared at him, belying not an ounce of fear. "Yet, in truth, you have forestalled your touch upon her, till the rituals could be completed that would gain you her powers. 'Tis the same as you wreaked on my own daughter, who was but a tender child when you forced your hideous self upon her."

"Strange that she has made no move to join you in your treachery, old one! If I have been so contemptible unto her, how is it she has chosen not to run with you?"

"Well you know she will never leave behind the son you fathered on her."

Lodur spat. "You are the one steeped all in lies, Sunniva Baardsdätter! Cannot be you have only pretended to serve me these years. Must be the nearness of these Vana Avkomling has revived in your heart some useless feeling for that upstart god who used and betrayed you."

"Never have I lost awe and affection for him!"

"Must be 'twas bitter for you then, to watch your daughter and know how well she loved and served me, the sworn enemy of your darling!"

Sunniva grew still suddenly, as if she feared to say more. Iseobel darted forward, wrapping the older woman in a fond embrace.

Lodur broke into wild laughter. "'Twill be more bitter yet for you, ancientness, for now your person is no longer of use to me, and I will be forced to splay and drain you!"

"You will have to kill *me* first, Lodur!" Iseobel's voice was hard, vehement.

"You, fairness?" Lodur laughed hard. "Nay! But the same fate shall befall your precious father if you do not recover the bind ring which he so cleverly has hidden. The lot of you have spent yourselves entirely in your childish tricks of magick this day. Do you not suppose 'twould be easy for me to smite him, here and now, even as we speak?" He thrust a sword tauntingly forward. Protectively, Iseobel moved herself in front of her father and glared at Lodur with unwonted fierceness, but with a short laugh Lodur signaled past her and two of his warriors, daggers drawn, took Dorflin in a captive hold from behind and dragged him, stumbling, back behind the darklord's line.

"By the gods, you quaver with uncertainty, Lodur!" Vanaash oathed, with a confidence he scarcely felt. "Never did you suppose the day would come when you would find yourself bested by dwellers of Midgard. Seems your presence here is threatened now, and it affrights you so that you must quash or capture all who have power to use against you!"

"Say you so?" Lodur opened his eyes wide with mock wonder and made a sweeping motion with his arm, drawing Vanaash's gaze to the men assembled behind them. "I have yet two score warriors here, heavily armed. Methinks 'twill be force aplenty to face the pathetic army from the village and the three of you. Four if you count the girl's father, who is scarce above a feeble magick trick or two, I suppose, were I to loose him!"

Lodur threw his head back and laughed, then grew sober all at once. "You hold no portion of immortality yet, Vana Avkomling," he hissed, "nor does any of your meager party. Can't be you suppose you can last long against me?"

Even as the last words escaped him, a rustling, as of lines moving stealthily in the fast lowing darkness, came from the northeast. One, then another, and another metallic helm appeared, like ghostly apparitions in the purple twilight. A booming voice rang out from the midst of them.

"They will last long enough, dark trickster, with the armed might of Swartalfheim massed behind them!"

Vanaash turned with a start. There was no mistaking the voice of Sivlir, though how he had come to be in Midgard with his massive darkelf army was a mystery. As Vanaash mused on it, gazing with wonder while the gigantic force marched brusquely into better view, he heard the familiar voice again, this time in the depths of his own mind. *'Twas Iseobel's thoughts which raised the alarm. Must be you touched the enchanted armlet to her brow; her fear and panic, fogbound though they were, summoned us hither!!*

Vanaash knew all at once that Sivlir had waited, crouched and ready, in the deeps of the forest, till the threat of sunlight was removed. How the darkelf had known to journey to Angland and wait at the ready, Vanaash couldn't guess. If the gods willed it, he would ask Sivlir when he had the chance. Swiftly, taking hold of his fillet, he lifted it a little, forcefully sending a message of thanks. Even as he did it, dozens of the darkelf warriors moved forward, surrounding Lodur's forces and absorbing him, and the two women with him, into their midst.

In the dim light, Vanaash reached for Iseobel and embraced her, showering her cheeks and brow with tender kisses. A moment later, he felt a staunch slap on the back and, turning, looked down into the earnest face of the darkelf chieftain. Stooping, he took Sivlir's shoulders, and the two embraced in the manner of blood-oathed brothers.

Lodur let go a bellow of rage that rent the night like thunder. "Aye! Take the Vana Avkomling, and the worthless old woman with them. Remember this, though! I still hold Dorflin. Already we have accomplished the trade which is the means of my restoration to god-form, therefore am I not shy to smite him!"

Iseobel gasped. Before Vanaash could stop her, she pushed forward through the sea of warriors to the front of the line. In the rising moonlight, Vanaash caught sight of her, standing, save for a half-score of yards between them, face to face with the dark-haired master who, scarce but a time's-breath ago, had almost made claim to her. Her voice rang out, strong and clear as Vanaash remembered it from times past, and his heart thrilled to the sound of it. "Be not swift to rob yourself of things greater, Lord Lodur, for the mere sake of spite!"

"How mean you?" Lodur's voice was cold, but held a note of interest. He had gathered Beatta to him and, even in the twilight, there was no mistaking the belligerence in the look of the two of them, twined of a sudden in a menacing closeness.

Iseobel cleared her throat. "Nights past, we have spoken of marvelous things, Lodur, the most amazing of all a magick ship of inestimable worth in Æsgard as well as here in Midgard."

Lodur said nothing. Iseobel continued, drawing forth a velvet pouch and holding it just out of his reach.

"Must be you know I have here the runestone which will invoke that ship, *Skidbladnir*. A most magick token it is, hand-carved for Freyr by the hand of Dvalin, wisest and most deceptive of the darkelves. By its very nature the stone is self-hiding, so that even the most strengthful of magickers can sit anext it and not feel its presence."

Lodur cut her off with a snort of anger, "I have no time for pretty speeches, fair one! If you mean to propose me something, be swift to do it!"

"I propose a trade, my lord. This runestone, which means the glory of returning to Æsgard not only with the chess thralls, which are Odin's due, but with the lost ship *Skidbladnir*, so garnering the thanks of Odin and all the gods there. Scarce could I offer this before, for I feared you would need me to invoke it, but now that I realize that Shiorvan, who serves you still, is also of the Vanir...."

"Name your price, fairest!" Lodur's voice, sonorous and smooth, had regained somewhat of its hypnotic charm, but now it held sway over Iseobel no longer, and she was thankful.

"Trade fair for my father. Let him step to me now unbound, and I will pass this to you!"

"Seems you will do a grave disservice to the Vana-gods, who have entrusted you with such power!" He said mockingly, but there was a sharpness in his tone which argued that his decision had already been made. Lodur's line parted grudgingly, and Dorflin, now loosed, came to the front of it.

"No, daughter!" Dorflin growled. "You will sow great harm!"

With a dauntless toss of the head, Iseobel stepped past her father, ordering Lodur's men back twelve paces. When Dorflin was well within in the perimeters of the grove and surrounded by dark-elves, she took aim, then tossed the stone, landing it squarely in Lodur's waiting hand.

His glinting, cherry-black eyes scarcely left her form as he examined the rune. Satisfied with its carven symbol, he signaled his housecarls back with a cold look.

"Must be you know I will miss you, fairest!" he breathed. "'Tis truth that I will ever hunger for you as I did those long nights, watching your innocent sleep."

But Iseobel had turned her back on him 'ere he finished.

# Chapter Twenty-four

*"... and when you share the marriage bed with your Vana Avkomling, fairness, you will ever long for the nights you spent in mine own. Fret not, my sweet, our paths shall cross again."*

Lodur's parting words to Iseobel looped endlessly through Vanaash's mind. The makebate persisted in touting an intimacy with Iseobel and Vanaash was still plagued by the lewd insinuations the darklord had made about her just before setting foot on his trek to Æsgard. Worse yet, however, was the evil one's assurance that he would return and be certain to put himself in their way.

An owl screeched through the trees overhead, flying high above Dorflin's sacred grove. Vanaash pulled Iseobel closer and, advantaging himself of the moonlight, looked side-long at her in wonderment. He knew she was exhausted. He had fully expected to carry her to the goddess hut, but she had resolutely refused, pulling away from the company and striking out alone on the path for home. He had caught up with her and she had finally consented to allow him to walk with her. But had she not in her fatigue stumbled time and again, surely Iseobel never would have let him support her as he now did. Now she was silent, scarcely aware of his arm around her, or of her father, Sivlir, and Sunniva following.

Iseobel found no joy in the warm, spring evening, though the deep loamy scents mingled with the fresh dew and the tang of the salt air was welcome after days of being shut away among attars and heavy perfumes. She paid no mind to the darkened footpath. If she fell, what did it matter? Today the pattern of her cloth with the Norns was established for all time.

To gain her own comfort, she had embittered brother and sister, endangered Shiorvan in Lokji's eyes, given the warlike Æsir a weapon of great power which might be turned against the Vanir, and, she winced, earned the wrath of her own dear father. She knew she did Vanaash no favors by clinging to him and forcing him to take her part to his own disadvantage. Oh, a fair day she had made of it!

Disgusted, she shook away from Vanaash and flung the cottage door wide. Moroseness supplanted her fatigue. It would have been better had she died on that field in Roric's stead!

Iseobel pushed past the chairs in the kitchening and, without bothering to light a candle, went behind the leather screen and dropped onto the pallet. Ignoring Machthild who had jumped into her lap, Iseobel buried her face in her hands. The sudden recollection of Roric's grim death made her misery complete, and for the first time since that horrid day, her full wits attacked her and she relived the moments of his dying ... the gaping death-wound, his ragged attempts at breathing, their final kiss.

So steeped in his own thoughts was Vanaash, that he had not grasped the reason for Iseobel's sudden bolting. While Dorflin, Sivlir, and Sunniva entered behind him rapt in low converse, he lit a candle at the guttering embers and contemplated how to comfort her. Standing at the hearth, he gazed at her lorn figure, hunched on the bed, so utterly despondent. He gulped at the shroud of pain that surrounded her. Uncertain, he searched her mind for a clue.

*Roric ... Roric in her arms.* He set his jaw. It would be impossible to fight the memory of his dead foster-brother! It was well enough, he fumed, feeling stupid, that Roric had stepped aside, freeing him to seek Iseobel once again. For though Roric had relinquished any claim on her, she was none but her own to give and 'twas plain she would not forgive him.

"Have you seen?" burst out Sivlir, touching a gnarled finger to his brow as if to indicate an invisible eye there. "Look you!! Look to Iseobel's thoughts. Might be 'tis not as grave as we had expected!"

"How mean you?" Dorflin asked, turning his concerned gaze immediately away from the partition that hid his daughter and to the excited darkelf.

"Iseobel," Sivlir prompted, shaking her shoulder roughly, "tell me. Whereby got you the *Skidbladnir* rune, the Boat-Beckoner?"

Blankly she looked up at the gnarled face. "'Twas in among my own stones ere I left Swartalfheim. Of what import is that?"

"Of great import," broke in Sunniva, turning from where she worked at mending the fire. Holding the tinder in mid air, she awaited the fuller answer.

"Aye, girl, and had the rune never left your side since first you found it? For I thought just now I read in your reverie that you took it away from the dying Roric Grim-Kill." He fixed his green eyes fast on hers. "Was it before or after the Valkyrie came that you reclaimed it?"

"Say you I stole it?" Iseobel stormed, standing so abruptly that the cat, forcibly dumped, yowled in surprise and the pallet banged into the wall behind her. "He had but vouchsafed it for me on his person, exactly as Dorflin had bidden him!"

Not waiting for an answer, Iseobel crossed her arms petulantly, her eyes crazed with sleeplessness. "Can't be you mean it would have been better for me to leave it to looters!"

Aware that she reached hysteria, but unable to stave it off, she brushed past them all in a rush for the door. Undoubtedly she had fallen gravely in everyone's estimation, but to heap the accusation of thievery on her. That was beyond insult! Further humiliation she could not suffer this day, and she meant to throw her tantrum outdoors in private.

Vanaash, acutely feeling Iseobel's misery, was certain that there was important purpose in Sivlir's unusually eager manner. Reaching as she tried to pass him, Vanaash gathered her to him and, stroking her hair, bade her be comforted.

"I think not that Lord Sivlir nor Sunniva Baardsdätter mean you hurt," he soothed.

"Nay!" exclaimed Sivlir earnestly, "'tis a hope we seek. For if the rune was on the man after his death, that would mean that the spirit of it has traveled with him."

Vanaash's head jerked up. Dorflin's brow lifted in surprise. Iseobel, embarrassed, stopped struggling and looked up from underneath Vanaash's chin. "I do not understand."

Sivlir took Iseobel's hand in his own. "Unlike the written runes of the FUTHARK, a quality of drawn-runes is that the soul of them will attach to the soul of the person, just as the body of them is carried by the body of the person. Thus, as your friend wore the rune when he died, he has taken the soul of it to another world with him. 'Twas but the empty shell of it remained here in Midgard and," he emphasized his meaning, "in that case, 'tis but a useless framework which Lokji has taken in triumph to Æsgard. The Boat-Beckoner will be useless to any until somehow the soul and shell can be rejoined!"

Without warning, Dorflin began to chuckle. Iseobel, startled, watched open mouthed as he leaned back in his chair, wiping tears from his eyes, then dried his dampened beard. "Perfect," he chuckled, "this news is the best sup of all."

"Father," Iseobel cried anxiously, "what are you about?"

"See you not, daughter?" he smiled, pulling her close. "You have out-tricked the very god of trickery! Because you knew not that the rune was useless, you have performed unwittingly the finest of all mischief on the master of treachery himself. Your name and deed shall be celebrated in all the Nine Worlds!"

All knew immediately that Dorflin's words were true. Had Iseobel suspected the rune was useless, Lodur would have culled the fact from her mind, and their victory would have been lost.

Thinking on all this afforded Iseobel a moment of satisfaction. Then she bristled and pulled away. Her torrent of words came swiftly as she eyed the company in turn. "Moments ago, before we knew that the rune was but a hull, I was the most unsatisfactory creature in all your eyes. And now—" She whirled for the door, choking on her confusion.

"Bide, daughter!" Dorflin waylaid her sternly, the surprise on his face genuine. "Anger had none of us for you in any wise for the trade you effected. Indeed, I found it galling that Lokji might claim so many prizes and truly return as the golden one to Æsgard, but none of us were wroth with you. Indeed, to a one, we all admired your staunch courage!"

Mouth agape, Iseobel stared from one to the other, rejoicing inwardly that she had not brought about total ruin by her impulsive bargaining with the darklord.

Still smiling, Dorflin added, "… though I warrant neither Lord Freyr nor the darkelves will think me a suitable barter for that hard-forged rune."

They all laughed heartily at that, then sat in happy silence while Sunniva, armed with wineskins and cups, poured out refreshment to accompany their meal. Iseobel eyed her happily, the playful banter having put her in mind of the fact that once the beauty of this powerful woman had drawn the approving eye of Freyr himself. Then, of a sudden, she remembered a promise of explanation on a thought that had been troubling her.

"I would know one thing, Vanaash," she started, even before she realized the question had been formed, "How is it that you know the Lady Sunniva?"

Vanaash exchanged a furtive glance with the old woman, as if to seek for permission to tell the tale. At her subtle nod, he smiled. "'Twas she who reared me at my father's choosing 'ere I came to be fostered by Aasa and Eirik Half-Dane. Since that time we have not until today met again," he explained, the fondness obvious in his voice and gaze. "Yet I would know her face anywhere, so dear it lies to my heart."

Sivlir's leathery face creased into a hearty smile. "Clever the woman, too, that she should call you Vanaav Komling. The name itself was a signal to those deserving to know it, yet uncomprehended by those who were not."

*Vana Avkomling:* Descendant of the Vanir.

Iseobel and Vanaash exchanged a glance—and in that single look, Vanaash read how his beloved had oft dreamed of his name, or heard it in said during moments of seith and magick, repeated over and over till the sound of the words seemed to merge with her heartbeat. *Vana Avkomling. Vana Avkomling.*

*Even so,* she apologized silently, *I did not recognize it when I heard you so called.*

Vanaash reassured her. Lifting the silver band slightly away from his brow, he sent her a comforting thought, completely forgetting that everyone in the room could read him, too.

*I did not recognize it myself until it was told to me.*

Then he moved close to her and, unable to resist longer, pulled her to him in a strong and commanding embrace, caring not that the others watched while he sought her lips.

Their affection seemed to warm the room and the hearts of all in it. When Dorflin proposed a raising of drinking horns, no one refused. The way each drained his brew belied how much in need all had been of soothing. Iseobel, finding the effects agreeable, re-filled them and emptied her own in one quaff. Soon, the sharp edges in her memory of the day began to mellow. *Perhaps ...* she fought her weariness ... *perhaps she would make more sense of it all after she rested.*

Pulling a bit away from the table and easing Iseobel from her stool into his lap, Vanaash settled to listen. Iseobel, spent and glad of a more comforting seat, pulled off his boar-headed fillet and pillowed her cheek against Vanaash's hair. Dreamily she traced the silver-work on the head-band, and Machthild curled up in her lap to purr while Iseobel drifted in and out from her surroundings, unable to fight off her languor.

Half-dreaming and ruminating on the obvious affection between the darkelf and Sunniva, Iseobel absently began to toy with the tow locks on Vanaash's neck that had escaped their fastenings.

"Father," she asked in a faraway voice, "is my bind-ring safe?"

Vanaash, hardly having dared to make any meaning of the fingers which thrilled shivers down his spine, could contain himself no longer, and held her a little away that he might look on her face. "Iseobel! Is't true? Mean you to be wedded with me?" He turned to face her, not caring a whit for the display he made in front of the others.

She lifted her heavy lids to look into his jewel-like eyes. "Wedded, is it?" she managed slowly, so tired that she was hardly able to follow one word with another, "wedded will you be? Ah ... what a notion ... but we must ask permission from both my parents," she mumbled finally, and sank dead asleep onto his shoulder.

"To a wedding in Swartalfheim!" Dorflin toasted. Vanaash raised an eyebrow.

"Mayhap you think Swartalfheim a strange place for a hand-fasting feast," Sivlir began, somewhat defensively, but Vanaash cut him off, shaking his head so hard that his white hair flew.

"Nay, Lord Sivlir! Methinks Swartalfheim would be the perfect place!" He was remembering suddenly how he had stood in front of the majestic, green-glowing waterfall there, seemingly a lifetime ago, and had vowed to make Iseobel hand-fast to him in that very spot.

"Good! For first both you and Iseobel must be proven at the Test Stone of Swartalfheim." Dorflin's voice was gentle, but it cut through Vanaash's reverie like a sharp-edged blade. "Only then will you know for certain that you have permission from Æsgard to exchange your bind rings."

Vanaash crossed his arms on the table and lowered his head onto them abjectly. Where a moment ago, he had felt secure in the obtaining of his heart's goal, now he wavered. What if—?

Feeling a hand upon his shoulder, he looked up, questioningly, into Dorflin's soothing smile. The magicker did not speak. His lips did not move, and his gentle look remained impassive. Vanaash heard the words clearly, though, in Dorflin's lilting and resonant voice.

"Have no fear that she shall not pass the test. For she, as you, is Vana Avkomling."

# Epilogue

It had been a strange life so far, this life in Æsgard, and Roric Grim-kill had only just begun to relax into the rhythm of it. Had pleased him right well to waken and find himself a virtual lord there, one of the elite guard of Lady Freyja. 'Twas a most exceptional brotherhood, this, for they lived all at Folkvang, her sumptuous manor. To a man, they had been hand-picked off the battlefield by her, and had each one been welcomed personally by her in a way which gave them all—men of great valor and good breeding—a great sense of solidarity.

'Twas whispered a lot by the Æsir and touted constantly amongst the multitudes of warriors in Valhalla, especially when deep in their sour grapes, that oft Lady Freyja slipped a little in her standards and chose this warrior or that strictly for his comeliness. At first, 'twas rumored of Roric, for he had grown exceptionally hale and well fit, and the nightly exercise of battle and sport agreed with him well.

This gossip was both a boon and a bane, and almost from the start, Roric realized he would constantly have to prove himself— a thing that was greatly to his liking. In a very short while, he had gained a reputation for boldness that was quite unequaled. It had by then become apparent that he was a great favorite of Freyja's, *as he traveled in her closest circles and was the one chosen most often for her notorious "special duty."*

*Unlike some of the guardsmen who lived in the hall of a god or goddess, Roric had no pretensions, and he counted as many comrades amongst the Einheriar as amongst his own high rank. Oft he went to drink or game with them in Valhalla, as much to enjoy their rough play as to appreciate the women who served there. Too, he liked to pass nights with his elder brother, Staag, who resided in that hall, though he oft-times found him boyish and tiresome, for the lad had seen but seventeen summers when he was welcomed to the other-world.*

*All in all, 'twas a happier time than ever he had known, and he was prone to attribute all his good fortune here to that charm he had carried with him—the Runestone he carried in the pouch round his neck. Much of his Midgard life had already grown hazy in his mind, but well he remembered how he had put this thing anext his heart so soon before he died. It had looked so much duller then, as if the phosphorescence had been shielded behind some surface half opaque. Now, it glowed in a dazzling variety of brilliances and an array of silvery hues. 'Twas his greatest favorite, for when he held it to his ear, he could hear most clearly the hum of the wind in fast moving sails and, apart from Iseobel, this was all he missed of his mortal life.*

# End Part One of *The Vana Avkomling Saga*

# Next, Part Two, *The Stranger's Son*

# Glossary

| | |
|---|---|
| Aasa | Healer of some repute in the Nor Way; widow of Eirik Half-Dane; mother of Beatta, Staag, Roric, and Rhus. |
| Æsgard | Realm of the Æsir. |
| Æsir | The warrior race of gods led by Odin. |
| Æthling | Prince |
| Alfheim | Realm of the Lightelves. |
| Angrboda | (Bringer of Distress) Giantess leman to Lokji; mother of Fenris, Jormungand, and Hel. |
| Avkomling | Offspring. |
| Badger | Vanaash's black horse. |
| Baldur | The most beautiful of all the gods; son of Odin and Frigga; twin brother of Hodur. |
| Baltha | Ivar Half-hand's stallion. |
| Beatta | Twin of Staag; sister of Roric and Rhus; daughter to Aasa and Eirik Half-Dane. |
| Beltane | May 1st—sacred day of the Cymric god of death. |
| Beobald | Roric's white-feathered gray horse. |
| Bifrost | The flaming three-strand rainbow bridge that connects Midgard to Æsgard. |
| Bodkin | Small knife. |
| Brisingamen | Magical necklace belonging to the goddess Freyja which was forged by four Darkelves: Alfrigg, Berling, Dvalin, and Grerr. |
| Cymry | Wales. |
| Dalmatic | Loose outer shirt with wide sleeves and open sides. |
| Danelaw | That part of Angland which was settled and ruled by the Danes. (ca. 835–1035) |
| Darkelves | A race of beings which were made at the time of creation and, because they are turned to stone by sunlight, condemned to live underground. Their domain is Swartalfheim. The gods put them in charge of the earth's gems and metals and they became |

master craftsmen by virtue of combining their smithing skills with Runemagick. There are no females among them.

Darkway | Tunnel that leads from Midgard to Swartalfheim.

Disir | Feast on October 11th wherein one celebrates ones maternal ancestors.

Dorflin | Both Druid and Runesman; father to Iseobel.

Druid | (Oakseer) Sacrosanct person of the Cymry who is seer, poet, priest, and judge and serves the sacred league of the oak and the White Goddess.

Dvalin | (Deluder) One of the wisest and most skillful of all Darkelves.

Dwarves | A race of underground beings who inhabit Nidavellir, a region within Swartalfheim. Not restricted to underground, but prefer to live there out of sight. They are unusually short and make excellent miners.

Effa | Iseobel's mare.

Einherjar | (Heroes) Dead warriors who dwell in Valhalla and Folkvang until Ragnarok. They do battle all day, the Valkyrie heal their wounds, and they feast all night.

Eireland | Ireland.

Eirik Half-Dane | Husband of Aasa; father of Beatta, Staag, Roric, and Rhus.

Fenris | Wolfish offspring of Lokji and Angrboda who became so ferocious that, when he threatened the safety of the gods, they bound him in chains.

Fensalir | Frigga's hall in Æsgard.

Fjanis | Darkelf who leads Dorflin to Sivlir.

Folkvang | (Field of Folk) Freyja's realm in Æsgard where her chosen warriors live. Equivalent to Odin's Valhalla.

Frankish | French

Freyja | (Lady) Vanir Goddess; Twin to Freyr; daughter of Njord and Nerthus. Brought to Æsgard as a hostage after the war. Exceedingly beautiful goddess of fertility and sex, she was also condemned by Odin to lead the Valkyrie as Goddess of Bloodshed, but her portion is a share of the glory slain who come to live with her in Folkvang. A powerful magicker, she is associated with cats and has a falcon cloak that allows her to fly.

| | |
|---|---|
| Freyr | (Lord) Vanir God; Twin to Freyja; son of Njord and Nerthus. Brought to Æsgard as a hostage after the war. God of sun, rain, and harvest, the shining Freyr lived in Alfheim as Lord of the Lightelves. Wild boars pull his chariot. |
| Frigga | Æsir Goddess; Wife of Odin; Mother of Baldur and Hodur. She is chief among the Æsir goddesses and the beautiful Earth Mother. She is the goddess of love, marriage, and motherhood. In her hall, Fensalir, she shapes the clouds from her spinning wheel. |
| Frisian | From Frisia, a land along the North Sea. |
| FUTHARK | Rune alphabet (taken from the first six letters: F-U-Th-A-R-K). |
| Gaard | Bastard son of Roric and Kirsten |
| Galdor | Runic, ritual magick |
| Geir Death-crooner | Anglish warrior; friend to Iseobel. Third son, fourth child of Harald and Græthl; younger brother of Stanus, Theda, and Eolh; elder brother of Cynedom and Emmela. |
| Gerda | (Field) Frost giantess and wife of Freyr. |
| Gladsheim | (Place of Joy) The gods' sanctuary where they hold Thingsteads. Only the principals have high seats. |
| Grey Sea | Anglish Channel. |
| Gullveig | Vanir seer goddess who is the first of her race to come to Æsgard. Lustful for gold, she purports that her superior magickal powers entitle her to take the riches she wishes. Odin and the Æsir move against her, and have her burnt to death three times; three times she emerges whole from the fires. Her ill treatment causes the war between the Vanir and the Æsir. |
| Gungnir | Odin's magic spear. |
| Haftor | Kinsman slain by Roric. |
| Halfling | Offspring of god and human. |
| Hauberk | Coat of chain mail or thick padding for protection in battle. |
| Heimdall | Watcher god who guards the Bifrost. |

# The Vana Avkomling Saga

| | |
|---|---|
| Hel (person) | Daughter of Lokji who, being half alive and half dead, is the queen of the inglorious dead. She lives in Eljudnir. |
| Hel (world) | Realm of Death. All mortals, save those who die valorous in battle, reside here eternally, judged according to the deeds of their lives—the virtuous in the highest level, the evil in the lowest reaches. |
| Hlidskjalf | (Opening in the Rock) Site from which Odin can see into all the Nine Worlds. |
| Hodur | Blind god of darkness; son of Odin and Frigga; twin brother of Baldur. |
| Hoenir | Æsir god of silence. Odin's brother-son known for indecision. Sent to Vanaheim as hostage after the war between the Vanir and the Æsir. |
| Hvaam | Darkelf guard. |
| Idavoll | (Field of Deeds) Site of Gladsheim. |
| Iseobel | Daughter of Dorflin; Runeswoman and healer. |
| Ivar Half-hand | Retainer to Vanaash and Roric. |
| Jarl | Earl. |
| Jord | (Earth) Daughter of Nott (Night) and her second husband Annar (Another); mother of Hoenir and Lokji. |
| Jormungand | Serpentish offspring of Lokji and Angrboda. Cast into the seas that surround the Nine Worlds, he encircles Midgard by biting on his own tail. Also known as the Midgard Serpent. |
| Jotunheim | Realm of the Giants. |
| Jutland | Peninsula from the Dane Mark. |
| Kirsten | Wife of Wulf Shin-griever; mother of Roric's bastard son Gaard. |
| Kirtle | Skirt. |
| Komling | Child. |
| Kvasir | (Spittle) A god created from the combined spittle of the Vanir and Æsir gods at the end of the war. In him was all the wisdom and poetry of both races. When two Dwarf brothers, Galar and Fjalar, hear of him, they contrive to kill him and catch his blood in a great cauldron, Od-Hroerir. They then mix it with honey to |

make a sacred mead of wisdom and poetry.

**Leman**  Concubine.

**Lightelves**  Petite beings of light and irreproachable character, they live in Alfheim and serve the Vanir god Freyr.

**Lodur**  Great jarl with holdings in both the Trondelag and Danelaw near Scarbyrig.

**Lokji**  Half-brother and son to Odin and Jord, the clever, handsome Lokji was an attractive light-hearted soul who loved to laugh and have fun. His many tricks at first brought much pleasure to the gods. Eventually a streak of evil began to show in him and he became more and more malicious. Along with his leman, Angrboda, he fathered Fenris, Jormungand, and Hel.

**Longhouse**  Main communal dwelling on a skaale often fashioned of thick turf walls and a sod roof with smoke holes. Access was through long tunnel-like antechambers. Only the very wealthiest owners installed windows, which were made from stretched, translucent animal bladders.

**Machthild**  Iseobel's cat.

**Midgard**  (Middle Earth; Middle Garden) Realm of humans.

**Mimir**  Wise Æsir god sent to Vanaheim as a hostage after the war. When the Vanir chop off his head and send it back to Æsgard, Odin preserves it and sets it near a well which becomes the well of wisdom—Mimir's Well.

**Mjollnir**  Thor's massive hammer, crafted by Darkelves Brokk and Eitri, which always hits its mark and always returns afterwards to Thor's hand.

**Moreen**  Heavy wool or cotton fabric with a watered finish.

**Muspellheim**  (Land of Fire) Realm of fire and the Fire Giants.

**Naglfar**  (Ship of Nails) Ship made from fingernails of the dead. When it is big enough to carry all the giants (i.e., when enough warriors have been slain in battle, yet not attended to through lack of correct observation of the rituals to the Æsir), they will attack Æsgard and Ragnarok will commence.

**Nastrond**  (Corpse Shore) The gruesome bank of the river Hvergelmir in Nidavellir where the bodies of the evil dead are strewn.

| | |
|---|---|
| Nerthus | (Earth) Vanir fertility goddess; Sister-wife of Njord; mother of Freyr and Freyja. |
| Nidavellir | (Dark Crags) Realm of the Dwarves. |
| Nidhogg | (Corpse Tearer) Voracious dragon of Nidavellir who chews up the bodies of the evil doers. |
| Nif-Helheim | (Fog World) Realm of eternal mist. Here exist forever all the thoughts, dreams, and ideas of mortal men, an eternal record forming a tangible mist. |
| Nine Worlds | The cosmos is formed in the shape of the great sacred ash, Yggdrasil, and along it are all the Nine Worlds: Vanaheim, Æsgard, Alfheim, Jotunheim, Midgard, Nidavellir, Swartalfheim, Hel, and Nif-Helheim. |
| Njord | Vanir God of the seas; father to Freyr and Freyja. One of the hostages sent to Æsgard after the war. His hall in Æsgard is the harbor and shipyard Noatun. |
| Norns | The three goddesses of destiny—Wyrd, Skuld, and Verthandi—who measure and control time and spin a thread for every living being and weave it into the web of life. |
| Od-Hroerir | (Heart Stirrer) The cauldron in which Kvasir's blood is brewed into the mead of wisdom and poetry. |
| Odin | Chief of the Æsir gods; the god of war and death. By sacrificing an eye to Mimir, he gained knowledge of the Runes and became the god of wisdom and poetry, as well. Known as All-Father, he is the father of Thor and Balder, and father-brother to Hoenir and Lokji. Married to Frigga, he lives in Valaskialf. From its high tower, Hlidskialf, he can see into the Nine Worlds. |
| Peaceweaver | Woman who is married off to help bring about harmony with a feuding clan. |
| Planch | Thick slab. |
| Ragnarok | (Destruction of the Powers) Final battle between the gods and giants where all Nine Worlds will be destroyed. |
| Rhus | Youngest child of Aasa and Eirik Half-Dane; brother of Beatta, Staag, and Roric. |
| Roric | Middle child of Aasa and Eirik Half-Dane; brother of Beatta, Staag, and Rhus. |

# Dorflin's Daughter

| | |
|---|---|
| Runes | (Secrets or Mysteries) Letter symbols attributed with magickal strength which later came into use as the Norse and Anglo-Saxon alphabet. Odin brought the knowledge of the Runes to humans. |
| Sark | Shirt. |
| Scarbyrig | Port city in northern Eworickshire in Angland. (Modern Scarborough) |
| Seith (Seidhr) | Shamanic trance magick, in which the soul can travel and the mind can project images (shapeshifting). |
| Sessrumnir | (Rich in Seats) Freyja's hall, which is so well built as to be impenetrable unless the goddess herself opened the doors. |
| Shimmel | Wulf Shin-griever's white horse |
| Shiorvan | Sunniva's daughter; leman to Lodur. |
| Singlet | Undershirt. |
| Sivlir | Darkelf. |
| Skaale | Farm. |
| Skidbladnir | (Wooden-bladed) Magick ship forged by the Darkelves who gifted it to Lokji, who in turn gave it to Freyr. It is reputed to grow large enough to carry all the gods and their weapons; fly through the air to the destination and then be folded up small enough to stow in a pocket. |
| Skiver | Soft thin leather shaved from sheepskin. |
| Skog | Farmstead in the Nor Way. |
| Skrying | Divination by peering into the glassy surface of water or wine. |
| Skuld | (Should) Youngest Norn who is the embodiment of what should evolve. |
| Sleipnir | Odin's eight-legged horse sired by Svadilfari and borne by Lokji. Often a synomym for pall bearers. |
| Sogn | Harbor town in the Nor Way. |
| Staag | Beatta's twin brother slain in battle at the age of seventeen. |
| Sunniva Baardsdätter | Woman of Uppsala. Mother of Shiorvan. |
| Swartalfheim | Realm of the Darkelves. |

| | |
|---|---|
| Thingstead | A place for public assembly or court of law. |
| Thor | Æsgard god of sky and thunder. Son of Odin and Fjorgyn; husband of Sif. His realm is Thrudheim and his hall, Bilskirnir (Lightning), has 540 doors. He is guardian of law and order in Midgard, yet cannot tread the Bifrost for fear of his mighty stride shattering it. |
| Thran | Beatta's late husband. |
| Trencher | Slab of bread so thick it can be used as a dish. |
| Trondelag | Remote region of the Nor Way. |
| Valhalla | (Hall of the Slain) Odin's hall in Gladsheim where the glory dead Einherjar battle daily and feast nightly until they will fight by Odin's side at Ragnarok, the final battle. |
| Valka | Servant at the Skogskaale. |
| Valkyries | (Choosers of the Slain) Beautiful young warrior maidens of Odin who, led by Freyja, pluck the strongest and bravest fallen warriors from the battlefield and bring them back to live in Valhalla. |
| Vana | Of the Vanir. |
| Vanaash | Foster child to Aasa and Eirik Half-Dane; Foster-brother of Beatta, Staag, Roric, and Rhus. |
| Vanaheim | Realm of the Vanir gods. |
| Vanir | A race of pre-agricultural gods and goddesses more ancient than the Æsir, who brought peace and prosperity to the land. After the war with the Æsir, they brought their knowledge of magick to Æsgard. |
| Verthandi | (Becoming) Middle Norn who represents the present moment of change. |
| Wallin | Darkelf guard. |
| Wenlith | Sheepfarmer and herder of Scarbyrig |
| Wenthur Crow-hair | Anglish warrior of Scarbyrig. |
| White Goddess | Threefold Cymric goddess—mother, bride, and killer—visibly appearing as the New, Full, and Old Moon. Lovely and slender with blue eyes and fair hair, she could be generous, fickle, wise, and merciless. |
| Windrider | Vanaash's dragon ship. |
| Woad | Blue dye extracted from the mustard plant. |

Wulf Shin-griever — Retainer to Vanaash and Roric; husband of Kirsten; stepfather to Gaard, Roric's bastard.

Wyrd (weird) — (To become) Eldest Norn who sees all that has passed and shapes that which should happen; fate or destiny.

Wyrd's Well — The sacred well of the Norn Wyrd which keeps the forces of evil from Yggdrasil's roots.

Yggdrasil — Great world ash whose roots and branches hold the universe together and wherin are sheltered all the Nine Worlds.

# The Futhark

ᚠ   Fehu ---------- cattle, wealth
ᚢ   Uruz ---------- aurochs, strength
ᚦ   Thuriaz -------- thorn, force
ᚨ   Ansuz --------- ash tree, ancestor
ᚱ   Raido --------- journey, leadership
ᚲ   Kenaz --------- torch, clarity
ᚷ   Gifu ----------- gift
ᚹ   Wunjo --------- joy, glory
ᚺ   Hagalaz -------- hail
ᚾ   Nauthiz -------- need, distress
ᛁ   Isa ------------ ice
ᛃ   Jera ----------- year
ᛇ   Eihwaz -------- yew
ᛈ   Pertho --------- dice cup, secret
ᛉ   Algiz ---------- sword, protection
ᛊ   Sowulo -------- sun
ᛏ   Teiwaz -------- Tyr, sign
ᛒ   Berkana ------- birch, regeneration
ᛖ   Ehwaz --------- horse
ᛗ   Mannaz -------- human
ᛚ   Laguz --------- lake
ᛜ   Inguz ---------- the people
ᛟ   Othila --------- ancestral estate, inheritance
ᛞ   Dagaz --------- day, breakthrough

# Mead Hall Press

www.meadhallpress.com

## Coming in summer, 2005, from Mead Hall Press
### *Unconquered*
### by Sieran Vale

By 1066, Earls Edwin and Morcar—brothers in their early 20s—ruled between them more than half of England, having weathered a turbulent upbringing characterized by alternating periods of privilege, tragedy, and undeserved exile at the hands of their rivals, the house of Godwine.

In the heroic tradition of *Braveheart, Unconquered* tells the incredible story of Edwin and Morcar. It follows them from highest favor to grimmest treachery, from castles to prisons to outlaw camps, from the blood feuds and enmities of the old Anglo Saxon kingdom to the harsh Norman oppression and violent rebel uprisings of the new. Meticulously researched and alive with authentic detail, *Unconquered* is peopled with unforgettable characters—William the Conqueror, Lady Godiva, Hereward the Wake, and many others.

The result is a spellbinding chronicle of top-notch scholarship which unabashedly redefines this momentous era and, in the process, restores a legendary family to its rightful place in the annals of history.

## Also coming from Mead Hall Press

### *Understanding Runes*
### by Eric Wilmoth
An illustrated manual exploring the archetypal principles of the runes and their practical use.

### *The Stranger's Son*
### by S. Leigh Jenner
The second exciting book in *The Vana Avkomling Saga*